SOUTH of EVIL

A Novel

by

Brian Dunford

For additional information or correspondence, contact the author at briandunford138@yahoo.com.

Cover by J Caleb Design.

South of Evil

For my mom

Chapter One

Curtis – Austin, TX

Walter Curtis was neither strong nor confident, and he was about to walk into a room full of men who were. They were armed and they were professionals and they were the best at what they did.

He pushed his glasses up on his nose. His hands were small and soft. He wore his best blue suit. Though he was in his thirties, he hadn't been eating, so it hung on him and made him look like a kid.

There was not one thing distinguishing about him. Overall, he looked boring and dependable. Reliable. Entirely unexciting. He looked like the world's ideal accountant, he thought, as he walked through the door to the Austin office of the Federal Bureau of Investigation.

"That's going to change," Curtis whispered as his phone began to buzz. He caught it on the second ring.

"Special Agent Curtis? Bill Montrose here."

When Curtis first arrived on the task force three years ago, he had been just another accountant from the Internal Revenue Service. Montrose would grunt and nod in his direction. That had changed. Montrose learned his name. It was after Curtis had told a region head out of DC that he anticipated a seven-figure seizure. It was after the IRS Criminal Investigation Division was told they couldn't have him back. It was definitely after Special Agent-in-Charge Montrose had introduced him to an assistant director from Homeland and simply said, "This is my guy Curtis."

Curtis was here for a deconfliction briefing. Curtis loved the sound of those words. It put him in the middle of everything. He'd first heard the phrase from an old friend, a Boston cop named Marc Virgil. "We make sure we're not all about to hit the same door at once," he'd said.

Montrose was eager to move. "I was just speaking with some people from Justice, and they wanted to confirm some small details with you."

"Fire away."

That was Montrose's expression, and Curtis had started using it. Bill Montrose was black, a climber, and in his fifties. He was known for his suits and his demeanor. He was friendly and outgoing when you were on his side. He could discard you in a second if you were not. He was always the best dressed man in the room.

"How soon are we looking to seize international assets?"

"I can't say, sir. As of right now, they are speculation. We know they exist, and we know they are substantial. We just can't pin them down."

"You're our accountant in charge. Even you can't find it?" Montrose meant it as a joke. He joked with Curtis now.

"We will know a lot more once we seize the books."

"I like it. By the way, how is Mr. Aston Martin?"

Montrose was terrible with names.

"Living large."

"You and I are in the wrong business."

Curtis had one more piece of information for the boss.

"You asked me several months ago about a certain picture of the target. About what kind of jacket he was wearing."

"I did?"

He did. Curtis had been told repeatedly: the easiest way to excite the boss was to show him how the target was spending all his money. "They need to smell blood," Virgil had once told him.

"Yes, sir. The target wore a very sharp, very unique sport coat. You asked me to find out what kind it was."

"And?"

"It's bespoke."

There was a slight pause.

"I'm not familiar with that brand," said Montrose.

"It's not a brand, sir. It's a term. It means the jacket was hand-made."

Again, Montrose gave pause.

"What does something like that cost?"

"I spoke with an excellent tailor here in Austin. He said most of that work is done out of state. He couldn't be sure without knowing the actual material, but he speculated based on the color and the apparent texture that it might be vicuna."

"Vicuna?"

"It's an endangered animal in South America. It looks like a llama. Very hard to find."

"And they make coats out of it."

"Extremely expensive coats, sir."

"How much are we talking?"

"According to my tailor, a hand made vicuna coat can run you thirty to forty thousand dollars."

Montrose whistled.

Eduardo – Austin, TX

Eduardo Mendes was a thing of beauty.

He wasn't just handsome. He looked like a Spanish sculptor's dream brought to life. His body was slim and exquisitely maintained, radiating wealth and entitlement. He sat at a cramped desk in his shabby office.

It was four o'clock, and the bell was ringing. It rang every time the door opened, and it was ringing non-stop. It did every Friday night. The floors were no thicker than the walls, and every whisper, laugh, joke, and curse from the first floor carried right up to his office.

Eduardo was revolted by the checks. They were grimy and marred by sweat and oil. Workmen were paid in the morning, stuffed checks in their pockets, and worked in the sun until late, finally wandering into the store with the now damp money orders. For years, he had worn gloves when he handled the checks.

At this point, the checks almost handled themselves. He had been moving another order. This one was to a new bank, a small one, and as always, in Mexico. Processing it was no problem, but he found himself picturing the bank itself as a clean stucco and glass fixture on an otherwise deserted highway, with not so much as a car in the newly paved lot, when he saw the address of the road and instantly recognized it. It was the same road he'd travelled. He knew where it led. Images of nastiness and wetness had flooded his mind and his ears roared with screaming and tears. And the begging. The begging was the worst.

Eduardo thought of Mexico and immediately ran to the bathroom. He walked stiff armed with his hands held before him as if covered in fresh gore, kicked the door open with his foot, and let the water run until it scalded.

He scrubbed forcefully and on both sides as the water turned scalding. He hated the tiny little bathroom. It had been crammed into a space where it didn't belong, and now he had to stoop over every time he washed his hands. He hated this building, but he needed it.

The soap was exquisite, extremely hard to locate, and very expensive. He let it all run over him until Mexico was out of his mind.

Sheldon Cashman came into his office and found Eduardo Mendes looking at two black and white pictures on the wall. One was Sheldon, fresh from Jersey riding a horse on his first day in Texas. He had a huge grin on his face and no idea what he was doing, but he was happy. He was older in the second picture, and his horse was a malevolent black Arabian named Maccabee. He had learned to ride in the years between these pictures. He was smiling confidently. Riding horses was where he found peace.

Sheldon knew Eduardo called him the Jewish Cowboy. He had a clever nickname for everyone. He suspected that Eduardo had let him know that on purpose, just so Sheldon would understand his place in Eduardo's world.

"The Hillbillies are done," said Eduardo. "They're erratic and unreliable. Split the difference among Looney Larry and the Astronauts."

The clients had nicknames too. Eduardo spoke only in code. The Hillbillies were out of North Texas. They were rough and trashy and had paid late for the third time. His other clients were reliable, and always begging for more. Until now, he hadn't been able to oblige.

Sheldon handled the books and the numbers. He made the money move, and he made it disappear. He nodded, and asked as few questions as possible. He shifted in his chair uncomfortably. His stomach hurt. The only thing that made it better was riding.

Sheldon hated this business. He hated himself for having any part of it. He hated himself for allowing Eduardo Mendes into his life. He put it out of his mind. Sheldon looked at his watch without realizing it.

"Are we running out of time?" Eduardo asked with undisguised condescension.

"No," said Sheldon. This was all because of the watch.

Sheldon had married a woman who was out of his league. She had been his guide to the finer things in life. Shortly after they were married, she had given him a gift. Inside the polished walnut box was the finest watch he had ever seen. It was leather and gold, and, below the finely engraved Baume & Mercier emblem the face of the timepiece featured a cut-away to expose an intricate series of gears and motors within the watch itself. Sheldon knew it was a nice watch, but he didn't know just how nice until he went to dinner with his wife's friends. The husband, who had made a fortune on a medical patent and seemed to know a little bit about almost everything, explained to him that this watch was an extremely rare tourbillon, an exquisite mechanism designed to offset the force of gravity itself. As this man spoke admiringly of the piece on his wrist, Sheldon's smile melted with the realization that this watch was far, far out of his financial reach.

He could afford the luxury condo she wanted, because it was a mere one bedroom. He could barely afford her European SUV. But when he realized that the watch had cost more than the car, he understood that he was in trouble.

Eduardo Mendes had appeared in his life shortly thereafter, as if he had sniffed out his desperation.

That night, Sheldon had gone riding. He pushed Maccabee until sundown. Across town, there was an arrogant little man who called him the Jewish Cowboy and convinced himself that everyone he met was his servant. Sheldon was great with numbers. He could ride the hell out of a horse. He'd give almost anything to see Eduardo Mendes put in his place. He'd give almost anything just to see the look on Eduardo's face when it happened.

It was a heavy leather wingback chair, just like the ones his father had in his office when he was a child. Eduardo Mendes was only one hundred and fifty pounds, and the chair was oversized, so when he sat on it, it felt like a throne.

His chair had dark wood legs and with a light antiqued leather. Odalys' whole room had been decorated in antiseptic white, just the way he wanted it. The chair was the only one of its kind though, and there was nothing else in the room like it. The bed and dresser and nightstand had been part of a set, but the chair was here because he wanted it.

Its place in the room was intentional. The chair didn't face the bed, nor did it look out the window. It looked directly into Odalys' bathroom. Eduardo watched her as she brushed her hair in just her tiny black underpants.

From this vantage, Eduardo could watch her shower and dress. He could watch her put on stockings. He often suggested she do just that, even while her hair was still wet, before her make-up was on. Odalys always indulged him.

His room was on the other side of the apartment, and had been decorated in dark, somber tones, like his father's office. As a boy, he had played in the office as often as he could. His father always had a short temper. Those chairs, with the handsomely carved wood and the old leather with the brass studs on the arms, sat in front of a huge mahogany desk. He would hear his father shouting on the phone, blazing in and out of Spanish into English and back once more as he grew angrier.

When he was ten years old, he had found his father in that office with a light skinned effete black man who was introduced to him as Mr. Patrick. Mr. Patrick appeared to be giving his father some sort of instruction.

"I would one day like to visit Saint-Tropez," said Mr. Patrick. His father repeated it word for word.

Mr. Patrick wore a gray suit with a flannel sweater vest, pattern leather shoes, and a pencil thin mustache. He enunciated each word like the teachers at his school. Effort and deliberateness were stressed into each syllable he spoke.

Eduardo was only ten years old and didn't know what a fag was really, only that you didn't want anyone to call you a fag because it meant you weren't a man, and if someone did call you a fag, you were going to have to fight him. He knew, without a shadow of a doubt, that the man in his father's office was a huge fag. He ran off to find his mother.

She was smoking on the veranda with a china cup filled with coffee at her side. She did not turn as he opened the door, or as his shoes clacked on the stone patio, but kept her gaze fixed on the gulf. Her hair was braided tight, as it was only at home, and he could see the edges of the tattoo on the back of her neck.

"Mother, who is that man in the office?" he asked.

His mother was always Mother, always formal, and always cool to him.

"That man is Mister Patrick. He is giving your father lessons," she said in her own distinctly European accent. Her lips returned to their usual grim position on her face.

"What kind of lessons?"

"He is giving your father speaking lessons," she said.

His father spoke normally, he had thought. He understood that his father did not speak like his teachers or his classmates or even like him and Mother. That was just his father, and until now there had been no reason to question it.

"Why does Father need speaking lessons?" he asked.

"Father needs speaking lessons so that he doesn't sound like a wetback drug dealer from Tijuana," she replied, and that was the end of that.

He never saw Mr. Patrick again, but when he returned from school, his father's accent was largely gone, then mostly gone, and finally, when he left for St. Paul's, it was gone altogether. In its place was a confident, booming voice like a newsman on television.

"Goodbye, Eduardo," he said with a handshake.

"When you get to school, I want you to do something for me," his father continued.

He would do anything.

"No one knows you there. No one knows anything about you. This is a fresh start. When you meet people, introduce yourself to them as Eduardo."

"I like Eddie."

"Eddie is cheap," his father said. "Be Eduardo."

11

Eduardo was most certainly not cheap, he thought while gazing at the woman he had built. She was, in her prime, without a doubt the most stunning woman in any room she entered.

She had been so young and so naïve — a young girl with no idea at the power her smile could wield. Maybe there were beautiful girls with no money all over the world, being worn down and taken advantage of and having their beauty wasted, but not this one. This one was his.

Odalys was looking at him now. He could see her lips moving. She wore only her underwear and it struggled to contain her. She looked amazing, and they were only going to dinner. With her long dark hair falling down her back, her warm-colored skin, and Latin curves, she was positively succulent.

"I wasn't listening," he said to her. It was not an apology.

"What was that man's name from the club?"

"Max."

"You introduced him by a different name."

"Max is his nickname from Saint Paul's. He didn't want his professional associates to know about it."

"Why not?"

"Perhaps he is a different person now."

"What kind of person was he then?"

"Arrogant and ruthless. Kind of a smooth operator."

"You must have been good friends," she said with a sly smile.

"Be nice."

"I didn't like the way he looked at me," she said, her smile fading.

"What way was that?"

"Like he could have anything he wanted."

"People who come from old money are like that."

"I don't like it," she said.

"You don't have to like it," Eduardo replied. "That's just how it is."

He lived on the top floor in one of the finest buildings in Austin. There was a patio on the roof that he enjoyed, and a pool several floors below that he never would. Odalys would lie out in the sun by the pool, but she attracted attention, so he always recommended the roof or a spa.

Some deals are signed in ink. Others are signed in blood. Luscious, breathing blood.

He'd once had a partnership of sorts. Angel had been a rough man, from the streets, and Eduardo had needed his connections. Angel had admired Eduardo's manners, his judgment, and his sense of propriety. Most of all, he had admired Eduardo's money. He had been born poor, whereas Eduardo had been born wealthy. At the time they had met, each had been teetering toward the middle. Each had something the other needed.

He noticed immediately that the man was proud to know him. He was a man from nothing who had built himself to a certain level. He needed Eduardo to get to the next one. He brought Eduardo to a family party to show off his new friend. Eduardo shook the hands of endless family members and forced a smile. It was loud and the music was Mexican and they were roasting a pig in a box and he might be expected to taste it if he stayed long enough. He had never imagined himself in a place such as this.

Then he saw her-a fifteen-year-old Odalys. She was fifteen and glowing, smiling with no idea of what she was. Eduardo looked at her and saw raw, unrefined beauty and sexuality. He looked at a fifteen-year-old girl and saw in an instant everything that she could become.

"Who is that?" he asked.

Angel beamed. "My little cousin Odalys. Isn't she something? She was always a shy little thing with her nose buried in a book. She suddenly became this beautiful young woman."

"Has anyone fucked her yet?"

Angel didn't answer. A man was shouting near the fire pit. A skyrocket exploded overhead.

"Has anyone fucked her yet?" Eduardo repeated.

When Angel quietly said that no, she was a nice girl, a good girl, very shy, the defeat in his voice could not have been louder. Eduardo knew then that he owned him, and their deal had been sealed.

"I would like to meet her," he said, and it was done.

They took the elevator to the garage. By his third day in the complex, he already couldn't stand opening the door to the garage on a used Cadillac with the handicap sign dangling from the rearview. Meanwhile, his car was in a dark back corner. Odalys had called it a rapist's dream come true. Eduardo had found the owner of the Cadillac, an older woman on the fourth floor, and exchanged pleasantries with her for almost twenty seconds before asking, "Exactly how handicapped are you?" A few negotiations later and his Aston Martin had the prestige spot in the front, so that when he opened the door, his exquisitely sleek, black car was the first thing he saw.

But on this day, when Eduardo Mendes opened the door to his garage, he saw shotguns and heard screaming.

Chapter Two

Strauss – Monterrey, MX

Strauss sat by the window, sipping coffee and thinking of all the men he had killed.

He didn't look Mexican, and he never had. His grandmother summed it up best when she spit on his head, tried to press his unruly blonde hair, and said, "Hundreds of years of perfectly good Indian blood, and you come out!" His grandmother had raised him. She had the same rough old hands as the men who came through this little café off the main highway. She had poor hands that had worked all her life, and would until the day she died.

Strauss hadn't heard it in a long time, but he had heard "You don't look Mexican" enough times to know it was true. He looked European. His hair and skin were lighter, and he had the bearing and countenance of the old world.

A man went into the small café. He made eye contact for a second with Strauss, but quickly looked away.

Sometimes, he thought of them by name. Other times, he gave them nicknames: The old man, the sad man, the fat man, the man who should have known better, the man who should have stayed dead the first time.

He preferred to think of a woman who had made him happy. She called herself Dulcinea. She was eternally clad in lingerie, or nothing at all, and whether smoking or sleeping or just peacefully letting him be, she'd had an old movie playing on the television.

The café was the only structure on this stretch of road, and Strauss sat a small table in the shade. He saw a blur of light appear on the desert highway. It was harsh to look at, but as the light faded, it became a Lexus, silver and freshly waxed. It pulled into the little road stop, its engine silent.

A well-built man in his late forties stepped out of the car wearing a fine gray suit. He looked around warily, though there was not much to see. When his eyes met Strauss's, he immediately sat down across from him.

Strauss placed a cup of coffee in front of him, and if he was surprised that Strauss, a man he had never met, knew exactly how he liked his coffee, he did not show it. He sat uncomfortably in his seat, watching the few other customers uneasily as they came and went. Strauss sipped patiently.

The man's name was Vicente Bonasera. He had the remains of a muscular body, but didn't work at maintaining it. He had played soccer well enough to play in college, but not well enough to play professionally. But wherever he went, he was an imposing presence.

On this day, he was sweating. He took a handkerchief from his pocket and wiped his face. He tried not to be nervous about it, but trying only made him look worse.

Vicente Bonasera cleared his throat.

"Is it safe to speak here?" he asked softly.

Strauss nodded. Bonasera began to talk. Once he began, there was no stopping him.

He was a lawyer, and worked for one of the largest companies in Mexico, with offices all over the world. His company had moved him to Buenos Aires, and later to Bilbao, Spain. He had four children with his college sweetheart, and they had spent many of their formative years in Europe, with the privileges and education of the old world. When his company returned them to Monterrey, Mexico, they found it a different place.

His eldest son went to college. His eldest son looked like his mother, who was very beautiful. The boy had been on a date when he was taken. The university called that night with the news. The kidnapper called the next morning. He said that he had Bonasera's son and the guard at the gate to his house had a package for him. Bonasera tried to keep him on the phone. "I will do anything you say," he told the kidnapper desperately.

"I know you will," was the response.

Bonasera raced out to the guard shack in his bare feet. The guard tried to stop him. He said he was going to call the police. Bonasera ripped the phone from the wall. Then he saw it. It was a brown envelope on the pavement. His name was on it. It was soaked through with blood. Inside was an ear.

16

Bonasera paid the money. He never questioned it. He met a man in town, who proved to be the most average man he had ever seen in his life. The man disappeared into the crowd. An hour later, his son was dumped naked and bound on the side of the freeway. Before they drove away, one of the kidnappers drew a knife and cut off his son's other ear.

Vicente Bonasera sat up straight in his chair and took a long sip of his coffee, like a spent athlete guzzling water. He breathed deeply, and he was no longer sweating.

When Strauss was a child, he suffered from a harelip. He talked strange and looked strange. Neighborhood children were so relentlessly cruel that he kept entirely to himself. He would hang around the church and watch hunched old women waddle into the confessional booth and spend more than twenty minutes confessing their sins. When people spoke to him like Bonasera did, this was what he thought of.

Strauss took out a pad, a pencil, and a Zippo lighter, and placed them on the table.

"The man who led you to me," began Strauss. "Did he explain to you the gravity of what you are doing?"

Vicente Bonasera nodded three times.

"You could back out now with no enemies. You and I met for a conversation. One of us decided that he did not like what the other had to say. There would be nothing wrong in that."

His voice slipped. It was the tiniest lisp. He heard it. He wondered if Bonasera heard it. He hadn't reacted.

"There is a man who I am going to contact. Once he is involved, it is impossible to stop him. Do you understand what I am saying?"

"Yes," said Bonasera.

"Then why don't you tell me precisely what you want from me, so that we are both clear of what it is we are doing."

Bonasera took a moment to think about what he was going to say.

"I want you to find the men who hurt my son and I want you to kill them."

He said it with calm conviction.

"Have you thought of which men? There are likely to be several."

17

"The man who called me on the phone. The man who said that he knew that he could have anything he wanted. I want him dead. And the man who touched my son. I want him dead too."

Strauss looked to his note pad.

"I want them to die badly," said Bonasera.

"That is reasonable." He slipped again. He despised his lisp.

Strauss took the pad and tore off the top page, which he placed on the table. He began writing a number on to the page. He would then take the page and show it to Vicente Bonasera, who would nod or balk, and a deal would be made or lost. Life was cheap in Mexico, but revenge was not. He was etching out another zero when Bonasera spoke.

"How much if I want to watch?" Bonasera asked.

His pencil stopped where it was. Strauss placed it on the table. He took the page and crumpled it into a ball and tore off another. When he handed the page this time, he did not wait for any sign from the man. There were no negotiations.

"Go home and sleep. Think on what we spoke about. If you wake up and change your mind, call the attorney. He will call me."

The lighter opened with a familiar metal cling, and Strauss lit both slips of paper on fire, dropping them to the ground where they burned to ash.

Bonasera nodded, but didn't shake hands. He walked quickly back to his car, but paused at the door. "Do you think you will be able to find them?" he asked.

"We will see," said Strauss, though it wasn't true. He remained in the shade and watched the rich man pull back onto the highway. He wondered if this well-heeled lawyer was prepared to see his blood lust come to life, if his grief was that deep. Bonasera's only concern had been if Strauss would be able to find out who they were.

He already knew.

"Get on the ground!" they shouted. "Show me your hands!"

Eduardo dropped, too stunned to do anything but submit. He got to his knees and was forced to the cement. His ear blurred with pain.

He felt an elbow to his skull. He saw a black shadow in his periphery and realized that it was the shotgun pointing right at his head.

He thought he was going to die.

His hands were pulled behind his back. He had dirt in his mouth. Dirt.

He heard Odalys screaming. She was crying in a loud and hysterical voice, pleading, and he wondered if the man was standing over his body was about to chop his head off.

"Darling, would you please shut the fuck up," said a voice. It was a command. That was when he stopped worrying about being murdered. These men weren't his executioners. These men were cops.

This was probably not how Eduardo Mendes had expected his evening would go, Curtis reflected happily. He walked up with Bobby Jordan as the team shouted at Mendes to put his hands behind his back. Curtis had requested the heavy take down on purpose. He wanted to soften him up.

The team was very fast. By the time they had walked to where Mendes was, he was secured, on his feet, and about to be loaded into a cruiser, which had been backed into the garage.

"Really, Curtis?" said Bobby Jordan disdainfully. Jordan was a Texas Ranger. Bobby Jordan had kept his hands in his pockets during the sting, but he took them out now and pointed. Curtis looked down and realized he was holding his gun.

"Did you think this guy was going out like John Dillinger?"

Curtis put it away and felt silly.

One day, two years back, as Bobby Jordan strolled into the office just before lunch, he had seen Curtis across the way, waving him into the conference room. The glass wall had blinds, which had been closed, blocking outside view.

Curtis had redecorated with a collage of dead bodies and broken glass.

The black and white photos were blown into eight-by-tens. The far wall was meant to be an overview, but it looked like a jigsaw puzzle of gore. A jagged line of broken cars and body parts led to a centerpiece of shiny metal, shell casings, and blood. Bobby Jordan laid his Stetson on the one empty chair and went straight to the center of it all. Then he sighed.

"I was hoping that last week's trip to Mexico would get this business out of your system."

"Are the latent print guys still talking about me?"

"Said you were the baddest accountant he ever met. Then he checked into a mental hospital. Something about being an accomplice to almost burning down a church."

"That church was still standing when we left. "

Bobby Jordan surveyed the damage.

"Did you sleep at all?"

"Not a wink," he said.

There were stacks of paper reports in Spanish all over the table. More photos spilled out of files and on to the chairs. There was a map spread out with colored tabs on it. There was a larger sketch of the street on top of that. He pointed back to the wall with the photos and the mess in the center.

"That thing right there. Is that Colon?"

Curtis looked just a bit wistful.

"Yeah. That was him."

"They bring him back to life after this?"

"No. He stayed dead."

"Then why are you doing this to yourself?"

Curtis thought about that reason.

"If we find the money, we can pick up our investigation right where it left off."

"Our investigation?"

"My investigation."

"Your pet project."

Bobby surveyed the damage.

"Curtis?" Bobby asked.

"Yeah?"

"Why are you doing this to yourself?" he asked quietly.

Curtis thought about this question too.

"I've never been really good at anything," he said. "But I'm going to be good at this."

They looked at one another for a long time without a word.

"Well," Bobby Jordan said finally, "if I can't talk you out of it, I might as well see what you've got."

Curtis took a photo from the wall. It was an overview of the street scene. Bobby studied it in profile against the window. Bobby Jordan was a legend in Texas law enforcement. He was in his late fifties but moved like a much younger man. He was a Texas Ranger, and had spent time in the army. He never spoke in specifics, but rumor had it that he had been Special Forces.

"Looks like an L-shaped ambush. We used to run these," Jordan said.

"Where was that? Back in El Salvador?"

"I could tell you. But then I'd have to kill you," he said distractedly.

He pointed. The photo showed five cars. They were surrounded by tiny cones. "Picture an L laying on its side in the street. Your shooters are lined up along the lines of the letter. As soon as your target enters the L, your shooters open up. There's no place to go."

Jordan tapped the Yukon.

"Who was in this truck? I don't need names. Just tell me about them."

Curtis crossed the room and tore into an even thicker file.

"Driver, age thirty-three. Minimal record. Served in the military for eight years. Cause of death: gunshot wounds to the chest and head with large and small caliber rounds. Check this out: blood alcohol content of point one one."

"What time did this happen?"

"Seven thirty in the evening."

"So he had a couple stiff ones that day, even though he was working. Tell me about the other guy."

"Ex-military. Three with the federales. Retired due to injury. He had an artificial knee and hip. Toxicology came back clean."

"I see one body next to the Mercedes. How many inside?"

"Two. The driver was in pieces behind the wheel, and the guest of honor was in the back."

"And them?"

"Former army. Attached to units that are known to work with the cartels. One was dishonorably discharged for conduct unbecoming."

"Jesus, what do you have to do to be dishonorably discharged from the Mexican army?" Jordan asked.

"Why are you asking about the bodyguards?"

"I don't know. You've always talked about how careful this Colon was. How smart. Now he's being guarded by a guy with a bum leg, a drunk, and some dude who can't cut it in the world's most crooked army."

"They're not his normal bodyguards," Curtis said.

"No. Then who is? And why wasn't he there?"

"He was fired six months ago. After twenty years of service."

Jordan thought on that for a while. "I would wonder where he's getting his bodyguards now. And who's picking them."

The Mexican cops hadn't released any conclusions, but by seven o'clock, Jordan and Curtis had a good idea of what had happened, and who had fired first. Curtis said he had access to a database listing all motor vehicles registered in Mexico.

"That car is burned to scrap metal by now. I wouldn't give it another thought. My best guess is this: sit back, relax, and see who picks up Colon's business from where it left off. It'll be someone who worked for him. That person will know a thing or two about what happened in Monterrey."

With that, Jordan stood, picked his hat up off the table where it had sat for many hours more than he had ever intended, and made his way to the door. He paused before he left.

"I'm going home for the night. I'm going to drink some beer, and I'm going to give advice."

"Fire away," said Curtis.

"Go home. Have a drink. Talk to a girl. Don't talk about drug dealers or meth or people getting their heads blown off. Be a normal person for one night. Come back on Monday with a clear mind and hope the cleaning lady throws all this crap in the dumpster and you never see it again."

"Yeah? Why's that?" Curtis asked.

"Because it ain't worth it, kid."

***

Curtis had asked the leading computer forensic expert to come on the raid of Eduardo Mendes' apartment because of the review he'd heard from Jordan. "He is the second biggest geek in the federal government," Jordan had told him. Curtis had almost asked who was number one, but he realized who it was and stopped himself. Even he didn't believe what the geek had to say.

"What do you mean?" Curtis asked.

"Dude, I mean, there's nothing on this computer," said the geek.

They had a search warrant to enter Mendes's apartment, as well as to seize and search electronics. Darryl the Geek was their digital forensic technician. His specialty was searching computers for evidence. Curtis wanted him on the raid so he could tear into the laptop immediately. He didn't want to wait. He didn't think he could.

"Have you looked around for an external hard drive?"

"This is a Mac Book. I went into the central drive, and from what I can see, the spreadsheet files have never even been opened. All he does on this is shop for clothes."

"Maybe clothes is a code or something?"

"Dude, it's no freaking code. Look. Websites about clothes and fashion designers and crap I can't afford."

He highlighted a field, and the screen went to an image of a man in skintight jeans with heavily gelled hair trying to look serious.

He had expected the laptop to be dirty. He'd seen it slung over Mendes's shoulder in a leather satchel time and again. There had to be something on the laptop.

"Is this website for real? Could it be a cover or a front?"

"Dude, I looked up these jeans on my phone. They're fucking six-hundred dollar jeans."

"Bullshit."

"Just because you and I can't afford them doesn't mean they aren't real."

That was all they found in the kitchen. Curtis stormed out and went into the main bedroom. The tech had opened the heavy drapes to let in natural light. The bed was crisply made. There was a long matching bureau with nothing on it.

"Did you clean this off already?" Curtis asked, pointing at the bureau.

"No. Your guy lives this way."

Curtis looked in the bathroom. There were droplets of water all over the glass door to the shower. Otherwise, the surfaces and floors were immaculate black marble.

"I thought you said this guy was rich," observed the tech from the other side of the bedroom. She had long blonde hair tied in a ponytail. Curtis thought her name was Susan.

"I did," said Curtis. "He is."

"Take a look at this."

Curtis stepped into the huge walk-in closet. He saw mostly dark bare wood. A line of suit bags hung from the rack. Two wooden hangers dangled uselessly. All of his shirts were wrapped in plastic. There were six pairs of shoes in the rack by his knees. Curtis scratched his head.

"Is it possible he doesn't live here?" he asked aloud.

"Aren't you the lead guy on this case?" asked the tech.

When it was clear that Curtis wasn't going to answer her, the tech marched over to the bathroom and began opening drawers. There were hair products and skin products and facial cleansers, all arranged in a very particular order and neatly stocked. There was a precision and an underlying order to all of it. Curtis spied a tiny bottle with Asian writing that he couldn't resist picking up without gloves.

"I would get suspended for that," said the tech.

"What is this?" Curtis asked.

"It's Japanese."

"What is it for?"

"Your eyelids."

"What does it do to them?"

"It cleans them. It's a cleanser for your eyelids. It's very expensive, and very hard to find."

"What does this mean?"

"It means he lives here."

"What's up with all this stuff?" Curtis asked, pointing at the bottles.

"Was our target in the Marine Corps?"

"No. Why?"

"I dated a Marine for a while. He ironed his socks. Then he folded them and stacked them in order in his sock drawer. If this guy isn't a marine, then he is your garden variety obsessive compulsive."

She opened the medicine cabinet. It was precisely, if sparsely, arranged as well. She took out a tiny blue bottle.

"See this? This is a mud mask emulsion therapy from Iceland. This costs more than two hundred dollars a bottle. It's supposed to soften skin while opening pores when you sleep. I would expect to find this in the bathroom of the most spoiled star in Hollywood. A female star. Yes, he lives here."

Curtis started to pace slowly around the room. The view showed the best of Austin, with a solid shot of the river and green flatland in the distance.

"Have you checked for hidden panels maybe?" he asked.

Susan the tech looked confidently at him and beckoned him over with her finger. She handed him a flashlight, but all he saw was a brand new screw.

"That screw has been used once, and that was when they bolted this wall. If this wall were coming off even once in a while, there would be signs of use. The edges of the screw would be worn. Or the wood might thread around it. Look at this one."

The screw was as clean as the rest of the house.

"Something is wrong," Sheldon said into the phone. There was panic in his voice. He was watching cars in the parking lot.

"I think they're on to me," Sheldon said nervously.

Sheldon had noticed a black Ford behind him on the way to work. Black Fords were the standard police car in America. Even a square like Sheldon Cashman could spot one. He saw it again before he turned into his lot. Now it was parked outside his office.

"Does anyone know about me? About what we do?" he asked.

It wasn't the first time Sheldon had experienced paranoia. He had never been comfortable in this business. This time, however, felt different. He had called Eduardo.

"Am I about to be arrested?" he asked.

Eduardo had answered the phone, but so far, he hadn't said a word. He hadn't been short. He hadn't been rude. Sheldon's mind went to its normal state of panic. He began to suspect that calling Eduardo had been a tremendous mistake. He desperately strained his ears for any sign of reassurance on the other end.

"Who is this?" asked Special Agent Walter Curtis.

Sheldon looked at the phone in his hand in horror. Outside, two black SUVs drove up to the door. Every door on the black Ford opened at once. Men wearing black jackets that read DEA raced into the building.

Sheldon hid in the men's room.

When Bobby Jordan walked in and announced that Mendes was willing to talk, Curtis jumped out of his seat and started to run down the hall before Jordan stopped him with a gentle hand to the chest.

"Slow down a minute," he said. "Let's do a little regroup before we rush in there."

Curtis was the foremost expert on Eduardo Mendes, and he realized that he had never so much as heard the sound of the man's voice. They had no phones on him. They had no video. What they had was Curtis, and for Curtis, watching, following, and stalking were things done with computers, calculators, and spreadsheets. Eduardo Mendes had been tracked by an accountant.

"Did you find anything on the book keeper?" asked Jordan, inclining his hat just slightly toward the stack of paperwork that Curtis had been attacking. Curtis shook his head.

"How about the money store? Did that yield anything?" Curtis shook his head again.

"Nothing that we didn't already know about."

"This raid isn't going so well, is it?" Jordan said. It wasn't so much a question as a wry observation.

"That being the case, this might be a gift from God. So let's not screw it up."

The forensic techs hadn't yet touched the machines that had been seized from either of the offices. There could be a treasure trove in there. There was a nagging sense of defeat creeping under his skin.

Curtis had his hand on the knob. He put his forehead against the door and listened. He heard nothing. The door felt cold.

Eduardo Mendes was sweating. Curtis came into the room stiffly. He nodded at Eduardo politely. Curtis sat down at the table opposite him and pretended to go through paperwork. He made his eyes roll over the words to mimic reading, but he had no idea what they said. He peeked at Eduardo Mendes.

He had pieces of hair clinging to his forehead. He was handcuffed by one wrist to a ring that protruded from the top of the table. The skin around the cuff was red and looked sore.

To his credit, Mendes hadn't said a word. According to Bobby Jordan, some prisoners were ready to confess to the janitor if he would stop and listen. Eduardo Mendes, though, was not the average criminal, so he sat quietly and in obvious discomfort, waiting for whatever was going to happen. Bobby Jordan came in, nodded, and sat in the chair behind Curtis.

He had thought about this moment. In slivers of dreams he was afraid to remember, he had even thought about sitting down in the box opposite Colon himself. Eduardo Mendes was a distant second, but he still quickened Curtis' pulse. Mendes was his. The case was his. The discovery was his. He had put time and effort into every minute detail, right down to the very first words he would say to the man. He thought of Marc Virgil's technique, where he called you by your first name like he'd known you for twenty years. Or Bobby Jordan's own familiar style, where he shot the shit with the suspect for so long he forgot he was in custody. He had actually woken one night at three in the morning and found himself agonizing over what his first words should be. It all seemed ridiculous now.

"Good afternoon, Mister Mendes," he said. He had gone with polite and formal, and it felt fine. He took a deep breath. "My name is Special Agent Walter Curtis. I am with the Drug Enforcement Administration task force." He always said task force, and he made sure they heard Drug Enforcement Administration before it. He never said IRS. "I apologize for making you wait, but we have a great deal of information to process. I understand you would like to speak with me."

"Yes, I would," said Eduardo Mendes.

27

The most beautiful words he had ever heard. Curtis said a silent prayer to whoever was listening.

The taxes were his undoing. It was taxes, money, mandatory forms, procedural filings, and little bits of paperwork that never ever went away.

For accountants, taxes are like a trail of breadcrumbs. For accountants like Curtis, they were more like red meat. Curtis had been on Colon's trail and had been closing in on a warrant for his arrest, pending the approval of the Mexican federal authorities, who had not yet been told of the far-reaching investigation when Colon's head had been taken off his shoulders. The Colon case was suddenly as dead as he was, but he had left several trails in his wake. One of those led to a quiet check cashing business in Austin, Texas.

The check cashing storefront was nothing special. It was ugly, yellow, and in a neighborhood where no one lived by choice. Its official name was West Avenue Check Cashers, but the huge, gaudy sign over the door flashed "The Money Store," and that was what you called it if you went there. If you had an interest in the business, or if you paid taxes from the profits from the business, then you would know that the parent company was Vanidad, International. There were five owners of Vanidad, International, and not only did they cash checks, but they processed money transfers, both big and small, into foreign countries like Mexico.

"You are part owner of this company, is that correct," Curtis asked.

"Yes. Absolutely."

"Your company is doing well."

"We have had some good years."

This was true. Since Eduardo Mendes had taken over the company, its profits had increased steadily.

"Do you know who your other partners are?"

"I do."

"How well do you know them?"

"When I purchased a stake in the business, thirty percent of the company was already spoken for at that time through the original investors."

"How much of the company do you own now?"

"I now own fifty percent."

"And you run the company?"

"No. I have a leadership role in the business, that is true, but I leave the day to day operations to Ronald Garcia, the manager."

"Who controls the rest of Vanidad?"

"A series of investors," said Eduardo.

"What are their names?"

"Their names are Jorge Lara, Sofia Quinones, Monica Cassavetes, and Sergio Nova."

"Did they all agree to allow you a leadership role, or was it acrimonious?"

"No, it was amicable. They preferred to be silent, and the arrangement appears to have worked out well for everyone."

This was true. Curtis had pored through everyone's tax records, which were filed dutifully and in accordance with the law. Each of the owners had given Uncle Sam his due.

"Did Mrs. Quinonez ever have a disagreement with you regarding your role with the company?"

"No. Not that I remember. "

"How about Mister Lara?"

"No. I do not remember anything like that."

"Was there any effort to strong arm your partners into allowing you to lead this company?"

"None."

"Are you sure? Not any of your partners?"

"No."

Curtis dove into his paperwork. He wanted to turn and look at Bobby. He wanted the silent head nod. He didn't think Bobby would nod yet. He looked at Eduardo Mendes, pretending to be polite and helpful, and all he wanted to do was to say to him, "I know you. And I know you are full of shit." Instead, he showed him an old document.

Eduardo read it aloud when he was asked.

"Male. Eleven years old. Body partially consumed. Cause of death: exposure. What is this?"

"That is Sergio Nova. Your partner."

"I don't understand."

"Sergio Nova died thirty years ago while crossing from Mexico into the United States. He died as a young boy. Several years ago, he came back to life, bought a check cashing company, and started paying taxes."

Eduardo didn't answer, so Curtis slid more documents across the table.

"Sofia Quinonez. Age eight. Dead. Found in the desert. Monica Cassavetes. Age nine. Cause of death: bullet wound. Her convoy was shot up. Found in the desert. Died three weeks later in America. Sergio Lara. Age six. He was in the back of a truck that broke down on a hundred-degree day. Died of suffocation. In America."

The sweat was back. His shirt was growing darker. Mendes wasn't looking at the documents either. He was staring at the table, past the papers, toward his wrist.

"Is this your signature?" Curtis asked as he held up another document. Eduardo glanced up and nodded.

"This is a certificate of incorporation where you entered into this partnership with a bunch of people who died over twenty years ago." Curtis reminded himself to speak softly, calmly, and, above all else, be friendly. Bobby Jordan had warned him on that. "No one wants to confess to a fella who hates them." But the excitement was building inside of him.

"Let me show you some more things," Curtis said. He pretended to look through the files, but he wasn't really looking. He could have done it blindfolded. He removed a ream of paper. The sheets were connected top to bottom and had been spit out from old government printers.

"These are money transfers from your company to individuals in Mexico. As the owner, I am sure that you know that any payments over ten thousand dollars are mandated by law to be declared to the government. You'll notice that there are a large number of transfers in the seven-to-nine-thousand dollar range."

Curtis now removed a stack of paper that was identical to the first. This one had been highlighted.

"You'll see that there is a series of accounts that are highlighted. The amounts transferred are never the same, but the people transmitting the money and the people receiving the money are the same. This repeats in a three-week pattern. That in and of itself is not so strange. What is strange is this: once you recognize the accounts, and begin to follow them, and you take all of the amounts transferred between them, you'll see that every three weeks a total of one point five million dollars goes from your office into Mexico."

Was he changing color? Was he turning gray?

Once upon a time, Marc Virgil had offered sage if drunken advice. "They turn gray sometimes. Be sure you're not sitting right next to them when they turn gray." Curtis had to ask how come. "'Cause that's when they start throwing up."

Curtis was secretly hoping Eduardo would throw up for him.

"Let's be very clear about this part. If I look at these accounts, the dollars change, Mister Mendes, but if I add them up, every three weeks, it comes out to a million and a half dollars. Every cent of it comes through your business. That is not a coincidence, and no jury is every going to believe it is a coincidence."

"Don't bring up the court system too early," he'd been told by Virgil. He regretted it as soon as he said it. He decided immediately to change the subject.

"Have you ever heard of a man by the name of Aureliano Colon?" Curtis asked.

The beautiful man in the handcuff sat slumped in his chair and said nothing.

"I have," said Curtis. "Colon was a very secretive man. He ran a very unique and very profitable business. Very quietly, and without being noticed, he began producing and shipping into America a very respectable amount of methamphetamine. He did it without fanfare or a gang, and most importantly, he did it without leaving dead bodies around to attract attention. I said he produced a respectable amount, because it wasn't particularly large. He ran what I would call a boutique drug operation."

Curtis had coined that term: boutique drug operation. He was proud of it. He'd seen the Dallas ASAC smile when he said it at a meeting. They were all using it now.

"It could have been much larger. Larger would have meant more money. A lot more. But larger would have attracted attention. Larger would have meant rivalry. Larger would have meant dead bodies. All of these things were bad for a boutique drug operation.

"I was looking for Colon when I found you, Eduardo."

He looked up now. Curtis could feel Bobby's disapproval boring into the back of his head, but he pushed along anyway. He couldn't stop himself.

"I became the world's foremost expert on Aureliano Colon. I knew him, and I know you knew him too. I can prove it."

Two of them were sweating now.

"I look at Colon's operation, at his entire approach, and even at the kind of person he was, atypical to the drug business. Then I look at you and I see the exact same thing. You've taken Colon's approach and you've recreated it on the other side of the border. And you're doing it very, very well."

"Not quite well enough," muttered Bobby Jordan for the first time from the back of the room.

"No," agreed Curtis softly. "Not quite well enough. You are in a great deal of trouble, Mister Mendes, but you do have options."

Curtis felt his blood rush when Mendes looked up at him: big lost eyes, beaten down with fear, and begging for a friend.

He had him.

"What kind of options are you speaking of?" asked Eduardo politely and in a voice that sounded fractured.

"That depends," said Curtis. "That depends on how much you would like to stay out of prison."

Prison, he had said. Not jail. Prison was a much more frightening word than jail.

Eduardo Mendes licked his lips, which suddenly looked very dry.

"I would like that very much," he said softly.

"I am an accountant by trade, Eduardo," Curtis began. He made a point of using his first name. "I don't always see people. I see numbers. I see accounts. I see how those things are linked to one another. I want you to think about who you are linked to, and what you can tell us about those people."

"Which people did you have in mind?" Eduardo answered immediately. His voice was awfully calm.

Once again, Curtis wished he could consult Jordan.

"I'm talking about people in the drug business."

"In this country, or another country?"

"In any country."

The handcuff rattled. Eduardo readjusted himself in his seat. He pulled the chair in closer to the table.

"Specifically, what would you like to know?"

I want to know everything, Curtis thought. And you are going to tell me.

"I would like to talk about what you have been bringing into the country, how you are getting it here, who you are getting it from, and who you are selling it to. We can start with any of those topics."

"And if I do have a conversation like this, what will you do for me?"

"That depends on your level of cooperation, Eduardo. If you are willing to share a little information, then we may be talking about a reduction in sentence and some asset forfeiture. On the other hand..."

He looked back to Jordan, who was stoically not moving. He sat there with his arms crossed and his back to the wall.

"You understand that I'm not promising you anything, but..." he paused for dramatic effect. "If you give us something big, you could be looking at a walk."

The handcuff rattled again. He was thinking about it. Mendes' eyes disappeared from view. His hair was matted with sweat. His shoulders weakened and sagged. Curtis could hear a shoe tapping nervously. He was mostly sure it wasn't his own.

There was a long moment where no one spoke. Curtis adjusted his chair as nonchalantly as he could. Over his shoulder, he could see a glimpse of an unmoving Bobby Jordan, a man who had never been nervous a day in his life. He was as patient as a mountain. Curtis felt like it was Christmas morning and he wasn't allowed to get out of bed.

Curtis wondered what the right move was. He had all day and all night and even tomorrow. Eduardo Mendes did not.

Nasty little thoughts had time to sneak into his mind. He had spent years on this, and it all came down to this interview. There were only a few eyes in the room, but many more would be watching. They would be waiting for results. His entire career rested on this case.

"Eduardo," he said.

There was no response.

"Eduardo." When he still didn't move, Curtis spoke anyway. "You could be a very valuable asset to us. Or you could be a solid prize in your own right. You're not stupid. You know we searched your home. We searched your business. We have all your computers. We have your car. We have your phone. We even have your girlfriend's phone. We have your accountant. We're going to get you one way or another. This is your chance to help yourself."

Nothing. He should be in tears right now.

"Think about yourself and your relationship with people. Are the people who work for you loyal to a fault? Are they blindly loyal? Would they be willing to go to prison for Eduardo Mendes?"

Curtis wondered if he had gone too far. He decided he hadn't gone far enough.

"Do you think Strasberg is willing to die in prison for you?"

Eduardo Mendes popped up. That got his attention fast.

"We arrested your accountant Strasberg at his office right after we arrested you. We have all of his computers and all of his books. You're both good to go for money laundering. His signature is on everything. When we walk down the hall and talk to him, he's going to take the deal and give you up. Then where will you be?"

"Strasberg?" Eduardo asked in a whisper.

"Yes, Strasberg," said Curtis. He knew he shouldn't have said it. Something was wrong.

"Strasberg," said Mendes, and when he did, there was a tiny flicker of life in his tone.

Eduardo Mendes suddenly had a spaced-out wistful look to him. He sat back in his seat and ran a hand through his long hair. A smile began to dance at the corners of his mouth.

Curtis came back at him with his tax documents, spreading them out across the table where Eduardo couldn't avoid them.

"Arlo Strasberg. Right here. And here. And here," he said, pointing out the man's signature on the same page as Eduardo's. "All of your money was laundered right through him. He has as much to lose as you do."

Eduardo stretched, as much as he could stretch with one arm chained to the desk, but he stretched, and his joints cracked loudly. Then he smiled broadly, glanced casually at Jordan, looked Curtis in the eye, and very confidently said, "I think I would like to speak to my attorney."

Curtis felt like it was Christmas morning, only to find that all his presents had been burned in a fire. His Christmas was a charred disaster.

Curtis pointed to a page on the table. "Look at this," he said to Mendes.

"Agent Curtis," Bobby Jordan said, cutting him off. "I'm afraid this man said the magic words."

With that, Jordan stood up, crossed the room, and turned the heavy metal handle of the door. It clicked loudly. Curtis began to quietly gather his things, as Jordan now held the door open for him.

"Agent Curtis?" Eduardo called as they tried to leave. He stopped.

"Was this your first time?"

Curtis stared back at him.

"How do you feel it went?" Eduardo asked.

Curtis dropped some papers from the stack. He'd packed it poorly and in a hurry and while he was distracted, but now he looked as ridiculous as he felt.

"Let me tell you something maybe no one's ever told you before," said Curtis. "We don't play fair. When the feds go through your books, they always find something to hang you for. You or your girlfriend or your friends. One way or another, you always lose."

Eduardo Mendes smiled. The son of a bitch smiled.

***

Montrose was on them as soon as they hit the hallway with even more bad news. He had a way of subtly abusing pronouns so that the successes were "ours" and the problems were "yours."

"You," said Special Agent in Charge Montrose, "have a problem in Interview Two."

A thin old man sat in the chair. His eyes were red from crying. He didn't look healthy. His skin was slightly jaundiced and hung loosely from his neck. He was unshaven and had been so for a week or more, from the looks of him.

"Good afternoon, Mister Strasberg," said Curtis as he sat down opposite the old man. He wasn't that old, thought Curtis. Not this old. He nodded, however weakly.

"Sir, my name is Special Agent Walter Curtis. I'm with the Drug Enforcement Administration task force. I understand that you are an accountant." He was speaking too fast. He knew it, but couldn't stop it.

"Yes," said Strasberg.

Curtis turned to Montrose, who was looking over his shoulder now. "He's been mirandized?" Montrose nodded.

"Mister Strasberg, do you have a client by the name of Eduardo Mendes?"

"I don't know," said the old man.

His hands were shaking. He was terrified.

Curtis went into the files once more and produced one of the documents he had shown Mendes.

"Mister Strasberg, is this your signature?"

"I don't know," said the old man.

"Mister Strasberg, I need you to listen to me very carefully. I am an accountant with the DEA task force. We have seized all of your business records. We have records of cash transactions and wire transfers, administered by you, with your signature, again and again and again. Now, you can tell us "I don't know," but eventually, you are going to have to answer to this in front of a jury. "I don't know" isn't going to be good enough."

A tear slid down the old man's face. It slowed Curtis. His heart beat so hard that he was sure his shirt must be shaking.

"Arlo, you're not the person we're after, and I think you know that. If you are willing to help us, we can help you."

Curtis noticed then that Strasberg was chained to the desk, just as Mendes had been, except that his hands were clasped together, fingers interlocked, as if praying.

"Arlo, who is the man you work for?"

"I just want to go home," said Strasberg haltingly.

"The sooner you help us, the sooner you can," Curtis said, but the thought raced through the edges of his mind that what he had said might not be true. "Who is the man you work for?" he asked again.

"My father," said Strasberg.

Curtis turned in his chair to look at Montrose. The boss made a gesture with his hand that said, "This is what we've been dealing with while you were gone." Curtis looked to Bobby Jordan, who gave him nothing.

"Your father?"

"My father is coming to get me."

Curtis looked at Arlo Strasberg. Curtis had done a background workup on him as well in the course of his due diligence. It was not nearly as extensive as the one on Eduardo Mendes, and it couldn't hold a candle to the treatise had written on Aureliano Colon. Arlo Strasberg was seventy years old and looked older.

"Your father is coming here?" Curtis asked him.

"Yes. I want to go home now."

"Mister Strasberg, you can't go home now. We have you committing tax fraud and multiple counts of money laundering. You're in a great deal of trouble. You're going to jail."

The old man began to cry in earnest now. There was an air of discomfort in the room now. Curtis was completely bewildered.

"Arlo," Curtis said, trying to get his attention. "How old is your father?"

"I don't know," said Strasberg. "Will he find out about this?"

Curtis pushed back from the desk. The door was eight feet away. He wanted to go through it. He wanted to walk out of that door, down the stairs, into the street, and never come back into this place. He wanted to run. He was chained to this case. He was chained to it irrevocably.

"Mister Strasberg," he heard Bobby Jordan say. "Could I ask you a question?"

Bobby Jordan had come to his rescue. Bobby Jordan had opposed this investigation from the start. Bobby Jordan had told him that Eduardo Mendes was not a drug dealer, was not a big fish, and was not the fast track to success. Bobby Jordan who had wanted nothing to do with any of this spoke up to save him, his voice calm and cool and unflappable as always.

"Mister Strasberg, could you tell me what year it is?"

Later, as Curtis sat in the conference room with Montrose and the rest of the team, surrounded by his research and spreadsheets and the montage of Colon's murder still taped to the far wall in glorious black and white, a memory he tried to forget came uninvited to the front of his mind. He thought of that day on the lake years ago, his family on vacation in New Hampshire, when his father decided that nine years old was far too old to be afraid of the water. Curtis saw what was coming and begged his father not to do it, growing louder and more panicked as his fear became a reality. As he was hoisted into the air, he opened his mouth to scream. Water rushed in before he could make another sound.

"Obviously," Montrose continued, "today was a significant disappointment."

Montrose wanted the money. He wanted a cash seizure. He hadn't been in Texas three years and had no roots here. It was no secret where his sights were set, and he had hoped to put an eight figure seizure on his resume.

"We still have a case against our target, and we will put resources into its continuation as necessary," he said. Curtis knew he didn't mean it. There was only one person in this room who would ever touch this case again, and every man in this room knew who that was.

"In the meantime, we are actively seeking new targets. Thanks for all your hard work today."

Curtis sat still in his chair as they began to file out, and he heard Montrose ask Bobby for a word in private. He was alone and surrounded by years of fruitless effort.

The old man thought it was 1952. They hadn't even bothered to process him. They called an ambulance and shipped him off for evaluation while one of the Austin cops was instructed to find a relative or, as Bill Montrose had put it, a caretaker.

There was a grainy photo of Colon, just to the top left of the one with his head taken off. He didn't sneer. There was no intensity about him. He looked benign. He looked like a well-heeled Mexican on vacation, not a drug lord.

Bobby Jordan came back into the room and stood in front of Curtis. "I suppose we ought to talk," he said.

I am being scolded, thought Curtis.

"I had an aunt," he began. "I loved her very much. When I was a kid, we realized that after dessert, if we cleaned up any trace evidence, we could ask for dessert all over again and she would happily serve it to us. She couldn't remember that we'd already had it.

"When she got worse, she would talk about herself as if she were seven years old. Same as Arlo Strasberg there. We found out years later that she had Alzheimer's and I don't need to be a doctor to know that Arlo Strasberg has it too."

He had his hat on his head. It was that same big cowboy hat he always wore, though it always looked crisp and clean.

"You never did any surveillance on Strasberg, did you?" Jordan asked.

"I was all over his books and monitoring his transactions."

"But you never did any surveillance. You watched his numbers go from this account to that account, but you never watched the man. That's the difference, you know. The difference between being a cop and being an accountant. I think we learned that today, didn't we?"

Curtis didn't know if Jordan expected him to answer.

"Why didn't you think of it?" Curtis asked.

Bobby Jordan shrugged.

"Maybe I did."

"You thought of it and never said anything to me?"

Bobby shrugged.

"Did you want me to fail?" Curtis asked.

"Maybe I just wanted you to learn a little bit of a lesson."

"What lesson is that?"

"That you may be the best accountant in the federal government, and an incredible researcher. But you're not cut out for the rest of it."

"What rest of it is that?"

"I think you know what I'm talking about."

"I'd like to hear it."

"I'm talking about street work. Hell, Curtis, you're always talking about your buddy Virgil back in Boston and what a great cop he is. That's his specialty. And the accounting thing is yours. I think once you recognize that, you'll find the success you want."

"What if it's not the success I want?"

"Then it's the success you'll have to settle for."

Curtis didn't speak for a while. He avoided eye contact with Bobby.

"You set me up to lose."

"You set yourself up, kid." He added the slightest intensity to it. "You over reached."

"A little guidance," Curtis said, and as he said it, he knew how defeated he sounded. He still couldn't stop himself. "A little goddamn guidance. Was that too much to ask?"

"Maybe it was."

When Curtis didn't answer, and it was clear that he had won this argument once and for all and forever, finally, Bobby Jordan walked out and left Curtis alone.

Curtis told the Austin cops that he would walk Mendes down to the deputies. They tried to tell him that they had it, but he sullenly replied that it was his mess and he would clean it up himself.

Mendes smiled when he entered.

"Is my attorney here yet?" he asked.

"Not yet."

"Please let me know as soon as he arrives."

"I will. You won't be here though."

A dent appeared in that arrogant smile. Curtis was too tired, too spent, and too distracted to notice.

"What do you mean?"

"You're still under arrest. You're on the way to jail."

"I am going to the police station until my bail is paid. I spoke with my attorney."

"Your attorney was misinformed. You're going to prison. Your bail is nine hundred thousand dollars."

Eduardo Mendes tried to comprehend that number. Curtis didn't have to look it up or make a phone call. He had arranged it weeks earlier. The bail would be more cash than Eduardo Mendes had on hand, and the prison he was going to had a fearsome reputation. Curtis' plan had been to steamroll Mendes. He wasn't tough and he wasn't street savvy. He was exactly the type of person who would be terrified of one night in prison. When Curtis placed the handcuffs on him, he could feel Mendes shaking.

"I've changed my mind," he said. "I would like to talk."

"Your lawyer already called us and demanded that we stop speaking with you. "

Curtis could see him racking his brain for any possible way out of this situation. Curtis had imagined their interview, and in his mind, it had gone differently. It ended with Mendes cooperating. It ended with seized assets, intelligence, and confessions. It ended with Curtis as the star.

"What if I know about a murder?" Mendes said as they entered the elevator.

"I'm sure you do," Curtis said. Just a few hours past and he would have killed to hear those words.

"What if I can give you a hit man out of Mexico?"

Curtis knew he could. But no one else believed him, and now it didn't matter.

"I still can't speak to you."

Curtis was skinny, and he was still larger than Mendes. Hanging Strasberg over his head had seemed like a real smart move a month ago.

"What if—" Mendes started to say, but he lost himself in thought before Curtis could answer. Curtis looked at the man and closed his eyes. Mendes had a volcanic desperation about him. He would have said or done anything.

"What if I told you there was three million dollars buried in the desert?" Mendes asked breathlessly.

The doors opened.

Curtis drove straight to a liquor store in a bad neighborhood. The cashier asked if he was having a party. He tried to smile and almost cried. When he got home, he drank until he couldn't drink anymore. He threw up, and then poured another. It burned his throat and stomach, but it didn't stop him. He fell asleep sitting up with a glass in his hand.

When he awoke, his head and his body felt horrible, and he was obsessed with a terrible new idea.

Chapter Three

Cashman – Austin, TX

After the agents left, when Cashman finally walked out of the bathroom, he found the hallway filled with people who worked in the building, whispering or on cell phones or peering through the window or sharing whatever they knew of what had happened, which was damn near nothing. He crept past them into his suite, and his secretary, a lovely woman when she was calm, practically exploded.

"Arlo has been arrested!" she yelled.

Of course he has, thought Sheldon Cashman.

Maeve Strasberg was Arlo's daughter. She was a chunky girl with red hair who had no problem asking other people to do things for her. She always smiled when she did it and said thank you so nicely that Sheldon just found himself doing these things anyway, even though he didn't want to. Even if it was a great imposition. Or even a little bit unethical.

"I know you spend time with my father," she had said years ago. "I'm sure you've noticed that he's not well."

He hadn't. Cashman had not noticed because he didn't know the man particularly well. Cashman was an accountant and Strasberg was an accountant, and they shared certain resources due to proximity and had a drink at the Christmas party every year. Beyond that, he was another face he said hello to in the hallway.

"My father has Alzheimer's. He's getting worse."

"Is he still working?"

"He works part time in tax season. He does taxes for a few old clients who have been with him for years. Older folks, mostly. Truth be told, we let him do it because it keeps him calm and gives him purpose."

No sooner had he asked what he could do to help, which he meant as a figure of speech, than Maeve Strasberg had handed him a stack of files. Would Cashman mind going over the numbers, just to make sure Mister Strasberg hadn't made any massive accounting mistakes?

While his mind had shouted, "You have got to be kidding me," her mouth was smiling and thanking him and she was standing and making her way to the door. She had dumped the files and ran. He went for a ride that afternoon.

It was years later, after he had continued to look over the old man's numbers, when Sheldon Cashman had realized that it would be infinitely safer for him if Arlo Strasberg went to work as Eduardo Mendes' accountant.

Eduardo - Beaumont Prison, TX

Eduardo was in line for food in the prison cafeteria when he looked down and saw a huge damp black head pressed upon his arm. He felt a warm, wet nose on his wrist, and it slid up his arm to his soft, gentle bicep.

The man pulled back and inhaled deeply. His eyes were closed, and his mouth hung open. On his face was a look of mild ecstasy.

"I smelled it too," said a voice behind him. Eduardo turned. Some fat white trash behemoth was in line behind him, smiling wistfully, front teeth long gone.

"Everyone in here smells institutional," said the behemoth. "You smell wonderful."

Eduardo had been processing all day. Normally at this time, he might be about to take his third shower. Today, he would not. He had been given a bar of soap. He was placed in his cell and promised himself that he was going to strip off all of his clothes and immediately scrub off any trace of good soap or cologne that might still cling to his body.

The head deputy was Nixon. He was black and hard and never took his hat off of his head. He had the deep, quick voice of military and back country. He was hard to understand and quick to anger if you didn't. He assigned the jobs. He had sent Eduardo to the kitchen.

When the group dispersed, Eduardo asked Nixon as politely as possible if he could have a word with him in private.

"You can have a word with me right here and now," Nixon said.

Eduardo didn't want anyone to hear this conversation. He didn't want to be noticed. He certainly didn't want to be noted for what he was about to say.

"Sir," he began. He had to call this man sir. He had learned this much already. "Could we please discuss my kitchen assignment?"

Nixon didn't speak, and he didn't react. He didn't so much as blink.

"Sir," he tried to speak as quietly as possible, in a voice that didn't sound condescending. That was the hard part for him. "Sir, if I have to work here, I think I might be of much more use in an office, or doing some accounting, or maybe helping in one of the classrooms."

Nixon began whipping through the papers on his clipboard until he found what he wanted.

"It says right here you got high school education."

"Yes, sir."

"You need college education for those jobs."

"I understand, sir, but I went to Saint Paul's."

"Saint Paul's. What's that now?"

"It is a preparatory school."

"What they prepare you for?"

"They prepare you for college."

"Well," said Nixon, "they shoulda prepare you for working in the kitchen."

On his first day, he saw how the food was handled.

The man who had sniffed him worked in the kitchen too. Fat, juicy beads of sweat hung tenuously to the edges of his beard, and as he leaned over the pan of fresh mashed potatoes, Eduardo watched six or seven drops fall from his beard directly into the food. He walked back out to the dining hall with the tray.

Eduardo tasted a sweetness in his mouth, and he knew he would be sick. He had eaten the mashed potatoes yesterday.

Bobby Jordan came into the office around ten in the morning. He walked slowly and kept his hat on his head. He carried a steaming cup of black coffee. He had a desk here with nothing on it, but he walked right past it and went to Curtis' cube. It was empty.

There was always half a library of books and spreadsheets on Curtis' desk, and this day was no exception. Boxes of papers filled with wrong turns and dead ends were stacked in corners. Folders and binders strewn across the floor. It looked like a random mess, but Curtis, to his credit, always knew where everything was.

Jordan walked down the hall to Montrose's office. It was in the corner and had tall glass windows. It probably impressed some people as much as it impressed Montrose himself. As he went, he noted that the whole building seemed quiet, even though it was a Monday. It seemed a little bit of life had gone out of the place.

Other people would have knocked, but Bobby Jordan strode right in.

"Is Curtis around?" he asked.

Montrose put his phone down from whatever he had been doing.

"I haven't seen him," said Montrose.

Curtis was usually the first man through the door to the office. He might have a powerful headache, smell like booze, or be dressed in yesterday's suit, but there he would be at his desk.

"Is something wrong?" Montrose asked.

"Yes and no," said Jordan, glancing behind him to see if anyone was listening. "You asked me to have a talk with him the other day. We had it."

"And?" asked Montrose.

"And it didn't go so well."

"It wasn't supposed to. It was a pretty big screw up. Big things were promised and not delivered. We didn't come out of that looking too good."

He knew what Montrose really meant. He'd known others like him.

"I think I was a little hard on the kid."

"Maybe he needed to hear it."

"Maybe he didn't need to hear it quite the way it was said."

He saw Montrose reach for his phone again, the surefire sign that he was losing interest.

"I don't blame the kid if he needs a few days away from work. I'm just a little worried about him. He tends to be a man of extremes."

That was the nicest way he could think of to say it. Montrose played by the rule of pretending he didn't know. Most bosses he had known carried the same philosophy.

"No, Curtis has been into the office. He's been busy from the look of it."

Good Lord, thought Bobby. What has Curtis gotten himself into now?

Montrose was on his feet and walking, and Bobby followed him down the hall at his own pace. Montrose stood in the door to the conference room that Curtis had taken over for himself. He'd turned it into his own personal war room. Jordan was slightly worried about what he was going to find in here, and of what intense and self-destructive off-shoot of his last obsession Curtis had immersed himself in now.

When he saw it, he wasn't sure what to think.

He saw the city of Austin. He saw clean streets and a blazing sun. He saw polished wood and faux leather chairs. He smelled pine sol.

The massive montage of Colon's murder had been removed. The boxes had been packed up and taken away. The random autopsy photos were gone. There was not a scrap of paper in the room.

Flan was coming.

Tobias Flan was a stooge. Eduardo Mendes had realized that the moment he'd first seen him. Flan looked like a freeze-dried jack o'lantern. His face was thin and ruddy, and when he smiled or laughed or attempted to ingratiate himself, he turned red. Eduardo had met him one October. He passed Halloween decorations on the way into his office where he made a sizeable cash deposit on a retainer for his services. Cash was against his better judgment, but based on who had suggested Flan's services, he was in no position to argue.

"Our mutual friend recommended you," said Eduardo.

"Who is that?" asked Tobias Flan. He smiled and grew redder. He was even shorter than Eduardo, who looked at him knowingly, not wanting to say Colon's name. Flan raised his eyebrows in a question.

He doesn't know, Eduardo thought. He is the stooge.

Flan must work for someone who prefers not to handle things like this directly, Eduardo realized. Colon had been very specific about hiring this lawyer, going so far as to hand Eduardo a business card on his balcony overlooking the Sierra Madre. It was a spectacular view, hovering over the city to face the broad side of the mountain, but all Eduardo had been able to see was Colon himself.

"What are you going to do with that?" Eduardo asked, pointing at the briefcase.

"Don't worry. It will be safe," said the lawyer.

"It had better be."

Flan had the early makings of varicose veins on his nose. The red spider web was just starting to bloom. Eduardo sniffed the air. He had an amazing sense of smell. He had expected alcohol, but smelled nothing.

Flan might be the man with the credentials who ran errands for those with money and power. He could just be the man whose job it was to float propositions and funnel contributions. But he was nothing more.

Eduardo said thank you because it was polite, but meant none of it. Inspiration struck him as he reached the door.

"Toby," he said.

"Yes?" Flan was still smiling.

"Toby. That's the name of the slave. In that famous movie about slaves, isn't it?"

The lawyer's grin was made of iron.

"I wouldn't know, Mister Mendes," he said.

"I think it is," said Eduardo. Then he left.

He never would have believed it, but on this day, he couldn't wait to see Tobias Flan. Eduardo had been here a week. He had called Flan and spoken to him on the phone, but the first thing Flan had said during the call was not to speak about the case or anything else.

He sat around the small, hot room for twenty minutes before they arrived. Flan shuffled in with the guard, talking foolishness the entire way, with a ridiculous smile on his face. He was babbling about boats and fishing with the guard, who was either too nice or too stupid to end the conversation by walking out the door. The guard stood there nodding as Flan rambled on about the outboard motor and the new anchor, wasting more of Eduardo's precious time. Finally, he seemed to notice Eduardo, said, "Say hi to your dad for me," to the guard, and shook hands with Eduardo, who felt he was being examined.

"Are you okay?"

Eduardo had a shiner around his left eye. He chose not to think about it and had most certainly decided not to talk about it with Flan. He went directly to business.

"Is it safe to talk in here?"

"It is," said Flan, smiling.

"There is no way they are recording our conversation?"

"No," said Flan. "That would be an egregious violation of the Constitution."

"Good. Do you have paper?"

"I do."

"Give it to me."

Flan obeyed and fished a yellow legal pad out of his bag. Eduardo tore off the top page and laid it on the desk. "Pen," he demanded. Flan obeyed.

He began writing. He had crafted this note in his mind many times, in between planning murders and laying food out for these animals. When it came time to put pen to paper, the letter wrote itself. He folded it three ways and pushed it across the table in front of the lawyer.

"When you leave here, I want you to purchase a disposable cell phone. Make one phone call with it. Call that number. Read this letter to whoever answers it. Then throw the phone away. Do you understand me?"

Flan's jack o'lantern face smiled. He nodded.

"Do you understand me?"

It had been so long since he had given an order that he missed the sound of it leaving his lips. He demanded an answer just to be sure his voice could pack authority.

"May I ask you a question, Mister Mendes?"

Eduardo was about to say no and tell Flan to run the errand as he was told when Flan asked the question anyway.

"Are you retarded?" Flan asked.

Eduardo sat back in his chair. He was stunned.

"What did you say to me?"

"I said, are you fucking retarded?" repeated Flan.

Eduardo put the pen down on the table. He felt his blood surging and swore there were bright halos around his eyes. He was not losing control of this. He'd lost too much control already. He would reassert.

"I don't care for the way you're speaking to me."

"Let me ask another way: do you think I'm retarded?"

"No, I—"

"Do you think you're making prison look sexy?"

Eduardo didn't answer.

"Listen to me. Anyone, and I mean anyone, who is so fucking stupid that they would take a list of instructions from someone in here wearing a goddamn orange jumpsuit would have to be legally mentally impaired. You left a large sum of money with me in exchange for future services. As your attorney. That does not include being your fucking errand boy. Do you understand me?"

Flan's face was red and maniacal. He looked like an evil jack o'lantern.

"Would you like my advice as an attorney?"

Eduardo flashed back to his interview with Curtis, and how he had felt. He had felt dirty and sick. This room was tiny, built for two people, and there was no privacy. He now feared that he was about to fill it with vomit. He felt dizzy. His head swam. He found himself saying yes.

"Take this piece of paper and whatever is on it. I'm not going to touch it. Destroy it. I suspect you won't want to explain whatever it says, and these people will look in your trash. They will look in your toilet. Would you like my second piece of advice?"

50

Eduardo did.

"Listen to your lawyer when he tells you to never, ever talk to the police. It doesn't matter if you're smarter than they are or cooler than they are or make more money. They're the police. Whatever you say will be used against you. So, in the future, shut the fuck up. Got me?"

Eduardo got him.

"Same with your cellmate. Or some guy who sits next to you at lunch. You don't have any friends in here. You have enemies and people who will sell you out for a nickel. You want my last piece of advice?"

Eduardo swallowed. "Please," he said. Eduardo hated saying please.

The jack o'lantern smiled as gently as he could.

"Someone, and I don't know who, recommended my services to you. That means you know someone with some sense to them. I hope you have some too. My services are expensive. You never see my name in the newspaper or on television. I don't want attention and neither do my clients. I handle things quickly and quietly. If you want a lawyer to go on the six o'clock news and rampage about his innocent client and racial profiling and the massive lawsuit he's going to file, then you need to find a new lawyer. I'll gladly recommend one. If you want this handled with what I call discreet intensity, then I'm your man. Am I your man, Mister Mendes?"

"Yes," said Eduardo, very quietly.

"Good. I've been after the feds all week to hand over their diligence on you immediately. They're not in a hurry to give it to us. My gut feeling is that there is a problem. From what I have seen, most of it is coming down to one IRS agent named Walter Curtis. I believe you met him."

He remembered Special Agent Curtis very well. He'd made a fool of himself in front of Walter Curtis.

"It's obvious that they expected to find ties to drugs or drug dealers or drug dealing. They haven't, and I don't think they're going to. Since that seems to have been their objective in the first place, we may get lucky and find that they no longer have much interest in you."

"That would be great," said Eduardo. He hadn't been excited in days.

"On the other hand, they might make you pay for it."

"Pay for it?"

"They have you on numerous financial violations. They have a pretty good case. If you want to plea this case down, they're going to want you to talk."

"Plea it down?"

"Yes. Mister Mendes, you do understand that you are looking at several years in prison for money laundering, don't you? I can take this to trial if you want, and we might shake one or two of the counts, but they have solid evidence suggesting that you've been playing games and funneling money into Mexico."

Eduardo was on his feet and walking. He had his hand on the door. He was trying to open it. He was trying to go back to his room. He didn't want to have this conversation anymore. He didn't want to be in this room anymore.

"Mister Mendes, are you alright?"

No. He was not.

"Mister Mendes."

He said several years in prison.

"What I am giving you is the worst case scenario."

Years. Prison. He felt like his head had lifted off his body. He held the door handle to keep from falling.

"Mister Mendes, as I said, we are just starting. This is a long process. Let's focus on the bail hearing."

I'll still have to come back, he thought. I'll always have to come back.

"I did manage to make one of the phone calls you asked me to make," said Tobias Flan.

Eduardo held firmly to the handle, but he asked.

"And?"

"It was a dead end."

He felt dizzy.

"I put my investigator on it. He's a talented man."

I am going to die in here, he thought.

"You're not going to die in here," said Flan.

Eduardo spun around. Was Flan reading his mind or had he been speaking aloud and not realizing it? Flan was still seated at the desk.

"There are different types of jails, Mister Mendes. You haven't been accused of murdering anyone. You've been accused of financial crimes. Granted, it is suspected that you have ties to narcotic distribution, but I am confident that those theories will be proven to be groundless. So this is a financial matter. It may seem like a big one now, but we'll talk to the prosecutors and compromise a bit here and there and when we are done it will be a small one. People who commit small financial crimes don't go to places like this. They go to different places. Ones that are not so confrontational."

"How did I end up here now?"

"I suspect someone took a personal dislike to you, Mister Mendes."

"Why?"

"I can't imagine. We'll talk again soon. In the meantime, I want you to think very seriously on what matters you are willing to compromise."

"I don't compromise. I never have."

Eduardo felt Tobias Flan size him up and down. His voice was lower when he spoke.

"Think about whether you should start, Mister Mendes. Also, you need to prove to me in the near future that you have more funds to pay me."

Eduardo thought of the heft of the briefcase that had been dropped on Flan's desk.

"I left a small fortune with you," said Eduardo, breathless.

"What you left," said Flan, "was a retainer. It was enough money to get things started. Not getting raped in prison is expensive. If you don't agree with how your money is being spent, let me know. We'll stop payment. I'll ask for a full refund."

Eduardo knew his mouth was hanging open. He was too stunned to close it.

"I thought so," said Flan.

***

In his cell, with the lights off and unable to sleep, Eduardo knew for certain that he could not and would not survive in this place.

He wasn't asleep when the door opened. He heard the footsteps, the keys, and the lock. As the newest prisoner, it wasn't the first time that he was bumped to breakfast duty without so much as a warning. He climbed off his bunk and followed the guard. He was steps into the hallway and heard the door close when he realized something was wrong.

The hall lights were dimmed. There were no other workers. All the other cells were dark and silent. There was no yawning, no screaming, and no crying. The rest of the unit was asleep.

"Let's go," said Nixon in his deep country voice. Eduardo had no choice but to follow.

They didn't go toward the kitchen. They went the other way. They passed the elevator. Nixon took his keys out. They went to the stairwell.

This is it, Eduardo thought. His whole body tightened. I am being delivered.

He knew he should run. He should start screaming. He should attack Nixon right now. There had to be witnesses. Eduardo knew what was going to happen. He saw it coming and knew what he should do, but a weak, cowardly voice inside of him said that fighting would make it worse. Just take it, whispered the voice.

Would they laugh at him now? They would. They would do anything they wanted to him.

Nixon led him to a hallway that had windows. It was early. The sun was coming up, and the sky was a deeper blue. Would they make him work in the kitchen later? Would he be able to? Nixon unlocked a door and stepped to the side.

Special Agent Walter Curtis was in the room. He wore a suit. Nixon closed the door and Curtis and Eduardo were alone.

This thin, nerdy agent was the last person Eduardo had expected to see.

"Tell me about the three million dollars in the desert," said Curtis.

Chapter Four

Curtis – Austin, TX

Marc Virgil had been a detective in the Boston Police gang unit. He handled investigations and ran informants. He trafficked in high level intelligence as well as street work. Virgil was everything Walter Curtis wanted to be.

Nine months ago, Marc Virgil had been working when a man tried to shoot him. He missed. Virgil didn't. His life as he knew it ended anyway.

The shooting happened outside a party, which quickly became a riot. After the riot, the dead man's gun couldn't be found. Everyone liked and admired the work Virgil had done before that night, but they still couldn't find the gun.

What Curtis and Virgil had in common was drinking. That's how it had always been. Virgil could wake Curtis at one in the morning on a work night, and Curtis would get dressed and meet him in a bar to hear of his latest adventure. Usually, Curtis had a lot of questions. Now, he had only one.

Curtis drank all the booze in his house. Then he walked down the street and ordered a whiskey. When he was drunk enough, he took out his phone and called Virgil.

"Remember the time," began Curtis, "I lost my job and I was broke and you took me out to eat. We got drunk and you paid for everything."

"Yeah," said Virgil. "I had money then."

"Let me repay it," said Curtis.

The Texas sun was still burning, and Curtis had the top down. He pulled his old Saab into Austin-Bergstrom Airport, and spotted him immediately. Marc Virgil stood out from the crowd. He had his things in a worn seabag. It was slung over his shoulder, and Curtis could see the tattoo on his arm of the Marine Corps emblem. He grinned as Curtis pulled to the side.

"Please tell me you're working undercover as a hairstylist and you didn't actually buy this with your own money," said Virgil.

"This car is a classic," Curtis said. Virgil tossed his bag into the open back seat.

"Thank God no one knows me here," said Virgil. Then they shook hands for the first time in years. Virgil was leaner, and all the softness had been stripped from his frame. He smiled, but his eyes were tired.

"Let me buy you a drink," said Curtis.

"Mi casa, su casa," said Curtis, though there wasn't much casa to be had. The apartment had a tight galley kitchen, a living room with one leather couch that had some miles on it, and the bedroom. There were boxes of paperwork everywhere.

"You don't spend much time here, do you?"

"No," said Curtis. "I've been at the office for the last few years."

"How's that working out for you?"

"I'll tell you about it later. I want to show you something."

Curtis disappeared into his room and came out a moment later with a gun in his hand. He laid it on the table.

It was a Kimber 1911 model forty-five. It was like Bobby Jordan's, but smaller. It was shined and polished, where Bobby's was worn and used. Virgil just looked at it for a while.

"You can pick it up if you want," said Curtis.

"When did you become a serious shooter?"

"A man needs a hobby."

Virgil still didn't touch the weapon on the table. It lay conspicuously between them.

"Are you sure you don't want to check it out?" Curtis asked. He sounded disappointed.

"Later," said Virgil. "I came here to be someone else for a while."

Perry's was an expensive steak house. It had a huge bar and wine racks that stretched from floor to ceiling, stocked the whole way.

Everything looked delicious, right down to the chocolate colored walls and ceilings.

"Do you remember that gift you gave me when I got out of agent school?" Curtis asked.

"No. I hope it was something good."

"It was a chain," said Curtis, surprised. "It had a medal of Saint Michael on one end and a handcuff key on the other. There was an inscription on the back. Your uncle gave you one. You said he was a cop. He told you and you told me to always keep it with you when you went to work. That Saint Michael was the patron saint of police officers. The handcuff key was for the things you could fix. Saint Michael was for the things you couldn't."

Virgil smiled at the memory.

"Yeah, that sounded real nice, didn't it?" said Virgil.

"Do you still wear yours?"

"I lost it years ago."

Curtis had his Saint Michael medal in his pocket. He always had it. He was about to ask another question he had been meaning to, but Virgil had turned his attention to the two girls who had slid onto the stools beside them.

They both smiled at him. Girls always smiled at Virgil. He immediately ordered drinks. Virgil told them that he was a professional mountain climber. He said Curtis was just a boring venture capitalist.

"He doesn't look that boring," said the one who looked vaguely Asian.

"He's not," said Virgil. "Just his work. Curtis actually saved my life once."

"How did you do that?" Curtis was just trying to keep up and didn't even know who had asked it.

"He found me wandering around in a snowstorm."

"What's so dangerous about that?"

"It was on Mount Everest."

"No way."

"Yes way."

"What were you doing?"

"I was climbing it," said Virgil.

"Did you climb it too?" one of the girls asked Curtis.

"No," Curtis said without thinking. Virgil shot him a look that said, 'Don't make me work harder than I need to.'

"Can you make money climbing mountains?"

"That was the problem. Everything else about it is awesome. "

"So how did he save your life?" She seemed genuinely intrigued.

"I guided a team up the mountain, and on the way down, I had to go back for a rich guy who got sick. Then I got lost in the snow."

He patted Curtis on the shoulder.

"Curtis climbed up to look for us and found me wandering around half dead in the storm. He dragged me back into camp and made me drink this strange Sherpa tea until I could walk again."

They ordered more drinks and the girls disappeared to the bathroom. The girls both asked for the same drink, which was pink, had a cherry, and came in a tall stemmed cocktail glass.

"You ordered four of them?" Curtis asked.

"It seemed like the smooth move at the time. Besides, I only know one person in Texas and he drives a Saab. Bottoms up."

"Know what story of yours I always liked?" Curtis asked. As he said it, he felt excitement building inside of him. "The story where you planned to rip off the Boston Beer Festival."

"I did what now?"

"The Boston Beer Festival story. You said you had the security detail. All you had to do was help security escort anyone who got too drunk."

"And listen to music and talk to girls. The only thing we couldn't do was drink. It kind of sucked."

"Remember it now?"

"No."

"It was in a huge tent that could hold thousands of people. So you started to watch. Then you realized that it was all cash, all day, and it all went to one small locked room."

Curtis could see the look of cagey recognition on Virgil's face. The look said, yes, I know what you're talking about, but I can't believe you remember. It also asked plainly, what else are you up to?

"Do you want to finish it for me?" Curtis asked. "You tell it better."

They had been in a bar in Boston called Foley's at two thirty on a Monday night. Marc Virgil had just gotten out of work. Curtis had to be up in a few hours.

"So here is my plan, and I swear it will work," said Virgil. "The average person in the Beer Fest spends about forty bucks. Some spend sixty. Then you have the serious drinkers, who spend eighty to a hundred. What you don't realize is that they have twelve thousand guests on a Saturday. By the end of the day, there's between six fifty and eight hundred thousand dollars in cash on site."

"And it's unguarded?" asked Curtis.

"That doesn't matter. I don't plan on doing a huge shoot out. What I did was I asked who the owner was, and he was right there. Young guy, went to the best schools, and instead of working on Wall Street or running for president, he started brewing beer."

He paused and drained half his pint glass.

"I'm going to walk right up to him with a phone and show him a picture of his terrified family in a closet at his own house. I'll explain to him in simple English that even a Harvard man can understand. I'm not a pervert. I'm not a sex offender. I am not jealous of your success and I wish none of you any harm. I have no desire to hurt you or your children, but so help me God, if you don't do exactly what I say, I will visit evil on this family tonight. From there, the two of us will casually walk the cash out in boxes to my car. Then, he never sees me again."

"Jesus H. Christ."

"No. Marc Virgil. At your service."

Years later, in a steakhouse in Texas, Virgil still had a skeptical smile. He finished his fancy drink.

"You realize that I was drunk and didn't mean a fucking word of that, right?"

"Of course I do."

"Because I'm not really going to rob and threaten to kill some guy's family."

"No. That would be nuts."

"Have a pink drink."

Curtis didn't even taste it.

"What if I had an easier way to make money?" he asked.

"You do. You have a job."

"What if I told you that I didn't like it?"

"I'd tell you to get over it."

Curtis looked up and down the bar. No one was looking at them. No one could hear them. He had no idea if the girls were coming back. He could feel his heart, despite how much he'd had to drink. Curtis figured it was now or never.

"What if I told you there was three million dollars buried in the desert?"

Virgil stood in line by the valet to wait for the car. The valet looked as if there was no way he was giving a car to a person this drunk. Curtis pulled him away.

"We parked down the street."

"I'm going to drive this fag-mobile," announced Virgil.

They had left the top down, and Virgil slid right into the driver's seat. Curtis began to protest, but he was in no shape to argue. He gave Virgil the keys. Virgil looked and looked again, but he couldn't find the ignition.

"How fucking drunk am I?"

"Saab's have the ignition in the center console. I know a good place up the street."

"I don't want to go to a good place. I want to go to a dump."

They found one. There was no sign over the door. Most of the other patrons looked like they had just graduated college and had no money or had run out of money a long time ago.

"What do you think of my plan?' asked Curtis.

"Doesn't sound like much of a plan at all."

"That's what's good about it. It's easy."

"How about the guy who told you about the money?"

"He's getting something out of it too."

"What's that?"

"A very reduced sentence and a one way ticket out of the federal system."

"I thought you said the case fell apart."

"He doesn't know that."

"If it's so easy, why didn't he go down and get it himself?"

"He doesn't know exactly where it is. I do."

"How did you manage that?"

"I did the one thing I'm good at."

"Police work?"

"No. Math."

The accountant came out of him. It was the accountant who Curtis hated, who he had never wanted to be. The accountant was studious and detail oriented and never quick on his feet.

"My source told me that there was three million dollars buried in the desert just outside of Monterrey. Out near the Sierra Madre. He was one mile south past a town called Salinas. He knew it was within twenty miles. He knew it had been buried with concrete walls. Monterrey is a busy city, but out there by Salinas is farm country. There isn't a lot of construction. So I looked into land permits in Mexico for new construction in that area. There was a little, but not a lot. Then, I started looking into who had bought that property, and who built a brand new house on it, and when. I had a few bites, but I found a corporation that doesn't own anything. They're a shell for a real estate company, which also doesn't exist. They exist on paper. They had exactly one transaction. When I looked into the origins, I found a thread to some money that I traced to a tiny little business that closed. No one else would have noticed, because it was just a little mom and pop operation, but if you were obsessed with a man named Aureliano Colon, and if you had spent years of your life tracking him down on paper and tracing his bank accounts and property and learning everything there was to know about him, you would know that this mom and pop construction company once imported a chemical from Hong Kong called anhydrous ammonia and that it is frequently used in the production of a very dangerous drug known as methamphetamine."

Curtis reached into his pocket and unfolded a sheet of paper. There was a color photo on it, blurry greens and tans and sandy here and there, surrounding an unmistakable monster of a red roofed house in the middle.

"That's from a military satellite."

"How did you get that?"

"I redirected it to look at the property."

"It's a good thing you're not obsessed with this. You didn't need an act of congress to get that done?"

"It's on loan to us. We use it to monitor smuggling routes over the border."

"Isn't it going to come back to you?"

"No. It covers huge swaths of land. This house is only part of it. I'm well within my province to request satellite images."

"How long have you been planning this?"

"A couple of weeks."

"You can do all this research in just a couple weeks?"

"You can if you don't sleep."

Virgil smiled broadly. Curtis suddenly thought they were in agreement, until he followed Marc's gaze and realized that he was smiling at a girl on the stool behind him. She was slim and wore a tank top. She was pretty with piercings and tattoos on her arms. She was with another girl who looked like she could kill any man in the bar.

"I want nothing to do with this," said Virgil. "I have enough trouble already."

"Where are you with that?"

"The story is finally out of the news, but that doesn't mean it won't come back. There's still talk of an indictment. Find someone who wants to make a name for himself and I could be on trial for murder."

"So the department is still backing away from you?"

"They are fucking running away from me as fast as they can. I tell you that the only good thing to come out of any of this mess is that you find out who your real friends are."

He gave Curtis a rough pat on the shoulder.

"What do you think of my plan?" Curtis asked again.

"Well, my plan about robbing the Boston Beer Fest was a sick joke I told you when I was drunk. Your idea is even worse."

With that, Virgil pushed away from the bar and began his stumble to the door. Curtis followed him out and caught him just as he was walking into traffic. The two of them fell into a cab, and as he sat down, Curtis felt as drunk as Virgil looked. Virgil dropped his head back against the seat and began to snore. Curtis laid his head against the cool glass of the window and felt himself unwind. Virgil wanted nothing to do with his plan, but that was fine for now. It was just another milestone of failure.

"Didn't we drive here?" Virgil asked, awake again. Then he put his head down and went back to sleep. Curtis's own eyes crept lower and lower to the sounds of snoring and the hum of the engine.

"What if?" Curtis said dreamily, "What if I told you that there was three million dollars buried in the desert?"

Eduardo remembered a time when he was seven and with his father. They watched a show about the Donner party, and Eduardo was shocked and disgusted to learn of cannibalism. His father showed only disappointment in him. "This is what you have to do to survive," he said.

His bed shook again. It was time for another set of fifty pushups. Eduardo saw his cellmate's head bobbing. It was lined with badly thinning blonde hair for such a young man. Eduardo didn't know his name, but his cellmate was a hulk of silent meat and muscle. He wore tank tops or no shirt at all during these sessions. His skin was pale and his back was dotted with huge pimples. He never spoke, but he was always eating, whether beef jerky or uncooked stews from a can. Eduardo had watched him eat a jar of peanut butter with just his fingers.

Eduardo was not a patient man. His mother had not been patient, and his father had not been patient either. His father was impatient that a seven-year-old did not see the practicality of eating other human beings. Eduardo had grown impatient with Special Agent Walter Curtis and his promises of movement on his case.

He expected a call from Flan. None came. He expected Curtis himself to come back, begging for more than the flat clues. He hadn't come either. He expected Odalys to be in the family room downstairs, dripping tears all over the glass and smiling. She'd tell him that she had found cash somewhere, somehow, and filled his account.

Flan had been dead serious on one point. If Odalys knew anything of his business, anything at all, if she had so much as served as eye candy at a meeting, then she should not and could not visit. Flan was not willing to take the chance of an offhand silly comment being played at trial and used against him.

During one of his calls, Eduardo had started to ask if part of the retainer he had given to Flan could be converted into a cash deposit for him in his prison account. He thought he heard Flan stifling a laugh.

On this day, when the bed stopped rocking, his cellmate looked up and caught his eye. He smiled broadly.

"Hi," he said.

Hi. As if they had just met. As if they hadn't been in this tiny cell together for weeks. As if he had just discovered Eduardo and thought he would like to make a good first impression.

"Hello," Eduardo said. This was the first friendly greeting he had heard in prison. The last greeting had been a man with a shotgun screaming for him to get his hands in the air. Everything else he had heard since had been another order.

"My name is Luke," he said. He was still smiling. He wrapped a towel around his neck and held it with both hands. His arms were massive.

"Brothers been giving you a hard time," said Luke.

It hadn't sounded like a question. It was more of an observation or a statement of fact. Eduardo didn't have a response. He shrugged.

"Happens to a lot of new guys," said Luke.

"I'm just minding my own business," said Eduardo. That seemed like the right thing to say. He'd been listening to people talk. Minding one's own business was a common refrain.

"Yeah, I like that. Doesn't always work though," said Luke.

Luke sat down on his bed and began to put on his boots. He even managed to flex while doing it.

"There was a guy here a few months ago, he tried to mind his own business. Brothers did some terrible things to him."

"Why are you telling me this?" Eduardo asked. It came out too quick, too sharp, and with too much emotion. There was a lot of emotion bottled up in Eduardo right now. He stood there in front of this hulk with no shirt on and nothing more to defend himself than a damp toothbrush. He put it away, lest even that seem too defiant. Luke didn't seem to notice.

"You seem like a good dude. I don't want to see you have any unnecessary trouble. Especially not with them."

"Thank you."

"Don't mention it. In fact, if there is ever anything I can do for you, let me know."

"Can I ask you one question?"

Luke's eyebrows raised, and his smile broadened more. "Anything," he said.

"The phones here are tapped, correct?"

"Yeah, they listen in. I wouldn't use one if you need to talk, you know, privately."

"What if you do need to talk privately?"

"There are other ways."

"Such as?"

"You could use a cell phone."

"Who has a cell phone?"

"Guys."

"What guys?"

"That's their business. I might be able to ask around for you."

"What would it take to use one of those cell phones?"

"Money. Usually money. They don't even pay you for all that kitchen work until the end of the month, do they?"

Eduardo shook his head.

"Could you introduce me to one of these guys who has a phone?" he asked.

Luke thought about it.

"Yeah. I suppose I could. You still don't have any money though."

He didn't. Two weeks ago, he drove a two hundred thousand dollar car and wore handmade clothes. He had enjoyed the best of the best. He was currently the poorest man in this prison.

"Toughest thing about prison isn't not having money," said Luke.
"No?"
"It's not having friends."
He thought about cannibalism and his father and what he was willing to do to survive.
"I need to use one of those phones," said Eduardo. Luke shrugged his enormous shoulders.
"Why don't you sit down and talk about it?"

Curtis stumbled out of his room in search of water. His head felt as if he had been sucker punched. His mouth felt like he had eaten dirt. On his way to the sink, he saw Virgil hunched over the Colon files.
"Who is this Chinese guy?" Virgil asked.
Virgil was holding a photograph. Curtis didn't even have to look to know who he was talking about.
"He's not Chinese. He's Japanese. And he's actually from Peru."
It was a grainy, dated black and white picture of a man in motion. It had been blown up from a surveillance camera. It wasn't the best photo, but it showed an intense man in a foul mood.
"What the hell is a Japanese guy doing in Peru?"
"Many Japanese people immigrated there."
"Why wouldn't they just come to America like everybody else?"
"I have no idea."
"Their loss. Who is he?"
"His name is Toshiro Matsumoto, and he is a very dangerous man."
"Dangerous how?"
"He was a captain in the Peruvian special forces. He ran a death squad."
Virgil looked at the picture, impressed.
"Tell me why you're collecting pictures of him. And you really don't spend any time here, do you?"
Curtis opened his freezer and removed a bottle of vodka.
"How can you tell?"
"The orange juice is the only healthy thing in that fridge."

Curtis began pouring the vodka. "It's about to get a lot less healthy," he said. It hurt to sit down. He could see that Virgil had been up for a while. His files had been carefully arranged.

"Toshiro Matsumoto," Curtis began, "was a very feared and respected man in their army. Then he suddenly resigned. A month later, he was implicated in the murder of a member of Shining Path. Back then, Shining Path was a real terrorist organization in Peru. The guy he killed was a professor from a prominent family. The professor was protected politically, so Matsumoto took matters into his own hands. After the murder, no one knew where he went for over ten years, when he popped up again in Hong Kong. Take out the other picture in that file. The wide shot."

The original showed Matsumoto as he walked through airport security. It was old technology and poorly copied. Curtis leaned forward and pointed to the first passenger in line.

"That's Colon," he said.

He was a small man with more weight than he needed. Colon was in his late forties and wore a suit with no tie and wore tinted glasses. In this one shot, he was exceptionally mild-mannered.

"He looks more like a teacher than a drug dealer," observed Virgil.

"It's not an accident. Toshiro Matsumoto left Peru and ended up in Monterrey, Mexico, where he was employed for many years as the bodyguard of an unassuming landowner and businessman by the name of Aureliano Colon, who was secretly a prolific producer and exporter of crystal methamphetamine."

Colon had been dead for years, but Curtis still loved telling his story, and all of its little branches.

"Did he get killed with the boss?"

"No. He disappeared six months before the hit. The Mexicans recorded him crossing the southern border into Guatemala. No one knows why. One theory is that he had cancer and went home to die. Another is that he quit due to his distaste with Colon's lifestyle."

"Was he touching kids or something?"

"God no. Colon wouldn't do that."

"I didn't mean to offend you. I know you guys were tight."

"It's not that. You spend this much time researching a man like him, studying his operation, trying to see how he thinks, you respect some of the things he's able to do. He went years without so much as an arrest. In all his time, there was no bloodshed traced back to his organization. They still don't know where he was making the stuff. Before I found the money trail, no one even knew he existed."

"A ghost," said Virgil.

"You've been reading my notes," Curtis said proudly. "Did you get to Colon's history?"

"No. Normal people sleep at night. And they have more food in the house than just orange juice. Tell me about it over breakfast."

They arrived at the Franklin Barbecue at ten thirty. They were seated at noon. By twelve thirty, they had been served, and by one Virgil was claiming that he was never going to eat again. He looked at what remained of his lunch and pushed his plate away.

"What really happened that night?" Curtis asked him.

He had wanted to ask him that since he arrived. He had wanted to ask the moment he had heard about it. Virgil had explained that he was fine but had a lawyer now who advised him not to speak about it with anyone, and certainly not on a telephone. There was a time when Curtis would have hopped on a plane back to Boston. That was before he had heard of Eduardo Mendes.

"That's the million dollar question, isn't it?" Virgil said. He took a long sip of cold water before he began.

"We had a case hanging over this guy's head. To work it off, he had to give up someone with a gun."

"Just like that? We can't work informants so easily."

"Neither can we. It was off the books. The guy was terrified of being labeled a snitch, so we did it unofficially. We've done it before. It always worked out fine."

"Until there's a bad shooting."

"Right up until the very second that there's a bad shooting. So, no matter what happens with the criminal case, at the end of the day, they'll hang me over the informant. One way or another, I am finished as a police officer."

Curtis suggested a little hole in the wall. Virgil said that he could sit in a dive back home. "I want some place big and bright, with

Texas written all over it," he said. They found a bar that looked over the river.

"I want to talk about your man Colon," said Virgil.

"What can I tell you about him?"

"Start with who killed him."

"Who pulled the trigger? No one knows for sure. I think Eduardo Mendes had a hand in it."

"Why?"

"His account ledger. It was steady for a long time. You could set your watch to the transfers. Right after Colon, it went up. Then up again. This is just the revenue stream we know about."

"How big are we talking?"

"Not big at all. Tens of thousands dollars per transfer. But it adds up. That's the thing about Colon and his disciples."

"He has disciples?"

"Another theory I have. Colon sought out people who would adopt his mindset. Slow and low. No bodies."

"How does a guy run meth in Mexico with no bodies?"

"That's the secret. That's what none of these thug crews can understand. Blood brings attention. Especially from us. How he did it? No one knows."

"You guys couldn't break into his distribution network?"

"We couldn't get past the money."

"Who was running this operation?"

"I was."

Virgil slowed down some. He refocused.

"Who are his other disciples?"

"His son-in-law, Augustus Villareal."

"What's he do?"

"He's an actor."

"Would I have seen him in anything?"

"By all accounts, he's a complete failure. Bad stage actor. He worked some circuit for tourists who wanted culture or some shit. No one comes to Mexico for culture."

"And this guy married the boss's daughter?"

"No one knows much about her either. Didn't have much to do with her father when he was alive, and nothing to do with his business. Supposedly, they spend their time in Oaxaca, which is quiet and poor and a nice place to live."

"I think she likes me," said Virgil.

"Colon's daughter? I doubt she likes cops."

He had meant the girl at the bar. She was cute, but had some late nights in her. Virgil crossed the room to start a conversation. Curtis followed.

"You talk funny," said the girl with a smile.

"I think you talk funny."

"Where are you from?" she asked.

"I bet you think you know."

"Only people from Boston talk as funny as you."

"You know, Boston was founded in the year fourteen-ninety-two. So by my math, this is how Americans talk, and as one of the new states, Texans should talk just like us, or we might have to ask you all to leave this great country."

"The rest of you wouldn't know what to do without Texas. We have lots of oil and the prettiest girls. And we're tons of fun."

"I can't argue with that," said Virgil.

She was smiling. Her friend hadn't said a word yet, but she was smiling too. There was a nice touch to the friend though, a sort of openness and friendliness that the girls at home never seemed to show him. Curtis smiled back.

"What do you do?" asked the first one. She was talking to Virgil.

"Me? I kill people. I'm here in Austin for a job."

"Oh no! Who are you going to kill?"

"A rodeo clown."

"I love rodeo clowns! Why would you kill one of them?"

"A circus clown is paying me. Rodeo slept with his wife."

"Is there a lot of money in killing people?"

"No. You really need to be dedicated. What do you guys do?"

"I'm a stripper and she's a Vegas showgirl."

"I strip when the money runs low," said the friend.

"How do you get started in killing people?" asked the first girl. "Is it a family business?"

"No. In fact, my brother is a priest."

Both girls laughed.

"How does a killer have a priest for a brother?"

"He wasn't always a priest. He was in finance, working for a fat cat in New York City. The fat cat got hired by the president for a big job in the Federal Reserve, and my brother went along for the ride. Later in life, he heard the call, gave away all his possessions, and became a priest."

The girls both stared at him, apparently stunned that they might have heard the truth.

"Well, what I should have asked was how does a priest have you for a brother?"

"Just lucky, I guess," he said, smiling.

Suddenly, one of the girls was addressing Curtis. It was the friendly looking one.

"He's not going to kill you, is he?" she asked.

"Me? No. I'm going to drown."

The conversation became awkwardly silent. Even Virgil didn't have a quick recovery, but the look on his face was clear.

"I almost drowned as a kid," said Curtis. "I took it as a premonition."

"Wow," said the friendly one. "What happened?"

"My father was teaching me to swim and threw me into the lake. He wouldn't help me. He didn't realize how much trouble I was in. My sister had to jump in and save me."

"Your big sister?"

"No. My little sister."

"Oh my God."

"That's why I moved to Texas."

"Why?"

"There's so much land."

They laughed, but not the way they laughed at Virgil.

The library at St. Paul's had been a beautiful room with a dark cherry wood on the walls. The stacks in Beaumont were plastic. There was no metal anywhere, for good reason. The men here would have used it to make knives.

A set of eyes caught his. There were sharp, conniving slits. The body attached to those eyes got up and walked casually into the stacks. Eduardo took a deep breath. He waited. Another man went into the stacks as well.

He found them at the end. The first was a thin greasy white convict in his mid twenties. He looked like his parents were brother and sister. He had cheap tattoos up both arms and the word "Taboo" was written on his neck.

"You Luke's friend?" the greasy man asked. He said it and smiled. It felt like more of a leer.

"Yes, I am," Eduardo admitted.

"I'm Avary," he said, still smiling.

Eduardo looked at the man behind him. He was small, young, and nervous. He had unmarked white skin and a haircut that was growing in at funny angles. He wasn't looking at Eduardo.

"Luke said you need something. I need something too."

Eduardo passed a folded up bill to Avary, who glanced at it like a card player and then made it disappear. He wore that leering greasy smile again. He made some gesture to the young kid behind him, who looked around nervously. The sound of velcro tearing apart ran through the room. Eduardo turned to see if they had been noticed. He turned back as the kid reached into the rear of his jumpsuit.

"Is this a safe place to use it?" Eduardo asked.

"The librarian is deaf. You good."

The young kid grimaced. Eduardo watched him. He was very young, maybe not even nineteen. On the outside, he looked like he could have made the bad boy image work for him. All Eduardo saw now was shame. The kid held it out to him.

It was a cloudy, filthy zip lock bag. It had never occurred to Eduardo where the phone might come from, or how it might be carried. In a pocket, maybe, or on loan from a guard, or in a fancy walnut case, bound in leather, and snuggled in velvet to look beautiful for generations of desperate prisoners. Luke hadn't mentioned that this was how it was coming here, slathered in Vaseline and nastiness and daring Eduardo not to touch it. The kid dangled it with his thumb and forefinger. He didn't do it to taunt Eduardo. He did it because he didn't want to touch it either.

Eduardo had come too far to turn back now. He grabbed it.

"Ten minutes," said Avary as they walked away.

The phone was warm.

Cashman – Austin, TX

Years ago, this horse would have killed him. Riding Maccabee was Sheldon Cashman's greatest achievement. Maccabee was a big, dangerous horse, and Sheldon had broken him. The sun was sinking low in the west and Sheldon pushed him to the edge of the ranch, pulling to a stop by an embankment that overlooked the river. The big horse grunted appreciably. This beast craved hard work.

Sheldon Cashman caught his breath. On horseback, away from his work and his wife and Eduardo, was when he was at his best. He could ride a dangerous horse and ride him well. This was where Sheldon came and what he did when he needed peace.

Without a thought or a worry, he found his phone in his hand. He remembered Eduardo's nickname for him. The Jewish Cowboy.

"Sometimes even a careful man makes mistakes," he said to the horse.

Sheldon had a number in his head. It had been passed to him unknowingly by Eduardo Mendes, written on the back of a series of payment instructions. Sheldon had seen the mistake immediately, and he had said nothing. Instead, he filed it away.

A man answered on the third ring. His voice was country, southbound, and rough.

"Do you know Eduardo Mendes?" asked Sheldon.

"Who is this?"

"A friend."

"A friend of mine or a friend of Eduardo?" Sheldon could hear the fight in this man's voice.

"You did business with Eduardo. It suddenly stopped, didn't it?"

There was no answer.

"He's talking to the police about you."

The line was quiet for a time.

"How do I know you're real?" the man asked.

"Eduardo has clever nicknames for everyone. He refers to your people as the Hillbillies."

Through the phone, Sheldon heard an exhale, and he knew, instinctively, that the man believed. Beneath him, the horse grunted.

Sometimes, he thought, even a careful man makes mistakes.

Strauss – Monterrey, MX

Unholy screaming filled Strauss' ears as he stood in the blazing hot sun. He had been thinking of a woman who wore black lingerie. She had her hair up, and was smoking a cigarette. The smoke was lit by the TV screen. The screaming brought him back to the factory.

Angel was the most frightening person he had ever encountered, in Mexico or anywhere else. Angel was responsible for those screams. He had been responsible for many screams over the years. He was inside the old station house now, doing what he did best, bringing new screams into the world.

He knew Angel's work for the day was done. The sounds had been far too intense for another round. There were men who can handle unthinkable amounts of pain. Fortunately, this kidnapper was not such a man.

Slowly, Strauss saw the shape emerge from the door. Bonasera, the lawyer whose son had been kidnapped, took small, uncertain steps as he came into the light. He approached Strauss in a daze. They had entered into a contract, and it had been fulfilled to his ghastly specifications.

"Did you find what you wanted in there?" Strauss asked quietly.

"I don't know," said the very stunned Bonasera. Strauss opened the car door for him. He sat and stared at the wall. Strauss's phone began to ring.

"I was given this number by a dead man," said the voice on the phone.

"What dead man?"

There was hesitation.

"His name was Colon."

"He gave it to you personally?"

"Yes."

"How?"

More hesitation.

"It was sealed in a white envelope. There was a religious card."

"What was written inside?"

"Nothing was written. It was only this number. He told me to memorize it and destroy the card. He said to call you if I ever need help."

"You sound like you are in America."

"Yes."

"Are you in Texas?"

"Yes."

"Is that where you need help?"

"Yes. It is."

Angel appeared in the doorway to the station house. His features were obscured in the dark, but the sun glistened off his arms. He looked black and wet. He was covered in blood. He stood in the darkened doorway, waiting.

"What can I do for you, Mister Mendes?"

They walked into a bar just as the sun was going down in the west. Everyone else in the bar was around their age.

"I think I like this place," said Virgil.

It was dark and mellow and had a restaurant on the other side. There was space to move without bumping their elbows. The bartenders didn't need to be waved down in traffic.

"Tell me something about Colon that I don't know yet," said Virgil. "Something that isn't in those boxes."

"He had a midlife crisis."

"How do you know that?"

"I don't want to say. You'll laugh at me."

"Everyone laughs at you. At least I like you. Why?"

"He bought a Bentley."

"If I were a Mexican drug lord, I'd get one too."

"That's the thing. He wasn't a drug lord. He was a secret drug underlord. He didn't want anyone to know what he did. He barely wanted anyone to know he existed. He had a system, and all of it was designed around the singular principle of not drawing attention. Then, one day, he buys a baby blue Bentley. When he died, I looked in his property bag. He had platinum cufflinks and a platinum tie clip. His suit had been hand made in England. His shirt cost three hundred dollars. He had started dining in fancy restaurants, very conspicuously. He was noted in the goddamn Monterrey society page. It was like he woke up one day and decided to be famous."

"How did you see his property bag?"

"When he died, I went to Mexico and took his prints."

"It's a good thing you're not obsessed."

Curtis ignored him.

"It didn't fit. Colon understood what was wrong with the business, and he did everything right for years. Then, he fires his fiercely loyal bodyguard and starts parading around town dressed like James Bond."

Virgil waved down a bartender.

"I'll have a martini. Shaken, not stirred."

"Right away, Mister Bond," said the waiter.

He turned back to Curtis. "Now I have James Bond's drink."

"This is why I didn't want to tell you."

"I'm sorry. Colon is a weird old guy who started dressing like a dandy. So what happened?"

"He lost his discipline."

"You were in his accounts. Was he doing something different?"

"Maybe. But I think he was doing more than that. The transfer amounts decreased over time, but they decreased in a strict, orderly fashion. When you add it up, the difference between what they had been making and what they were making equals about three million dollars. That's the money that I think is sitting in the desert."

"Why would a guy who can afford a Bentley start burying cash in the desert?" Virgil asked. When he said it though, it wasn't a real question. Curtis could see that he was just speaking his own thoughts aloud. He could see Virgil was thinking about it too.

"He was going to retire. He was going to disappear," said Virgil.

Curtis beamed.

"Finally, another person sees it. I'm not crazy."

"That remains to be seen. What went wrong?"

"I think, and this is just my theory, but I think that his son-in-law Villareal found out that he was going to close up shop, and he had him killed. Then Villareal started over right where Colon left off."

"Let me ask you one thing. You're screwed at work, maybe. They'll never put you in charge of anything ever again. But you still have a job. They pay you good money to do the basics, right? You can do the basics in your damn sleep. Why in the world would you want to throw that away on a trip to Mexico to find a pile of money that you don't need?"

"I do need it."

"Not the same way I do."

"No, but I need it. And it is there. I know Colon."

"I believe you. For the first time, I saw you actually become great at something. I understand. It all went up in smoke."

"I'm a laughing stock at work. I'm the accountant that reached too far and thought he was a cop."

"Who cares?"

"I care. I can sit at a desk and do nothing for twenty years. I can get old and wear the same clothes every day and grow cobwebs from my elbows. I'll watch people who aren't half as smart as I am but have social skills climb up the ladder while I sit at the bottom and take orders from them, but you know what? I want to be laughing on the inside. I want to be quietly sitting on a pile of cash that grows larger every day, and while they're busting their asses to get a slightly bigger pension that's going to be taxed into oblivion, I'm sitting there with more money than I need, not a care in the world, untouched by their rules, and with a secret that they will never, ever know."

The bartender placed a cocktail glass in front of Virgil, who pulled a messy stack of mixed bills from his pocket.

"That's been taken care of, sir," said the bartender.

"By who?"

"The ladies."

There was a drink for Curtis as well. The two ladies, like everyone else, were in their mid-thirties. They said their names were Liz and Caroline. Curtis noticed that Caroline hadn't taken her eyes off of Virgil.

"What do you do for a living?" she asked him.

"I'm a disgraced Boston Police officer, but probably not for much longer."

"What's not for much longer? The disgraced part or the police officer part?"

"Either."

"My dad was a cop," she said. "He swore his entire career that he hated it, and when he retired, he spent all his time talking about the good old days on the job."

"It happens to the best of us disgruntled cops."

"You're not from here."

"No, I'm not."

"How did you end up in Austin this weekend?"

"Old friend," said Virgil, pointing a thumb at Curtis. "He thought I needed to get out of town for a while."

"What do you do?" asked Liz. She was talking to Curtis. She was thin and had blonde hair. She smiled nicely. She looked like an athlete.

"I'm just an accountant," he said. "I'm with the IRS."

"How did you get into that?"

"I asked for the most boring job on the planet and this is what they came back with."

She laughed. They both laughed.

Liz had a tiny crook in her nose, like she had broken it years before. Curtis wanted to ask her about it, but didn't. Her pants were fitted, and she had strong, solid thighs. She said she had ran a marathon. Curtis asked her which one, but she was listening to something Virgil said. Curtis couldn't hear what Virgil was saying, but his girl seemed to like it. She smiled and laughed all the way back to Curtis' apartment.

She stopped laughing there. She showed Virgil big round serious eyes, and the two of them disappeared wordlessly into Curtis' bedroom. Curtis kissed Liz on the couch and she tasted delicious. Her thighs were solid. He could feel their power and potential. He had unbuttoned her shirt when the ungodly moaning began to pour through the thin walls. The moaning was replaced by screaming. The black and white photo on the wall of the CITGO sign that loomed over Fenway began to clatter. Liz stopped him and smiled and the two of them looked awkwardly at one another as her friend screeched as if she was being murdered.

"She just got out of a bad relationship," said Liz.

Curtis didn't have any response. He inched closer to her mouth.

"I have to get up early in the morning," said Liz. She was still nice.

"Okay," Curtis said softly. She called for a cab after the screaming had stopped. Curtis remembered seeing her in the doorway as he was falling asleep. There was a bright light from outside that lit her up, and she didn't turn back.

In the morning, Curtis heard the clacking of heels and the door open and close. It was daylight, and his mouth felt as if it had been filled with sand. Then he heard bare feet on wood. He opened his eyes. Virgil looked invigorated.

"I'm in," he said.

Chapter Five

Curtis – Austin, TX

Curtis' phone was ringing. He was ignoring it as he pored through pages of documents from the boxes that overwhelmed the small apartment. Curtis silenced the ringer and went back to work.

"You can't bring your phone to Mexico," said Curtis.

"Do Mexicans have something against cell phones?" asked Virgil.

"Your phone will bounce off the nearest tower everywhere we go. There will be a record of it. It will be like a trail of breadcrumbs leading right back to us. When we leave, your phone stays here."

As Virgil spoke, Curtis had his phone in his hand. He looked at it and pressed buttons quickly, immediately deleting a message.

"Who was it?"

"Work," said Curtis.

"What did they want?"

"Did you see me answer the phone?" he asked, annoyed. This was the Curtis who Virgil had never seen: a man with runaway intensity and omnipotent powers of concentration. Once he started, he put his head down and didn't move for hours. This was a man who could find a drug lord hidden in a sea of numbers. This was the man who could find three million dollars buried in the desert.

Virgil had never been made for this type of work. He grabbed the phone.

"Bobby Jordan," announced Virgil.

"He's a Texas Ranger. We work together on the task force."

"You've mentioned this guy. He's a legend down here, you said. I thought you guys were friends?"

"We were."

"Not anymore?"

"We're running out of time," said Curtis.

Curtis was busy. He had a series of photos he had printed from the computer. He arranged them across the table.

"My theory is that it's either a corporate retreat or a spot where some bigwig can bring his mistress."

"What if the mistress is there?" Virgil asked.

"She won't be. That's why we're going on a weekday. I've seen satellite footage from several days and there's never been a car. No one lives there. "

"But what if she is?" Virgil asked softly.

Curtis looked at him and wondered what had happened to the man he knew. The man on the other side of the table worried. He was nervous and hesitant and unsure of the direction in which he was headed.

"Then we wait for her to go shopping. And since there is nothing around there and nothing to do, she'll be gone for a while. Good enough?"

"Tell me again how Eduardo Mendes knows about this place?" Virgil asked.

"Mendes was the one who wired the money to Mexico. He would quietly transfer a portion into cash and send it across the border, just like Colon asked. It was always small amounts, but over time, it came to three million dollars. Then one day, Colon asked him to handle some business. Find two men who can handle concrete and who won't be missed. And bring muscle.

"He asked Eduardo to field it to his people. Instead, Eduardo came down there himself to do it personally."

"That doesn't sound like the guy you described."

"It doesn't. I think he was trying to discover Colon's secret. He wouldn't tell me the rest. Whatever really happened down there made him very uncomfortable. Haven't you ever done something out of character?"

"I'm doing it now," said Virgil.

"Phone call," Nixon the guard said to Eduardo. He barely understood him. Eduardo saw the annoyance on his face and hurried.

"Mister Mendes," said the voice on the phone. It was Flan, the lawyer. There weren't many people left that would call him Mister Mendes, and he couldn't decide if Flan was using it condescendingly himself.

"What can I do for you?" asked Eduardo. He hated those words.

"You can tell your unit supervisor that you will be unable to work in the kitchen tomorrow morning, Mister Mendes."

Nixon wouldn't like that. He hated change. If it were written in ink on the page in his hand, it might as well have come from God himself and been carved in stone.

"How come?"

"You are due in court tomorrow morning for a hearing."

"You said it would be months."

"I said it might be months. There's a reason why you hired me and not someone else."

Eduardo sighed into the phone.

"Relax, Mister Mendes."

"That is easy for you to say. What are we doing tomorrow?"

"I requested an emergency evidentiary hearing based on systemic problems with the investigation, as well as misidentification of the accused, namely, Eduardo Mendes."

"The feds allowed this?"

"Hopefully, they're just finding out about it now."

"How were you able to arrange this?"

"I asked nicely," said Flan.

"You expect me to believe that you simply walked into a court house, asked to have a hearing made up out of thin air, and it's just because you asked nicely?"

"You've paid handsomely for my services, Mister Mendes, and there is a reason for it."

"What reason is that?"

"People like me," said Flan.

It was the watch.

Sheldon Cashman awoke on the couch again with the ticking in his ears. During sleep, his hands always crept up to his face, the watch and its tourbillon components and its incessant ticking crawling closer and closer to his ears until his eyes opened. This happened every night.

This watch had gotten him where he was now: awake in the dark on the couch and wondering what Eduardo Mendes was going to do.

His wife was asleep in the master bedroom. They had a beautiful king-sized bed with a massive oak headboard. She had bought room darkening shades, and the room had become a tomb. Sheldon had slept in there only three times.

It was the thrashing. And the snoring. He hadn't known he did either of these things, but it kept his wife awake endlessly, despite her pills. She was dead to the world now, and he was on the couch listening to the ticking of the fabulously expensive watch that he couldn't afford.

Eduardo Mendes had seen this watch and refused to even acknowledge it. Eduardo could have it now if he would promise to never have come into his life. The watch could keep Eduardo up all night.

He stood, and his head smashed into the floor.

As Sheldon Cashman's brain stopped bouncing off the side of his skull, he realized that he had been struck. He tried to get to his feet when he was struck again. He landed half on the couch, the rest of him kneeling. A man pounced on him and grabbed his face.

Cashman began to scream, and the man pulled his head upwards. His voice was strangled by a hand on his throat. He felt the weight of the man and his strength. It was willful and relentless. There was a smell of waste.

"I have money!" he shouted as he twisted away from him. The man relented. It was the slightest, most incremental hesitation, but he relented. This was his chance. He could talk his way out of this. He could bargain.

"I have some money," he said. "But I can give you all my cards."

What else did he own?

"I have a car downstairs. An Audi."

The man said nothing. He didn't grunt or nod. His fingers remained gripped on Cashman's jaw, and he gave no sign of understanding or acceptance. Cashman wore pajamas, but felt naked. His toes nipped uselessly at the rug. He waited for a response. That was when he realized why this man was really here.

"My God, did Eduardo send you?" he asked. It was a plea. The man said nothing.

"Tell Eduardo that I am no threat to him at all. I am his friend. I have as much to lose as he does." Cashman struggled to think of what might appeal to this man. He tried to conjure a child who could make his life worth saving. He couldn't do it.

His mind went to another place.

"Look at this watch," he said desperately.

Cashman moved his hands together, and he felt the grip on his jaw tighten. His head raised against his will.

"No, no, no, just look. Let me show you."

His hands were shaking and missing their marks. His fingertips found the tiny clasp and pulled the leather away from it until the watch dangled invitingly from his hand.

"This watch is ridiculously expensive. It's extremely rare. No one else has one. It's worth money anywhere in the world. You can have it."

With that, Angel pushed the blade through the soft flesh of Sheldon's neck until metal struck bone. Angel took the watch from the air as Cashman's hands lunged helplessly for his own throat. Angel stood and regarded the item in his hand as Sheldon convulsed on the floor.

Blood spread quickly across the hardwood floors, and the rug formed an island in the growing dark flow. There was a subtle thrashing from Cashman, but that stopped soon enough. Then there was silence except for the tiniest, most delicate ticking from the elegant timepiece.

Angel didn't look at the body. Instead, he put the watch into his coat pocket. Then he went into the bedroom where Cashman's wife was sleeping, and he slit her throat too.

Judge Granary was a large woman with sad eyes that lit up when she saw Tobias Flan. He smiled that same smile that he had shown Eduardo years ago, when Eduardo was free and had money to spend. He remembered thinking once upon a time that Flan and that old grin of his had indicated that he was a push over and a simpleton. Somehow, that same grin had become flat out carnivorous.

The judge was a plain woman. She had ancient bifocals perched on her nose and a ten year old hairstyle. After greeting Flan, her mask went back on. It was pure seriousness, just as Flan had warned.

"Do I want that?" Eduardo had asked hesitantly.

"If I am your attorney, yes, you do. While we're on the subject, what are you wearing?"

Eduardo had been led into court wearing his orange prison jumpsuit and shackles. The shackles stretched from his handcuffs to a chain that led to matching bracelets around his ankles.

"What happened to the clothes you were arrested in?"

"That's a good question," Eduardo had said.

Flan had left a request with a guard he knew to have Eduardo changed into his own clothing for his court appearance. The clothes had been worn for days and bore the sweat of fear and interrogation, but the judge wouldn't be able to smell him from the bench. But when he was handed a large plastic bag containing his things, what he found instead were vintage slacks that had been passed along a dozen halfway houses and a flannel shirt that smelled like vomit.

"What is this?" Eduardo had asked. He realized at that moment that he had learned to automatically remove the entitled air of disgust from his voice. Not that it mattered to Nixon, who sucked on his toothpick and simply replied, "Your clothes." So he went to court in his prison jumpsuit.

The prosecutor, a woman of thirty who was new to the office, was on fire.

"Your honor, the government believes its case against Mister Mendes is solid and it will present evidence that he is guilty of laundering money across the Mexican border and into the hands of drug cartels."

"Name one," chimed in Flan.

The prosecutor shot him a death look for interrupting. She wore her ambition on her sleeve. Just from listening to her in the courtroom, and watching her interact, Eduardo knew that she spoke loudly and forcefully, giving orders instead of asking.

"Miss Tibideau is speaking, Mister Flan," stated Judge Granary. Though she seemed almost pleased when she said it.

"Thank you, your honor," Tibideau continued. "Mister Mendes has been implicated in a scheme to launder money for drug cartels and is in fact believed by my office to be the head of a methamphetamine trafficking operation. He has dual citizenship in the US and Spain. He is considered to be a flight risk, and we feel his bail is justified."

"Your honor, respectfully, Miss Tibideau may have the best intentions, but she has been misled by an overzealous team of agents that focused on Mister Mendes, who has no criminal record and is a self-made businessman. He has no link to drugs or drug money and no drugs or money were found during the deeply invasive search of his home and place of business. All that was found was that his accountant seems to have mental health issues, unbeknownst to Mister Mendes. I would request an immediate reduction in bail to ten thousand dollars."

"Ten thousand seems low, considering the charges your client is facing, but I will consider one hundred thousand dollars."

"That's ridiculous, Your Honor," blurted the prosecutor.

"Pardon me, ma'am?" said the judge.

"That is an insignificant amount of money for Mister Mendes."

"I will point out that not a cent of cash was located in his apartment during the search," said Flan politely.

"Mister Mendes is a drug dealer and a money launderer."

"Accused of such."

"He lives in a luxury building and drives an Aston Martin."

"Have these assets been seized by the government, Miss Tibideau?"

"Your honor, if I may," interjected Flan. "Mister Mendes rents a two-bedroom unit in a very nice building and he leases his vehicle. I will concede that he lives beyond his means, but that is likely a product of his upbringing. His father died when he was young."

"His father was a drug dealer too," said the prosecutor, in a voice that was too loud and too direct for the judge's taste.

"Does that make Mister Mendes a drug dealer, Miss Tibideau?" asked the judge.

"Well, ma'am, the apple doesn't fall far from the tree."

Flan lowered his head. Eduardo stood in shackles and watched, not understanding anything of what he was seeing. He felt the eyes of the judge on him. He tried not to look back. He followed them to Miss Tibideau, where they lingered and smoldered, before going back to Flan once more.

"I am setting Mister Mendes' bail at fifty thousand dollars," said Judge Granary.

"Your honor, that's ridiculous!"

"Miss Tibideau, I'm not in the habit of being called ridiculous in my courtroom and I don't think I care for it."

"Your honor, fifty thousand dollars is a joke. This is a man who has laundered millions of dollars into Mexico through his business and may even be implicated in several murders."

"Murders?" Flan asked. "My client is going to be charged with murder now?"

"Is the indictment against Mister Mendes going to be amended, Miss Tibideau?"

"Your honor, I may have misspoken. I've had meetings with several officers on this case who tell me that Mister Mendes—"

"Your Honor, if I may," began Flan. "This harkens back to our central theory that Miss Tibideau has been duped into thinking that she has a drug kingpin on her hands when in fact she may have only a kid who grew up rich, took what was left of his inheritance, and invested in a check cashing business in a bad neighborhood. Frankly, I feel the prosecution is a bit delusional."

"Don't you call me delusional!" shot Tibideau, who was on the edge of fury.

Real fireworks now, thought Eduardo, still in the dark.

"Your Honor," said Flan in calm, friendly tones. "Miss Tibideau appears a little overwhelmed at the moment. Perhaps we can return later in the morning in order to continue with the hearing. I think a lot of Miss Tibideau's confusion in the matter could be cleared up by calling the officer at the center of this case."

Flan looked at his notes. Eduardo peered at them. There was nothing on the page.

"An IRS agent by the name of Walter Curtis."

"An IRS agent?" asked the judge.

"Your Honor, we believe this is a tax matter relating to an accountant who has a mental disability and has been blown well out of proportion."

Tibideau opened her mouth as if to speak, but thought better of using the word ridiculous again. Instead, she was quiet.

"Will Agent Curtis be here this morning, ma'am?"

From where Eduardo was standing, there seemed to be a little less of the prosecutor now.

"I don't know, ma'am."

"You may want to find him," said Judge Granary. "Bail is set at fifty thousand dollars."

"Your Honor, we have a woman here who is willing to post the full amount."

That part shocked Eduardo. That part he definitely had not see coming. He turned and scanned the courtroom. There was no missing her. She sat perched at the end of the bench, touching as little of it as possible. She had her hair down and long, despite her age, as she always did, so no one would see her tattoo. Her pale legs were crossed and slid out from beneath a stunning black dress that had probably cost more than the rest of the clothes in this room. He hadn't seen Elodia de la Cueva Mendes in five years, and he hadn't spoken to her in three.

"Where did you find her?" he asked Flan in a stunned whisper.

"Hamburg," said Flan.

"Can this woman account for the funds she is providing for your client, Mister Flan?" demanded the judge.

"Oh, yes, ma'am," said Flan. He looked like he had been licking his lips. They glistened. "She is his mother."

In the hallway to the cells, Eduardo Mendes sat on a metal bench that was affixed to the wall and watched as the unthinkable happened: the court officer unlocked his handcuffs and let them fall loudly to the ground. What a wonderful sound, he thought, as he rubbed his wrists and ignored everything that Flan was saying to him. His skin felt almost like his own once more. A month ago, if those shackles had been on his wrists, he'd have run to the nearest sink with his arms outstretched to douse them in scalding hot water and disinfectant. Now he ran his fingers pleasantly along the trenches and ridges caused by the digging metal frames.

"How did you find my mother?" Eduardo asked.

Flan had been speaking when he said it. He had been speaking about procedures and next steps. He had been speaking about not leaving the state or associating with anyone who could cause conflicts for him if this matter should fail to resolve as succinctly as expected.

"I have a very talented investigator at my disposal. He followed an account that was generated after you wired some funds to her just last year. Good things happen when you're good to your ma."

"I was paying a debt," Eduardo said wistfully.

"No doubt, Mister Mendes. I am going to ask you to sign some documents."

"I need to make a phone call," said Eduardo.

"Is it urgent?"

"Very."

"I wouldn't recommend using any of the phones in this building."

"Good point," said Eduardo. He was still cruising through disbelief.

"How did you pull this off?" he asked.

"Pull what off, Mister Mendes?" asked Flan innocently.

"Two weeks ago, I had a massive cash bail and was doing federal time. I'm walking out the door on fifty grand."

"These are the services you've retained me to provide, Mister Mendes."

"I would like to know."

"When you were a child, did you ever see a magician?"

"No."

"They never reveal their tricks."

"I insist."

Flan could see that it was useless.

"The judge and I enjoy having a drink together from time to time."

"You're banging the judge?" Eduardo laughed. Too loudly, it seemed, because Flan's eyes searched the hall.

"Not at all. We're friends. I know her well. I know the clerk. I know the magistrate. I know the secretaries who assign which cases to which courtroom. And I knew enough about the prosecutor to get what I wanted. The prosecutor has a reputation for a short temper and a quick tongue, and both turned out to be true. It was easy to get her to say something to fire up the judge."

"How?"

"If you had demanded this sort of detail from everyone in your service, you might not have needed me today," said Flan.

"How?"

The lawyer sighed.

"Judge Granary comes from a very modest background. Her father was executed forty years ago for gunning down a police officer. She has always been quite sensitive about the stigma attached to a thing like that."

"Ah," said Eduardo, remembering the prosecutor bringing up his father, and being more glad than ever that his mother was there to hear it. "So that was the trick?"

"The trick, Mister Mendes, is getting the right people into the room at the right time."

Tobias Flan had a red nose with red varicose veins perched upon it. The deep red veins looked ready to burst. Eduardo reminded himself that he had a phone call to make.

"And how did you do it? How did you get them all into the same room?"

"I asked," said Flan simply.

"You asked?" scoffed Eduardo. Eduardo didn't ask. Neither did his mother. They told people what to do. Flan licked his lips and showed his canine teeth again. It was his version of a smile.

"People like me, Mister Mendes."

Odalys's heart exploded when she saw the flowers. Her eyes instantly became wet. A sound came from her lips, and it was a gasp of deep and genuine surprise, from the very bottom of her heart, where wishes she'd given up on had suddenly come true. Eduardo had sent her flowers.

It was a spectacular bouquet of bluebonnets with white roses. They weren't pristine. They were vibrant and messy and colorful and alive and perfect. She reached out for them.

The delivery man punched her in the stomach. She landed on her backside with the air sucked from her lungs. She saw blood on her hands and bubbling from her belly.

Angel calmly closed the door behind him. He dropped the flowers on the ground. He took Odalys by the neck so she couldn't scream and dragged her into another room.

Odalys' last rational thoughts, before being overwhelmed by pain and horror, were of Eduardo Mendes. She thought of how Eduardo would eventually find this man and kill him for what he had done to her.

A heavy gold crucifix dangled from the border guard's neck as he leaned over his station. Curtis thought of his St. Michael medallion. He had held it in his hand while getting dressed and asked himself if the patron saint of police officers would really be watching over their errand into Mexico. He doubted it, but he shoved it into his pocket anyway. His fingers touched the handcuff key, and he remembered: for things you can change, and for those you can't.

"Be careful down there," said the guard. "Mexico ain't like home."

"That's what I'm hoping," said Curtis.

The guard waved the beaten down Jeep through the gate where they were clear to merge with the highway. Virgil exhaled as if he'd been holding his breath.

"I thought you were supposed to be the cool, calm, and collected one," said Curtis.

He saw the sign as they approached. "Mexico Only. No Return USA," it read. They went right under it.

There were two phones on Walter Curtis' kitchen table. One was set to ring, but no one had called it. The other was set to vibrate, and every time a call came in, the whole table shook lightly. They had started out next to one another, but were now on opposite sides of the table. Curtis' phone buzzed impatiently, then buzzed again and toppled on to the floor.

Angel barely seemed to notice. He moved silently amongst Curtis' things. He took no notice of the files or the printed e-mails or handwritten notes. His eyes glanced over the map of Mexico covered with red ink. Finally, he focused on a small framed photograph. This interested Angel very much.

It was a picture of Curtis and Marc Virgil. They were in a bar and laughing. It was a few years old, but it would do.

Chapter Six

Ordo – Nuevo Leon, MX

Ordo Beltran was on a private lake talking to a man whose hands were nailed to an Adirondack chair. Ordo had never seen a chair like this, and it had been perfect for his needs. He had demanded that the man tell him what it was called and grown impatient when the man only cried.

The Russian plodded over in just his shorts. Blood was spattered across his torso. The Russian had told him to take his clothes off, but Ordo hadn't listened. He would stop by this man's closet in the main house before they left. Ordo's phone began to ring. He knew the voice immediately.

"I just took a call from a man with TS. Do you know who I mean?"

Ordo did. Texas Syndicate was a necessary evil. Men had to know that they weren't safe anywhere.

"He says he needs some work done."

"No problem."

"On an American."

"Here or there?"

"Here. You have someone who can handle this immediately?"

Ordo looked at the Russian.

"How important is this?" He was busy with Laredo.

Ordo cupped the receiver again. The man in the chair had begun wailing, and he couldn't hear the phone. He indicated to the Russian that he no longer needed this man.

The Russian pulled the hand axe from one of the small bodies in the sand and headed toward the Adirondack. The wailing grew louder.

"Who do I need to kill?" asked Ordo.

The answer was immediate.

"An American named Eduardo Mendes."

***

Juan Dossantos Diaz was his Christian name, but everyone at work called him Juan Two Saints. He was thirty years old, married, and had two little boys. Juan was a state policeman in Nuevo Leon, Mexico. He had become a police officer because he wanted to believe in something greater than himself. Lately, Juan Two Saints had been having trouble holding on to that principle, and the main reason was sitting next to him.

Jefe smelled even worse than usual. It was a toxic combination of oniony food, old sweat, stifling heat, and body odor. Jefe sweated like other men breathed.

"Do you know where we got this truck?" Jefe asked.

They were sitting in a black Ford Expedition with smoked out windows, crouched just off the highway behind a grove of shrubby trees. Juan knew where the truck came from. He knew, because Jefe had told him a hundred times.

"The government of the United States bought this truck for us," Jefe said with a beaming smile. "International narcotics interdiction."

Jefe stood six foot four, though he preferred to sit. He was well over three hundred pounds, and when he did stand, his belt disappeared under his belly, with only his sidearm poking out desperately at the side. Drips and stains of food from days past decorated his uniform shirt, and the pits of his shirts were permanently soaked. He managed to appear for work unshaven every single night, his beard extending down the huge flaps of skin under his jaw.

To Juan's knowledge, Jefe was the only full-fledged gringo in the Nuevo Leon police force, which was why, Juan supposed, Jefe had been so excited to learn that he was fluent in English.

When he was a boy, there was a police officer in his town who everyone called Don Fernando. It was Don Fernando who had made him want to be a police officer. They had never spoken, but it was his demeanor. Don Fernando was cool and tall and impeccably well dressed. Don Fernando, in hindsight, never seemed to do much in the way of police work, but he was always around. Since nothing ever happened in his town, around was enough. Juan Two Saints told Jefe that story one night after he had been transferred to the task force.

Jefe howled with laughter. The next night, he had made Juan his driver.

Jefe made Juan sit in the truck with the windows rolled up, trapping him with his stink. He made Juan handle money from shops and garages that never seemed to open, handed to him by men whose rough lives were written on their faces. A man who was missing the tips of two fingers once passed him a stack of bills. Juan imagined they had been chopped off at some point. He certainly didn't ask.

Fast moving blue lights lit up the highway. That would be Dejo. Jefe smiled.

"Looks like we're in business," he said.

Dejo had a blue work van stopped going North. He pulled his shotgun from the cruiser and walked up to the window. He held it crossed in front of his chest in the most confrontational manner possible. Juan stood in the back. A small young man climbed out from behind the steering wheel.

"Hola, Santos. Que pasa?" asked Jefe.

"Nothing," said the nervous man.

He was in his early twenties. Juan had seen him before on the highway. He was small and wiry and in the day time had an obvious athleticism about him. Tonight, he just looked scared.

"How many friends you got in there?" he asked.

"Ten," said Santos, and Juan exhaled a tiny bit.

"Any pretty girls?" asked Jefe.

The question had surprised Santos. It didn't surprise Juan, whose stomach was clenching on him. "No," was Santos' answer.

Jefe had been chewing on an unlit cigar. He took it from his mouth, inspected it, and then slid it into his shirt pocket.

"Can I meet your friends?" asked Jefe.

"I don't want anyone to get hurt, Jefe."

"Why would someone get hurt?"

Santos didn't respond. Dejo was suddenly at the back with the keys in his hands and sprung open the lock. He threw open both doors.

"Oh, look at this," Dejo shouted dramatically.

Juan hated Dejo. In the back of the van were ten men and women. More men than women. They were young and old and middle aged. One woman held a child.

"I thought you told me there were no pretty girls back here," said Jefe.

Santos shrugged.

"You're not a faggot, are you?" asked Jefe.

At that, Santos stiffened. Dejo laughed loudly. Santos was dwarfed by the huge man, and the huge man was the law. His anger had risen to his face and looked to be creeping up his throat. Santos swallowed hard and held it.

"Get them out," said Jefe.

They lined the whole group up on the side of the road in the blast radius of the headlights. The boy caught his eye. He was older than Juan's boys. His eyes were large and scared.

"What do you say about her?" asked Jefe.

There was no doubt as to who he was talking about. The woman held on to the boy's shoulders. She looked tired and terrified. She wore lipstick but no other makeup. Her hair was tied back in a ponytail. Jefe's eyes climbed all over her. She had the slightest bulge in her tummy, and he could see clearly this boy was hers. His wife's body had been the same after she'd had their boys. He loved that little tummy on her. He loved his wife. He wished he were home with her, and not here.

"She looks good, Jefe," said Santos. He said it flatly, and with defeat.

"What's he got on him?"

Dejo went straight to the pockets and then to the waist band. He checked Santos' groin and shoes. When he was done, he held out a wad of green bills.

Jefe looked at the bills. Then he looked at Juan Two Saints. His meaning was clear. Juan knew what was expected of him. He wanted to ignore it. He wanted to get back in the car to go home and see his family. He would lie on the floor between his sons' beds and listen to them sleep. He should take his uniform off, hang it in his closet, and never wear it again. Instead, he took the money.

96

"Count it up for me," Jefe said in an offhand way, as if distracted. Juan knew he wasn't distracted at all.

"You were crossing this group tonight. Why are you trying to run bodies over the border without doing the right thing?"

Santos shrugged. Jefe grinned.

"Juan Two Saints," Jefe called. "How much is it?"

He gave Jefe the count. Jefe didn't respond. Instead, he walked his huge frame over to the woman.

"Come with me," he said.

The woman clutched the child even tighter. "Your boy will be fine," said Jefe.

He never touched her. He didn't have to. She went with him, and twice she looked over her shoulder, as they walked behind the scrub trees. Her eyes were pleading. None of her group moved. Santos looked at the ground. Dejo laughed. Juan Two Saints pretended to count the money again.

When they came back, she walked ahead of Jefe and walked quickly. Juan didn't look at her directly, but in his peripheral vision, he saw her hug the boy to her chest. Jefe told them all to get back in the van. Then he addressed Santos.

"I asked the pretty girl if she wanted to go to jail or go north. She chose north, so this ride is on the house. Are we going to have a problem with you holding out on me in the future?"

Santos shook his head.

"No what?" said the big man.

"No, Jefe."

When they got back in the car, Juan could feel Jefe's eyes on him. The big man had a way of leaning sideways in the truck to watch him. Juan hated every second of it, and it went on and on.

"You have my money," Jefe said.

Juan passed it to him, glad to be rid of it. It disappeared somewhere inside Jefe's clothes.

"I gave her a choice," he said as he lit up his cigar. His stubble filled face was illuminated for seconds. "We all have a choice."

***

Curtis had driven this road many times before. The landscape went from green to tan to dusty before green gradually began to poke through once again. There were signs of civilization. They passed homes that seemed beautiful at seventy miles per hour, and they passed shacks that remained shacks at any speed. The big mountain was looming over them when Curtis pulled off the road.

"It's better that we eat now instead of later, when we're closer."

"I don't think Mexican food is what I need."

"I don't think you know what Mexican food really is," said Curtis.

They pulled into a gas station that had a large empty lot next to it. There was a trailer with an open window. Curtis was excited when he found out what they were serving. He said it was liebre pozole, but wouldn't tell Virgil what was in it. It was a thick, red stew filled with a shredded meat that he couldn't identify. Each spoonful he dug out had a small vegetable that appeared to be corn. He started to ask one more question before Curtis yelled at him to shut up and eat it. When Virgil finished, he demanded to know what liebre was.

"Bunny rabbit," said Curtis. "Everything here is fresh catch or fresh kill."

Virgil licked what little meat was left on his spoon.

"This was not what I expected," he said.

Eduardo – Austin, TX

"Te amo," said Elodia into the phone. She was talking to a man. A man from another place who spoke a language he didn't know was spending time with his mother in Hamburg. Finally, she hung up, put the phone into a Hermes handbag, and looked at her son for the first time in years.

"I met a man, Eddie," Elodia gushed. She looked thirty years younger when she said it.

"What's this man's name? Where's he from?"

She looked self-consciously into her hands.

"His name is Laszlo. He's from Vienna."

"Does he import cocaine?"

"No, Eddie. He's a count."

"A count! I love it. Does he live in a castle?"

"He lives in a very well appointed condominium in downtown Vienna. It's very European. I think you'd like it. You can see the Opera House from our apartment."

"Our apartment," Eduardo repeated. "Can you hear the opera too? You wouldn't have to buy tickets. You could open your windows and listen for free."

"Very funny, Eddie," she said, showing the girlish smile again. It was a smile Eduardo had never seen growing up in her house. "Laszlo was well provided for, and he's managed his accounts well. He can take me to the opera if I want to go."

"Do you?" Eduardo asked.

"When the right people are there," said Elodia. She regarded him for a moment, then reached out to touch his face. Eduardo pulled away from her.

"I'm not clean," he said.

"You're still my boy." She reached again. He reached out and stopped her.

"I mean it." He did, and she saw that. She was silent for a long time as they drove. When she finally spoke, she was serious, and the girl in her was gone.

"Did you think I was cold, Eddie? When you were a child?" she asked.

"Yes," said Eduardo.

"I was for a reason," she said.

Eduardo didn't respond. He didn't know what there was to say.

"When I was young, I thought I was special. I thought I had things because I had a right to them. I was entitled to the things that were mine. I behaved as if rules didn't apply to me. "

He found himself looking at the knees of the orange jumpsuit he was still wearing.

"I did whatever I felt, and I flaunted it. That is what entitlement will do to you. I thought that there were no consequences for me, because I was above consequences. I was wrong.

"I believed that I was special and that my father's love was unconditional. His love was. His affections were not. I had finally disappointed my father so profoundly that he could not forgive me. Instead of forgiveness, he taught me a lesson. I could live a life with nothing, or I could have a life with rules. He married me off to a pig of a drug dealer half a world away. Seven months later, you were born."

Eduardo knew this. She had told him before, when she had told him that his father would not be returning from Mexico.

"I was cold to you because I didn't want you to believe that you were too special for the rules of the world."

Elodia regarded her son coolly.

"Why are you telling me this again?"

"Because there are times that I wish I had taken nothing," she said.

"Sir," called the driver in a quiet voice that said he was doing his damnedest not to listen to a word of their conversation. "We've arrived at your first destination."

"I'm getting married, Eddie," said Elodia. She was smiling. Not beaming like before, but smiling. "Married for real this time."

"Congratulations. You and The Count can make lots of babies and be happy."

Elodia's eyes fell to the floor. Eduardo regretted saying it immediately, but did not apologize.

"You and I made a pact, didn't we, Eddie? A long time ago."

"You told me The Count was rich."

"He is well off, but I will not go empty handed. I won't be that woman again."

"Doesn't he love you?"

"This isn't about him. This is about you and me."

Eduardo got out of the car and strode into the second-floor office in his prison clothes. The lawyer was taken aback by his appearance.

"Mister Mendes...I was not expecting you," said the lawyer from the small firm of Holden, Glanton, and Brown.

"Well, here I am," said Eduardo. The old man was examining him.

"Are you okay?" the old lawyer asked.

"Why? Is something wrong?"

"I...I don't know...if there is..."

"Something you can do? Yes, there is. I left a package in your care some time ago. Please fetch it for me."

Fetch it. He loved the way that came out of his mouth. He hadn't even planned it. Like riding a bicycle, Eduardo thought. The befuddled old man stammered a bit, then came to his senses and left the room. When he returned, he had a sealed manila envelope in his hand.

"Forgive me, Mister Mendes. I was quite surprised to find you here."

"The important thing is that you were exactly where I expected to find you." With that, Eduardo turned to walk back to the elevator. He was at the receptionist's desk when he heard the lawyer calling for him.

"Sir, you don't plan to go to the bank dressed like that?"

"I certainly do," he said.

"Your father is gone," she had announced when he came home from school. It was Christmas break. He was wearing a St. Paul's jacket. All the guys wore their jackets home then.

"Gone where?" he had asked. He was embarrassed he had said that. Not immediately, but as the years passed and he had time to reflect on that day, he'd become more and more embarrassed at his naïveté. When his mother didn't answer, and he'd begun to realize what she meant, he asked what had happened.

"The phone rang," she said. She lit a cigarette. She only smoked on the balcony, and the smoke never clung to her. It was on her breath, but the wind took the rest.

"He was told to go to Mexico for a meeting. He went to the meeting, and he never returned."

Eduardo thought about this for a while. He wondered if there wasn't something being kept from him. "Could he maybe just be in hiding?"

Elodia's glance was both dismissive and withering. He never forgot it.

"No, Eduardo," she said. "He is never coming back."

His father had lost all of his money. He had invested profits into the stock market, and after profits, he had invested operating capital. When he had invested the capital, he had invested money that was still owed. When the unbeatable market finally burst, his father's wealth burst with it. His father had spent a lifetime illegally accumulating money and possessions that were beyond his reach, and in just months, legally, it was all gone.

He cried. He sobbed and ran from her and discovered half of the home's possessions had been sold already. When she found him, she stroked the crown of his head and told him they would be fine. She also told him she was leaving to begin again. She told him who his father wasn't.

"You're better than this, Eddie," she said in her ancient, old world accent. "You're better bred."

Inside the bank, the guard eyed him suspiciously. Eduardo waited for him to leave before opening the box. He saw money. He saw stacks of hard work and sweat he detested. He saw stacks of things he did without for years. He saw a past he thought was behind him.

He saw a pile of money that he couldn't carry out in his arms. Eduardo realized that he had neglected to bring a bag or a box or any sort of container. Grabbing one green stack, he went behind the tellers' counter and scanned their feet, until his eyes landed on it.

"I like your bag," Eduardo said to the unsuspecting teller. "Louis Vuitton."

"It's fake," said the teller, very surprised.

"It's perfect," said Eduardo. "I want it."

At first, she said it wasn't for sale. It was her bag and she needed it, but her eyes widened as he tore off the first bill, and then another before she could react. By the time he had laid down the third bill, she blurted out, "That's enough to get a real Louis bag!"

"Almost," he said, picking it up and dumping the contents onto the ground.

He realized then that he had two deposits to make, and one bag wouldn't be enough. He looked around the inside of the tellers' counter, seeing nothing that suited hm.

"Tell me something," Eduardo asked. "Did you bring your lunch?"

When he climbed back into the Town Car, he saw his mother's quizzical look at the small pink Hello Kitty lunch bag that was in his hand. It was zippered tight and still bulging. "This is for you," he said, handing her the brown leather bag covered in little intercrossed counterfeit gold LV's. His mother took it from him as if it smelled bad.

"It's fake," she said.

"I know," replied Eduardo. "I can't wait to see you wearing it."

Curtis – Monterrey, MX

They entered the city of Monterrey surrounded by towers of glass. The city was modern and clean, and everything was painted white. There were new buildings and old churches, and most looked more like they belonged in Europe instead of Mexico. They drove past the great plaza, over a spectacular blue canal, and then found themselves by a sea of green grass. Wherever they went, the mountains loomed over them.

"That's the Bishop's Palace," said Curtis almost absentmindedly. "That's the Gran Plaza."

Virgil was barely listening. He looked on with amazement.

"I had no idea," muttered Virgil.

"No idea about what?"

"I pictured Mexico differently," he said. "I pictured shacks and dirt roads. Tin roofs and kids with no shoes. Not this."

"I can find some poor people if you want."

"No. This is fine," said Virgil. In the distance, the city ended abruptly, and the mountains rose out of the earth. "A man could get lost down here," he said.

Eduardo liked Puro because they had Asians. He liked Asians because they were cleaner than Mexicans. Mexicans, of course, were in plentiful supply down here, and could be hired dirt cheap, so Eduardo appreciated the effort Puro made to find Asians to scrub him and clean him.

"Welcome back, Eduardo," said the manager in her deep whisper. He didn't care for the familiarity. "Will Miss Odalys be joining you today?"

"No," he said. "We're not together any longer."

"Well," said the manager, with a smile he didn't care for. "Perhaps you will be again."

Eduardo wondered if there was a spa where he could have a blood transfusion. He wanted to use his own blood, but from before.

"I want to be scrubbed," said Eduardo.

"We have a wonderful coconut scrub that you should definitely experience."

"I want to begin with something harsh," he said.

"We have a dry brushing therapy that may suit you. We could combine it with a citrus blend exfoliant."

"What do you use to scrub the floors?" asked Eduardo.

She was briefly taken aback, but composed herself. He could see her thinking of how to proceed, so he placed the lunch bag filled with money on the desk. His expression made it clear that he was completely serious.

"There was a woman here before. She said her name was Lily, but I know it wasn't. Is she here?"

He read her hesitation and her nervousness. She said yes anyway.

"I want her to scrub me."

"Very good."

"And another thing."

She looked unsure of what would come next.

"I want to know her real name."

Lily appeared dutifully with a bucket and a bottle of cleaning product from the closet. She said her name was Qiao, and Eduardo repeated it twice, making her do the same, until he had the pronunciation correct. Then he made her scrub.

He liked the clear wrapper, discarded on the floor, from which she had drawn the thick yellow sponge. He liked new things used on him. The cleaning fluid had a lemon scent, and the texture of a light oil. Qiao had immediately grasped what it was he wanted and used force on him. He tried not to wince.

He soaped and showered as she waited, and he eventually took the manager's suggestion of the coconut body scrub. It was delightful, and he didn't want it to end. Qiao suggested the detailed parafango treatment, which was pure wonder, followed by a coconut mini-facial, which rotated cool smooth stones and hot towels against the skin of his face. It was the Vichy shower that he wanted though, and the Vichy that had brought him here. It felt like a storm, controlled, and compressed just onto him. Warm rain ran over him and through him, and once again, Eduardo felt like the reigns of his life were back in his own hands.

Qiao laid a fresh dry towel over his body and told him softly that his delivery had arrived and was waiting for him in his private room once he was ready. Eduardo rolled over and let the towel fall to the floor. He watched Qiao's eyes fall on his body. Her face showed neither shock nor apprehension. It was disappointment mixed with equal amounts of resignation. Eduardo knew that she didn't want anything to do with this. That made it so much better for him.

There was one dry spot on the floor below the sink, and that was where he stood, barefoot. Everywhere else in the bathroom was a flood of piss or dirty water or both or worse.

It was a discount gas station so cheap that it had no name. The lights on the sign faded and flickered, and so did the lights in the bathroom. That didn't bother Angel.

Tufts of black hair fell to his feet. Whiskers landed in the puddles. He was nude and had hair all over his body, which he shook and padded off of himself. With scissors, he cut his hair short. With a comb and water, he neatened it.

He dressed in plain khaki pants and a plain white shirt. His shoes were brown and used. On his wrist, he wore a watch that was worth almost as much as a house. It had a tiny device on the inside of it that spun and twirled miraculously. It was called a tourbillon, though he paid it no notice. He pulled a sport coat over his shirt. It was a deep brown and made of a material called vicuna. It had once belonged to Eduardo Mendes. He left everything else in the trash.

Angel walked the last quarter mile to the border, where he crossed unnoticed into Mexico.

Chapter Seven

Virgil – Monterrey, MX

Curtis' ridiculous yellow shirt lit up like a beacon. It was a short sleeve yellow button up Hawaiian shirt that hung past his waist. "It covers my gun," Curtis had said when he felt Virgil's dismay. The shirt had little hula girls dancing with a guitar before a red flame. The girls were all shaking their bottoms either left or right, one after another, all across the shirt.

"Are you under the impression that they have hula girls in Mexico?"

"When the task force goes to Mexico, they don't want to look like cops. They want to look like tourists. They want to blend in."

"You think that shirt blends in?"

"I think I look like someone who came to Mexico to have a good time."

Virgil kept his head low and his voice low. Curtis was staring into his binoculars.

"Anything?" he asked.

"Nothing," said Curtis. Nothing was good.

Before them lay the grand white house they had envisioned. It was a large home, but not by modern American standards. It was not ostentatious. It was rectangular, with four solid corners and no additions. The roof was red tile. There was a short staircase to the first floor, with tiny windows just above ground level.

"A basement!" Curtis had exclaimed. Inside Virgil, the nervousness grew. Most importantly, and the only thing which made him feel better, was that as the sun sank lower in the sky, the windows in the house remained dark.

"Any sign of the old man?"

"No," said Curtis. "No sign at all."

The big house wasn't the only structure on the property, but it stood in contrast to everything else. There was a huge old barn a few hundred feet from the house. In the light, it looked much older than the house. When they had arrived in the late afternoon, they could see its paint was faded and peeling. Like the house, it was two stories, but the roof was in need of repair. Its two main doors could open wide enough to accommodate a tractor or a wagon, but had been barred from the outside by a wooden beam. No real farming was done here anymore, save for in the vineyard, and the forest had been allowed to encroach behind the barn.

The vineyard was the one thing they hadn't expected. It was situated in a triangle from the house and the barn. When they had first arrived, they could see a little old man walking amongst the stalks, clutching tools or a watering can. He went back and forth between the vines and a small shack with a tin roof off to the side of the vineyard. They had taken it for a tool shed until the old man went in and didn't come out. As the sun dipped, they saw a light in the window.

"What do you suppose he's doing here?"

Curtis shrugged in the dark.

"He's the caretaker. Some old man living rent free. Gives the place character."

"He wasn't part of our plan."

"He isn't screwing it up either."

"How is he not?"

"Some company owns this place as a retreat. The old man takes care of it and lives free. I used to audit companies that did stuff like this all the time."

"Really?"

"Yeah, really. The Boston Police Department doesn't have a corporate retreat in Italy or Lake Tahoe, but lots of successful companies do. They send their clients away for the weekend to wine and dine them. Come January, they write the whole thing off in taxes."

"Companies do this?"

"It's commonplace."

Virgil scanned the property with the binoculars. It was dark now. This was countryside dark, and totally unlike night in the city. There was no escape from this kind of night. He watched the house, the vineyard, the shack, and the barn. As he went to repeat the cycle, his mind clicked, and it took a moment for his eyes to register the change. It was the shack. Curtis saw it too, without binoculars.

The lights went out.

Eduardo had had a fine suit delivered to the spa, and he wore it now as he walked over the bridge into Mexico. He spotted a man standing by a black Navigator. He was dressed formally, like a character from an old Hollywood film, and his clothes were very well pressed. His hair was smooth, and he wore a goatee. Eduardo saw immediately that it was meant to cover the deep scar on his lip. He looked like a man from another time who didn't belong where he was.

"Mister Mendes," said Strauss.

Without another word, Strauss took the pouch from Eduardo's hands. Then he opened the door.

The truck was clean, and almost unused, save for the coffee mug in the center console. From time to time, Strauss sipped from it, and paid Eduardo no attention at all.

"The man you sent…what is his name?"

Strauss didn't answer immediately.

"The less you know about him, the better."

"I understand that. All the same, I would like to know."

"His name is Angel."

"Angel fucked up."

"It was a short notice."

"I needed a person dead, and they are still alive."

"For now."

"He is still a danger to me."

"If you like, I can arrange a meeting between you and Angel, and you can voice your complaints directly."

Eduardo glared at him. The words themselves were polite enough, as was the tone, but he understood their meaning. Strauss sipped his coffee.

"You knew me. Didn't you?" he said to Strauss.

"I did."

"How? We've never met."

"You've never met me, is what you mean."

"Have you followed me?"

"Mister Mendes," said Strauss. "When we're done here, do you want me talking about what we're about to do?"

"I would think not."

"I show all my clients the same courtesy," he said quietly.

Eduardo thought about that. He thought of Colon.

"Did you know him?" Eduardo asked.

"Did I know who?"

"You know who I mean," said Eduardo.

He nodded.

"What did you think of him?" Eduardo asked.

Strauss sipped his coffee again. He drove, and Eduardo thought he was going to be ignored again before Strauss finally spoke.

"He was a man who valued discretion."

And surrounded himself with men who barely spoke his name, even after his death. Eduardo had spent a good amount of time pondering Aureliano Colon, his life, his business, and his lifestyle. Or, more to the point, the tight glimpses of these things that he had been granted. He was not prepared to pass up an opportunity to make inquiries with someone who had known him well.

"Before Colon died, did he tell you to do what I asked?"

"You could say we had an understanding."

Eduardo felt something stir inside of him. It was an evil thing. He felt a tingling rise in his skin. He felt himself giving life to a certain demand.

"You know Monterrey well, don't you? Not just the city, but the city below it."

Strauss shrugged. The shrug was a modest yes.

"Tell me. Is there a place in Monterrey where you can have sex with a child? A boy, preferably."

Strauss didn't answer. This time, he didn't sip coffee either.

"Is there?" Eduardo asked.

"I wouldn't know."

"But you could find out if there was, couldn't you?"

Strauss nodded. He did it almost automatically, as if it were entirely against his will, but couldn't help himself.

"Find out," said Eduardo.

Virgil – Monterrey, MX

They stood on the steps of the big house. It was dark. The barn was dark. The shack was dark. Yet still they whispered.

"We can get back into the Jeep and drive home right now. We haven't done anything wrong yet."

"Do you want to go home?" Curtis asked.

Now the time for being quiet was over, and the red door stood between them and a point of no return. Virgil held the heavy sledge hammer in his hand.

He knew what Curtis meant. He meant, Do you want to go home to shame, as a criminal, as a man unable to support himself?

The sound exploded over the silence. Wood broke and splintered. Tiny shards flew into the air. The door blasted wide open and crashed into the opposite wall.

No, Marc Virgil thought. He did not want to go home.

Juan Two Saints entered his house and went straight to the room in the back where the boys were sleeping. One was tucked in his bed with blankets pulled to his neck. The other slept on the floor.

Juan looked at the empty bed and sighed. When the floor sleeping had begun, his wife had been distraught.

"How can he be happy? The floor is so hard," she said.

But Juan understood.

As a child, in church, he would go to confession with his mother. His mother would be in the confessional for two minutes, tops. When Juan went in, he liked to stay for a while. When he ran out of sins, he made up new ones, no doubt unconvincingly. The priest seemed to understand and punished him accordingly. Most everyone knelt at the padded brace, but he had once spotted a man, a strong looking beast of a man, praying and crying on his knees. Juan couldn't resist trying it too. He liked it. He'd run into his house at the end of the day with blood running from his knees. His mother would gasp and say, "You've been in church again!"

He was on the verge of his fourth double this week. Jefe had become more erratic and unpredictable in his demands. He had come home to enjoy his first quiet night in a week, and his phone began ringing.

He didn't even need to look. It was Jefe. "Change of plans," he growled.

Virgil thought of a moment from a thousand years ago when he had entered a dimly lit room and been electrocuted. He had entered a room with no lights, but he could see by the daylight streaming in through the partially shuttered window. He had ignored his training and moved. For that, he was shocked.

The instructor touched his arm with the device. He only touched it, and the electric pulse ran wild. Pain seared through him. It was August. He had been sweating. The current jumped through the sweat and raced across his skin.

"When you enter a dark room," said a calm voice that was holding the prod. "Turn on the lights."

Years later, Virgil instinctively ran his left hand along the wall. It was covered with paper. It was paper with fine, rich, tiny details. Most light switches are five feet off the ground, he reminded himself. Even in Mexico.

The room lit up white. It was occupied by plain red furniture. There was a wood coffee table in front of the couch. There was Mexican artwork on the wall.

Then came the dining room. He could see it all, but found the switch anyway. The lights went on in the kitchen at the same time. He heard Curtis' step and called, "Clear."

He found the base of the stairs. The stairs are the most dangerous place in the house. He could feel Curtis behind him. He didn't have to look. For the first time in almost a year, he drew a gun.

He climbed just far enough to see the floor. There was no one on the landing. The rooms were all dark. All the doors were open. He leaned backward as much as he could while still watching the second floor.

"When I go up, you stay low on the stairs. You watch those three doors," he whispered.

The only thing he saw was the six stairs to the top and the three blackened rooms beyond them. Virgil almost felt Curtis' hesitation. He thought about telling him that it was fine, that nothing was going to happen, and that the house was empty. Instead, he took the stairs in two steps and jumped into the darkness.

It was Curtis' turn. He ran into the last dark room on the second floor. He fumbled for a light. It had to be there. His hand swept the wall. He imagined a machete slicing through his neck at any moment. He felt only wall. He imagined being shot in the stomach. His nails scraped the wood.

The light went on, and before him was what looked like a hotel room. It was on the nice side of bland, and the colors were neutral. The bed was made. The furniture was bare. Curtis looked deeper. He looked at the bureau to his side. There was a neat lamp, and there was something else. He ran a finger along the top of the bureau and saw a line he had drawn in the dust.

"Unlived in," said Virgil.

"What do you think?"

"I think we should look in the basement."

The higher end appointments throughout the house ended at the stairs to the cellar. The floors were unfinished. The walls were plain. In the ceiling, pipes were exposed. There were four sets of lights. They could see a bulkhead leading out at the far end.

Curtis found himself staring at the floor. He was looking for a weakness. He wanted to see one portion that looked newer, softer, less worn, or recently added. He wanted to see a space that had been tinkered with, camouflaged, or covered over hastily. He found himself wondering if he had expected to walk into the basement to find a big black X on the ground.

"What's that?" asked Virgil. At some point, they had stopped whispering, but he couldn't remember when.

Virgil had been staring over his shoulder the whole time. Virgil never took his eyes off whatever he was looking at. Curtis turned.

There was a door under the stairs.

Virgil made a line straight for the door while Curtis wondered how he hadn't seen it. He imagined a stream of Mexican gunmen piling out of the little room to cut and kill him. He imagined being shot in the back. He imagined all the things that could go wrong in the seconds it took Virgil to cross the room.

He stood to the side of the door and felt the handle. He did it naturally and without thinking, while Curtis realized he was still standing right in the kill zone, the perfect place to get shot.

"Locked," said Virgil.

He dropped to his stomach and peered under the door. There was no light on the other side. Virgil took a flashlight from his back pocket, but the door was flush with the ground.

"Can we open it?" Curtis asked.

"Every door opens," said Virgil. "It's just a matter of how hard it's going to be."

"This could be a safe room."

"It could. Aren't they supposed to be hidden?"

"They're supposed to keep people out long enough to get help."

Virgil felt the door. He ran his fingers along the face of it. He pushed it with his palm. He rapped it with his knuckles.

"Good solid door," he said. "I'll be right back."

Curtis stood staring at the lock now that he was alone. Gently, he pressed his ear to the side. He stopped breathing and listened.

He heard a loud thump. His whole body tensed. Then he heard another. By the time he heard it three times, he realized that it was Virgil upstairs dragging something heavy or clumsy across the floor above him. He heard the boards creak when he reached the top of the stairs. Then there was a terrible crash.

Curtis looked over to see the sledgehammer come to a rest at the base of the stairs. It was on top of the shovel and the pick axe. Virgil pounded down the stairs after them, grabbing the hammer in one motion.

"Get back," he said to Curtis.

Just as he had upstairs, he slammed the sledgehammer into the space just below the lock. The sound was enormous. The door was undamaged.

He hit it again.

"This is a lot stronger than the front door," said Virgil, as he took a deep breath.

Curtis thought about that. He thought about a person who had a stronger door in their basement than they did on the front of their house. The weight of the sledge struck again. Who would make the whole of their home less safe than a tiny room in the basement? he asked himself. He saw more and more of the hammer disappear into the frame each time it landed. What would you keep in the basement that was more important than where you slept?

"This door wants to open," huffed Virgil. He put the hammer on the ground, bent his knees, and stretched. "All doors want to open."

"What if it's not to keep you out?" said Curtis. Virgil never heard him, and a moment later, he forgot he ever said it. His words were lost in the sonic violence of the lock blasting off the frame. The room stood wide open.

Curtis wanted to be the first to enter, but Virgil dropped the hammer and walked under the stairs. Curtis supposed he had earned it. He began to follow when he heard Virgil shout. That was when he started to run.

He saw Virgil from behind. His arms hung loose at his sides, like they didn't know what to do. He had always thought of Virgil as the person who could commit to any decision, in any amount of time. He stepped around him.

There was a young woman crouching in the corner.

She kept her back to the wall and moved sideways to get away from them. Virgil put his empty hands up and said he wasn't going to hurt her. He said it in English. She didn't stop.

She grew closer to Curtis. He didn't know what else to do. Virgil was speaking even louder. Curtis reached into his front pocket. She watched his hands with panicked eyes. He withdrew his badge and identification.

"Policia!" he said.

She backed quickly away from him. Of course, he thought. The police aren't the good guys down here. He racked his mind for more Spanish.

"Yo no soy un hombre!" shouted Curtis.

"I'm not going to hurt you," said Virgil.

"Yo no soy un hombre malo," shouted Curtis.

She stopped moving. Her back was pressed to the wall, her hands out to her sides. She looked back and forth between them. Virgil stepped backward.

"Hombres buenos," said Curtis. Good men.

Curtis watched her eyes. They were searching. Her eyes tracked to the door, then to them. She was looking at the guns on their waists. He held up the badge.

"Policia Americana," he said.

She spoke to him in Spanish, but it was too fast. She was too excited, and his Spanish wasn't good enough.

"No tu quiero," he said.

She looked at him quizzically.

"What are you telling her?" Virgil asked.

"I'm trying to convince her that she shouldn't be afraid of us."

Virgil took his shirt and pulled it over his gun. He put his hands in the air. He walked toward the door. He smiled.

"No problemo," said Virgil.

He pointed to her and then back to himself.

"Me. You. No problemo."

"Que quieren?" she shouted.

"No tu," said Curtis.

"Que quieren?" she shouted louder.

"No soy a hacerte dano," said Curtis.

"Que quieren?" she almost screamed.

"Dinero," said Virgil calmly.

She stared at him incredulously, but this answer, whether it caught her off guard or just struck her, quieted her.

116

Curtis tried to smile. He knew it was crooked. He backed away from her. As he did, he crowded Virgil out of the doorway. It was Curtis and this woman in the room. He could see in the calm that she was beautiful. She was Mexican, with pale skin and dark hair. She wore no makeup and needed none. She looked like she would fight if she had to. He extended an arm into the main basement.

"Bienvenido," he said.

She didn't laugh exactly. It was an exhale that caught her off guard. Curtis smiled.

"Mi espanol no esta bueno," he said. He covered his gun with his shirt like Virgil had.

She came away from the wall slowly, but some part of her always touched it. Curtis left the tight little room and backed away from her. The young woman contorted her body around the frame, casting a side glance at the broken door as she did. Curtis realized what Virgil had done. He had blocked her way to the stairs.

"Por favor," Curtis said. He had her attention.

He tried to think of the word to sit. His mind was blank. Curtis motioned for her to sit. He did not say por favor this time. She sat.

"Gracias," he said.

With that, Curtis immediately entered the little room.

There was a carpet with a design on it. The carpet was green, or greenish, and had a black pattern running through it. There was a hardbacked chair and a bed that didn't look much more comfortable. A tiny sink and toilet were squeezed into the corner.

"What is this?" asked Virgil from right behind him.

"Are you watching her?"

"Yes, I'm watching her. What is this?"

"I don't know yet," said Curtis. He looked to the girl, who was sitting across from the door with her back to the wall, looking confused and overwhelmed. She looked lovely.

"Que esta?"

She didn't answer.

There were clothes in the little room. They were piled neatly and folded on the floor by the bed. She was wearing a black tank top and light pajama pants. The clothes on the floor looked to be the same.

He heard Virgil fiddling with metal. He saw his hand on the lock. Curtis looked out and saw the girl in a haze.

"You still think this is a safe room?" Virgil asked.

"Maybe. I don't know. Why?"

"Did you see this lock?"

"You busted it."

"It's still worth seeing."

It was a thick deadbolt lock on a solid wooden door. The wood was bent and dented, and the wood around the lock was torn and broken. Curtis looked closer. The wood was new. The lock was new. There was oil on it. He looked back to Virgil.

"Which side is the lock on?"

Curtis looked again. The handle was plain on both sides. The lock was twisted and would never work again. He stepped back into the room and closed the door.

"Shouldn't a safe room lock from the inside?" asked Virgil.

Curtis wished he knew more Spanish. He wished he knew what the hell was going on in this little town outside of Monterrey, Mexico.

Then he noticed the floor.

It was a cheap rug. It wasn't a piece that anyone would love. It was a plain off green with a black print pattern running through it. The pattern formed boxes that stacked at angles, building from the center and edging to the four corners. Virgil must have seen him grinning. He leaned in to see what was the matter.

"No way," said Virgil.

When viewed from above, the pattern on the run formed a large black X.

Virgil tossed the chair effortlessly behind him and into the basement. It landed loudly. The girl jumped. Curtis waved his hand, motioning for her to be calm, apologizing.

"How do you say I'm sorry in Spanish?" Virgil asked.

"I don't know," said Curtis. He was straining to move the bed. Virgil grabbed the mattress and dragged it with one hand.

The rug was flush with the wall at the very edge. Virgil drew out a knife and began digging at the edge by the door. He scraped and swore as he worked. Curtis wondered why he hadn't thought to bring a knife. The girl watched them in confusion. Virgil ripped the rest of it away and clumsily pulled it into the basement. All they saw now was a floor of dull gray cement.

"What do you think?" asked Virgil finally.

"I don't know." And he didn't. Curtis had no idea what to do.

"This cement is a different color than the rest of the basement."

The main room had a light gray floor. It was fresh poured, clean, and level. The floor in the little room was none of those things. It had been there for a while.

"I was picturing a stash that he could get at if he needed it," said Virgil.

"I was too."

"If I had that kind of cash, I would keep it where I could get to it."

Curtis didn't answer.

"Unless I was thinking long term. And I was hiding it."

Curtis said nothing. His mind was full of thoughts. They were not good thoughts. They were puzzled and criticizing. Had he come all the way down to Mexico so Eduardo Mendes could make a fool of him?

Curtis suddenly swung the hammer. Virgil jumped out of its way. He heard the collision. It was metal on stone and hard. Virgil rose up, the sledgehammer clutched in both hands. He swung it directly into the ground. This time it broke.

Curtis was moving before he heard the next collision. It was the sound of more stone breaking. He chose the pick. Curtis pushed himself into a corner and aimed for the cracks in the floor. He dug the pick into the ground and pulled.

They dug and they picked, and when there was just a big pile of dirt and broken rock, Curtis used the shovel. Virgil sat down and caught his breath, but Curtis was possessed. He hauled dirt out of the little room until he realized it was a waste. Then he just threw it. Dirt piled up in the little bathroom. Virgil kicked it out of the doorway.

Curtis found himself on his knees, clawing from the ground a rock the size of a bowling ball.

Curtis didn't tire. He didn't notice that he had dirt on his face or in his hair. He didn't notice that he had dug a pit to his knees. He didn't notice that Virgil had stopped helping.

"Curtis!" Virgil said sharply.

Curtis looked up surprised.

"What are you doing?"

"I'm digging."

"It's not here."

"What do you mean?"

"Look how deep you are."

He looked. The pit was now almost to his pockets. It was halfway to his thighs. It was an ugly pit in a tiny room and surrounded by jagged concrete.

"It's not here," Virgil said. He was trying to reason.

"It's here somewhere," said Curtis.

There was a trigger in Curtis' mind that he even he didn't understand. He climbed out of the pit and started toward the girl. He picked the hammer up off the floor.

"Donde esta el dinero?" he said to her. He swung the hammer and it crashed into the plaster wall. The girl put her hands over her head. Curtis pulled it out with intentional carelessness. He made an even greater mess of the wall. He pulled more away with his hands. There was only stone of the other side. He swung again somewhere else. Then he started on the other walls. He swung the hammer and didn't stop until one whole wall of the basement wore a wild, crooked grin.

Virgil and the girl stood next to one another. They both looked frightened.

"He said he needed men who could work concrete," was all Curtis could say. It didn't make sense to anyone else, but he was thinking aloud. He scanned the room. He looked beyond it. He thought he heard Virgil speaking, but he ignored it. He ignored the searing, burning sensation in his shoulders. He ignored the pain in his hands.

"Concrete," he said.

He started to the bulkhead. Curtis didn't pause, striking the wall in stride. He swung and swung again with the hammer, until chunks of rock fell to the ground and dry brown dirt poured on to his feet. He swung until the air filled with dust. He swung until his arms burned and blood raced through his torso. Then he dug deeper and swung some more.

One side was gone. He reached into the hole and dragged dirt free. He reached and pulled and felt around in the dark, and when he came back with nothing, he set his sights on the other side.

"Curtis, let's get back in the car."

He couldn't swing it so hard to his right. He felt like his arms weren't working the way they were supposed to work. He couldn't swing side to side, but he could swing up and down. He unlocked the bulkhead.

"Curtis, let's go home. Now."

The cold air struck him. It was refreshing. He felt sweat drying on him instantly. He hadn't realized that it had been a cold night. He thought it had been warm.

"Ask her in Spanish if she wants to come with us." Virgil was on the stairs now.

"I think you should move back."

Virgil was off the stairs, level with Curtis, closing distance between them.

"Curtis, I need you to listen to me. Tell this girl we will not hurt her. Ask her if she wants to leave with us. I want to do the right thing here."

The right thing. Curtis thought about an answer. He heard a distinct noise not far away. He'd heard it before, but couldn't place it. Virgil had heard it too, because he spun around nervously. A part of his brain found a faint memory that recognized the sound of a shotgun chambering a round.

"Basta!" a voice shouted.

Curtis was struck in the face by a beam of light. It caught him every bit as off guard as an actual punch. He put his hand to his face. He saw Virgil spin and reach for the gun on his belt. More voices rang out from all around him. They were harsh and foreign. A man came into view, and he was pointing a gun at them.

His clothes were dark. Curtis saw something familiar. There was a soft twinkling over his heart. It was where his badge was catching the light.

Others joined, and they began shouting in earnest. "Muestrame tu manos!" one shouted over another. Virgil put his hands over his head, and he didn't speak Spanish.

Curtis reached into his pocket.

"Get your hands up," yelled Virgil, his own hands held high.

He could see the figures rushing toward him. He quickly held up his credentials.

"Soy policia Americana!" he called out to the group. He had his other hand held high displaying his credentials.

Curtis saw an officer approach from his left. He held a shotgun in both hands. The officer had a slightly American look to him, though he had a bad haircut and buck teeth. Curtis thought for a moment that the officer was about to turn and walk away, that the problem was solved and there would be no more need to explain who they were or what they were doing here. He didn't turn away though. He was gaining momentum. He brought the butt of the shotgun up suddenly and smashed it into Curtis' nose.

Curtis came to on the ground. His nervous system was running wild, and his mind was just beginning to make sense of what had happened when a huge mass of man appeared over him. The mass of man spoke English.

"Not down here, you're not," said Jefe.

Eduardo jerked awake. He was in a car next to Strauss. Outside, it was dark, but the lights were lit, and there was movement inside a café.

"There is one more thing I thought you should know," said Strauss.

Eduardo looked around the car. He did not see the money that he had given to Strauss, and it wasn't in his hands.

"There is a man in Mexico who very much wants to kill you," said Strauss.

Chapter Eight

Juan Two Saints – Monterrey, MX

The American didn't look like a cop to Juan. He had blood pouring out of his nose. It had to be broken. He didn't look like a man who needed to be put down as hard as he had been, but that was Dejo's style. Juan had noticed the man's glasses and put them back on his head.

The other man looked like a fighter, but he wasn't fighting. His hands were chained up behind his back. He looked resigned to his fate.

Juan reached into the American's pants. He felt money and saw a roll of bills. He looked up to see Dejo watching him. Juan put it in his pocket and was disgusted with himself. He reached again and felt a chain. It was a religious pendant of Saint Michael. Dejo wasn't looking. Juan shoved it back into the American's pocket, thinking he might need it.

"Get these two out of here," said Jefe impatiently.

Juan Two Saints was watching the Americans as they drove away in the back of the police car. He wondered if they would ever be seen again. He turned, and Jefe was gone. Then he saw light pouring out of the bulkhead. He was about to go down the stairs when he noticed another house on the property had its lights on too.

"We're attracting attention," he told Jefe when he found him in the cellar.

"So what?" said the big man. He was distracted. Dejo was with him, and there was a young woman on the ground. She looked scared. She was beautiful. Suddenly, Juan Two Saints felt scared too.

Jefe's attention was on a little room under the stairs. Dirt was piled ankle high and a deep pit had been dug just past the door. Jefe's attention was on the walls.

"Ever build a house, Juan Two Saints?"

"No, Jefe."

"Know what I know about building houses?"

"What?"

"Less than you. But I know just enough to know that this isn't usually how one builds a wall."

Juan was curious. He leaned to where Jefe was standing. He could smell him, all sweat and bad food. Juan's eyes stung. Plaster and dust drifted through the air. Inside the wall were rows of cinderblocks.

"Was something valuable kept in here?"

Jefe sniffed. He turned his attention to the girl on the floor.

"Maybe," he said.

His huge body lumbered across the basement floor until it came to a stop and towered over her. Sweat ran down Jefe's back in a dark river. Juan thought about the woman who had been with the smuggler.

Jefe held out his hand. It was almost gentlemanly. The girl looked to the ground and looked back up in surprise. She put her hand in his hopefully.

"What were these boys looking for in there?" he asked in English.

She didn't respond. Jefe watched the woman. He turned her hand in his, with care, studying it, and studying her. She had dust and dirt on her, but Juan could see her nails. They were a glowing red. Her skin was soft and pale. Her hair was thick and had body. Someone had cared for this woman.

Jefe shook her hand away with clear disgust.

"Want me to talk to her, Jefe?" Dejo asked. He sounded eager.

"No," said the boss. "We won't learn anything from this…senorita."

The girl looked at the floor.

Jefe's footsteps pounded slowly up the stairs of the house. Dejo nudged him. His mind swam with terrible thoughts of what Dejo might suggest, but Dejo was handing him money.

"What is this?"

The girl could see all of it. Dejo was too dumb or too reckless to care.

"The American had it on him. I took a cut off the top."

The girl watched them. Juan felt naked. He took it and shoved it into his pocket.

"What did you do to your hand?" Dejo asked as Juan walked away.

"Nothing," Juan muttered as he stepped into the air. He felt dirty. He saw the little house in the distance. The lights were on still. An old man stood at the edge of the field, watching.

"Do you know a man by the name of Ordo Beltran?" asked Strauss.

Of course he did. Strauss knew he did.

"What do you know about him?" Strauss asked.

"He is with the Zetas."

"Have you done business with him in the past?"

"Maybe."

"Very well then."

"I want to know something," said Eduardo. Strauss nodded.

"Why do you ask questions when you already know the answer?"

Strauss seemed to think about it. When he answered, all he said was, "Old habit."

Eduardo wondered what Colon would have said about old habits, or any habits at all.

"What do you know about him?" Eduardo asked.

"I know he's middle management and was promoted by attrition. I know he has been assigned the task of taking Nuevo Leon for the Zetas. I know he has hired muscle. And I know he has been paid to kill you."

"Paid?"

"Asked? It is a business arrangement. One day, the man will himself be asked to return the favor. It seems someone thinks you are a liability."

"Where did they get that idea?" Eduardo asked.

Strauss did not care for the implication.

"You entered into an agreement with me, Mister Mendes, and I can assure you of the utmost confidence. In fact, aside from a guarantee that the work will be completed, that is all we have to our names."

"Where I come from, your name doesn't mean much," said Eduardo.

"Where I come from, it means everything," said Strauss.

Strauss left the truck without another word. Eduardo could see him at the counter through the window. As he thought of more questions he wished Strauss had asked, he found his new cell phone in his hand. He looked down and saw his fingers dialing the numbers. They dialed from memory.

"Who is this?" said the man on the phone.

"Eduardo Mendes."

The voice on the phone laughed. "What a coincidence," said Ordo. "I am going to kill Eduardo Mendes."

"Maybe we could make a deal?"

"No, I don't think so."

"Do you know that my girlfriend was killed as well?"

"You will be reunited soon."

"Do the facts matter to you at all?"

"No. Tell you what. Why don't you make this easy on yourself? Why don't you tell me where you are and I will come find you. That way, when I get there, I will shoot you in the face and then tear your body apart, instead of the other way around like I was told to do. It can be our little secret."

"Why don't I tell you exactly where I am and we can talk about it?"

"Have it any way you like, Eduardo."

"I am in Monterrey."

He heard laughter on the phone.

"Is this really Eduardo Mendes?"

"Of course it is. Why?"

"The Mendes I knew didn't have the balls to come to Mexico. Never mind to Leon. And never in a million years would a coward like him come to Monterrey."

Eduardo looked around the landscape. He saw freight trucks whipping past in the distance. That must be the highway. He saw Strauss coming through the door. Steam rose from the cup in his hand.

"The mountains are behind me and to my left. The city is in front of me. I do not know the town, but I do know how to answer my phone. Call me when you are here."

Ordo Beltran seemed to think about the offer for a moment. Strauss climbed into the driver's seat. For a man whose face didn't show much, he looked alarmed when he saw Eduardo on the phone.

"The Eduardo Mendes I know is clever. If you are trying to be clever, don't. I made a promise to a man."

"When we're done doing business, you'll be having him killed for me," said Eduardo. He hung up. He could feel the eyes of Strauss boring into him.

"Tell me you did not just call Ordo Beltran."

Juan Two Saints walked silently through his little house. It was too early for him to be home, but he didn't want to be where he was headed.

He checked on the boys. They were where he expected: in bed and on the floor. They made their sleeping sounds. He could have stayed there all night, just listening to them.

He crept past his own room. If he opened the door, she would hear, so he kept it shut. She snored a little. She denied it. She would curse him for saying it. That didn't mean she didn't snore. He stood and listened for a while.

Then he built a fire in the cast iron stove. It wasn't especially cold, but he lit it and waited until the top of the little door glowed orange.

Juan Two Saints sat on the floor with his legs crossed, just as his boys did. He unwrapped the bandage on his hand. It was still sore, and the skin looked tender. He let it breathe. With his other hand, Juan Two Saints touched the handle on the stove. It was warm but not hot. When he pulled it open, he felt the heat on his face. He fished in his pocket for the money that Dejo had handed him. He hadn't so much as counted it. It disgusted him. So he made himself count it.

It wasn't much. Little bites, as Jefe would say. There was a time when he would give the little bites to his wife. He found himself growing angry as he watched his boys eat, knowing how the food got there. He tried giving his little bites to the church. He found himself drifting into anger while the priest spoke.

He took the bills and threw them into the stove. Whenever he gave his little bites to the fire, he always felt better. Not much, but a little. He began to recite the Hail Mary in whispers. The flames grew taller and brighter as they devoured the money. He watched the bills shrivel and turn black.

"Pray for our sinners," he said so quietly that no one would hear it, and he stuck his hand into the stove.

"Would you mind telling me what you were thinking when you called Ordo Beltran?" Strauss asked.

"My mother had a rule for the staff in our house. They didn't ask questions."

"I am not your butler, Mister Mendes."

"I came here to finish a job that you couldn't handle. I expected you to have a team in place. I find it's just you. No offense, but I think we need more men."

"We have all the men we need."

"I doubt that."

"And what will you do when Ordo decides to kill you?"

"I am going to talk him out of it."

"You don't know him very well, do you?"

"I know him well enough. I've paid you to find out where these men are. Why don't you focus on that?"

"I already know where these men are," said Strauss.

"You're joking."

"They are being held in a police station a few miles from here."

"Why didn't you tell me?"

"You were busy making speeches."

Eduardo looked out the window.

"Have they been arrested?"

"It seems so."

"How do we get them out?"

"Why do you want them out?"

"So I can kill them."

"As you say, Mister Mendes."

He had never expected it to be so fast, or so easy. He found himself sneaking glances at Strauss, who either didn't notice or didn't care. Eduardo wondered how deep his loyalties ran.

"I asked you to do something else for me, didn't I?" Eduardo asked.

"You did."

"Did you get it?"

There was long pause before Strauss spoke.

"Are you sure you want to do this?"

"Give me the goddamn number."

Strauss handed him a slip of paper. On it was the address and phone number of an apartment where a man could have sex with a child. Felipe was scrawled at the top.

"Is Felipe the boy or is he the man who sells him."

"Felipe is the man," Strauss said wearily.

Eduardo slid the paper into his coat pocket and smiled.

It was a cement building with no windows. It had been painted once when it was built, then allowed to fade and peel. There were many cars, but none of them were police cars. Eduardo saw a man in a uniform sitting on one. He was young and looked very bored.

"They have an officer watching their own cars in their own parking lot?"

"Yes," said Strauss.

Eduardo's phone began to ring. He looked at the number. He realized that Strauss was looking too. They both knew who it was.

"I do not recommend this."

Eduardo answered it anyway.

"You are either very brave or very stupid," said Ordo Beltran.

"I am very rich. You can be rich too. How does that sound?"

"I am always looking for more money."

"We should talk."

"I better like what you have to say."

"You can't afford not to."

"Where are you?"

"You realize I am not alone."

"I don't give a fuck who you're with. Where are you?"

Eduardo covered the receiver with his hand. He looked to Strauss.

"Where should we meet him?"

"Nowhere."

"Pick a good place."

"Good for what?"

"For not getting killed."

"You picked the wrong country, Mister Mendes."

Strauss saw only agitation on the young man's face. He let it boil for a moment.

"There is a bar called La Hermosa Pasado. It is in an alley off Corrando. Tell him to meet us there." Eduardo repeated it into the phone. Ordo asked who he was with.

"None of your business," said Eduardo as he hung up the phone.

The garage door began to open. Two headlights came to life. A police car rolled slowly out of the garage. It took its place in line behind one that had just sped into the parking lot. An enormous man in a police uniform stepped out of the garage. The front of his belt was hidden by his belly. The cars waited for him. Eduardo could see that there were two officers in each car, but the car that had just left the garage had two men in the back as well. Police didn't ride in the back.

He knew who was in that car.

What he felt now was compulsion. He felt compelled to put his hand on the door handle. He felt compelled to pull it open. He stepped into the street with a numbness, and he must have been overwhelmed by the blood rushing into his ears, because he never heard Strauss telling him to stop.

He wanted to run, but he walked. He walked slowly and carefully in his black suit in the middle of the street so the cars couldn't move. An officer jumped from the car and drew a gun. Eduardo held his hands up and out from his slim frame. He kept walking. Then he smiled.

Walter Curtis was in the back of the car. Now his hands were behind his back.

Curtis had dried blood on his face. He wore a ridiculous yellow Hawaiian shirt. He wore a white undershirt under that, and it had been soaked in blood. His clothes, however, could not compete with the look of fear on Curtis' face.

It was more than Eduardo could have hoped.

"Special Agent Curtis. Here is something maybe no one has told you before. I'm going to have you released from prison. Then I am going to have you stabbed in the belly. I'm going to let you bleed to death in a dumpster behind a whorehouse where American men go to fuck little boys. When people hear that, and believe me, I'll make sure they hear it, everyone who has ever known you, even your own family, is going to be glad that you're dead."

With that, he walked away, overwhelmed and afraid and very proud of himself. Strauss was out of the truck, and knew something was wrong. Eduardo supposed he had impressed the man, but as he approached, he realized that Strauss was not looking at him at all. He was looking through him. He turned and saw the fat man. He was watching them with a look that straddled anger and amused curiosity.

"Who is that?" he asked Strauss.

"Get back in the truck," Strauss said quietly.

Virgil didn't speak a word of Spanish, but he understood quickly who Jefe was. Some jumped when he barked, while others left as he entered, but everyone moved.

He could see the cells, but they weren't in them. Not yet. They were seated on a metal bench that was bolted to the wall in a concrete holding area. It was like every other cell Virgil had ever seen. It smelled of shit and sweat and hopelessness.

The chairs the cops sat in were old and wooden. They creaked. They were uneven. The paint on the walls was chipped. There were heavy metal desks with little bunnies of dust around their legs. Most of the men who worked here looked much like the furniture.

"This is a retirement home," Virgil whispered to himself. This was a local police station. The cops here were old men. If they had ever cared, they had stopped long ago. There were a few young faces, but they were painfully young. Young faces were impressionable.

He heard the voices from the office again. There were loud throaty gargles, and then a soft whine that followed. After a while, the little whine seemed less like weakness, and more like passive stubbornness.

A small man bounded from the office. He had steadfastly refused to look at them when they had been brought into the station. He did now though. He was a slim little man, and very neat. He had a mustache and thinning hair. His chest was overflowing with medals, but he looked to Virgil like a man who had never done an honest day's work in his life. The little comandante looked at them and huffed with resignation. Then he crisply put his hat on his head and walked out the door.

A young clerk in the opposite corner was typing a report on an old-fashioned typewriter. He didn't know how to type, Virgil guessed, by the long pause between each single metallic slap. A truck went by the windows. Metallic slap. There was laughter on the street. Metallic slap. The phone rang, and the very nervous cop picked it up quickly. Then he slammed it down, grabbed his hat up off the desk, and left the room in a hurry.

Jefe came out of the office. He sauntered slowly. Virgil could hear the big man's footsteps as the old floor bent under him.

Two other officers stayed. The one who looked decent stood when Jefe entered. He looked apprehensive. The one who had crushed his nose looked even meaner in the light. Slowly, Jefe sat down in front of them. The nails and wood groaned.

The big man smiled.

"Call me Jefe," he said. He had a grin on his fat, stubbly face. "Which one of you is a federal agent?" Jefe asked.

He had Curtis' credentials. It didn't appear to mean much at the moment.

"I am," said Curtis.

"FBI?" asked Jefe with his eyebrows raised.

"IRS," said Virgil.

"A tax collector," said Jefe.

Curtis didn't answer him.

"Tell me this, Special Agent Walter Curtis," Jefe began. "How does one become a special agent with the Internal Revenue Service?"

"I just applied," he said.

"I mean, was it your lifelong dream to arrest people for not paying their taxes?"

The mean cop snickered. Jefe looked annoyed and turned his head to the slightest degree. The look disappeared, and so did the snicker.

"They were hiring when I needed a job," said Curtis.

"Good answer," Jefe said, and he sounded sincere. "I take it you boys haven't slept much since we met."

It wasn't exactly a question.

"I'd like to find you some place to get cleaned up and sleep. Someplace you can relax and not be chained to the wall. Have some hot food. How's that sound to you?"

Neither of them moved, but all of those things sounded wonderful. They didn't move because they didn't believe him.

"Before we can do that, we have some things to talk about. How long we talk is entirely up to you. Do we understand each other?"

Virgil looked at the floor. He was looking at the big man's belly. He was looking at the suffering chair legs. He was looking everywhere but in his eyes. He felt those eyes now. They were calm and demanding. They were waiting for him. He nodded.

"Agent Curtis," Jefe said, capturing his attention. "When did you cross the border?"

"Yesterday," squeaked Curtis. His voice was hoarse, and his mouth and throat were dry.

"Yesterday," he said in a louder voice.

Jefe waved, and Juan Two Saints approached, grabbing a bottle of water from the nearest desk. The bottle was half empty. An unknown person had been drinking from it, but that didn't matter. The cop held it to Curtis' mouth, and he drank gladly.

"Better?" asked Jefe.

"Thank you," said Curtis.

"I'm human," said Jefe.

Virgil turned and saw how badly Curtis was sweating. The dried blood on his face was liquefying and beginning to run down his face and into his mouth.

"Agent Curtis, what made you go to the country house last night?"

"I was told by a source that there was evidence buried in the walls. I thought that if I attempted to get a search warrant in Mexico, the cartels would be tipped off and they would move it."

Jefe seemed to believe it.

"What sort of evidence?"

"Financial transactions. I'm an accountant."

"An accountant?" Jefe smiled.

"That's what I do for the IRS."

"An accountant with a gun. And you didn't give Mexican authorities any sort of heads up?"

"No."

"Because the cartels might be tipped off."

"Yes," said Curtis.

"Because the police in Mexico are corrupt."

Curtis didn't know what to say. Jefe laughed.

"You don't have police corruption in the states, do you? You don't have any issues with federal agents breaking and entering luxury country houses. Or carrying unlicensed firearms."

"Those weapons are licensed to me," said Curtis.

"Back home, maybe. Not in Mexico," said Jefe. "And that's just you. I'm still trying to figure out what he's doing here." He was looking right at Virgil.

"I'm here to help him," said Virgil.

"Uh-huh," said Jefe, his attention elsewhere. He was reaching for Virgil. Virgil wanted to jump back, but he couldn't. He wanted to flinch or duck, but he was afraid. Jefe's fat, damp fingers touched his skin. The edge of his tattoo was poking out from his shirt. Jefe pulled it up to reveal the eagle, globe, and anchor, with the letters USMC printed below them.

"Uncle Sam's Misguided Children," said Jefe. "How long did you do?"

"As little time as I could."

"Spoken like a true veteran," said Jefe. "What did you do for them?"

"Infantry."

"A foot soldier. Let me ask you this. When the Marines ask you to go do something, were you allowed to ask why?"

"No."

"In the Marines, you do as you're told, don't you?"

"Yes," said Virgil, not sure where this was going.

"How about in real life?"

"I don't understand."

"What I mean is, if you're a Marine, and they order you to drive six hours to a little house in Mexico and rip it apart, you get in your truck and you do it. You don't ask why. You don't care why. You follow your orders. Isn't that right?"

Virgil shrugged. He heard the chains rattle when he did it. He knew where this was going.

"But this isn't the Marines, is it?"

"No," he said.

"Forgive me for saying so, but you don't look like the type of man who'd drive to Mexico in the middle of the night to break into a house without knowing a little more about it."

Jefe reached into his shirt pocket and removed a plastic card.

"What kind of work were you doing?"

"Construction, mostly."

"Construction, mostly," repeated Jefe. "So what would a construction mostly worker be doing all the way down in Mexico with a federal IRS agent?"

"He said he might need help taking apart the house."

Jefe laughed loudly.

"From the looks of that place, I'd say he got it." He continued laughing until his chuckle wound down to nothing.

In one quick motion, he had Virgil's hand in his own. Virgil couldn't believe the big man could move so fast. Jefe had his hand upturned, examining it.

"Construction mostly?" he asked, skeptically looking Virgil in the eye.

Jefe turned over the card. Virgil could see it for what it plainly was: his own driver's license.

"According to this, Marc Virgil lives at 15 Rita Road in Boston, Massachusetts. That's you, isn't it?"

"Yes."

"And that's your address, isn't it?"

"It is."

"I have an idea," said Jefe. "My idea is that if I go into that office and call up the Boston Police Department and pretend to be the sack of shit who runs this house, when I ask if Marc Virgil is a Boston Police officer, they're going to say, yes, he is. What do you think about that?"

"Do whatever you want," said Virgil.

Jefe smiled. His teeth were brown.

"I will, thank you," he said, sitting back in his chair. He seemed to notice at that moment that there was a phone on the desk beside him. He looked at it, then looked back to Virgil with a twinkle of excitement. He picked it up and dialed one number.

"Por favor, senora. Me llamo Commandant Lucid con La Policia de Monterrey. Yo quiero la Policia de Boston en Massachusetts en los Estados Unidos. Gracias."

He covered the receiver with his hand.

"This will just take a moment," he said with a smile.

Virgil glanced over to Curtis. He saw a bead of sweat drop from his nose to the bench between his legs. He found himself wondering what time it was at home. He didn't even know what time it was in Mexico. He heard the phone ringing.

"What do you think? Want me to make this call?" asked Jefe.

"No," said Virgil.

Jefe dropped it back into the cradle.

"Know what I do think?" asked Jefe. He slid the plastic license into his shirt pocket. Both Curtis and Virgil hung on his words now, knowing that their fates were about to be determined.

"I think you two need to work on a better story."

Eduardo didn't look up when the truck stopped. He was lost in his phone.

When he did look up, he almost jumped out of the car.

"What are we doing here?"

"I have business inside. It will not take long."

"You're going in there?"

"I am."

"What am I supposed to do?"

"You cannot go with me."

"I don't want to."

"Then it's settled," said Strauss, and shut the door.

Eduardo watched in stunned silence and wondered if this man Strauss was suicidal. No sane person, doing what he does, would have come here. Then Eduardo had a revelation. He remembered that he was in Mexico, and he burst out laughing. He laughed, and he realized that it should have occurred to him from the start.

Fifty feet in front of him, Strauss disappeared into a building that was clearly and professionally marked Federale Policia.

Strauss didn't make eye contact with anyone in the office. It was getting late, and there were fewer people there. He walked with purpose through a sea of desks, looking forward, not into them, listening to the clack of fingers on keyboards and the occasional faceless voice on a telephone. Someone was smoking, and the name Dulcinea slipped through his mind. He found one desk in a dark, deserted corner and immediately began to rummage through the drawers. He found a file, looked inside, and put it down again. He thought of Dulcinea's hair and how the light from the screen filtered through it.

"What do you think you're doing?" a man asked him.

Strauss turned. The man who had accosted him was tall, and younger than himself. He wore a tie and a shirt with the sleeves rolled up to his elbows. He had bushy hair and tired, honest eyes.

"Who are you?" Strauss asked.

"Who the hell are you?" the man asked back. "And why are you in my desk?"

"Who told you this was your desk?" Strauss asked calmly. The other man's temperature had risen noticeably.

"The goddamn Federal Police, that's who. Who do you think you are?"

"I think I'm Inspector Strauss, and I think this is my desk."

That stopped him cold. The man looked for something to say.

"In fact," Strauss continued, picking up the file for which he'd been looking. "I know it is. My things are in it."

"Inspector Strauss, I apologize. I was told——"

"I know what you were told."

"They said you didn't come to the office, so I should make myself at home."

"Is this your home?" Strauss asked.

"No, Inspector, I understand now this is your desk."

"I mean, is this where you are spending all of your time?"

The man didn't quite know what to say. His whole body teetered indecisively.

He stammered, but Strauss knew the answer. He could see it in his clothes and in his hair and in his worn eyes. Behind a coffee mug was a two-fold frame. In one, the man posed with a pretty woman. In the other, two very young children smiled.

"Can I tell you a secret that the Federal Police don't want you to know?" Strauss asked.

The man, who clearly knew Strauss by reputation, wasn't sure if he wanted to hear it. That was evident. Another part of him turned his ears up in the slightest way, unable to resist.

"Yes," said the man.

"It isn't worth it," Strauss told him. Then he left.

"What do you think?" Jefe asked when they stepped back into the office. Juan Two Saints shut the door behind him.

"I think they're full of shit," said Dejo, dropping himself into a chair. Juan stood.

"Everyone is full of shit," said Jefe. "Just depends what they're full of shit about."

Dejo looked confused.

"Juan Two Saints," called Jefe, as if he were announcing his presentation. "What do you think?"

Juan shrugged.

"You buy this business about cartel papers buried in the wall?"

"No," said Juan.

"Me neither," said Jefe. "I think they were after another kind of paper. The green kind."

"Why there?" Dejo asked.

"Good question," said Jefe. There was a slight inflection in his voice, and it said that Jefe might already have a very good idea as to why that house had been torn apart.

"What do we know about the owner of the house?" said Juan. Even as the words came out of his mouth, he didn't know why he'd said them. Jefe looked surprised. Not at the question, but at the pointed way Juan had spoken. Juan swore he saw a slight glint appear in the big man's eye.

"Nothing," Jefe said. And it was gone. "Some company owns it. Probably a little spot for the boss to bring his hugger. You know what a hugger is?"

Juan did. "What?" said Dejo. Jefe never looked at him.

"A hugger is some little chicky mama you keep on the side so your old lady doesn't find out about her. That country house would be a good place to bring your little chicky mama. Wouldn't you say?"

Dejo said yes, but Jefe wasn't talking to him.

"How long you been married now, Juan Two Saints?"

"Five years," Juan said. Jefe never asked about his family, and he didn't like him doing it now.

"Five years," repeated Jefe. "Maybe we ought to find you a little chicky mama?"

Strauss was on the phone as he approached the truck. He stopped outside to finish his conversation in private. He hung up and dialed again. This time he got behind the wheel.

"Why didn't you tell me?"

"Tell you what, Mister Mendes?"

"That you're a cop."

"It's not really your business."

"I've put my life in your hands. I'd say it is my business."

"You've put the lives of other people in my hands, Mister Mendes, and I've seen to it that your desires were carried out. Your life is another matter."

"You haven't fulfilled that promise yet," said Eduardo.

"Yet," said Strauss, purposefully.

"I'd like to know what you're doing about it. If anything."

"You seem intent on provoking me, Mister Mendes," Strauss observed dully.

"I'm intent on having my enemies broken. I'm intent on having those two corrupt pig cops—no offense—released from jail and brought to me and killed."

"Brought to you. You want to watch now?"

"I want to see that it's finally done right."

"I can arrange for you to do it yourself if you prefer."

"Thank you, but I'm not interested in having blood on my hands. I'm just starting to feel clean again."

"Don't get used to it."

"Who did you call?"

"In regard to what?"

"Having them released."

"Why would you want that, Mister Mendes?"

"So I can have them killed," said Eduardo.

"And you need to have them out of jail in order to do that?" asked Strauss.

As he said it, a set of headlights came into view and grew large and dominating. Eduardo squinted. Strauss got out and walked towards them. Eduardo followed. He saw fleeting globes of light. Behind them was a white BMW with a crooked grill. It gave the car a demented, buck-toothed happy face.

A man popped out of the passenger seat, pulling a loose silk shirt over his shoulders. He didn't button it. He was very lean and muscular and had a tattoo of a snake that wrapped around his body so the head and tail appeared on opposite sides of his torso. He wore sunglasses and smiled.

"Hello, Eduardo. I can't believe you came," said Ordo Beltran.

The driver's door opened, and a thick man in a gray track suit stepped into the street. He was known in Mexico as the Russian. His hair was chopped short, and his eyes were slightly too close to one another. The Russian cased Strauss with his eyes. Turning toward

Eduardo, the Russian's eyes filled with surprise and recognition. He nodded to Eduardo respectfully.

Ordo spoke first.

"What do you say, Eduardo? Let's go for a ride. We can make this easy."

"Would you like to have a cup of coffee?" asked Strauss.

Ordo looked at him for the first time, and his surprise was evident. The thick man with him whispered in his ear.

"I am impressed," he said to Eduardo. "But don't think he can save you."

"I didn't come here to save anyone," said Strauss. "I came here to have coffee. You can have some with me if you like."

"This is a bar. I drink whiskey in bars."

Strauss's phone rang. Eduardo watched in shock as he drew the phone from his pocket, opened it, and began speaking. Ordo laughed.

"See, Eduardo? You are not even his priority." He made a motion to the Russian that was no more than a flip of his hand, but it was made in Eduardo's direction. Its intent was obvious.

"Si," said Strauss into the phone. Then he handed it to Ordo. "It is for you."

Ordo paused, then showed his teeth in a large smile. He took the phone. He listened. He nodded. Then he stopped smiling.

A black Range Rover pulled onto the small side street and came to a stop beside them. Strauss didn't even glance at it.

"What is this?" Eduardo asked.

"You have an appointment," said Strauss. He held open the door to the truck.

Eduardo had his back to the wall. To his left was a dark city at night that he didn't know. To his right was the short hulking Russian. He knew what the Russian was capable of.

"Where am I going?" he asked.

"I don't know," said Strauss.

"Do I have to go?" Eduardo asked.

"You could stay here," suggested Strauss.

Eduardo looked around himself again. Ordo Beltran wasn't smiling anymore. The Russian never smiled. He could smell the truck. It was rich, clean leather. He slowly slid himself into the seat as if sitting would be painful. He and Strauss looked at one another for a moment. He looked to Strauss for any sort of reassurance. Strauss closed the door and the truck pulled away quickly.

The three men were left standing in the street as if the Range Rover had never been there.

"Let me ask you something, Juan Two Saints," growled Jefe. He spoke slowly, deliberately. "What would you do? If you were me?"

"I would let them go. I would tell them to go home and never come back to Mexico."

Dejo made a noise. It was loud and sounded disagreeable. Jefe just chuckled.

"No, that's what Juan Two Saints would do. What would I do?"

"I would just go into that cell and pound on them until they talked," said Dejo, as if the answer were obvious.

"Yeah?" asked Jefe casually. "What do you think that would get you?"

"Whatever you want," said Dejo, not understanding how everyone else couldn't grasp this.

"Pound on them until they talk," repeated Jefe wistfully, as if he were rolling the idea through his mind. "What do you think about that, Juan Two Saints?"

"I don't like it."

Jefe raised an entertained eyebrow.

"No? Why not?"

"Your average man doesn't like pain," said Juan.

As soon as he said it, he watched Jefe's eyes travel down his body to his bandaged hands and back again. Juan folded his arms.

"Your average man?" asked Jefe.

"He has no tolerance. Not for direct pain, and not for sustained blows. Or physical damage."

"What's that mean to you?" asked Jefe.

"It means if you hit him long enough, he'll tell you he killed John F. Kennedy. That doesn't make it true."

"Who is John F. Kennedy?" asked Dejo, but they ignored him.

142

"So tell me, Juan Two Saints, in your expert opinion, what does work?"

He thought about whether he should answer. He thought about walking out into the street and never turning back. He thought about Jefe laughing at him.

"You don't need to break a man physically. You need to break him mentally. Break his will."

"Break his will," said Jefe. "How would you do that?"

"Put the fear of God into him," said Juan.

Jefe sat with his hands folded on his belly. He spun his thumbs in little circles. He turned the idea over in his mind. Dejo looked confused.

"This is Mexico," said Jefe. "What if God isn't around?"

"Then put the fear of you in him," said Juan, who regretted it immediately.

"Which one would you start with?"

"The little one," said Dejo, struggling to get back into the conversation.

"Yeah?" said Jefe. "How come?"

"Did you see how he was sweating? How he folded up when I broke his nose? Walk in there, whack him around a little, he'll give up his whole family if you promise to stop."

"Is that what you would do, Juan Two Saints?"

Juan knew the conversation had gone too far. It had gone miles too far.

"No," he answered, in spite of himself. "I would let them go home."

"But we're not talking about you. We're talking about me. What would you do if you were me?"

"If I were you," said Juan Two Saints, "I would work on the one with the tattoo. He's the strong one. Let the little man watch. The little man is afraid. Let him know he is next. Make sure he watches his friend suffer. Let him think about it. After a while, separate them. Sit the little man down, put him in a quiet room with a glass of water. Let him wash his hands. Convince him that he has no options. After that, he'll belong to you."

"That's what you would do?" asked Jefe.

"If I were you."

"If you were me," said Jefe.

Jefe made a face, and Juan supposed it could have been called a smile. He had never seen so many of Jefe's brown teeth at once.

Chapter Nine

Virgil – Monterrey, MX

Virgil had realized long ago that every man in custody would test his handcuffs to see if his freedom was really gone. The bars would shake, the metal would clang on metal. When they chained him to the bar in his cell, after they left the room, he did it too.

They locked Curtis into the cell behind him. Virgil had to twist back to see him. Curtis sank to the floor. His handcuff didn't make a sound.

They were together, at least, though in different cells and cuffed to the rails with metal bars and a ten foot ocean of cement floor between them.

Virgil gave Curtis one more glance. He could see the blood all over his shirt. His head was down, and his eyes were closed. His shoulders had collapsed. He barely looked like he was breathing. Virgil thanked God he wasn't crying.

The jail was a long room with two large cages, placed side by side, separated by one row of bars. If they hadn't been locked to the bars, they could have sat next to one another and spoken in whispers. Instead, Curtis was on the other side of the room by himself, and Virgil was in his cage with three snoring drunks to keep him company.

Virgil sat on a metal bench. A drunk in a tan coat had curled up on the second bench in Virgil's cell, facing the wall. Two vagrants huddled next to the toilet, one leaning on the other. He could smell them from here. There was a sink next to the toilet. A gray bar of soap had melted into the flat surface over the faucet. Virgil shook his cuff once more. No one moved. The toilet wouldn't do him much good.

"Hey," he called out in a hoarse whisper. He looked at his cellmates. One of the vagrants poked his head up and sniffed, then settled back into the other's shoulder. The tan coat didn't move. Another drunk, thought Virgil, snoring away into oblivion. He was afraid to sleep.

"What?" said Curtis.

"What can you hear on the other side of that door?"

It was seven feet down a dark hall. It led to the booking area, which fed into the room where they had been questioned. The door was closest to Curtis.

"I can't hear anything," he said.

"Try," said Virgil.

He did. For a moment, it was quiet. Then, Virgil heard the soft snoring of a drunken vagrant.

"I don't hear anything," said Curtis.

"Then they can't hear us," said Virgil in a normal speaking voice. "How is your nose?"

"Broken."

"I broke my nose when I was a kid."

Curtis didn't answer.

"Is anything wrong with you other than your nose?"

"No," said Curtis, in a voice that sounded like everything was wrong with him. His voice was weak and nasally.

"Have you tried to fix it?"

"I'm not a doctor."

"You don't need to be. It's going to hurt more to fix than it did to break. But you need to."

"Why?"

"Because you need to be ready for whatever they're going to do to us."

After Virgil said that, he heard nothing but snoring for a long time.

"What do you think they're going to do?" Curtis asked finally.

"I don't know."

"Are they going to hand us over to Mendes?"

"I don't know. But it won't be good."

"We only broke into a house."

"They moved us around for a day until they found a police station that would take us. Know how many times I've done that? Never. That's not normal in Mexico. That's not normal anywhere. And look where they finally took us. What do you see?"

"One of the dirtiest cells in this country," said Curtis.

"One of the oldest. Look who works here. Old guys. If you're an old cop in Mexico, it's because you learned a long time ago how to mind your business. Wait for your retirement. Did you see what they don't have here?"

Curtis didn't answer, but Virgil barely noticed. He was almost talking to himself.

"Cameras. Not a damn one in the entire station. No one's looking in this place. No one is going to remember anything either. Or ask any questions. Jefe brought us to this place for a reason, and that reason is he can do anything that he wants to us here."

Virgil twisted around in his cell to look at Curtis. Curtis was in a daze. Dried brown blood formed a goatee around his mouth.

"Fix that nose," said Virgil. "You might need it."

The man driving the Range Rover had a tattoo on his elbow of a spider web. Eduardo had expected a thug with scars and bad skin, a cartoon evil man with no front teeth and a sinister laugh. This man was anything but that. He was neat and young and wore glasses. He was muscular and clean cut except for the tattoo.

Eduardo sat in his seat and stared at the traffic. They were headed out of the city, and by the time he realized that he should have been tracking the road signs, it was too late. Suddenly, the driver veered right for the exit, a horn blaring behind them. Eduardo saw nothing but a blur of colors and letters, all moving too fast to make any sense.

"Where are we going?" he finally asked.

The driver looked at his phone. He had turned down the brightness of the display so it emitted very little light.

"You have an appointment, sir," said the driver. He said it firmly and politely.

Eduardo could see the driver clearly. His clothes were nice without any flash. He had no jewelry, but wore a gun on his right hip. It was black and plain and as unflashy as the rest of him.

There were fewer cars on the roads now, and Eduardo could hear gravel colliding with the front of the truck. The gravel gave way to dust, and soon Eduardo realized there was only dirt beneath the tires. They entered a green corridor of trees. Then civilization in the form of a well kept home burst in front of them. The door was open and bright warm light poured through it.

The truck pulled onto the drive and stopped beside a black Porsche. The moon shone brightly off its hood and roof. The driver manipulated the phone again. Eduardo watched as the driver scanned the area around the house. The phone beeped once.

Eduardo studied the sports car. The windows were tinted so he had to peer through them and squint. The interior was black as well, and he thought he was seeing things. At first, the small Porsche didn't appear to have a steering wheel, but then he found it on the right side of the car.

"Did he buy this car in England?" Eduardo asked.

"Right this way, sir," said the driver. He motioned toward the open door of the house. It wasn't just open, Eduardo realized. It was broken. Broken wood surrounded the lock and the door appeared to be off its hinges, so it would never close. He understood now where he was.

Eduardo breathed deeply through his nose.

Strauss — Monterrey, MX

This was no place for winners. A red light lit the room. La Hermosa Posado had been the spot once, long in the past. The same customers came in, but their fortunes had drifted dramatically. They wore the same clothes, told the same stories, but drank cheaper booze. They were a collection of gray and graying, brown and dusty, and eyes that had long stopped fighting. With his silk shirt completely unbuttoned, Ordo Beltran stood out from the rest.

"I told the bartender to put it on your tab," he said to Strauss.

It could not be more clear who Ordo Beltran was. Strauss looked down the bar and saw a man placing cheap beers on the counter. That man would know, and he wasn't about to argue. He knew a couple beers weren't worth it.

"Tell me who was on the phone," said Ordo.

"It was a friend of Eduardo's. I presume they asked that you leave Eduardo in peace to continue his business. You can kill him when he returns," said Strauss matter-of-factly. He didn't know whether it was

148

the content or the tone, but he saw the Russian turn an eye in his direction.

"What can I get for you?" said a voice Strauss knew. He saw Guillermo's eyes widen in recognition. He saw the hand reach across the bar. He felt the grip. Once, Guillermo's arm had been a heap of raw muscle, fueled by youth and science. In the years since, that same body had deflated, and skin now hung loose from his bones. His eyes were weary. The smile, however, was still warm.

"How long has it been?" the bartender asked.

"A lifetime," answered Strauss.

Guillermo suddenly had a bottle of whiskey in his hand, and said it was on the house. Ordo turned around for that.

"Johnny Walker. I remember you used to drink this like water. What do you say?"

"I say no thank you," said Strauss. "But I will take a coffee."

Guillermo was not offended.

"I heard that about you," he said, putting the bottle on the shelf. Guillermo pointed to his nose. Strauss shook his head as if the idea were impossible.

"Not since Juarez."

Guillermo turned to Ordo.

"I have never in my life seen anyone do more coke than this man," he said, pointing at Strauss.

"Him?"

"He was the craziest bastard I've ever met."

"What kind of company did you keep?" Ordo asked skeptically.

Guillermo shrugged. "We were cops," he said. For a moment, he seemed to get lost in his memories. A man at the far end of the bar was trying to get his attention, but Guillermo was in another place.

"Hey," he said finally and with a smile on his face. "What was the name of that whore you were always mooning over? The gorgeous one. She had you wrapped around her finger. What was her name?"

"I don't remember," said Strauss.

"Yes, you do," said Guillermo, seeing right through him. "I took you to that brothel. It was for high rollers. We'd leave a week's pay there in an hour, and I had to drag you out every time. What was her name?"

Strauss stared into his coffee. There was still a smile on his face, but it seemed to have frozen there.

"Dulcinea," said Strauss.

"Dulcinea," said Guillermo, his smile growing. "She was something. How much of your money did she take from you?"

"Whatever it was, it was worth it," said Strauss.

"Yeah," said Guillermo. He had seen the thirsty man at the end of the bar by now. He just didn't care at the moment. "Where do you suppose she is now?" Guillermo asked rhetorically.

"Arizona," said Strauss. Guillermo had clearly not expected an answer. He looked deeply surprised.

"She cleans floors in Phoenix," Strauss said.

"How does she look now?" he asked as he began to fetch the man's beers, only half listening for the answer.

"You'd never know what she once was," said Strauss quietly.

There was a thick, heavy, humid smell. When Curtis tried to inhale gently, he felt a tightening sensation that began behind his eyes, reached out for the muscles in his face, and grabbed. It felt like his face was about to be pulled into his head.

One of the two drunks who lay against the wall in Virgil's cell sat up and yawned. He opened his mouth and displayed a mismatched set of rotten, scraggily brown teeth. He laid back down against the wall like it never happened.

The drunk next to him hadn't moved. He hadn't snored either. Curtis hadn't seen him move since he'd been here. Curtis found himself wondering if they would leave a dead body in the cell.

The man on the cot had nestled into himself. From time to time, he adjusted, his shoulder blades shifting inside of the tan jacket, but he never stirred or yawned or stretched.

"I used to love getting drunk like that," said Curtis aloud. He was hoping Virgil had heard him. If he had, he didn't move. He wasn't asleep exactly, but he was resting.

He touched his nose, and the pain stood up. He gently ran his finger along the edges, and his skin felt like it belonged to another person. It sent butterflies of pain through his belly. Pain sparked everywhere their wings touched. That had been a thumb and a forefinger. He thought doctors used a tool, some long thin pole they pushed into a nostril. He didn't have one of those.

"It's going to hurt," Virgil told him. He said it in a sleepy, dreamy sort of way. It was the last thing he said before drifting off. He might not have been aware that he said it. It certainly didn't help.

The thumb and fore finger squeezed harder this time. It felt like blood was squirting into his eyes from the inside. He let go. His nose felt wet and loose. He could feel the exact place where it was out of line and needed to return.

He thought about his sister and her huge house and perfect kids. He imagined her finding out that he'd been killed in a brothel for pedophiles. He touched his nose again. He imagined his sister hearing that and pretending he had never existed. He thought about wasting years of his life chasing the ghost of a drug dealer. He felt the blood pooling in his head, ready to burst. He thought about the life he had failed to build for himself and watching men like Eduardo Mendes repeatedly succeed. He thought about every bad decision of his miserable life and how they had all individually and microscopically contributed in their own tiny way to him being chained to a wall in the filthy jail cell in Mexico.

He squeezed hard and pulled. A volcano of pressure erupted inside his head. He saw black.

Eduardo saw him immediately. He leaned over the mantle, with one arm resting and his head in his palm, acknowledging no one.

He wore a thick beard that hung well past his chin. He was bald on top, and his eyes were hidden by tinted glasses. He had on a cream-colored suit with an elegant brown shirt. He was a large man and seemed to be aware of his own presence.

Eduardo had never seen this man, but knew who he was. This was the man who had married Colon's daughter. This was the man who had inherited his business. This was the man who had provided him with the means to become rich. This was Senor Villareal.

At his side was an angry looking woman. She wasn't beautiful by any means, and while her black dress was simple, it was expensive.

Her fingernails were freshly painted, and her toes, laid bare by sandals, were as well. Her legs were crossed, and one foot tapped the air impatiently. Eduardo had never met her either, but he knew this was Senora Colon, the old man's daughter.

The driver directed him to have a seat. The room was new, but old-fashioned. It could not have been farther removed from the sleek, ultra-modern box where he'd last met with her father. The couch on which he sat rested on tall, delicate, hand-carved legs. This room was bold, formal, and filled with classic Mexican charm. Eduardo hated it.

Unlike Senora Colon, the woman sitting next to him on the couch was beautiful, but she had been crying. Her eyes were red and worried, and mascara covered her cheeks in smudges and smears. She sat up obediently.

There was a little old man in another armchair, and he too sat straight and quietly. He was dressed in drab work clothes, old pants with touches of paint cut into shorts, and his shoes were rough and dirty. He bore scars like Eduardo had never imagined. His face had been torn apart at some point, then put back together carelessly.

These are the servants who work for Villareal, Eduardo realized, and we have all been assembled for a dressing down of some sort. Eduardo realized to his horror that he had been lumped in with them.

Villareal spoke to his wife, and she spoke back to him. It was Spanish, but it was a Spanish so quiet and fast that no one else would have understood it. It was Spanish but just for them.

"Service," said Senora Colon impatiently. She said it to the woman seated next to Eduardo, but she said it without looking at her. The woman jumped to her feet and rushed out of the room.

Villareal and his wide frame brooded. His bulk exuded impatience. His head was buried in his hand between the two glowing sconces. His hair and beard were reddish. Even the two drivers, who Eduardo recognized less as drivers and more as professional bodyguards, appeared to show him deference with their distance.

The woman appeared in the doorway. She held a tray like an untrained waitress. On it was a bottle of wine and a bottle of scotch, each with the appropriate glass. Villareal looked to her and impatiently took the scotch, setting it on the mantle. The woman handed the bottle of wine to Senora Colon, but when she attempted to pass the stemmed glassware, Senora Colon snatched it from her before she could touch it. The senora quickly examined the glass, looked at the woman with certain disgust, and issued a wave that could only have meant her dismissal. The woman left the room quickly. A driver closed the door behind her.

When it was closed, there were only four of them in the room: Villareal, his wife, Eduardo, and the old man. Villareal held his head up expectantly. He looked to his wife. She looked back, and Villareal nodded. He took the scotch by the neck, ignored the glass, and soundlessly left the room through the opposite door, closing it shut behind him.

Senora Colon had a small elegant black purse on her lap. From it, she retrieved a long cigarette and pressed it between her lips. Then she held a small gold lighter and ignited it. It was a cigar lighter, Eduardo noted. The room was quiet. After she lit the cigarette, she inhaled and let it out. Then she spoke.

"I understand you knew my father, Mister Mendes. Personally," she said.

"Yes. I did," he answered.

"Then you understand who I am," she said.

"You are Senora Colon."

She nodded as if it were of no interest to her.

"What did you think of my father?" she asked.

"He was a great man."

"He sold drugs, Eduardo. There is no reason to romanticize it."

For once, Eduardo had sense enough not to answer.

"What did you think of him as a man? I ask for your honesty. Please remember that there are things that you want from me."

"He was generous with his knowledge," started Eduardo. He watched as Senora Colon raised an impatient eyebrow.

"And a hypocrite."

The shape her mouth formed was as close to a smile as he would see.

"You knew him in his extravagant phase, didn't you? Did you visit any of his glass houses? Did he invite you to one of his mansions for a lecture on the dangers of excessive living? Was he wearing a hand-made suit while telling you to dress like a farmer? It doesn't matter. He was having fun with you. He was having fun with the whole world."

Senora Colon poured for herself. She filled the glass up to the rim with red wine. She did not offer any to Eduardo.

"Would you like to hear a story about the great man my father was?" she asked. Eduardo said that he would.

"When I was nineteen years old, I was in love with a boy I met at school. At the time I thought he was a man, but I understand now that he was just a boy. He believed that we were a family with some property outside of Monterrey, and that was all he knew. This was the first boy I had ever brought home to meet my family. Are you familiar with my mother?" she asked.

"No," said Eduardo. It had never occurred to him that this woman existed.

"She's dead," stated Senora Colon without sentiment. "She was a troubled woman. I'm sure you know the story or a story of how my father rose from poverty to being murdered in a Mercedes Benz, but I'll tell you regardless, because this version is the truth. As a girl, my mother took seizures, and she was not mentally well. This was not a secret. One day, my mother had a seizure while swimming. She would have drowned if she had not been saved by a boy on the farm. After that, my grandfather took an interest in the boy, realized he was intelligent and capable, and granted him increasing responsibility. As you no doubt have realized, this boy was my father.

"As time passed, my mother's mental health worsened. My father's responsibilities increased. He expressed interest in my mother, and my grandfather allowed it. He allowed it because she was a mentally ill woman who had seizures. No one else wanted her. They were married, and she gave birth to me. My father's place was now secure. Once my grandfather died, the business and the property belonged to him. Not bad for a penniless boy from the farm.

"Were you witness to any of my father's perversions, Mister Mendes?"

"No," said Eduardo, stunned.

"Of course not. You are a business associate. Perversions are for your loved ones. When I was a girl, my father delighted in tormenting my mother. One of his tricks was laughably simple. He would watch her set a place at the table, but when she turned her back, he would silently grab the silverware and hide it. My mother would come back to the table and just stare in disbelief. At times, she would simply get more silverware. Other times, she would crumple into a ball on the floor and weep for hours. Until she was medicated, which, as time went on, and by her own request, was more and more often.

"So, I was nineteen and hopelessly in love, and despite my father's efforts and what you see before you today, I was a sweet and loving person. I was happy, and I loved my mother. I had asked my father to meet us in the city for dinner, just the three of us, but he refused. He said a young man should come to the home of the man whose daughter he is courting. He used those very words. Courting. Pretending to be genteel and traditional was part of his great act.

"My father greeted my boyfriend graciously, toured the property with him, and even opened a rare whiskey he'd been given as a gift. When it was time for dinner, my mother came to the table. She was in a wheelchair at this point. It was obvious to anyone that she was an extremely fragile personality, and she didn't engage in conversation much. Despite how much I loved her, I was aware that my mother's appearance could be striking. Still, I loved her, and she was a part of me, but I was in love and naïve and thought love was all that mattered.

"We sit down to dinner, and my father, the gracious host, launches into a speech about love. I remember it vividly. He said love is eternal. The bonds you form in this life never dissolve, he said. They follow you forever, and they are unbreakable. Then, he got to the heart of his speech. He told my boyfriend, who was only twenty, to remember one thing: no matter how they may appear different, no matter if they argue or disagree or if one is blonde and the other brunette, ultimately, and without exception, every girl one day turns into her mother. He smiled at my mother and said, "Isn't that right, my love?"

"I don't suppose you have a place in your heart for tragic love stories, do you, Mister Mendes? No, I thought not. You are an intelligent man, so you can see for yourself where this story is going. The boy never came to the house again, and soon, he called less often, and wasn't as gentle, and then, abruptly, for me at least, he was gone. He was the love of my life, and for that, I have to thank my father."

Senora Colon lit another cigarette.

"You should have him killed," said Eduardo with a smile.

"Who?" asked Senora Colon. "The boy? What would that prove?"

"Just the indulgence of a wealthy woman," suggested Eduardo playfully.

"He did nothing wrong. No normal human being would knowingly betroth himself to a house full of sickness and madness. No, that was the last time I was happy, and that was what my father was after. Do you realize where you are? What you are sitting in right now?"

"No," said Eduardo truthfully.

"This house was built to very particular specifications. It was decorated in the same manner. You see, this house is a replica of the large house on the property where my father lived as a boy. This is the house as it was and as it looked, to the best of his memory, when he was poor, when he worked on the farm, and when he saved my mother's life. According to him, a man who made millions upon millions of dollars selling drugs, that was the time when he was happiest. When he had nothing. What do you think of that, Mister Mendes?"

"Not much," said Eduardo.

"And why is that?"

"I've had nothing, and I have no desire to relive it."

"What if I told you that this perverse fantasy grew worse? What if I told you that my father had this house constructed with no intention of ever living in it himself, and that his true intention was to live in a filthy shack in the fields? Just as he did as a boy, the last time in his life that he was truly happy?"

156

"I'd say your father was a madman."

"Well, today is your lucky day, Mister Mendes."

"Why?" asked Eduardo, now growing uneasy with the direction of the conversation.

"Because now you can tell him yourself."

She said it plainly and without showmanship, but she waved her empty hand toward the other armchair. The old man with the gnarled face still sat there, still upright. Eduardo had forgotten he was in the room. Eduardo recoiled as he saw the light in his eyes.

The old man was laughing.

The car raced past Juan Two Saints and missed him by only a foot. It was a small dark hatchback and it sped off with the horn blaring. Juan hadn't looked before he jumped out of his car, and he hadn't looked when he stepped into the street. He didn't bother looking at the hatchback as it drove into the night.

He wore uniform pants and a t-shirt. He stepped up to the phone booth and dropped three coins into the slot. There was a number in his pocket, taken down hours ago when the idea had been only a seed. The number was fresh in his mind.

It rang four times before he heard a voice. It could have rung twenty. He wasn't hanging up the phone.

The voice was bored.

"Policia," it said.

"Listen to me. Men are coming to the station right now. They are going to kill the Americans, and they are going to kill any officers who are in the station when they get there, whether they try to stop them or not. Do you understand me?"

There was silence. Then:

"Who is this?" demanded the voice.

"This is someone who is going to be alive tomorrow. Did you hear what I said?"

"Yes, but—"

"What did I say?"

"Men are coming."

"Get out."

"Who are you?"

"Your guardian angel."

Juan slammed down the phone.

Curtis opened his eyes and it was as if he had been staring at the sun. He saw only huge globes of light surrounded by darkness. The blinding pain had passed through him, up his nose, into his brain, and down his spine. It had been total and overwhelming. He still saw darkness around the globes, but soon he saw more and understood it was blood.

His nose still throbbed, but in comparison, calling it pain was laughable. What he felt was relief. He was on his knees on the floor. His free hand was on the cement. One hand was still cuffed to the bar.

"That's just a little runoff," said Virgil with a morbid laugh. "How did that feel?"

"It was the worst pain I've ever felt."

"Yeah, I knew it was going to hurt. Did I mention that?"

"Once or twice."

He saw Virgil was turned around, twisted, and had a smile on his face. It was a grim smile, but it was a smile nonetheless.

Curtis stared at his friend, not able to place his finger on what was wrong. Then he saw it. It was the movement. It wasn't Virgil. It was behind him. The drunk on the bench in the tan coat rolled over and sat up.

Virgil's eyes were elsewhere. His thoughts were inward. Curtis couldn't hear anything, but he watched as the drunk on the bench got to his feet. He didn't move drunk. He didn't look drunk. His movements were quick and confident. His face was lean and hard.

It came to him suddenly, in the midst of all that was wrong. It was just a small footnote in Colon's story, and he was the only one who cared. He'd seen this man before, seen traces of him, and read a solitary description. He instantly knew this man was called Angel.

Curtis opened his mouth to shout a warning when Angel broke into a run at Virgil. A sound did come out of his mouth, but it was too late. Angel kicked Virgil in the back of the head. His face smashed into the bars.

Eduardo stared in horror at what had become of the man he had known. His Colon had been clean and stylish man, well manicured and mannered. The giggling madman in the great armchair beside him looked like he'd been torn apart by animals and put back together with the worst of medieval medicine.

His daughter, Eduardo noted, appeared completely unaffected by his looks. Both of their reactions seemed to delight the old man.

When no one spoke, and Eduardo couldn't bear the orgiastic smile on what was left of Colon's face any longer, he had to ask a question.

"You survived the shooting in the car?"

This seemed to make the old man even happier.

"Don't be ridiculous, Eduardo," Senora Colon said with mild impatience. "He was never in the car."

"How did you do it?" asked Eduardo with genuine intrigue. "I know the Americans checked."

"Tell him," said Senora Colon. "You want to."

"Years ago," said Colon in a rusty voice. "My cousin, his friend, and I went for a ride in a car that was stolen. We all ran, but my cousin was caught. He gave them my name, because I was young at the time. He went back to his village immediately after and never had any trouble again. He was very soft. I told him I would pay him back one day."

"Eduardo," began Senora Colon. "Has it occurred to you to ask why my father is living in a filthy shack?"

"I would think because the authorities or competition had begun to pose a threat?"

"You would think, wouldn't you? When you met my father and his fancy homes, you were impressed. That is what you aspired to have, and he was who you aspired to be. What you didn't realize, what you never could have known, was that persona—the wealthy, sophisticated drug dealer—was my father's joke. Why retire peacefully to a country that will never extradite him or hold him responsible for his crimes when he could have a plastic surgeon disfigure him and live out a demented fantasy with that creature he keeps in the basement. My father never cared for money and he still doesn't. My father changed himself a long time ago. He changed himself from a poor boy on a farm to the comfortable husband of a woman no one else wanted. He changed me from a loving, happy young woman to a shadow of himself. Has he had any fun with you, Eduardo?"

"No," he answered quickly.

"Are you sure?" asked Senora Colon. "Has he asked you to run an unusual errand for him? Or do anything that was a little out of character? Did he make you think it was actually your own idea? Maybe he's having his fun with you right now?"

Blood squirted into Curtis' cell when Virgil's head collided with the bar. The gash split him just over his left eye. Before he could react, or fight, or stand, Angel had him by the collar. He ripped Virgil to the other side and banged the back of his head against the bars. Curtis felt the vibration. Angel threw Virgil to the floor.

Curtis saw Virgil kick. Angel backed off, and Virgil got his one free hand under himself. As he rose, Angel kicked him again in the stomach. Curtis heard a gust of air rush out of his lungs. Virgil collapsed onto the floor.

Curtis could see him on the ground beneath the bench. He had rolled on to his side to shield himself as best he could. He was gasping for air. His head was bleeding. He looked scared.

Curtis knew then that if he had hurt a person like this, he would stop at this point. There was no greater victory to be had, and no further point to make. Virgil was helpless, and he was beaten. But Curtis wasn't Angel.

Angel raised his shoe and brought the heel down on Virgil's ear. He did it again. Then he hit his side, under the ribs, by the organs. Virgil rolled on to his back, unable to control himself. He was completely exposed.

Angel didn't stop.

***

"Why have you brought me here?" Eduardo asked, finally feeling more confident in his surroundings. He looked sideways at the old man's scars.

"That is a good question," said Senora Colon. "You've been profitable for us, Mister Mendes, but other people have been profitable for us, and I haven't chosen to meet them. I suppose you've intrigued me with your recent exploits. One of my father's genuinely brilliant ideas was to have layers of insulation from those who might do him harm. My layer of insulation is down the hall drinking whiskey right now. My father's layer of insulation is that he looks like he stuck his face in a lawn mower. Your layers of insulation were carved up on the floor of your apartment."

Eduardo swallowed hard and tried not to show it. He thought about smiling, but didn't.

"She was very beautiful. I'm sorry for your loss," Senora Colon dryly.

"Thank you," said Eduardo.

"I understand that there are people who want you to be held accountable for this."

"I'm dealing with it."

"The way you dealt with your legal problems in America?"

"I don't understand," said Eduardo.

Senora Colon sniffed.

"You were arrested. Suddenly, the agent who arrested you is here in this house, tearing it apart, looking for something. Or someone. It would appear to be a tremendous coincidence."

"It isn't."

"No?" she said, faking intrigue. "Tell me how it isn't."

"The man who was here was Agent Curtis. He was the agent who interrogated me."

From the look on her face, he gathered that these were things she already knew.

"But Agent Curtis miscalculated."

"About what?" she asked.

"About me. When he realized his investigation into me was going to be revealed as a massive failure, he apparently decided to pursue some other leads. I've met the man. I don't know much about him, but I know he is an accountant. I would expect you left a paper trail for him to follow to this house."

"We…" said Senora Colon. "Left a paper trail?"

"How would I know about this place?" he asked.

Senora Colon appeared unconvinced.

"Ask your father," suggested Eduardo.

Senora Colon never took her eyes off of him.

"My father and I don't speak," she said.

Virgil wasn't moving. Curtis could hear him though. A low-pitched painful sound was crawling out of his throat.

Angel stood a few feet away, watching, his chest rising and falling without a sound. Curtis knew his friend wasn't getting to his feet, but watching Angel watch him, he knew this man was a patient killer. This man would wait all day.

Angel grabbed his own jacket and pulled it off. He dropped it to the floor as if he would never see it again. He wore a strange old shirt. It was plaid and tight on him and looked older than the man wearing it. Angel unbuttoned it, and it fell on top of the jacket.

He was bare from the waist to his neck. A light layer of sweat covered him. There was an ugly greenish burn mark on his right shoulder. It looked like a tattoo that had been burned and melted. There were ragged scars and sharp scars on his chest. He turned, and there were scars on his back. They were long stripes.

He wore a watch. It was gold with a leather strap and, even in this light, it looked very expensive.

Angel paid no mind to Curtis. He didn't even seem to know he was there. He crossed the room to the sink where the two drunks snored, ignoring them too. He took a gray, gnarled brick of soap from atop the sink and inspected it. He tossed it into the sink and turned on the water.

Curtis heard a faint sound of metal on metal. He saw Virgil's arm begin to rise, then fall weakly to the ground. He kept moaning. He saw the two drunks lying on one another. He saw Angel unbutton his pants.

162

***

"I wanted to meet you," said Eduardo. "Not you, specifically, but you nonetheless."

"Why?" asked Senora Colon.

"Because I want more," said Eduardo.

"Why would I give you more? You have enough trouble handling the business we've already provided you."

"This will all go away, and when it does, it will be business as usual."

"That's what I'm afraid of, Eduardo."

It wasn't her voice. It was the old man. He wasn't laughing, and there was no mirthful look in his eye. He was very serious.

"You were given tools, Eduardo. You squandered them, and you ignored my advice. You drew attention to yourself. You, your personal style, your orders, all of these things incite emotions in people. Emotions like jealousy. People see what you have, and they want it for themselves. They see how you treat them, and they seek to treat you like that. They want to trade places."

Colon spread out his arms.

"Do you suppose anyone wants to trade places with me?"

"I can do better," said Eduardo.

"At a certain point in a man's life, there is no being better. There is just what the man already is."

"If Strauss can kill these men here in Mexico, I can go home and start anew."

"Can you? Authorities in America know what you are now. They know what you do for a living. Even Strauss cannot fix that. Perhaps what you need is not new people. Perhaps what you need is a new Eduardo."

"You need me too," he said aggressively. "If you dismiss me," he said, choosing his words carefully, "it will take time to rebuild your entire operation."

"Our entire operation?" observed Senora Colon. "Mister Mendes, are you under the impression that you are our only distributor?"

Eduardo said nothing at all. He could feel the old man's eyes. He felt as if he were sinking into his chair. He had thought he was the only one. Colon shook his head.

"We've enjoyed your success, Eduardo. We have. But you are one of seven. Our operation will not rise or fall with you."

Suddenly, Eduardo's mind began to do calculations. It was entirely involuntary, and he tried to stop. He couldn't. He suddenly found himself entirely overwhelmed.

"Tell me what I need to do," he said softly.

The old man sighed happily. He stood. He gazed at his daughter. She looked back at him with a quiet hatred in her eyes.

"Sacrifice," said Colon. His voice sounded content when he said it.

Angel walked barefoot on the cement floor. The two drunks hadn't moved. He had taken the gray bar of soap from the basin. It was now a frothy mass of bubbles in his fist. He tossed it on to the bench above where Virgil lay.

Angel wore only his underpants. It was red bikini underwear with a leopard print band. It looked obscene.

Angel studied the man on the ground for a heartbeat. Then he leaned down and slapped Virgil in the face. It was gentle at first, and Virgil shuddered, but when his eyes didn't open, Angel hit him hard.

Virgil rolled onto his stomach. His knees and shoes scraped on the floor. He tried to get under the bench. He reached for the bars. He reached into Curtis' cell. Virgil's eyes were fixed on him, begging for help. One side of his face was coated with blood. The other side was coated with confusion and fear. Virgil dug in and pressed his face into the bars. It looked as if he were trying to squeeze himself through them.

Angel pulled him away and dragged him out from under the metal bed. Wordlessly, and without even a grunt, he picked Virgil up and dropped him chest down on to the bench. Singularly focused, Angel locked his left hand on the back of Virgil's neck, holding him in place. What tiny bit of light there was in the room glinted off the watch for the thinnest of seconds. Virgil, weak and exhausted and unable to defend himself, reached with his free hand, but Angel slapped him away uselessly. He used his hand and feet to push down Virgil's pants. Virgil's eyes rolled upward, and he coughed. "No," he said desperately.

Angel reached down for the soap and stopped suddenly. His eyes met Curtis' eyes. They were inches away, just on the other side of the bars. Angel's cool, distant eyes looked into those of a man possessed.

Angel's glance shot down to his arm as two hands locked onto him from the adjacent cell. His arm was coated in sweat. Curtis gripped, and his hand slipped. They slid just a fraction of an inch and no more. His grip was held fast by the expensive watch on Angel's wrist.

Angel looked up in shock. It was a look his face was not accustomed to making. Curtis, normally methodical and prone to hesitation, had no time to think. He pulled back with everything he had and ripped Angel face first into the iron bars.

Curtis saw life in slow motion. He saw Angel's jaw fall open. He saw Angel's eyes lose focus. He felt the muscles in his arm soften. It was only for a fraction of a second. He felt a jolt of electricity as Angel began to awaken. So he pulled him again.

Blood spurted from Angel's head and struck Curtis in the face. It didn't stop or slow him. Curtis pulled him again, his fingers circled around the expensive watch. He felt the collision of bone and metal deep in his ears. Curtis felt numbness in his extremities. He put a leg up to the bench. It was leverage. He pulled Angel's body as hard as he could. He pulled until his whole shoulder was in his cell. He pulled until he heard that shoulder pop. He felt Angel go limp, and felt his body falling. He pulled again. He heard a crunch. He pulled again and again until Angel stopped moving. Curtis pulled until he couldn't breathe.

Angel's arm reached up from his cell and into the next, held in the air by Curtis' hands. His body lay slumped atop Virgil. His head had imploded, and a purple mush-filled dent was all that was left of where his hair and forehead had been. Dark blood leaked from him. Curtis stood with one foot on the bench and felt himself shaking. He let go, and Angel's arm fell loosely. His body slid helplessly off of Virgil and landed with a limp, meaty slap on the floor.

Virgil rolled his eyes upward without lifting his head off the bench. He looked at Curtis as if he expected to see someone else. Then he lifted his head up, not far, but enough.

"How?" he asked, still trying to breathe.

Curtis looked back at what had been his bench. Just above it, between the bars, a dull silver Saint Michael pendant dangled in the air, hanging from the end of a long chain, which was clasped onto the end of a tiny handcuff key, twisted into the lock of an old pair of cuffs, which had become stuck on a bolt instead of falling to the ground. "For the mistakes you can fix, and for those you can't," were inscribed on the back.

"Thank you," Virgil said in a whisper, before putting his head back down again.

Curtis was shaking uncontrollably, and it was the proudest moment of his life.

The front desk at the police station was empty. Plexiglas separated the desk from the lobby. Scratches lined it from top to bottom. Juan peered through it to the big room beyond. He saw nothing and no one.

He heard papers ruffle and turned sharply. A fan was blowing on a desk. Two sheets of paper skidded about on the floor. He glided through the big room toward the office, looping to the back to see the parking lot. All of the cars were dark.

Back in the big room, Juan looked at the metal door to the cells. He had never cared for the cells. From the start, he had hated to see men inside them. He had always avoided their faces. All he ever saw in the cells was rage or begging. Neither was fit for a man.

There was a mug, filled to the brim with black coffee. Juan touched it. It was still hot. A little wisp of steam floated away from the brim. He set it down and entered the cell.

He smelled blood.

He saw the bare legs. He saw the red briefs. A crazed thought went through his head that the briefs were white, soaked with blood, but that was impossible. The legs were very real. The legs lay bare and vulnerable and unmoving.

He saw blood. He moved closer. It was in splatters, then in a pool. He inched forward. The ring of keys jingled in his bandaged hand. He stood in the doorway and soaked in his failure. He began to shuffle through the ring for the correct key when he felt the presence on him.

A hand raced past his face. It had a hold of his shirt, gripping him, pulling him off balance and into the bars.

His face touched metal. He tasted blood. Juan heard his shirt tear around the neck. He felt another hand grasp his belt.

"Give me the keys," said Curtis.

Juan Two Saints brought his eyes up to the man speaking. He was wild eyed and covered in sweat and blood. His grip was relentless. Their faces were inches away from one another. Juan could see teeth, and he had no doubt that this man would chew his face off if he didn't do what he told him. He held the keys behind himself, awkwardly, stretched out and away from the bars.

He could have tossed the keys. He could have thrown them into a corner. He could have dropped them on the floor. He had a gun in his pants. He could have shot this madman. But the more he looked at him, the less Juan Two Saints wanted to do that. The madman before him was one of the Americans. Juan had thought he was the soft one. He looked at the man on the ground. Juan didn't know if he was dead or alive, but he could still smell blood. Slowly, deliberately, he passed the keys through the iron bars and into Curtis' hands.

***

Senora Colon stood alone in the doorway. The warm light from the house kept her as a dark shadow.

"I will be interested to see how you deal with this situation, Mister Mendes," she said. "And whether or not we have a long term relationship."

It was exceedingly clear to Eduardo what she meant.

"I think you'll be calling me to congratulate me on a job well done."

"After this, you and I will never speak again. Good night, Mister Mendes."

She began to move away when Eduardo called to her.

"Senora?"

She paused, annoyed, since the last word had been hers and already spoken.

"Tell me one thing?" he asked.

From the dark figure in the door, Eduardo saw an almost imperceptible nod. Eduardo pointed to the Porsche Carrera in the driveway.

"You drove here, didn't you?" he asked. Maybe she could see him smiling, but when she spoke, her voice was cold.

"Good night, Mister Mendes," she said.

Juan Two Saints had a needle in his hand. He had thread in the other. The contents of the first aid box had been spilled over the nearest desk. It was as old as the rest of the station. Curtis thought of asking if they should boil some water for the needle.

Instead, he asked, "Do we have time for this?"

Juan looked at the clock. Then he looked at the mug of coffee on the desk. He poked his finger into the coffee.

"No," said Juan. "But we have to."

He had poured clean bottled water over the wound and was mopping it with a bandage. He took the needle then, ignoring the very skeptical looks of Virgil and Curtis, and stabbed the hematoma. He clotted it immediately with a bandage. Virgil winced and then sighed. Juan began to massage the wound.

"Better?" Juan asked. Virgil nodded.

Juan clotted the wound with bandages and then laid them on the desk. Virgil saw the mess and reflected that it had all come out of him. A vision occurred to him of the man lying in the cell behind them.

"Is he dead?" he asked.

"Not yet," said Juan flatly.

"Do you know who he was?"

Juan Two Saints nodded.

"A man you do not want to meet."

He thought of the way that man's head looked, and hoped his own head looked nothing like it. It occurred to him then what had almost happened. It occurred to him then what he now owed to Curtis. He watched his slight, skinny friend pace.

"We need a car," said Curtis, coming back to them.

Juan reached into his pocket and threw his keys to him.

"It is in front," he said. He handed a stack of bandages to Virgil. He told him to finish patching himself up in the car. He handed his radio to Curtis.

"Habla espanol?"

"A little."

"Listen to this. It will work for a few hours, but it is not fully charged. Make a straight run for the border until you hear them talking about the highways. Then get off."

Virgil was picturing the man on the floor of the cell. He was picturing himself naked and bleeding in his place.

"What is your name?" asked Virgil.

"Don't tell him," interrupted Curtis. "In case we get caught."

He didn't say that they would be tortured and killed. He didn't say what he knew, which was that no one could withstand torture, and when enough pain was applied, he would answer any question they asked.

These were things Juan knew too and wished he didn't.

"They call me Juan Two Saints," he said.

"Thank you, Juan Two Saints," said Virgil.

"Juan, the big man, Jefe…he took our guns and our passports. All our ID's."

Juan walked into the office. They could hear desks and cabinets opening and closing. The sounded like the old metal kind that could be found in every municipal building all over the world. Juan came back with a brown paper bag. He handed it to Curtis. It was heavy and filled with their guns.

"Where are the passports? And the wallets?"

"Jefe will have them."

"Why did he leave the guns?"

"Guns are common. A US passport is valuable."

Juan reached into the back of his waistband and brought out a revolver, placing it on the desk. Virgil slowly climbed to his feet.

"You're not coming with us?" Curtis asked.

169

"No, he's not," said Virgil, understanding.

"What are you going to tell them?" Curtis asked.

Juan Two Saints walked to a nearby desk and began rifling the drawers. He slapped a pair of handcuffs on the desk. The coffee in the mug rippled. He rooted through another drawer until he found what he needed. He held out a heavy nightstick to Curtis.

"Nothing," he said.

Curtis felt sick as he began to see it. He wanted nothing to do with this.

"I was overpowered as I entered the cell. I was severely beaten," said Juan. "I was lucky to survive, but I don't remember anything else."

"I'm not going to do this," said Curtis.

"If you don't, he will kill me."

"There has to be another way."

"Not in Mexico."

Juan walked back to the cells and waited in the doorway. He looked patient, but there was little time. Curtis looked to Virgil, who could barely stand up straight. Virgil understood.

"You have to," said Virgil.

"How can this be right?"

"Without him, we would still be in that cell."

Curtis felt like he was in a trance. He had forgotten about the urgency. He had forgotten about the police, who would no doubt be returning soon. He had forgotten about the weight of the bag until he set it down with a heavy thud and started across the room. As he did, Juan clicked one handcuff around his wrist and put his hands behind his back. Curtis heard the other bracelet click.

"I'm so sorry," said Curtis, with the bat in his hand.

"It's all right," said Juan. "I actually want it to hurt."

"Why are you doing this?" Curtis asked.

Juan Two Saints smiled as he walked into the cells.

"Because I'm a police officer," he said.

Chapter Ten

Virgil – Monterrey, MX

Curtis wasn't speaking. Before tonight, Virgil had never even seen Curtis in a fight. He thought of Curtis with the heavy night stick in his hand, and then Juan Two Saints saying, "If it's not convincing, they will kill me." He had smiled gently when he said it. Virgil knew his friend and knew what he was made of, so when Curtis finally hit him, the man took it and said, "I have a family. Do this for me." A flurry of violence exploded from Curtis, the stick striking the man as he stood, the man falling, and the stick following him to the ground. The stick continued to fly. It flew again and again until Virgil caught Curtis by the wrist. A single drop of blood rolled down the stick and on to Curtis's hand. It stopped before it reached Virgil.

"I think he's covered," Virgil said.

He ushered Curtis out of the cells, and though he tried not to, he glanced down at the man who had attacked him. His face was a mess. His arm hung awkwardly. He looked at Angel, naked except for his underwear, and remembered how close he had come to being that man. He stole one last glance at Juan Two Saints. Suddenly, he felt bad for neither of them.

Virgil had a terrifying thought. He kept it to himself, imagining that he was being hysterical. He didn't speak Spanish. He didn't know where they were. He looked into the sky for the moon. He found it, but it meant nothing to him.

Finally, he saw another sign, and he knew he wasn't crazy.

"Where are we going?" He realized he had yelled.

"Back to the house," said Curtis.

"What house?"

"Colon's house."

"Are you out of your fucking mind?"

"No," said Curtis. "I am absolutely clear."

"About what?"

"About everything. Finally."

"I want to leave Mexico now."

"We have to stop first."

"Why?"

"We're going to pick up Aureliano Colon, and we're going to bring him back with us."

"He's dead. You told me all about it."

"No. I was wrong. Everyone was wrong. Colon is alive and well and living a quiet life."

"I don't care what he does. I don't care if he lives or dies. I want to go home."

"You just don't understand." His voice was strangely calm. Virgil knew Curtis was prone to excitement. He was one to get carried away.

"Help me understand."

"I bet on Aureliano Colon. He outsmarted me. I bet everything I had and I lost. I tried again, and Eduardo Mendes beat me. This time, I was ridiculed. I was put out to pasture. You know what? I have a chance to prove I wasn't wrong. That I'm not a joke. Imagine if you suddenly got the chance to prove that guy had a gun, and he was pointing it at you. What would you do to prove it, to get your name back?"

Virgil looked again for the moon. He had lost it in the clouds. There were no other cars on the highway, and the roadside was growing thick with trees. He remembered the bag of guns at his feet. He rubbed the wound on his head.

"How far away are we?" he asked.

Eduardo paused as he touched the door. He tried to smile arrogantly, but his lips were filled with nerves. He was painfully aware of how much he had to lose.

"What did I miss?" he said with a smile upon walking into the bar. He saw the Russian size him up again. The Russian nodded.

Ordo was eyeing him as if he hadn't eaten in years.

"You have bigger balls than I thought," shouted Ordo.

"Is he still planning to kill me?" Eduardo asked quietly.

"Eventually, yes," said Strauss.

"I don't suppose you would talk him out of it?"

"You have about two minutes before Ordo finishes his drink and comes over here. While we wait, do you want to tell me how you and the Russian know one another?" asked Strauss.

Eduardo's eyes darted automatically for the nearest washroom. Strauss waited patiently.

"It was a favor for Colon," said Eduardo.

"A favor?"

Eduardo looked at Strauss for the first time. He was tall and stoic and impassive and patient.

"Colon asked me to send two men for some work. Instead, I hired the Russian and I came myself."

"What were you thinking?" asked Strauss incredulously.

"I was looking for his secrets," said Eduardo, in a voice so heavy and deep that it could only have told the truth. He felt better saying it aloud, and worse all at once. He waited for Strauss to ask what had happened, but he never did. He saw Ordo Beltran and his quickly draining glass.

Eduardo exhaled long and loud. He hoped to drive out every nervous cell in his body. When he breathed again, the air was smoke and liquor. He thought of his father and his summons to Mexico. He walked directly toward Ordo Beltran. Then he smiled.

"I've seen a lot of men before they died," said Ordo. "None of them looked as happy as you."

"Today is not my day to die."

Ordo laughed. He looked to the Russian, who did not smile.

"Where is your man?"

"My man?"

"Your protection. Strauss. He is hiding across the room with his creepy friend. He washed his hands of you."

Eduardo could see Strauss, and he could see the distance between them.

"He doesn't need to hear what I am about to say."

"He's heard men beg before."

"You won't need to beg. You just need to say yes."

Ordo looked puzzled. He wasn't sure if he should be amused or offended. Instead, he looked at the Russian and laughed.

"Say yes to what?"

"My offer."

"What is this now?"

Eduardo exhaled. This time, he did it through his nose, so no one would notice. He had a fleeting thought of his first meeting with Colon.

"I had a woman in Texas. If I said she was beautiful, that wouldn't do justice to what she was. Imagine God having a fantasy of the most sexually perfect woman, and then breathing life to her. That was my Odalys. She was my creation, and I loved her. Last week, I had a man tear her apart with a knife."

"Why?" asked Ordo. It seemed he was genuinely intrigued. Eduardo felt his steam rising.

"Because I am a survivor. Many men in this business like the idea of being ruthless. Very few truly understand it. To be genuinely ruthless is not to be cruel to your enemies. To be genuinely ruthless means to be cruel to those you love most, including yourself, if that is what it takes to survive and to succeed."

Ordo looked into his glass for inspiration. Eduardo took a chance.

"My accountant is dead. My woman is dead. My connection is alive, and my customers are alive. I am alive. My money is alive. I have work ahead of me. I cut ties between me and every single living human being who could hurt me. I am alive, and they are not. Tomorrow, I am going to make money, and they will stay dead. What do you think about that?"

Ordo said nothing.

"This business is filled with talkers. Men who have a lot to say about what they will do if, and what they might do when. I have already told you what I did when I needed to do it. What I am willing to do is now obvious. Your friend will vouch for me, will he not?"

Ordo looked uncomfortably at the Russian. He nodded.

"So what are you saying?" asked Ordo, suddenly sounding unsure.

"I'm saying I need new people. A new organization. One that is tight and ruthless, made of men who have no problem making lots and lots of money. Would you like to be part of an organization like that?"

Ordo stared into his drink. He pretended to be mulling over the offer, but Eduardo could already see his offer taking effect.

"I notice you're not still threatening to kill me," said Eduardo.

Curtis turned the lights off while he was on the main road and slowly, silently rolled the car through the driveway. The house rose up before them. There were no cars and no sounds. The entire property was still.

They found the front door open a few inches. Virgil looked nervously before he remembered that they had broken it. The room behind it was dark. He reached out to push it open when a voice spoke from behind them.

Virgil spun, his hand on his weapon, thumb breaking the catch and ready to draw. He saw Curtis had dropped to a crouch. They looked across the empty field, all the way to the trees. There was no one there.

They voice came again. It was speaking Spanish in harsh static. Curtis laughed. He reached into his back pocket and removed the radio they had taken from Juan Two Saints. Curtis looked like he wanted to laugh. He clicked the off button.

Then they heard a woman scream. It wasn't the radio. It was inside the house.

"You should get rid of the old man," said Ordo to Eduardo. They all turned and looked toward Strauss, except for the Russian. Guillermo was refilling their glasses.

"You still don't know who he is, do you?" Guillermo asked.

"I know what I need to know," said Ordo dismissively.

"You think you do," Guillermo responded. He saw the look coming from Ordo. "Twenty years ago, in Juarez, if you needed a man dead and it couldn't be done, he was the one to do it."

"Why couldn't it have been done?" asked Ordo.

"Some people were protected."

"There's no such thing," said Ordo.

"No," agreed Guillermo. "Not anymore."

175

Eduardo saw Strauss returning his phone in his pocket as he approached.

"That was the call," said Strauss. "But it was not the call you wanted."

It was an awful, desperate, choking cough. It was tough and clear and followed by a plea. Then the plea disappeared.

They made their way up the stairs. Curtis went first. He heard water. It was splashing roughly, spilling onto the floor. They heard gasping. The woman was begging for air, begging for reprieve, begging for it to stop, all of it in desperate, unfocused sounds.

"Por favor," came the first articulate sounds. A man screamed at her.

"In English!" he shouted.

"Please," she said. They heard a splash, and there was no more talking.

They followed the screams to the master bedroom. The bureau drawers had been opened haphazardly. Gaudy lingerie spilled forth. He saw a long black phallus with straps on it. A machete rested on top of the bureau. Blood glistened on the blade. The bathroom glowed bright white and pink. A filthy man held a woman's head under the water.

He wore old khaki shorts with huge pockets. He wore a simple work shirt, and it was gray and wet. He had thinning hair. His skin was tanned from being outdoors. He didn't look at Curtis.

Curtis heard her voice again. It was Maria. It was the woman they had found locked in the basement. She was on her knees now. There was water all over the floor. Her hands were bound behind her back with metal bracelets, and she was dressed like a prostitute, in only a skirt and a bra. Her hair was soaking wet.

"What were you told?" he demanded.

She took a long breath before she answered.

"You are very brave," she said quickly.

"And?" he demanded.

"My father would like to offer a gift to honor you," she said. She gulped more air.

The man froze. He said nothing. The girl breathed deeper and deeper, but stopped, sensing that something had changed. She rolled her eyes. Curtis brought up his gun. He watched as the old man turned his scarred face to his. He had been butchered by a surgeon, and he was wearing rags, but there was a sparkle in his eye that Curtis recognized immediately. He knew without doubt or hesitation that he was looking at Aureliano Colon.

"Let go of her," Curtis said. He tried not to sound nervous.

Colon didn't move. He had one hand free and the other entwined in Maria's hair. She was watching. She had been made up garishly and now it was running down her face in blue and black streaks. Her lips were bright red.

Curtis began to repeat himself when suddenly, Colon complied.

Then he smiled at Curtis.

Jefe stood over a puddle of blood in the cells. Then he locked eyes on Juan.

"What's the name of the officer?" asked one of the paramedics.

"Juan Two Saints," said Jefe in his slow growl. Juan broke his gaze.

"Only superficial injuries," said the paramedic.

"Superficial injuries," repeated Jefe.

"He's ugly, and he's going to stay that way, but he'll live."

"And the other?"

The medic groaned. "Not so superficial."

"Is he going to die?"

"If he's lucky."

"If he's lucky," repeated Jefe.

"I need a name for him," said the medic.

"Sorry," said Jefe. "It's not my jail."

**

"Take them off," said Curtis. He said it seriously. He wanted to sound forceful, but the old man had a playful look about him.

"I don't have the key," he said.

Curtis remembered the St. Michael chain in his pocket, and the key on the other end of it. He thought about tossing it to the old man and repeating himself, but he didn't. He felt an impulse not to let that chain go.

"Yes, you do," said Virgil from behind him. Virgil sounded like a man with no patience. Colon must have heard it too. The look on his face remained, but he slowly reached into his pocket and removed a long key on a wide ring. He held it out to them.

"You do it," said Curtis.

Curtis saw Maria and her soaking wet bra and breasts. He watched Colon's hands. As soon as her left hand was free, Maria pulled away and retreated to the corner of the bathroom.

"I know who you are," Colon said to Curtis.

"I know who you are," Curtis replied.

Colon didn't care enough to react.

"When I heard that a lawman in Texas had discovered me, I drew a picture of him in my mind. He was a tall cowboy of a man, rugged and hard. Imagine my surprise."

Colon started forward. "Get your hands up," said Curtis.

"You've been roughed up a bit, but in the end, you're nothing more than a bookworm."

"I'm taking you back," said Curtis.

"No, you're not," said Colon. "You're not policemen here. I'm not a wanted man. Down here, we're both nobody."

"Take the handcuff off of her," Curtis said, "and put it on yourself. You can explain why you keep a girl locked in your basement."

"She's here of her own free will, just like you."

Maria slapped him. She slapped him right in the face and drew blood. Curtis stepped back. He could see the surprise over Colon's face. His eyes went wide, and his voice cut off. Curtis realized immediately that she hadn't slapped him.

Maria had one hand held over Colon's throat, the remaining metal handcuff plainly visible on her wrist. As Curtis came forward, he could see the other handcuff in her fist. It was held open by the force of her hand to form a jagged toothed metal hook. She had plunged it into his throat and was holding it in place.

Colon's fingertips had almost touched her hand when she whispered to him. He stopped before contact. She whispered again.

Curtis could see it clearly. He could see what was going to happen. "Don't," he said.

Maria looked at him. It was a face wholly without pity. She ripped out the metal hook, pulling it toward her and with more force than any woman her size should have been able to summon.

Blood sprayed into the air. It arched and rained down onto the bathroom floor. Colon turned and painted the wall of the bathroom. Maria slid away from him but didn't scream. Colon crashed into the sink, spraying blood on the mirror and the basin. Then he fell to the floor.

Curtis came to the doorway but didn't enter. Colon put his hands to the wound. It wasn't spraying now. It was leaking. A dark mass was pooling underneath him and running along the threshold. He made a gurgling sound. His feet kicked.

Curtis heard the water. He looked to the tub, and saw Maria stepping out. She stepped onto the toilet on her toes. Droplets of blood dotted her breasts. She looked to them expectantly, and with fear, and they looked back with awe. Then, without words, they all looked down and watched the old man die.

When it was done, when it was clear beyond all doubt that this time, Colon was dead, and he would never rise again, Curtis took stock of himself. His thoughts ran briefly toward his old life, and how far away it seemed.

Curtis reached out a gentle hand to Maria, and she took it. He helped her climb down and out of the bathroom. She disappeared into the house behind them.

"Come on," he said to Virgil. "Let's get what we came here for."

***

Curtis left the big country house and never looked back at it. He walked straight into the field. He knew the layout like it was a picture in his head. He went to the little old shack.

It was a simple one room wood and metal affair thrown up with limited skill. They let the flashlight roll over it. The roof was old and rusted iron. The wood on the sides had been weathered for years. Even the small glass on the window was scratched.

Virgil knew what he was thinking.

"This has been here for more than two years."

"Yeah," muttered Curtis. He touched the walls and roof. This was where Colon had been all along. He had been hiding in a one room tin shack.

Just as he touched the door, he heard Virgil call to him.

"Do you think it could be trapped?"

Curtis paused with his fingertips on the doorknob.

"He was pretty crafty," said Virgil.

Curtis got down on one knee. He studied the door. It was solid enough and it shut cleanly. It was faded red with chipped paint. It would keep out the weather and keep out the bugs. He lowered his head and saw it was tight at the base.

Curtis poked around the foundation. He was pulling weeds away from the frame and sifting through the dirt. He worked his way to the corner and, finding a soft spot in the earth, went to work, shoveling away with his hands. He began tossing dirt behind him. Virgil stepped out of the way. Curtis reached with both hands now, using his arm as a plow, moving loose handfuls of dirt away from the shack.

"In answer to your question, no, I don't think this has been here for two years. It's been somewhere, but not here."

"I think maybe we should go."

"I think he found a shack that looked just like the one he was born in, picked it up, and moved it here. That's what I think he did."

"Good for him. He's dead now. And we will be too."

"In your experience, are old shacks built with new bricks?"

Virgil peered over his shoulder and into the hole Curtis had dug. Curtis dusted loose soil from the foundation. In the light, it was clearly a fresh concrete brick, far newer and more professionally laid than the rest of the shack. It was stacked atop an identical brick, and descended into the earth.

"What do you think?" Curtis asked. He stood. He didn't dust himself off. He turned the door knob as if Virgil had never said a word about traps and walked right into Colon's house.

There was a cot along the wall. Clothes were stacked neatly in the corner. A crucifix hung from the wall. The lights came on as Curtis pulled on the string that hung from the bald overhead lamp. Colon had a few things to cook and eat with, but that was all. A coat was on a hanger on a nail in the wall. There was a shirt underneath it. Curtis was on the floor.

He threw an old dirty carpet into the corner. He was pushing at the floor boards, shifting, trying to find the loose one. Virgil backed out of his way as Curtis picked up the cot, emptied the blankets to the floor, and launched it into the night. He was on his knees for seconds when the floor came up with him.

It was in one piece. It extended directly below where the bed had been. A dark hole stared back at them. Curtis almost laughed because he was so excited. He didn't though. He knew he would look insane. Instead, he took his gun out.

"Just in case," he said to a visibly nervous Virgil.

Curtis and Virgil were beyond words now. They both understood. Curtis, with a flashlight in one hand and his gun in the other, dropped into the hole feet first.

It was a concrete vault, for lack of a better word. It was a concrete floor with walls and a ceiling that led straight up to the shack. When Curtis landed, he felt his knees hit an object.

He heard Virgil land. He heard his feet scuff the ground. He never lifted his eyes. They were fixed on what he had found. He had travelled hundreds of miles, almost been killed, located his arch enemy, and now found himself staring at a blue and white cooler.

He was struck by how mundane it was. It was a small cooler. There was one at every beach. There were three at every cookout.

"What is it?" Virgil asked.

Curtis lifted the cover. He suddenly thought of a severed head. The madman who lived upstairs could have been saving it. He opened the lid. He found his hands inside the box.

It was green.

His eyes burst open. He realized his hand was shaking. He gripped the flashlight with his whole hand and focused. It was all green bills. The number "100" flashed at him, and he counted it five times. He saw the words, "The United States of America" written large. A fat brown paper wrapper ran straight down the middle, and Curtis didn't have to tear it off to know that Ben Franklin would be staring back at him.

The whole room lit up, but Curtis' nervous system had already been too stretched, too overwhelmed, run too thin to react properly. He looked up with interest and squinted at Virgil, who was holding a handheld lamp, which had hung from a nail in the ceiling.

He leaned over Curtis' shoulder.

"Oh my good God," he said.

Curtis looked back at him.

"You're welcome," he said.

"This is the most money I've ever seen."

"This is more money than most anyone ever sees," Curtis whispered.

Curtis reached into the box. The bills were crisp and smooth. They had probably never been touched since they left the treasury.

He was suddenly filled with urgency. Curtis strained his ears, hoping against hope that he wouldn't hear the sound of a police siren in the distance. Adrenaline flooded his system, his feet preparing to run.

"Get up there. I'm right behind you. Just start the car."

"What are you saying?"

"We need to get the hell out of here." Curtis had crawled backwards and was under the hole in the floor.

"What about the money?" Virgil asked.

"I have it."

"Curtis!" Virgil yelled. It was an impatient voice. He felt Virgil's grip on his arm. There was too much going on right now. There was no time to tell him to slow down.

"Do you not see where we are?" Virgil asked.

Curtis looked about himself. They were still in the cinder block grave under Colon's shack, only now the lights were on and shining bright. Curtis clutched the blue cooler in his arms. His jaw almost slammed against it when he really opened his eyes.

There were nine more coolers just like it.

Virgil raced from cooler to cooler, flipping open the lids as if it were Christmas morning. He gasped each time he looked into one, each time a little higher, and with a little more excitement, occasionally looking back at Curtis with wild eyes, until he finally came to the last one, which he stared into with silent amazement. He took a deep breath.

"Holy Mary, Mother of God," he muttered.

"What's that?"

"Something my father used to say when we were kids. When he just didn't know what else to say."

Curtis wanted to look, but he didn't have to see to believe. He knew what was in those cases. He had always known. He had always been right about Colon.

"Curtis?" Virgil asked carefully. "You're my math guy. How much money are we looking at?"

Curtis looked into his box. It was mostly full, but there were stacks missing. Colon had needed money from time to time. He had no idea what for.

"I don't know," he said.

"Guess." Virgil's tone was pointed.

He peered into the first container. He touched the fresh, clean sheets. They were spotless. Slowly, he poked a finger into the pristine stack and pulled one loose. Then another. He counted, and as he counted, he realized he was talking aloud, whispering as he went. It was money that didn't belong to anyone. Not anymore. It was money that could buy anything. It could buy a new life.

"Are they all just as full?" Curtis asked, looking down the line.

Virgil went to the end for him. "Yes," he said with excitement.

"Are they all hundred-dollar bills?" Curtis asked. But he already knew.

"Oh yeah."

Curtis paused respectfully before he said the words.

"We are looking at almost twenty million dollars."

Virgil sat back on his heels. The number sunk into his head. It was twenty million dollars.

"Holy Mary, Mother of God," he whispered.

"This call is for you," said Guillermo.

Strauss looked at the phone.

"Who is it?' he asked.

"You know who it is," Guillermo said.

He did know. The call had been placed to the bar so Strauss would understand in no uncertain terms that his whereabouts were known. It would have rattled some men. Strauss looked at Ordo and Eduardo.

"Your friend from America just asked a Mexican gangster if he could bring more men here tonight," said Guillermo.

Strauss eyed them both seriously.

"Does he have any idea who he is dealing with?"

"None," said Strauss.

Guillermo waited a moment for his next question.

"Are you coming back?" Guillermo asked.

"I don't know," said Strauss.

Curtis was trudging through the field with the first cooler in his hand. It was a short walk, but the cooler had begun to feel heavy. He felt himself sweating. He realized that the events of the night were wearing off, and the unholy energy which had propelled him was taking its toll. Yet he walked through the field with the grass to his knees, his forearms beginning to burn, and he didn't stop until he came to the barn.

When he got there, the door was open, and the old maroon pickup truck was parked end first, just as he had promised.

"Adios," said Maria. Curtis hadn't heard her and had no idea she was there. She smiled shyly.

Maria wore a coat that wasn't hers. It was a man's coat and too large. Her legs were bare, and she wore sandals. She had washed the blood off of herself.

They both regarded each other for a long moment. Curtis was very aware that he had a broken nose and blood all over his shirt, and that didn't bother her in the least.

"Thank you," said Maria in English, and it seemed to Curtis that he had never heard anything more genuine in his life.

"I don't know how to say 'you are welcome' in Spanish," he said.

"Con mucho gusto," said Maria. This didn't sound genuine to him. The way she said it, it sounded like trouble.

"Are you going home?" he asked.

She shook her head no.

"Why not?"

"I cannot go home. Not like this."

I cannot either, he thought fleetingly, knowing in his heart he didn't mean it.

"Colon said that you were here of your own free will. Is that true?"

Her face was puzzled.

"I do not know free will," said Maria.

"It means that you decided to be here. That you could leave."

Maria understood, and she looked at the ground.

"He does not mean it the way you mean it," she said.

Curtis did not ask more. He suddenly remembered the box at his feet and felt guilty about it.

"I have something for you," said Curtis, as he bent and opened the box. Some part of him was careful not to open it all the way, and not to let her look into the box.

"Is it money?" she asked.

Curtis paused.

"Yes. It is money."

"It is his money, isn't it?"

"It was."

"Then I do not want it."

"You earned it," said Curtis.

"I do not know earn," she said.

185

He didn't explain. Instead, he took one of the stacks of hundred dollars bills and closed the case. He shoved the money into her coat pocket. Curtis caught himself looking into her dark eyes as he did it. She was passive.

"To help you get out. When you get there, if you don't need it, you can give it away."

"You knew him, didn't you?"

He thought about that question, and he thought about what she really meant.

"Yes. I studied him. Too much, maybe."

"Are you glad you did?"

"I don't know. It changed me," said Curtis.

She smiled. She was sad and lovely at the same time. She started to leave.

"He changed you?" she said whimsically and over her shoulder. "I am really a boy."

At the top of the stairs, Strauss thought of another time when the phone had rang and Guillermo had said that a man wanted to see him. He had been young and stupid and very, very drunk, and Guillermo had known all of these things. He remembered, after it was over, racing to the brothel, and falling asleep in Dulcinea's arms while an old black and white movie flickered in the background.

He opened the door and stepped into the night.

"Buenos noches, Inspector Strauss," came the wet rumbling from Jefe's throat. Strauss turned and saw Jefe coming from the corner of the parking lot. His gun was still holstered. His huge belly hung over his belt. Jefe zipped up his pants.

"Been a long night," said Jefe.

"For all of us."

"Not much gets past you, Strauss, so I suppose you heard about what happened at the station a little while ago."

"I've heard only rumors," said Strauss. "What can I do to help?"

Jefe laughed. It wasn't his rueful little chuckle that made Juan Two Saints cringe every time he heard it. It was an honest to God caught off guard laugh.

"What can you do to help," he said. "That's a good question, Strauss. You know I don't mind a little bloodshed, even if it's in a police station, but there is a time and a place for everything, and I like to be in control of it."

Jefe reached into his shirt pocket and took out a half finished cigar. The end was still wet and discolored, but he put it into his mouth anyway.

"I wasn't in control of it today," he said as he lit it.

"Are you here to ask if I was?"

"No, I don't think you did this. Not intentionally. The funny thing was that we were going to have a talk with the Americans. So we put them into a cell with a guy who we thought might give them a little trouble. We didn't know him, and he didn't say much, but when a mean looking bastard covered in scars comes into your life in a Mexican jail, it's not usually hard to put two and two together."

"I wouldn't know, Jefe."

"It isn't," he said, and there was a touch of anger to his voice. "Funny thing about this Mexican in my Mexican jail is no one can really remember how he got there. No one remembers talking to him. I've known a good deal of drunks in my day. They kind of run off at the mouth. Not this one. Silent as a church mouse, if you know that expression."

Jefe chewed on the cigar, watching Strauss. Strauss was impassive.

"Reminds me of a rumor I heard. Didn't you once have an employee who didn't say much?"

"I don't have any employees."

"But I think you know very well who I mean. So before we sent him off, I made sure we stopped and took his finger prints."

"How did that go?" Strauss asked.

"I think you know how it went, Strauss. I have a finger print card in my truck full of ugly black smudges. I have two Americans on the run and a district captain who has already thrown me under the bus to his superiors. I have people to answer to now. And you do too."

"Why am I sharing your problems, Jefe?"

Jefe smiled his brown smile. There were flecks of tobacco stuck in his teeth.

"I hear you have an American in there with you? Who is he?"

"He is nobody."

"You don't work for nobodies."

"Times are tough."

"I'll find out who he is."

"I'm sure you will, but he will be gone before you do."

"No matter. He'll be back. After all, this is Mexico."

Jefe spread his arms out wide as he stood in the center of the empty piss-scented parking lot behind the bar and laughed. It was his deep, dangerous belly laugh for when nothing was really funny. Strauss turned to leave.

"And Strauss, before you go, answer one last question."

Strauss' hand was on the door. He was tired, but he stayed.

"I heard a rumor about you once. I always wanted to know if it was true."

Strauss felt worn. He hoped Guillermo had more coffee brewing. "What was it?" he asked.

"I heard that when you moved to Monterrey, you tried to go straight," Jefe said, the mirth in his tone unmistakable. "Is that true?"

Strauss wanted to find the Americans. He wanted to send Eduardo Mendes back where he belonged. He wanted to be done with this conversation.

"Yes, it is true," he said. Jefe laughed loudly.

"The Assassin of Juarez comes to Monterrey to clean up the joint. What did you offer them?"

"I told them that there was a disgrace of a police officer who worked for the cartels or anyone else with money and we should arrest him immediately to send a message."

"How did that go?" Jefe asked with delight.

"You're still here," said Strauss.

Even when the door slammed shut, he could hear Jefe laughing.

Virgil stepped out of the little shack with the last blue and white cooler in his arms. There was a full moon overhead. It was enough to see Virgil across the field, but not much else.

The truck was waiting for Curtis. The handles on the door felt old fashioned. He pulled it open, and the hinge creaked loud enough for

Virgil to hear. It smelled of use. There was a scent of oil and gas, with a hint of nature on the side. The interior was threadbare. The seats had holes, some of them stitched.

It was old and rough, but it was clean and well cared for. Curtis felt along the steering column, groping blindly with his hands, until he found a set of metal keys above the visor. The engine came to life.

He jumped into the driver's seat and pumped the gas. It roared. This was a healthy truck. He fumbled for the headlights and found them, lit them up, and saw the open road of the driveway before them. All he had to do was back into the field, load up the flat bed, and drive as fast as they could to the border.

There could be some awkward questions at the border. He was a federal agent, but his credentials were somewhere in Mexico. He had a flat run to the border and a story ready to go when he got there. A phone call announcing that he was coming wouldn't hurt. He wouldn't be the first man to lose his passport in Mexico.

What he needed first was to leave this place. They could sort out the details on the road. They needed rope. They needed a tarp, or, as Virgil suggested, a heavy blanket.

"And something sharp. A machete," suggested Virgil.

Curtis had looked at the bandage on his head and wondered if he were planning to carve up Colon. He imagined a hand in a plastic bag as a souvenir when Virgil seemed to read his mind.

"To cut the goddamn rope," he said.

A rope. A tarp. A blade. He climbed out the truck and walked to the back of the barn and suddenly drew his gun.

"Virgil!" he screamed.

He brought his gun up, sights to his eyes, and screamed again for Virgil, no longer caring who might hear him. He heard Virgil's footsteps come to a halt behind him.

"Jesus," he said.

In the barn by a set of stairs lay the body of a man whose throat had been cut. The body was that of a man about forty. He had a ghastly wound on his neck, and his eyes stared into the ceiling. He was a plain man and not prosperous. His clothes were well used but sturdy. He had a good pair of boots. A long hunter's knife was on his belt, still in the holster, where it had done him no good. Virgil touched his wrist and examined his hands.

"A working man," he said quietly.

There was an inherent honesty on this man's face, thought Curtis.

Virgil kicked a bag at his feet. It was a dark green backpack, stuffed with belongings. There was a small satchel near that, and further still, by the other side of the truck, he found shotgun in a carrying case with a strap. Curtis opened the bag. Food, neatly wrapped in napkins, some in cans, both full and empty. Socks. He found clothing. It was too small for a man. It was a child's clothing.

"What in the name of God went on at this place?" Curtis muttered.

"We need to leave," said Virgil. The way he said it made Curtis believe that he would get into the truck and drive whether he was in it or not.

Strauss hated to admit it, but he needed the help. He was trying to tell Ordo to head north fast and double back, but Ordo was barely listening. He was busy giving orders to the Russian.

Strauss felt Guillermo by his side.

"You're working with them, aren't you?"

"For the moment, I have to."

"These kids are no good."

Strauss looked at the Russian and his passionless face.

"No," he said. "They are not."

"Look at this," said Guillermo.

He was holding an old green canvas bag with dust clinging to it. It was worn, and its straps hung loose. Guillermo pulled it open. Strauss smiled.

"Where did you get that?"

"Juarez. Years ago. I never got rid of it."

"Why not?"

Guillermo shrugged as if he knew and didn't want to say.

"May I?" he asked.

Strauss took an Uzi submachine gun from the bag and examined it carefully. Strauss felt the familiar heft of the weapon.

"Let me come with you," Guillermo said.

"Why?" Strauss asked disdainfully.

"Look at this place," he said.

Strauss slid the gun back into the bag. He walked away from Guillermo without saying yes and without saying no. Guillermo fastened the old green bag shut. Then he followed.

They loaded the coolers onto the bed of the pick-up truck. Neither one of them said a word as they did it.

They had backed up right to the front door. The coolers slid on to the bed. After the first few, it became clear that they would run out of room very quickly. Curtis did the math with his eyes. They were not leaving any coolers behind.

He had found a big blue tarp, dirty and dusty, and spread easily. There had been plenty of rope. He had also taken the small satchel from the ground. It was full of shotgun shells. There was an old compass too, and a greasy plastic bag stuffed with matches. He grabbed the shotgun as well.

Virgil was standing beside the truck in the view of the headlights. He watched as Curtis tied off the end of the ropes to the bed.

"We need water," he said.

"I know."

"Are we out of time?"

Curtis heard a gunshot. It was a loud, crisp pop. He watched Virgil's eyes widen, then his hand slapped his belly. Virgil slapped it.

"What the fuck?" he said.

Curtis pushed him, and another shot sounded. They heard glass break over their heads. Virgil stumbled and fell lightly onto his back. He landed and looked to his stomach, then they rolled to cover behind the truck.

He heard another shot and put his head down. He saw Virgil, on his knees now, crouched behind the tire. Another shot went into the night. They heard the bullet bouncing inside the engine.

Virgil had positioned himself behind the engine. Curtis found himself at the bed. He had cover from twenty million dollars.

"Can you see him?" Curtis asked. He was whispering.

Virgil was looking at his hand. Even in the moonlight, Curtis could see the blood.

"How bad?" he asked, hearing a shot and then metal being struck.

He could see blood soaking into Virgil's shirt. It was the left side of his abdomen. He thought about what organs were on his left side. His mind was blank.

"We can't stay here," said Virgil. He looked again. He started to pull the shirt away and winced. "I can move," he said. "But I can't run."

Curtis looked at the injury. It wasn't good, but it wasn't that bad either. He wasn't going to bleed out in the field. He could function.

"I'm going to run to the trees. Shoot as I'm running. Reload when I get there. Keep him busy while I'm gone."

He thought for a moment that Virgil would argue, that he would offer a better plan. Instead, Virgil studied the blood on his hand, and then looked painfully at the wound on his belly.

Virgil nodded. He wiped his hand on his pants and left a red smear. He took his gun out of his holster and nodded again.

Curtis stood and heard a shot as he did. He ignored it. He thought he felt the sensation of the bullet flying past his face. He brought his gun up and fired. He fired three times and ran.

He was ten feet from the truck and heard no more shots when the subtle sense of panic emerged. What if Virgil couldn't shoot? What if Virgil had just been shot? He saw the dark tree line emerge before him, growing bigger and bigger. He felt the acid rise in his chest. All the sniper had to do was land one decent shot to slow him or take him off his feet. He'd never crawl to the trees.

The night exploded behind him. He heard it and accelerated as if he were in the blast wave. He felt his feet stomp through the uneven ground, with grass nipping at his shins, and with each shot he pushed hard until he was surrounded by brush and felt thin branches scratching his cheeks. He slid to his stomach as the last shot sounded.

The shots from Virgil were so much louder and more powerful than the shots coming at them. It hadn't occurred to him before. He had no time to reflect on why, and he began to crawl. He knew where the shots were coming from now.

The shots had come from the barn. There was a window on the second floor. That was where the shooter was.

As he ran along the side of the barn with his gun in both hands stretched out before him, it occurred to him with perfect clarity. The sniper was shooting at Virgil specifically. Curtis had fired, just a few rounds to push his head down, and then run into the open. The sniper had hit Virgil. He had almost hit him again. He was skilled. There was no way he hadn't seen Curtis sprint to the trees. He had to know he was out there. He hadn't turned toward him. Curtis watched the flashes, and the more he ran, the longer they were. They were pointed toward Virgil.

He entered the dark barn quickly, hooking into the room, moving away from the door. He remembered being told to do that, to never stand in any entrance. He moved through the open space where the truck had been, could see the dead man's body, and looked into the staircase at the end.

He heard another shot. His body constricted. The shot was from upstairs. No one was shooting at him.

He stared into the open space at the top of the stairs. He told himself not to look at the body. The threat was above. The dead man lay on the floor, his limbs loose, blood no longer pouring out of him, but still all over the ground. His eyes were closed. Curtis thought they had been open.

The stairs were just a frame and the steps. They were narrow and rose sharply. Curtis put down one foot and pressed. He listened. He was waiting for the telltale creak. When he pressed with his whole foot and stepped up with all his weight, he braced himself for the loudest creak of all time. It didn't come. The stairs were solid.

Another shot was fired. By now, his ears and body had become accustomed to the gunshots. He heard it distinctly after the round. Metal on metal, a latch closing. He knew immediately what it was and knew immediately why the shots were timed. The shooter had a bolt action rifle.

Slowly, Curtis peaked over the rise into the second floor. It was dark. There were shadows and dark forms. He could make out nothing. The window loomed large. He thought it had been dark outside, but now, it seemed to blaze light. He realized how exposed he was. He realized that if the sniper had any idea that he was coming, then this was the moment he was waiting for, and Curtis had served himself up to be executed. He clenched and waited. It didn't come.

The shot came for someone else. It came for Virgil. In the flash of the muzzle, Curtis saw a man lying prone, peering over his rifle, his head barely exposed. He was right there, and his back was to Curtis.

He should have shot him, Curtis thought, as he bounded over the top of the staircase. He had a gun full of bullets and even with his eyes closed, some of them would have hit. It was too late. He thought it had to do with seeing the sniper's face, or the sniper seeing his before he died.

He heard the slide of metal as the sniper worked the bolt. His feet were no longer silent, and the sniper turned just in time to see Curtis in the air, the bolt of the rifle open and useless. Curtis landed on top of him, ready to kill him, planning to do it, and brought his gun right into the sniper's face.

The front sight of the gun was right under the sniper's nose. It touched slightly. Curtis' finger was on the trigger. If he pulled it, he knew a bullet was going to travel into the sniper's face, through his brain, and come out the back of his skull.

He was glad he didn't.

The sniper let go of the bolt. He raised his hand, palm up, fingers loose, in the universal sign of surrender. He let go of the rifle with his other hand. It dropped out of sight, through the window and into the darkness below.

It was a boy. He was a child of twelve or thirteen at most. He was thin and Mexican. His skin was brown, and his eyes were red. Curtis remembered the face of the man on the floor below, and he saw that face in this boy. He knew immediately and without having to ask that the man had been this boy's father.

Curtis had no idea what to say. There was no reason to ask why. He knew why. He just didn't know what to do next. He sat up. He motioned with his gun, and the boy sat up too. He remembered Virgil then, who had been firing in this direction very recently.

"I got him!" he shouted.

"Is he dead?"

"No. I got him alive."

Curtis didn't take his eyes off the boy. This boy had just shot Virgil. Curtis had no idea what condition Virgil was in, or how badly he was wounded. When he heard the truck slowly rumbling through the field, Curtis stood and pointed where he wanted the boy to go. He pointed with the gun. The boy spoke no English as near as he could tell, but he was fluent in this language. He was small and scared. There was no fat on him.

As the boy took the stairs, Curtis finally examined where he was. It was a loft above the barn. The walls were the roof, with its bolts and nails exposed. There were two bedrolls and no furniture. A few items of clothing were stacked neatly on the deck. A camping bag hung from the ceiling. Hunting gear was arranged on the floor by an empty pack. He took to the stairs, and as he did, he noticed a few books. It was clear, even in the dark, that the boy and his father lived here.

Virgil didn't look good. He was standing straight, but had his hand to his side. The bleeding appeared to have subsided, but there was a large red stain across his shirt. He was pale. Curtis sat the boy down before him.

Curtis could see Virgil's face. Virgil understood what had happened.

"Jesus Christ," said Virgil, seeing it too. "Look at his eyes. He thinks we did it!"

There was a growing visible rage in the boy. Tears were flowing, but not just of sadness. Anger was flowing out of him.

"Tell him it wasn't us," Virgil pleaded.

Curtis hadn't slept in days. "I don't know how," he said, searching for the words. He couldn't find them. He couldn't locate the denials. Even a simple phrase, such as we did not do this, escaped him.

They didn't have time to wait.

"What do you want to do with him?" Virgil asked.

"We're not going to kill him," he said.

"I wasn't suggesting it."

"Some things need to be said aloud."

"Should we take him with us? Drop him off on the road?"

"Like in the desert?"

"I don't know."

"I'm not leaving him in the desert."

"We can't leave him here."

"I need you to tell him something for me."

Curtis looked at the boy. He had no idea what they were saying, but it was clear the two strangers were discussing his fate. That alone should have scared him.

"Tell him I didn't kill his father."

"I don't know if I can."

"Try."

Curtis' mind had been erased at some point of all the Spanish he ever thought he knew. Still, he tried to piece it together.

"El hombre," he said, pointing at Virgil. "No muerte tu padre."

The boy's eyes raged. There was a fire in him. It did no good, and they could both see it. Virgil grabbed him by the collar and lifted him to his feet, dragging him from the barn. The boy swung and hit Virgil right in the place where he'd been shot. Virgil cried out but didn't let go. When they were out of the barn and under the moon, Virgil spun him around and looked at the boy face to face.

"Listen to me. I don't know if you can understand me, but remember these words. I did not kill your father. I am sorry he is dead."

"Sorry," said the boy.

Virgil took his gun out. He didn't point it, but held it in his hand. Then he pointed to the field.

Curtis knew what he meant. "Vamanos," said Curtis, but he said it flatly. There was no threat in his words. The boy turned and looked and then looked back at Virgil. Then he walked, slowly, sulking, looking over his shoulder, until Virgil shouted, "Run!" and fired into the ground. The boy's walk exploded into a sprint. Within seconds, he was lost in the night.

Virgil looked tired. He was starting to look sick as well.

"How far to the border?" he asked.

Chapter Eleven

Curtis – Nuevo Leon, MX

The clouds were moving in heavy, and there was just a piece of the moon left. Tiny wet dots glistened on the road. Curtis tied the rope where it had come loose. He looked at the wet spots and remembered that he was in Mexico.

He ran his hand under the car and brought it back. It was dark and wet. Not soaked, but there was fluid down there. The truck was leaking. He thought of the bullet he had heard bouncing aimlessly around the engine.

He opened the door to the truck and saw Virgil. He was leaking fluid too. He'd been examining himself in the dark, and now that the interior light was on, he looked guilty.

"I think I'm okay," he said.

His face was soaked with sweat, and his skin was shades lighter than healthy. He thought the bleeding had slowed, but now there was blood in the truck and on the seat.

The police radio chirped. It came in waves. When they got on the road, there was a flurry of conversation, tense, demanding, and too quick to follow. Then it was more or less quiet. Curtis hit the gas and rejoined the highway heading north just as the rain drops began to fall.

"One of the driest places on the continent, and it has to start raining while we're here," said Curtis. Virgil didn't reply, and that made it worse. That was when Curtis knew how much pain he was really in.

They were on Highway 85, the big road that had taken them here. It was the big road taking them home. It should have been the busiest, though at this hour, there were few other cars on the road. They had hoped to blend into the traffic. They hadn't planned for this.

"Who do you think killed that man?" Virgil asked.

Curtis remembered the machete on the bureau.

"Colon killed him," replied Curtis.

"Did he know who Colon was?"

Curtis thought it was a good question. He thought about it. The rain began to strike harder.

"No," he finally decided. "He was just some poor guy. Colon figured he had seen or might have seen what had happened that night, and figured there was no reason to risk him telling someone. I think that's all there was to it."

"Why didn't he kill the boy?"

Curtis pictured himself with his gun to the boy's head. He pictured Virgil being shot.

"Maybe he just hadn't had the chance," said Curtis. "Or the boy might not have been that easy to kill."

"I imagined someone else," said Virgil.

"Who?"

"I imagined a fancy pants drug dealer living in the lap of luxury."

"He was once."

"But he was a vicious bastard."

"He was that too," Curtis agreed.

"What did you see in that guy?" Virgil asked with a laugh. It was a laugh that tried to make light. It didn't succeed. But Curtis didn't even have to think about his answer.

"He was the best at what he did," he answered. "He was the best, and he went to great lengths to make sure no one knew it. Can you imagine the discipline?"

When Virgil didn't answer, Curtis looked over at him. Virgil was looking at the bullet hole in his side.

Eduardo looked into the shack. He felt rage building as he saw the trap door thrown open and the cellar exposed.

It was gone.

"Here," said Strauss without excitement.

Eduardo burst into the field where he found Strauss in a squat. He expected another hole, different, deeper than the first, which had been meant to mislead. Strauss pointed to something that glimmered. It was yellow metal. He thought of gold.

"Brass," said Strauss.

It was a tiny cylinder. It looked altogether worthless.

"It's the cartridge from a bullet. There are more of them. There are more in the loft above the barn."

"What does that tell us?" Eduardo asked.

"They didn't leave without a fight."

"Does it tell us where they are now?"

Strauss kept looking.

"It might," he said.

Eduardo walked away. Strauss looked to Guillermo. Guillermo shrugged.

"What do you see?" he asked.

Strauss pointed into the grass. Guillermo squatted with him. Eduardo watched silently.

"Blood," said Guillermo.

"Someone was hurt. My guess, it is one of the Americans."

"Why?"

"They came here for something," he said, pointing to the tracks. "They got it. Then someone tried to stop them."

"Should we see the dead man in the house?"

"Eventually."

"Who is he?" asked Guillermo.

Strauss looked at the bloody grass at his feet, then at the shack behind him.

"A man whose luck ran out," said Strauss.

When Virgil awoke, a man was speaking Spanish in the truck with them. Virgil looked in the small cabin and saw only the two of them. When the man spoke again, his voice was harsh and broken. He realized it was the police radio.

Curtis had it in the center console and had cranked the volume all the way. The signal was touch and go, but at the moment, it was clear.

"What's he saying?"

"They have a road block on highway thirty five. Another highway too."

"Are we going to run into it?" Virgil asked.

"No. The roadblocks are way to the east. They're on the shortest routes out of the country. Just like we said."

"So we're okay?"

Curtis looked at the dark mass that spread over Virgil's shirt. It was no longer moving.

"We're going to be fine."

But when he looked up, his eyes met Virgil's, who knew he had been examined.

"I should get a new shirt before we get to the border."

"You think a new shirt will do it?"

"I can make it. We'll get a doctor when we're home."

"What will we say?"

"Anything. We'll say anything. Just not the truth."

"I've been thinking about the border," said Curtis.

"What have you been thinking?"

"That we have enough to worry about just getting you over it."

"I'll be fine."

"I don't know anymore."

"We're not leaving the money."

"No one said we were."

Virgil started pressing at his stomach. He made a sound like it hurt.

"What were we going to do with the money in the first plan?" Virgil asked. His breath was short. A cargo truck passed in the opposite lane. In the light, his face was wet.

"Originally? We had three million dollars. You can hide three million dollars. Look in the back. We have ten cases with two million each. I'm an IRS agent with no credentials, and I'm going to try to cross the border with a cop from Boston who has a bullet in him. Telling me you'll be fine is one thing. Being capable of being fine is another."

"I'm sorry," said Virgil.

"It's not your fault."

"The kid picked me."

"What's that?"

"He knew his father was dead. He saw the two of us. But he decided I was the one who killed him. He had a chance to kill you, and instead, he kept shooting at me."

Curtis knew that Virgil was right.

"Why?" Virgil asked.

"I guess you just look like a killer," Curtis said.

Virgil laughed, and then he cried out in pain.

Strauss was behind the wheel with his phone in his hand when he glimpsed movement to his right. Eduardo was closer, but hadn't seen it. Guillermo was in the back and looked like a tourist.

Strauss strode off toward the barn. As he walked, he remembered what he had seen at the top of the stairs. He stopped at the edge of the barn door.

"Come out," called Strauss. "I saw you run inside."

"Who is it?" Guillermo asked. Strauss could see that Guillermo had reached into his sack. Strauss leveled his hand to calm him. He did not want any guns.

"You can come out," Strauss said again. He listened. He listened for creaking in the ceiling above him. He listened for the sound of a body dropping from the second floor. He listened for the sound of a metal bolt sliding a bullet into the barrel.

"If I wanted to hurt you, I would burn down the barn. Come out now. I only want to know what happened here."

Slowly, a foot emerged from the top of the staircase, moving with unimaginable caution. Finally, the boy was in sight. He held a small rifle. The body on the ground lay between them.

The boy was a mixture of terror and anger. At once, he was a boy with a weapon who wanted to kill every one of them, while at the same time, he was a boy who desperately needed help. His eyes kept falling to the man on the ground.

"Is that your father?" Strauss asked.

"He's dead," said the boy. That was his way of saying yes.

Strauss noticed the rifle was inching its way into the air.

"I need you to lower that," he said.

"I am not putting it down," said the boy.

"I am not asking you to," said Strauss.

It was lowered, and Strauss stepped into the barn. When he saw the boy in focus, he could see his face was streaked with tears, though his lips didn't tremble, and his hands were steady. He thought of the men behind him.

Strauss heard a car traveling down the driveway. It was traveling fast and coming for them. He hoped it was Ordo and the Russian. He hoped Guillermo looked. Strauss didn't take his eyes off of the boy.

"Who killed your father?" he asked.

"A white man," he said.

"Tell me about him."

The boy shrugged.

"Was he alone?"

"No. There were two men."

"What were they wearing?"

"The one who killed my father had a dark shirt and blue jeans."

"And the other?"

"A crazy yellow shirt. And he wore glasses."

"Were they hurt?"

"Yes," he said.

"What the fuck is this?" he heard Ordo shout from behind them.

"I shot him," said the boy.

Strauss felt his attention being drawn in two directions. Ordo was demanding to know who the boy was. The Russian carefully stayed by the door of the car. Strauss thought that the Russian was no fool.

"Which one did you shoot?"

"Shoot who?" Ordo asked.

"I shot the one who killed my father."

"Was he wearing glasses, or was he the other?"

"The other."

"Is he dead?"

"No."

"Where was he hurt?"

The boy pointed to his side, just above his hip.

"You did this?"

The boy nodded.

"With that rifle?"

He nodded again.

"Was he able to walk away?"

"Yes."

"Who is this kid?" Ordo demanded.

"This boy did what you have not. He shot one of our Americans."

"I would have shot him dead. Where are they now?"

The boy did not know.

"So what good is he?"

Strauss shrugged, and Ordo walked to the BMW.

"What were they driving?" Strauss asked.

"My father's truck."

Strauss looked around himself. He could feel the impatience burning off the other men. He looked back at the boy.

"What are you going to do now?" he asked.

"I am going to bury him."

Strauss was afraid that the boy would ask him for help. He was afraid because he would have to say no. At first glance, the boy appeared frail and small. He wasn't though. Strauss could see that too. He could see that this boy would never ask for help.

"Get in the back of my truck," said Strauss.

The boy refused to move.

"We are going to find the men who killed your father."

The boy ran into the Navigator. He sat with his rifle butt down and with the barrel to the sky.

"What are you doing?" Eduardo demanded. As they began to speak in private, Ordo joined them.

"I'm bringing the boy."

"What for?"

"Because I want to."

"Are you a fag?" Ordo asked.

Strauss sighed.

"That boy has seen us," said Eduardo. "He has seen me."

"So he has," agreed Strauss.

"Call that boy over here," Ordo said.

"No."

"Call him."

"He stays where he is."

"He's seen all of us. We're not letting him go."

"I'll take responsibility for him."

"It will be like this," said Ordo. "Call him over here. Smile at him. Tell him you have a special job for him. I'll have my Russian shoot him in the back of the head. He won't even know it happened."

"How many men are you bringing here?" Strauss asked.

"I forget."

"However many there are, not one of them knows what the Americans look like. Not one of them can identify them. This boy has seen them. This boy has proven that he can put a bullet in a man. He survived a gunfight with two trained American law men. All I've seen from you is scary tattoos and a lot of talk."

There was no more greasy smile. It was replaced with greasy anger. Part of Strauss enjoyed embarrassing the proud young fool, but memories flooded his head, and he immediately turned course.

"After you kill the Americans, I'll let the boy shoot their remains. That way, he is as guilty as the rest of us." He looked at the boy, sitting in the back of his truck. There was nothing childlike about this boy.

"When this is done," said Strauss, "I will deal with him myself."

"You look awful," said Curtis.

He was sweating, and his color had changed to gray. Virgil had crossed a line.

"Tell them I'm drunk."

"Drunk people don't bleed."

"They do if they got in a fight. We'll make up a story when we get there. Tell them we were mountain climbing."

"I can't climb a mountain," said Curtis.

"We were climbing a mountain and we were jumped by a gang that said they were federales. They said to give them our guns and our money. When we didn't, they shot us. We fought back, and we got away. We got to our car and we drove all goddamn night because we were afraid they really were corrupt federales and we'd be framed for murder. We drove straight to the border to plead our case to honest lawmen. How's that?"

"We have to get rid of the money," said Curtis.

"How is the story?"

"It's fine. We can't pull up to the border with twenty million dollars cash and you with an extra hole in your body and no explanation for the money. They'll take it on the spot and they'll never give it back."

"Is it worth dying for?" Virgil asked.

Curtis saw what he was asking. He wasn't asking if Curtis would die for this money. He was asking if Curtis would let him die for this money. It wasn't the question that bothered Curtis. It was his own hesitation.

"No," he finally said.

"Look out!" Virgil screamed.

They crashed.

His ribs hurt, and the world was fractured before him. Then Curtis sat back in his seat and breathed. The windshield was cracked from top to bottom in two places. Rain still pounded the roof, and from the crack closest to Curtis droplets of water began to trickle down the inside of the glass.

Virgil moaned. He was on his side and rolled to his back.

"What did we hit?" he asked.

Curtis peered through the broken glass. Ten feet ahead was a small black beaten sedan. Its rear bumper was on the ground, and the trunk was popped open wide.

"Some shitbox."

"How did you hit it?"

"I don't know. It was just there."

Virgil sat up and looked for himself. He was clutching his side. He looked at the wreck and then looked at his hand. He wiped his hand on his shirt and ran it over the wound again.

"Are you okay?"

"I'm bleeding again."

"Worse than before?"

"I think so."

Curtis could tell he was worried. He wasn't complaining, and he wasn't asking for help. He opened the door.

"Where are you going?" Virgil asked.

"To see what we hit."

"Has anyone come out of the car yet?"

No one had. There was no movement inside the car. Rain pelted the roof and was now pouring into the trunk. No one had come out to stop it.

"You say this car came out of nowhere?" Virgil asked. He stared at the car. Then he scanned the night. There was no visibility.

"It's like it was parked there," said Curtis, starting to realize what Virgil was implying. He took his gun out of the holster and kept it tucked under his shirt. He opened the door and rain hit him in the face. He looked back to see Virgil trying to slide out of the door on his side. It was slow, awkward, and painful.

The flashlight showed an almost empty trunk. There were tools and some pipes. Water was collecting in a puddle. He looked into the backseat. There was a large dark shape. It was just a bag. The front seat was empty as well.

Curtis looked up and down the big road. He could see one hundred feet in either direction. There were no cars or trucks or people moving in this weather. He had been out of the truck for sixty seconds and his shirt and pants were already soaked through. There was no one coming at the moment, but that would change. He walked over to where Virgil was to help him back in the truck.

"We need to be moving," he said.

Virgil reached out and stopped him. A jut of the chin to the side of the road cut him off immediately. A lone figure stood in the dark, watching them.

He stood not ten feet away, covered from the head to knees in a poncho. His hands were invisible. If he had a face, it could not be seen.

Curtis remembered that he had a gun in his hand. He thought about ordering the stranger to show his hands.

"Hola," he said instead.

The poncho nodded ever so slightly.

Beyond the figure in the poncho was rain and darkness. There could have been a hundred men out there waiting for them. They would never know until it was too late. If they were there, then it was already too late.

"Como se llama?" he said.

Rain bounced off the poncho. His feet had sunk into the mud. His hands were invisible.

"Rodrigo," said the man in the poncho.

"Esta tu coche?" Curtis asked.

"Si," said the man very simply. It was his car.

Curtis began to doubt that there were hordes of men in the dark. Curtis asked him what was wrong with his car. He saw the man's eyes fall to the gun.

The man removed his hood and immediately winced as the rain struck his face. He was an exceedingly average middle-aged Mexican. His face was fleshy and heavy. Curtis motioned for him to put the hood back on. Rodrigo nodded.

Curtis moved to put the gun back into the holster. He turned his body, but he saw Rodrigo's eyes move to Virgil's waist. Virgil's big forty-five stuck way out on his belt, his bloody, torn shirt unable to hide it. Rodrigo didn't react.

"El coche no esta funcionando," he said simply. Rodrigo was also exceedingly calm.

"Que esta roto?"

Rodrigo shrugged. He said it never works in the rain.

"What are we going to do with this guy?"

Curtis looked at the car. It was fifteen years old and didn't run when wet. Rust crept up the base and along the wheels. There were no hub caps, and the brand emblems had been stolen long ago.

"We're going to over pay and hope he forgets us," said Curtis.

He walked around to the car side where Rodrigo could not see what he was doing and reached up under the tarp. When he came back, he handed Rodrigo ten one hundred dollar bills. They were wet by the time they changed hands.

A horrid cough sounded and Virgil threw up on the street.

"Terminado?" asked Curtis.

Rodrigo shrugged. His hands had disappeared into his poncho again. "Si," he said in the same simple manner he had said everything else. He seemed to understand Curtis' meaning, and he stepped back to his original perch, ankle deep in the mud.

As Curtis helped Virgil to his feet, he could feel him shaking. He didn't climb into the truck so much as he fell upward into it.

He didn't look at Rodrigo again and started back to his side of the truck. He kept his head down from the rain. Then he stopped. He looked at what Virgil had retched. There was blood in it.

"Senor," he called to Rodrigo. "Donde esta el medico?"

"No hay un medico aqui," Rodrigo replied. There is no doctor here. Curtis asked him where he would go if he were sick.

Juan had only been to the hospital as a police officer, and he had never liked it. He especially hadn't liked it when he was there with Jefe and they were visiting people who had been put there by Jefe. People in the hospital were sometimes given a syringe full of drugs. Juan wondered if he had his own plunger, just as Jefe's face appeared over him. Jefe stared and worked a dip around his mouth until Juan counted four tiny brown drops that left his lips in slow motion, hung in the air, and landed somewhere on his face. He never felt them land.

"I found out something about you, Juan Two Saints."

Juan Two Saints didn't answer.

"Something you didn't want anyone else to know. I had a conversation with your doctor before I came in here. Funny guy, this doctor. He asked me if you were a brawler. I said absolutely not. He's a gentleman, I said. Then this doctor told me a secret. Something you've never told anyone about. He said, underneath your clean, pressed uniform, you have scars and marks and burns all over your body. Some very new. Some very old. Doctor says, this man, he's endured some real punishment.

"Real punishment," Jefe said again. Brown juice worked its way out of his mouth and down his chin. Normally, Jefe would have wiped it away with the back of his hand, but not tonight. Tonight, he just left it there.

Jefe took a few steps and reached out his giant arm. The lights dimmed, and he pulled a curtain behind him.

"Where are they?" Jefe asked. He didn't say who.

Juan realized then that he couldn't speak. So he shrugged. Through the haze of the drugs and the impact of the beating, he didn't know if he was moving enough to be noticed, but he tried.

Jefe noticed.

"Did they say where they were going?"

They didn't.

"What did they take with them? Did they take anything?"

He told his fingers to make the shape of a gun.

"Did they take anything else?"

He thought about it. He thought about lying. He also thought about the look on Jefe's face and that brown juice drying on his chin and the curtain pulled tight and keeping them out of view. He knew Jefe. Jefe already knew.

"Radio," he said. It was a whisper.

"They got your radio? What do you suppose they're going to do with that?"

It wasn't a real question. Sit in a car with a man night after night, and you'll learn his inflections. Juan shrugged, because it was faster.

"I misjudged you. Now, I don't know what happened in those cells. But I do know this: those boys aren't leaving Mexico. And while they are here, they might have plenty of talking to do, and some of it might be about you."

Jefe sniffed. It was a huge, fluid, phlegmatic readjustment. It should have gagged him.

"It goes without saying that any conversations these two boys have are going to be persuasive."

Juan Two Saints whispered. He was trying to shout. He wanted Jefe to know. The whisper was all he had. Jefe bent over him and held close to his mouth, stinking of sweat and onions and smoke and chew.

"What was that?" he said. "Say it again." He sounded almost gentle.

"I told them to run," Juan said as loud as he could.

"You did?" Jefe whispered back.

209

Juan nodded. At least he thought he did.

"Do you think they listened?" Jefe asked, trying his hardest to sound like a co-conspirator.

Juan moved his head. Jefe imitated him. Then Jefe stopped and began shaking.

"They didn't," he said, still in a whisper, still terribly close. "Here is how they repaid your kindness. They went back to that ranch out in the country, and they shot the hell out of it. Then they chopped up two people and left them there. But you want to know the best part?"

Juan did want to know. Even though one of his eyes was swollen shut, Jefe could see it plain in the one that wasn't.

"After they killed everyone, your amigos took something out of the ground. Something that had been buried and hidden that no one was supposed to know about."

"What was it?" Juan croaked. He said it suddenly and it hurt.

"That's what I want to know, Juan Two Saints."

"I don't know."

"Why did you let them out?"

Juan didn't answer.

"What did they promise you?"

"Nothing."

"Why were you at the station?"

Juan opened his mouth, and even that hurt. Nothing that came out of it would make either of them feel any better. He remembered the plunger and wondered if he had one.

"We stopped by your house," Jefe said.

His thoughts raced to Jefe in the desert stopping cars after midnight.

"Your family is very worried about you."

He should have killed Jefe. He should have shot him in the face one morning and been done with it.

"Know what I told them?"

He found his arm. It was useless. Jefe was still close. He was still whispering. He was still vile. Juan began flapping his hand open and shut, trying to hold on to whatever he could.

"I said, Don't worry, Senora. We think they stole a radio, and we're using it to make them think we have all the other roads closed, when in fact, we're driving them right up 85, into the desert. We've already got men at the border waiting to take them. They're trapped. And you know what she said, this nice girl of yours? She said to me, Good, Jefe. I hope you kill them."

Jefe snorted. He cleared his throat.

"Now that's my kind of woman," said Jefe.

Through the rain and mud and dark, Curtis was surprised to find the old stone wall where he had been told it would be. He had run out of Spanish, and in the groggy haze of sleeplessness and the realization that Virgil might be dying, his capability of locating words in his mind came to an end.

They pieced it together in single bits, one off ramp, and one street at a time, until Curtis found himself driving on a long dark road that had only been paved once, Virgil sleeping beside him, and convinced that he was lost in the rain in Mexico until the old stone wall rose up before him. He damn near drove into it.

Rodrigo had pointed, though Curtis still knew left from right, and he gestured, waving with his arms like a third base coach, that Curtis should keep driving.

"Arbol," said Rodrigo.

It was obvious that Curtis had no Spanish left in him. Rodrigo stretched out his arms and stood on his toes, cranked his neck to the side, and drew wide his fingers.

"Arbol," he said.

They found the old dead tree just where he said it would be. It had two long branches and not one leaf. Curtis turned right.

Before them was a ranch house. It was only one floor, and the windows were dark. There was a squat barn behind them that led out to a field.

"Listen to me. I think this is a vet. It's not as good as a doctor, but it will have to do. We'll get you fixed up and we'll get back on the road."

He waited for a reaction, but none came. Virgil was unconscious.

He stepped out of the truck into the rain and looked at the dark house. He thought of his broken Spanish and pantomimed directions. Like a doctor, he had said. He thought about who could be inside this house.

Curtis took off his glasses, folded them, and put them in the pocket of his yellow shirt. He opened the truck and pulled out the shotgun. It was the double barrel that they found on the floor of the barn. He popped it open, put a slug in each chamber, and closed it up again.

He pulled Virgil out and felt his weight land on him. Curtis took one last look at the tarp covered pile of money and started the slow walk to the porch.

He saw a tiny shovel, a pail filling with rain water, and a little wagon, painted red, white, and green, only large enough for a child.

When they stood on the porch under the overhang, finally out of the rain, Curtis breathed, turned the shotgun in his hand, and used the butt to loudly knock on the door.

He gave it a moment, and then knocked again. This time, he heard the sounds of the house. There was the soft creaking of wood and bare feet on floors. He saw a dull glow in the windows, and a light went on in the back of the house. He heard metal touch metal from inside the door. A woman's face appeared.

It was a stern and suspicious face that opened the door, and opened it just a crack. Her hair was cut short and from what he could see, her build was not feminine. She wore a long nightgown that went to her shins. He came back to her face. There was anger in it. But he saw intelligence too. If this woman were some kind of doctor, she would be educated. He took a chance.

"Do you speak English?" he asked.

Virgil grunted in his ear and said yes. Curtis ignored him. The woman did too. He said it again, this time with less patience.

"Little," she said. She had an accent, but not a heavy one. From one word, he could tell she spoke English just fine.

"Are you a doctor?"

She began to say no, but he saw the lie on her face, and she knew that he saw it. They hadn't come here by accident.

"I cannot help you," she said.

"My friend needs help," Curtis said.

"I will call the police," she said, and with that, she began to close the door. Curtis pushed the shotgun into the door jam so it could not close. He could see one of her eyes.

"No, you won't," he said.

They stared at one another. Curtis was soaking wet from head to toe, unshaven, his hair matted to his head, and he hadn't slept in two days. His t-shirt was brown with blood and his nose rumpled under his skin. His glasses, which normally made him look bookish, were safely tucked away in his pocket. He imagined that he looked like a dangerous man.

His mind was finished with Spanish, but he sank back into his memory and found an old speech from a drunken Marc Virgil. It was one he'd often repeated, because it was exciting, and because it was so completely foreign to the life Curtis had actually lived. He also remembered the little car in the yard. He pushed the door open just enough to see her whole face.

"Listen to me," Curtis began. "My friend needs help, and he needs it now. You can help him. Once you do, we will leave. I'm not a psychopath. I'm not a sex offender. I have no desire to hurt you or your children, but so help me God, if you don't do exactly what I say, I will visit evil on this family tonight."

He liked to think that thunder might strike in the distance after he said it, but all he heard was the rain coming down on the roof. He liked to think that he would have felt like a hero as the door opened and the stern woman stepped back, allowing him to enter, but all he felt was disgust.

Chapter Twelve

Curtis – Nuevo Leon, MX

The stern woman had hard hands. They were rough and callous with nails worn short. Her knuckles protruded, and the backs of her hands were tan. Curtis thought he would have been proud to have hands such as these.

He caught her looking at him. Her eyes were as hard as her hands.

"Let go of him," Senora Uto said. It was an order. She said it again, impatiently, when he didn't move fast enough. "You are in my way."

He pulled his hands away from Virgil's arms. The flesh burned white where his grip had been, though only for a second.

"He has lost too much blood," she said aloud, though not to Curtis.

"Is he going to die?"

She didn't answer. She moved to the side with a sharp cutting tool in her hand. Curtis had never seen this tool before and didn't know what it was. It was too small for a garden tool, and too large for a medical instrument. But this wasn't a place to ask questions.

At first, while Virgil screamed, he watched her hands and her tools carefully. He watched her wash, dipping her hands into the water, watched her scrub and come to the table prepared. He watched to see what went into her pockets. He watched her roll up her sleeves. Angry as she was, he came to understand that she just wanted them gone. There was no doubt why.

As he had carried Virgil through the house, the stern woman had pointed to the rear and told him to follow. They had passed an open bedroom. In the doorway, a lovely young woman with long dark hair had held two scared children. They were both little girls. They didn't stop. She had led them into a clean room with a long table. There was old Mexican art on the wall. There was dust on the floor and on the table. Virgil had screamed when they put him down. Virgil had kicked and tried to twist away as the woman cleaned and studied the wound in his side. Eventually, he had stopped kicking, and finally, he had passed out from the pain.

He looked at the young woman and her girls, and he doubted that this woman was their grandmother. In fact, it seemed very clear that she was not.

Soon her hands were soaked in blood past her wrist. The screaming hadn't affected her. What had affected her was the shotgun, on the counter behind him and unloaded, and the words he had said. They were words he now regretted, and words he was glad he had said. She peered into Virgil's side.

"There is light bleeding inside of him," she said.

"Light?"

She wiped a finger on her apron, inspected it, and pushed it into the hole in Virgil's side. His neck twitched slightly. She pulled it out again. It was red. She held it up for him.

"If it were dark, he would be in trouble."

"Can you take the bullet out?"

"I cannot even see it."

"What does that mean?"

"It means I do not know where it is inside of him."

"If I move him, will it kill him?"

"It could," she said.

When she spoke, she spoke in a flat voice. There was neither passion nor anger. She spoke of Virgil as if he were butchered meat.

"That bullet needs to come out eventually, doesn't it?"

"Yes," she said.

"How soon does it need to come out?"

"That depends," she said.

He wanted to scream himself, but Virgil had screamed enough for the both of them. That, and he knew it wouldn't help, and would only scare the girls more. Scared people were unpredictable. Virgil was unconscious. Everyone was calm now. Everyone except him.

"What do you want me to do with him?" she asked impatiently.

"I want your advice," he said.

"My advice is that you should leave Mexico immediately."

He could see the young woman in the kitchen. She was sitting in a chair, holding the girls, and watching them closely. He had heard her whispering to the girls. He didn't understand what she said. It wasn't

Spanish, but she certainly looked Mexican. Curtis wondered who she was and how she came to be here.

"Stitch him up. Get him ready to travel," Curtis replied. He said it like an order. He looked at the stern, defiant woman. He thought about saying please and decided not to.

Senora Uto had stitched up the hole in his side with a thick thread that didn't look like what they used in emergency rooms back home. She had taken a paste from a small pot and smeared it over his wounds. It was grayish green and earthy looking. It didn't smell good either, but she touched it with her bare hands and didn't seem to mind. He asked her what it was.

"It is difficult to say in English," she replied. She had stitched the wound over his eye, and smeared some of the paste over that as well. On Virgil, it looked like war paint.

They eyed him closely, and it did not matter if he tried to put them at ease. The woman in the other room didn't seem to understand any of what was happening. She was very Indian looking, he thought, though her daughters were less so. When he turned back, he found the stern woman staring at him with a renewed rage.

Curtis picked up the shotgun and loaded it. He felt the tension rise as he touched the gun. As a veterinarian, there should have been some guns here, but he saw none. He held it by the barrel with his weak hand, hoping to disarm the women. It didn't.

He roused Virgil, who came to fast, but not all the way. When Curtis realized that full and clear consciousness wasn't going to come for him, he gave up trying, and pulled Virgil to his feet. He pulled and tugged and shoved him back into his torn and bloodied shirt. He carried him to the car in much the same way that they arrived: slowly, stumbling, and in pain.

Curtis heard Virgil whispering.

"Agua," Curtis said to Senora Uto. She didn't budge.

"Could we have water please? For the road."

It was clear that she didn't want to give them anything, but she wanted them gone. They stood on the porch for a moment. The sun was coming up in the east. The two Americans watched the pretty woman and her girls. They looked back silently. Senora Uto reappeared with two handled jugs.

"Thank you," said Curtis.

She said nothing back.

Strauss hit the brakes hard. Eduardo was wearing a seatbelt. Guillermo rushed forward in his seat. The boy was in the back was in the tail gunner position, and he turned to see what had happened. There were no cars on the road North. He turned around to see a vehicle on the side of the road. A man was pushing it.

"What?" said Eduardo.

"Did you see that man pushing the car?"

"Another Mexican in a shit box."

"How many other Mexicans have you seen on the road?"

"Sounds like a stretch," said Eduardo.

"Guillermo?" Strauss asked.

"Follow all leads, even the small ones," Guillermo said.

Strauss hopped out of the truck and walked toward the man who was pushing his car. He had a raincoat on, but the hood was pulled down to his shoulders. He hadn't stopped pushing and only looked up when Strauss approached. He smiled. He had no front teeth.

"Buenos dias, senor," said Strauss.

"Buenos dias," said Rodrigo.

"What's wrong with the car?" Virgil asked in a clear voice. He turned to see his friend sitting up and conscious.

"How do you feel?" Curtis asked.

"I feel like the car sounds," he said.

The clinging and clanging from the engine had grown worse since they left the house of the stern woman. After settling Virgil into the passenger seat, Curtis had peeked under the car. The ground was wet and muddy, but in the morning light, he could see some black fluid puddled below the engine.

"The truck is getting worse. You're getting better."

"It didn't sound this bad when we left Monterrey. Could someone have messed with it?"

"No. The vet who worked on you would have ripped the transmission out with her bare hands, but she was never out of my sight for more than a few seconds."

"Maybe she put a curse on it?"

Curtis laughed.

Virgil began to unfold the map. "Where are we?"

"We're close."

"How long?"

"An hour." It felt great to say it.

"Nice job," said Virgil. He meant it.

"Thanks," said Curtis.

"With me passed out and not yapping in your ear, you've had plenty of time to figure it out," said Virgil. "How are we and the money getting across the border?"

"We're not," said Curtis. "We're driving into Nuevo Laredo, and we're going to rent a storage facility. We're going to leave the money right here. Then we are going to walk over the border and declare ourselves Americans who are lucky to be alive."

"A storage facility?"

"A big building where you rent space by the month to store shit. You lock it up and come back to it later."

"Is it safe?"

"It's safer than driving up to the border with it."

"So we'll come back and get it in a week when I'm healthier."

"No. I'll do it myself. When I get my credentials back, I can come and go as I please. It might take twenty trips, but I'll do it."

Virgil let out a deep breath and pinched his eyes like it hurt.

"There's another problem with this plan. I don't know if you can get past the guards. We'll buy you new clothes. I'll be just a few bodies in front of you. Once I tell them I'm a federal agent, I should fast track."

"And me?"

"Just tell them you're an American. You were robbed. Say nothing more."

"Is that good enough?"

Virgil's eyes were pleading with him. They were begging for reassurance. They wanted someone to be in charge. It was a new role for Curtis.

"It'll have to be," he said.

Strauss looked in the rearview and saw the boy's head and his rifle. Beyond that, he saw two cars approaching fast, kicking up great plumes of dust from the road. He cracked his window, and he could hear their engines. That meant anyone in the house could hear the engines. He put the truck in drive.

The second car meant that more of Ordo's promise of men had been fulfilled. He had regretted calling him at all, but it was a necessary evil. The two Americans had fought their way out of two messes. They would fight a third time. He needed Ordo's men.

A gaudy late model Cadillac with white stencil on the side skidded to a stop in the soft wet ground. The doors opened, and five skinny boys spilled out in the yard. They had gold chains or huge belt buckles and blazing new white sneakers. One of them carried a pistol grip shotgun that looked as if it would knock him over if it ever went off. The Russian walked past calmly, paying them no mind.

"I heard you coming from a half a mile away," Strauss said. "They already know we are here."

The Russian shrugged.

"Ordo said drive fast, so I drive fast," he said. He kept his hands in his pockets.

"What if he told you to go inside and kill everyone in this house?" Strauss asked.

"His dime," he said in English.

Strauss surveyed the property. He saw no vehicles. The house was small, but there could be a car in the back. He doubted it, but he didn't chance it.

"Guillermo," he called. "Watch the back of the house."

Guillermo nodded. "What if they come out?" he asked.

Strauss looked at the bag with the gun slung around Guillermo's neck. "If they are the two Americans, kill them. If they are a bunch of girls with their hands up, tell them to get down on the ground."

"It's been a while," said Guillermo, apologetically.

"It comes back," said Strauss.

Strauss walked toward the house. The ground was still damp, and mud clung to his shoes. By the time he reached the edge of the yard, his shoes were coated. It was impossible not to get dirty.

Strauss stopped and stared at the black puddle in the ground before the steps.

"Boy," he called out.

The boy ran up faster than any of the men would have.

"Was there anything wrong with your father's truck?"

"No," said the boy. "It ran well."

"Did it leak oil?" he asked. He glanced up at the windows as he said it. He knew the Russian was watching.

"No. He would have fixed it."

Strauss studied the frame of the house. It was a good run to the slim tree line. Whoever had been inside when they arrived had not left.

"His truck was here," said the boy.

"How do you know?"

"These tracks," said the boy, pointing at the mud. "Those are his tires."

A z-shaped pattern had dug into the wet ground. It had driven smoothly into the yard and then driven smoothly out.

The front door opened just wide enough for a human being to slide through the opening, and Senora Uto came onto the porch. She closed the door with her hand behind her. She wore work pants, boots, and a long-sleeved shirt.

Ordo started right over to her. He started to call out.

"Send them out," he said loudly. "It will be better for you."

The woman didn't budge and didn't look like she would. Ordo was still walking toward her. He was smiling and clenching his fists.

"Ordo," Strauss said. "Do you mind if I try first?"

He walked back to his truck and reached inside, bringing out an object and keeping it close to his leg. He could see the woman clearly. She was dressed like a man and cut her hair like a man. She had a face that declared her intelligence and her backbone. Still, he watched her brace herself as he came to the bottom of the stairs. Then, he stopped.

"Good morning, senora," said Strauss.

He could see she was searching him with her eyes. He held an object in his right hand that she couldn't see. He showed it to her.

"Good morning," she said back when she saw Strauss holding a thermos.

"I am out of coffee," he said.

Senora Uto looked at the men gathered in front of her house, and especially the men who displayed guns.

"You," she said, meaning all of them, "came here for coffee?"

"No," said Strauss. "I am the only one who wants coffee. And I would like to have a quiet conversation."

As she led him into the house, she slipped behind him and locked the door. Strauss made a note to watch this quick little woman very carefully. He saw a much younger woman, dressed to travel, with two little girls clutching her skirt. There were bags behind them.

"Senora," he said with a nod.

"This way," came the stern response from the stern woman, who clearly did not want them speaking.

The coffee was brewed quickly and without conversation. Strauss sat at the table and waited patiently. She kept her back to him as much as possible, but he still had the feeling that he was being observed.

"Senora, I don't mean to pry into your business, but I noticed your luggage in the hall. Are you going away?"

Her reply was short and sharp.

"I knew you were coming."

"I am sorry for being here, and I am sorry for bringing these men. This is not how I like to do things."

"How do you like to do things?" she asked. She was mocking him.

"Quietly," he said.

She turned with the pot in her hand. He could see the steam rising from the lid. He slid forward the thermos and let her pour. She had rough, worn hands. They were not hands for making coffee.

"Thank you," he said.

"Is that all?" she asked, knowing it wasn't.

"No, senora. I believe you already know why I am here. I am looking for two men. They are Americans, and one or both of them is injured. I know they were here. I am not angry with you for helping them. If two dangerous men come to your home and make demands, threatening to hurt the people you care about, then you do what they ask so they will leave you in peace."

He thought of the man whose son had been kidnapped and mutilated. He thought of how much that man had to say. Most people did, he had found. He waited for this woman to find her moment.

"He had no right to speak to me the way he did, not in my home," said Senora Uto.

"Why do you suppose they came to you?" he asked.

"Because some fool told them I was a doctor."

Strauss looked at the artwork on the walls. There was an ancient looking bird done with a red clay-like paint and another of the sun with a man's face blended into the rays of heat. The paintings didn't look old, but they had an old feel to them.

"Were they both injured, or just one of them?"

"Just one. The other was running his mouth."

Strauss glanced down the hallway toward the young mother and her girls. The mother was terrified, and it was contagious. The girls were crying and hiding. Strauss screwed the lid back onto his thermos.

"What sort of treatment did he receive?"

"I stitched his wounds. He still has a bullet inside of him."

"Where is it?"

"His abdomen and his groin."

"That must be very painful."

"I hope it is."

"Can he walk? Is he conscious?"

"He needed help."

"Which way did they go?" he asked.

"North," she said.

"And how long ago did they leave?"

She looked through the window.

"The sun was just coming up when they left."

"Thank you, senora," said Strauss as he stood.

"He had a tattoo," said Senora Uto.

"Which one? Which man had a tattoo?"

"The man who had been shot. It was on his arm."

"What was it of? Had you seen it before?"

"Never. But I would know it again. It was a bird standing on the earth."

Strauss looked at the two pictures on the wall. Then he looked at the young woman in the next room. He had scarcely noticed how lovely she was.

"Thank you, senora," said Strauss. "I apologize for intruding upon your family. If I meet these men, I will give them your regards."

"There is no need. He is not going very far," said the stern woman.

Strauss could feel the heat of the coffee trying to burn through the metal of the thermos. He nodded goodbye and showed himself out.

"How much of a lead do they have?" Eduardo asked. His nervous energy had returned. Strauss noticed that the Russian was now close by and listening.

Strauss looked at the sky. Then he looked at his watch.

"Two hours at most," he said. He looked to the Russian for a reaction. There was none.

"Do you have more men coming?" he asked the Russian. Ordo answered for him.

"All of my men are coming."

"Tell them to stay on the main roads. And to just be themselves."

"What does that mean?"

"Tell them they don't need to hide. Make sure they are seen."

"Why?" asked Eduardo.

"I want to keep them on the back roads if I can."

He took his map from the truck. He looked to the Russian.

"How fast can you get to here?" Strauss said, pointing. The Russian shrugged.

"Are you talking to me or to him?" Ordo demanded.

"I'm talking to whoever is driving," said Strauss, though it wasn't true. He tapped the map with his finger.

"Get up there as fast as you can. Take your men. We'll block them in."

They all made for their cars, and the engines burst loudly to life.

"Does Jefe have them already?" Eduardo asked. He was nervous but sincere.

"I don't think so. I sent them away for a reason. If we are lucky, we will find them pushing an old broken pickup truck down the road."

"Then we'll have to deal with them ourselves."

"I thought you wanted to?" Strauss asked.

Eduardo swallowed.

"I don't want to enter a gunfight that we might not win in a landslide."

Strauss pointed at the boy. He was already in the back, his rifle pointed to the sky.

"This is why I brought him," he said.

Guillermo approached. No one had told him to come out, but he had heard the engines and seen the mud flying. He looked disturbed.

"What is this place?" he asked.

"This is Senora Uto's home."

"Do you know her?"

"No."

"There were dogs back there. They were all dead. They were stacked up on one another. The dogs had been cut open."

Strauss patted him on the shoulder and told him to get back in the truck. Guillermo put the machine gun away and did as he was told.

"Who is she?" Eduardo asked when no one else was listening.

"She is Nahautl," replied Strauss.

"What in the world is that?" asked Eduardo.

"The Nahautl were the people who were here before you and me."

Strauss saw that the stern woman had emerged from the house. The door was open behind her. She was motionless and watching. He opened the thermos and poured the coffee on to the ground.

"Clever old woman," he said.

***

224

The engine took long slow belabored breaths, choking on its own smoke. The truck heaved along, and no matter how hard Curtis pressed, it wasn't going faster.

When there was so much smoke pouring from the engine that Curtis couldn't see the road, he pulled over and opened the hood. It burned his fingers. The engine smelled of rubber and chemicals.

Virgil hobbled along from his side.

"Look at that," he said.

Two tiny holes stood out clear in the thin metal, and with daylight poured through them. Virgil tried to trace with his finger where they had ended up in the engine. He was quickly lost.

"They bounce around," said Curtis.

"Yeah," said Virgil. "I noticed."

They were in clear flat country. There were short tough trees and some grass, but no hills. Otherwise, the ground was brown and burnt with flecks of green here and there.

"How much more can we get out of this truck?" Virgil asked.

"Five minutes? An hour? Do you want to break down in the middle of Laredo with this on the back?"

Curtis stepped backward, but he stared down the damaged truck. He stared at it like an enemy, as if this truck were responsible for everything that had gone wrong.

"You want to explain to a bunch of starving Mexicans waiting to cross the border why we have twenty million in cash and why it's ours and not theirs? You want to explain to the cops up there that we understand them, but those other cops, the crooked ones who tried to kill us in Monterrey, those guys are no good? By the way, let us walk over the border. Can you help us carry some of these coolers? Don't look inside.

"And another thing. Don't ask why my nose is broken, or why my friend here looks like he got shot. Or why we don't have any passports. It's no big deal. Trust me. I'm an accountant with the IRS."

For a moment, Virgil thought he was going to see an explosion, the hood being slammed, the grill being kicked, glass being broken. He expected the events of the last two days had finally taken their toll. Instead, Curtis walked off the road and into the grass. He walked out until the grass covered his knees. He walked until his pants blended with the ground below, and the only thing that stood out in the landscape was his ridiculous yellow shirt with the tiny hula girls all over it.

Virgil had expected screaming and yelling, but the further Curtis walked, the more sure he became that it wasn't coming. He looked up and down the road. It was empty, but it wouldn't stay that way. He held his hands over his eyes, suspecting that Curtis's mind was working.

"Curtis," he shouted. "What do you say? Let's drive this thing until it dies. Then we'll push this truck into a storage container in Laredo."

"No," said Curtis, and from his tone, that was the end of the discussion. "I have a better idea."

Curtis reached for the seatbelt, but his hand grasped at air. He turned and found nothing where a seatbelt would have been.

"Are you sure about this?" Virgil asked again.

"This is the best idea I've ever had."

He put the car in drive and slowly drove up the road. The truck heaved and the engine stuttered, but it slow-rolled as needed. Curtis carefully inched it from the paving to the sand, and back on to the paving and onto the wrong side of the road. From there, he stared down the embankment.

It wasn't much of an embankment. It was really a small rise. The average jeep would have sailed over it, but the average jeep wasn't leaking oil and didn't have a bullet lost in its engine.

He just had to clear the embankment.

"Hundreds of miles of flat landscape and I have to find the one spot that rises up," he said to himself.

He turned on the radio. It was static, then more static, until he finally found music. It was loud Mexican country music. He turned the volume up as high as it would go.

He hit the gas. It was ten or fifteen feet before the engine seemed to catch, and another twenty before he felt acceleration. Virgil was growing larger and larger. Finally, with speed, he veered over the middle lane, turned as sharply as he dared, then drove straight up the embankment and into the air. All four wheels left the ground.

The coolers full of money became weightless for a second. He watched them lift in the rear view. It was for the faintest of moments. Then, it all crashed down to earth.

The back window cracked loudly in his ear. There was an awful screeching of metal that sounded like the chassis breaking in half. The whole truck surged upward on the bounce, but the truck kept rolling.

Virgil chased it through the desert. He hopped along on one foot, calling for Curtis to stop.

"Are you okay?"

"Did the money stay in?"

"Yeah, it's all still there. Will you stop?"

"No. I'm afraid it won't start again."

"I can't get in if you don't."

There was a smoke from the engine, and they drove no more than seven miles an hour. The load behind them had shifted, and it was moving. The ropes squealed, trying to hold it in place. The truck didn't so much drive as it moved in a sustained bounce. He saw the dust flying from the edge of the road. "Are you sure you're okay?" Virgil asked again.

"I've never been better," Curtis said.

The road was behind them, and the highway was even further than that. They drove west into the desert.

The engine died whimpering, huffing and puffing and pushing until it had nothing left. The land was silent, save for a light breeze. Virgil closing the door of the truck sounded like a racket.

"This is a good place to start," said Curtis.

"No more storage containers?" Virgil asked, knowing the answer. Curtis shook his head.

The knots had been expertly tied. They were frustratingly tight.

"Were you a sailor in another life?" Virgil asked.

"No. Why?"

"These knots are brutal. How did you learn to do this?"

He thought of his father. He'd also had a boat. He had taught Curtis to how to handle rope as a kid.

"Didn't you tell me once that you hated boats?"

"I did. I do. I spent time on the rope so I wouldn't have to go out to sea."

The tarp came down loudly. They laid it out flat and finally saw the stacks of coolers for the first time in the light. They stood higher than the truck. Wind caught the tarp and blew it into the air.

They held it down with rocks at the four corners. Virgil climbed painfully and slowly onto the truck. He took a cooler from the top and opened it. It was stacked with money. They were clean, fresh, virgin bills, in the sun for the first time. Virgil walked to the edge of the tailgate and dumped it all on the ground.

"How much money was that?"

"Don't think about it," Curtis said.

The stack, when it was done, was unruly, spilling out of the corners and refusing to stay in one place. Just when he thought he had it, one stack would slip out the side, while four or five stacks jumped out the back. Virgil cut holes into the tarp. "Just slips," Curtis said, looking over his shoulder while holding the pile in place. "The tarp has to hold." The ropes that held it to the truck were threaded through, held, and then knotted to form great loops. The loops lay in the sand. Virgil folded the knife and put it back in his pocket. He coughed loudly. Then it was quiet.

"This is what twenty million dollars looks like," said Curtis, looking at the fat, blue, overflowing bundle before them.

"This is what a new life looks like," said Virgil.

They each picked up one of the long loops of rope. Virgil watched Curtis sling it over his head and across his chest. He did the same, except it hurt when he did it.

Virgil leaned into it and pulled. He heard the tarp crumple. He heard Curtis grunt. Then he felt movement, and he realized they were moving forward.

The money was heavier than he ever thought money could be. It was just paper. Paper is the lightest thing in the world, second only to feathers. Anyone can move paper.

"How far do you think we need to drag this?" he asked. He probably asked much too soon.

"As far as we can," said Curtis. "We'll drag it as far as we can until we can find a landmark."

"And when we find a landmark?"

"We bury it," said Curtis.

They pulled further. Virgil felt pain in his side. His head was beginning to throb. He pushed.

"I think I left my shovel at home," he said.

"Me too."

"How are we going to dig this hole?"

"With our hands," said Curtis.

Virgil stopped. He looked at the size of the bundle of money.

"It's going to take forever to dig that hole."

"Do you have someplace to be?"

"Then what?"

"Then we go home. I'll come back in a few weeks and dig it up."

Virgil thought about it. It was like his thoughts were visible.

"Once we bury the money, we're free of it," Curtis said.

"Are you sure?"

"I am. They're looking for two men in a car heading North with a ton of cash. We'll bury the money, and that won't be us."

"What about the trail?"

"This is drug money. There is no trail."

"Look," said Virgil. He pointed. The truck was still visible, though a ways off in the distance. It wasn't hard to find. The ground was still soft from the rain. He could see their footsteps. He could also see the wide, flat path the money had laid in the dirt. It started at the truck and led right to where they stood. It might as well have been an airport runway.

"We don't have much time. What should we do?" Virgil asked.

Curtis leaned into his rope, making it clear that this conversation was over for now.

"Pull," he said.

***

Eduardo had shouted for them to stop because he saw something in the desert. It turned out to be an old trash bag overflowing with food and dirty magazines. He felt ridiculous until Guillermo shouted for them to stop and jumped into the sand.

"What is it?" Eduardo asked.

"It's nothing," said Guillermo, climbing back. "My mistake."

"There is something there. I see it too."

"It is just trash. Let's drive."

It looked familiar, but Eduardo couldn't place it.

"It's a portable toilet," said Strauss. "It's tipped over on its side and blowing around on windy days."

They drove on down the road heading north, or as north as the road would take them. Outside, the temperature climbed, while Strauss turned up the air conditioner in little increments. The colder it was, the easier it was to stay awake. It was miles and miles of brown and green dotted land with little or nothing in between. When the boy shouted out, no one bounded out of the car or climbed onto the roof.

The boy was still in the tail gunner position, facing the back, as the truck slowed. "What do you see?" Strauss asked, but the boy had already rolled out and was running down the road.

Eduardo watched him in the side view mirror. The boy sprinted with passion, carrying the rifle in one hand. He watched as the boy stopped, studied what it was he had seen, and looked to his feet. Then the boy grabbed the rifle with both hands and brought it up to his shoulder.

They were all out of the car and running. The boy was already climbing the embankment. He dropped to his stomach, peering over the rise, gun first. Strauss put his arms up and motioned for them all to get low.

The boy cut a very low profile. Eduardo knew nothing of hunting or surviving in the wild, but even he could see that this boy did. His body loosened and moved in tiny unnoticeable steps, slithering up and over the rise until they could only see feet. Then those were gone too.

"What did he see?" Eduardo asked.

Strauss pointed to the mound of earth. It had been demolished. Something large had crashed into it. There were thick tire tracks in the dirt where it hadn't been churned.

"How do we know it's them?" Eduardo asked.

"Look where you are standing," replied Strauss.

He looked down and saw nothing except his expensive shoes. These shoes were never intended for the desert. Even prolonged periods of direct sunlight were discouraged. He thought about getting his feet into the shade, as if there was any.

When he moved his foot, he saw that he was standing on a wet spot of oil.

He felt the heat on the back of his neck. His clothes were wet. Sweat fell around his head, collected on his brow, and dripped drop by drop on to his glasses until he was effectively blind. He couldn't see Virgil, but he could hear him. He sounded like he was in pain.

He looked back at the load. It was twenty million dollars. How much did twenty million dollars weigh?

"Nothing," he said aloud. "It's the lightest thing in the world."

He had hoped Virgil heard him. They would talk about the money and what they were going to do when they brought it home.

But Virgil said nothing.

Strauss held the glass to his eyes. The desert rose up for him. He scanned, but saw nothing except scorched brown earth and tough green plants.

Strauss walked back to the truck and got the map. He studied it as he walked and didn't especially like what he saw. He didn't dislike it either.

"Can you read a map?" he asked Guillermo.

"I'm from the slums of Juarez," said Guillermo.

"I can," said Eduardo. He came over and squatted, his heel rising out of his loafers. He still wore his jacket.

"You're joking," said Strauss.

"I took a geography course in high school," said Eduardo. "It included a portion on topography."

He pointed at the map. "We are here," he said. The boy had discreetly joined them.

"If they drove off into the desert, where are they most likely to come out?" asked Strauss.

"These are just the marked roads," said Eduardo.

"And?"

"There are bound to be many more, smaller, unmarked roads. We go around," said Eduardo.

Strauss hesitated.

"But what?" asked Eduardo impatiently.

"What if they didn't make it through?"

"What if they did? They'll cruise right through another border station."

Strauss was thinking of oil.

"But what if they broke down? What if they are still out there?" Strauss pointed toward the desert.

"If we follow them and they did then they are gone," said Eduardo.

He was right. Eduardo Mendes was a fast learner. He could read maps, he could give orders, he could act like a spoiled prick, and he could see the angles.

The boy was right behind him, but Strauss hadn't noticed. There was an eagerness to him, but it wasn't childlike. There was no innocence on him.

"What would you be willing to do to find the man who killed your father?" Strauss asked.

"Anything," said the boy.

Strauss looked into the desert.

It was midafternoon when Virgil finally fell. Curtis was on a single-minded track, staring straight ahead, eyes cast to the ground, only occasionally looking up to the horizon. He kept pulling. He dragged the bundle right over Virgil.

Virgil tried to stand, digging himself out from under the money. Curtis pulled him free.

Sand had caked all over Virgil's face. It was even on his eyelids.

Curtis rifled through the bundle for the water. The money was in his way. There was so much of it, and now it was loose. He made Virgil drink. Then he made him put his head back, and he washed some of the dirt from his eyes.

"What are you doing?" Virgil asked suddenly.

"I'm cleaning you up."

"Why?"

"Because you fell."

"Where?"

"Are you okay?"

"I need more water."

Curtis drank some himself. When he was done, he was still thirsty. His eyes stung. He could feel his tongue drying already. He wanted more, but he gave it to Virgil.

"How much more do we have?" Virgil asked, realizing the bottle was empty.

"Not much. We need to be careful."

"How much further?"

"Until we can bury the money?" Curtis asked.

"Until we can stop," said Virgil.

"Drink some more water," said Curtis.

"Why?"

"Because we can't stop."

"I feel sick."

"The sun does that to you."

"It's not just the sun. I've been in the desert. Something is wrong with me."

"Nothing is wrong with you. You're the strongest man I've ever met. Keep walking."

Virgil was leaning on the bundle of money, but Curtis pulled him to his feet. He felt heavy and weighted. Curtis put the loop around him.

"Who told you that woman was a doctor?" Virgil asked.

"Rodrigo."

"Who is Rodrigo?"

"Someone we met."

"Was I there?"

"You were sleeping."

Virgil thought about it and then agreed. That made sense.

"Go that way," Curtis said, pointing. Virgil started his slow walk. Curtis threw the rope around his shoulder and started grinding his way forward.

The load was heavier this time.

The boy didn't need much preparation. He had his pack and he had his rifle. Strauss had given him two bottles of water.

"Do you have food?" Strauss asked.

The boy said yes. He had dried meat in his bag. He wanted to go.

"You need to remember, these are dangerous men. They are the police."

"I know," said the boy.

"They killed more men than your father. They killed the old man at the house. They killed a man in jail. He was an especially dangerous man."

The boy simply nodded.

"If you engage them, you can't let them live. You can't let them get close to you. From a distance, you have the advantage with this rifle. Up close, they will kill you. Skill has nothing to do with it."

The boy's face was the same stoic expression of readiness. If the gravity had sunk in, he didn't show it. This was a serious boy. Strauss went back to the truck.

"We need to be moving," said Eduardo.

"I need to see your phone."

"What for?" asked Eduardo as he handed it to Strauss.

Strauss walked over to the boy and handed him the phone. He lit it up and showed his number to the boy, then gave him the phone.

"If you can kill them or wound them, do it. If you can't, you need to call me. If they kill you, they will get away. Not just from Mexico and from us, but they will get away with killing your father."

The boy took the phone and said nothing. Finally, when he realized that Strauss was done, he turned and walked into the desert, following the trail in the sand.

When he climbed into the truck, Eduardo was annoyed.

"The boy is a danger to all of us," he said. "It might be easier this way."

"Not for him," said Strauss, and he put the truck in drive.

They pushed until dusk, when Curtis realized the sun was going down and they wouldn't see where they were going. He pushed on blindly. The load had shifted as the day wore on, with more and more of the weight falling on Curtis' narrow shoulders. But the money kept moving.

Virgil moved like a zombie. He dragged himself forward, one step at a time. Curtis looked over to him, and his eyes were closed.

"Hey," said Virgil, suddenly, without prompting. His voice was dreamy.

"What?" Curtis asked. He felt the ropes biting into him.

"Remember that time we got that innocent guy killed at that ranch in Monterrey?"

It wasn't getting lighter.

"Yeah. I remember."

"I deserved to get shot."

"No, you didn't. It just happened."

"I killed that guy in Boston too."

"You had to do that."

"Yeah," he said. "That doesn't matter. He's dead. I have to pay for it."

"We didn't kill him."

"We did. As sure as I killed that guy in Boston, I killed him too."

"Stop thinking like that."

"When are we going to stop?"

"When we are safe. When we can bury the money."

"When will that be?"

"We'll find a landmark. Something we'll know. We can find it again. We'll bury the money when we find it."

"Where is it?"

"I don't know. It's nothing but flat desert out here."

"I can't see. Do you still have your flashlight?"

"Yeah."

"I need some light."

Curtis clicked the light on to see Virgil with his hand inside his shirt. He was reaching right where his wound was, right where he had been shot. He took it out and held it up to the light.

There was blood on his fingers.

The boy wanted to run, but he had been taught never to run in the desert. It was too hot. Water was limited. Walk slow. Be patient. Never rush.

So he walked. Strauss and the other men thought he was a tracker. There were two deep sets of footprints that occasionally disappeared under a wide gouge in the earth. The gouge never disappeared. It pushed on and on. Any fool could find it.

They had something with them. The boy didn't know what it was. He had watched them take it out of the old man's shack. His father had told him to avoid the old man. He seemed harmless and hapless. He fiddled about in the yard all day. The boy had listened, but he didn't know why.

Then he'd heard the screams from the big house. His father heard them too. The boy had leaped to the window to see where they had come from, but felt his father's hand on his shoulder, pulling him back. His father shut the window.

"What is that?"

"I don't know," said his father. The boy thought he did know.

"She might need help."

"We will mind our own business." He said it so firmly that the boy laid down on his bedding and shut his eyes. He didn't shut his ears though. Soon, he heard more.

The boy had a question. He waited some time before he asked it.

"You told me one time that if we found someone who had been hurt that we had a duty to help him."

"That was in the mountains."

"Why not here?"

"Because it is different here."

"Why?"

"It just is."

He was twelve then. He was thirteen now. He had tried to tell himself that "it just is" was good enough. There were days in the mountains when it was. There were nights when he heard screams when it wasn't.

He wanted to sprint across the desert and catch up to them. There was the man in the yellow shirt. He had taken him for a fool the first time, and it had almost cost the boy dearly. The other man, the dangerous looking one, was the one the boy sought. He had hit him at least once. He would be slowing them both.

When the sun was low enough that it filled his eyes and he couldn't see anything else, he lay down on the ground until it disappeared. When it was dark, he felt the cold creeping in, so he took off all of his clothes. He opened his pack and dressed in thermals. Then he put on his clothes again, and after that, the rain poncho.

Then he cleaned his gun.

He thought about his father. He loved him desperately. His father had been his whole world. He put his whole world out of his mind.

He focused on the men he was hunting. He'd had the man who had killed his father in his sights. He had shot him and wounded him but not killed him. He knew what he had done wrong. He had been crying.

Never again, thought the boy.

The desert had dried his eyes and dried his pores. He was ready. He slept, though just a little. He wanted to see the sun rise. Today was the day that he would find the man who killed his father.

Chapter Thirteen

Strauss – Nuevo Leon, MX

"We have one of them," said Ordo.

They found them in a field at the end of an unmarked road a quarter mile past a dying gas station. The white and red lamps from their cars were impossible to miss. Four men stood in a field with the light to their backs.

"Take a look," said Ordo. There was a man in the dirt at his feet. He was face down and there was blood on his back, on his shirt, and on his pants. He had been wearing a backpack. It had been opened and rifled through, its contents had been dumped and were now blowing about.

Ordo's men were well armed. One had a shotgun slung over his shoulders. The other wore sunglasses and cradled an AK-47.

"He got the American," Ordo said.

"Roll him," said Strauss.

One of Ordo's men grabbed an arm and turned the body over roughly.

"You've got to be kidding me," said Eduardo.

"Is this one of them?"

The man on the ground had a large ragged hole in his chest. A round had gone through his body and burst out from the other side.

"How old do you think this man is?" Strauss asked Ordo.

"I know how old he is now."

The man on the ground had thin, wispy facial hair. It was a weak attempt at a beard. His hair was blond and tied back into a tiny bun. He wore shorts and layers of shirts. He had hiking boots on his feet. He had a gauge in each of his earlobes.

"Did you hear me say that we were looking for two police officers from America?"

"I told my men to find Americans walking out of the desert."

"They did a great job."

Strauss picked up the backpack and looked at what had been left inside of it. There was blood on the pack. There were two bullet holes on each side. Strauss found a copy of Moby Dick. A bullet had gone through that too. He dropped it.

"So it's not one of them. We keep looking," said Ordo, glancing at Eduardo.

"Look at this, you idiot," said Strauss. He held a small red book in his hand.

"What is that?" Ordo did not reach for it.

"It's a passport. From Holland. He's Dutch. Did you bother to look at what was in the bag?"

"My men don't read so good," said Ordo.

"Or think so good."

Ordo shrugged.

"He ran from them."

"I wonder why."

"What more do you want?" asked Ordo.

"What I want is a man with a little common sense who can follow simple directions," said Strauss. He started toward the car.

"Hey," said a voice from behind them. When Strauss turned, he saw that Ordo's man was no longer cradling his AK. Now it was in his hands.

"Who the fuck do you think you're talking to?" the man asked.

Strauss said nothing back to him.

"You're a cop, right?" the man asked.

He held the rifle loosely, but it was pointed at Strauss's lower body. He made a few slow steps to his right. Behind him, Ordo was enjoying himself.

"Do you know what I don't like about cops?" the man asked. He was moving closer. Strauss didn't answer.

"All my life, I seen cops do things that I do too. Except they put me in jail for it. They give me a beating for it. They look down on me for it."

"I think we're in for a first tonight, boys," said Ordo.

"It's that cops think they're better than everybody else," said the man.

He flipped the sunglasses off of his face and let them rest on his head. The rest of him was still and controlled, but his eyes were pure rage.

"Except you're not," said the man. He was a few feet away and inching closer. He brought the rifle up and used it to cross the distance. When the barrel touched Strauss's belly, he stopped.

"I've never heard a cop beg for his life," called out Ordo.

"You won't tonight either," said Strauss.

He had understood that one day he would die, and for a long time, he had expected he would die badly. He had never imagined the how or the why, because he knew it wouldn't much matter. He braced himself for what he knew was going to be an awful, excruciating blow. He hoped he would bleed fast.

"What do you have to say now?" the man asked.

Strauss racked his memory. He wanted to imagine himself breathing through Dulcinea's hair, with her arms around his neck and a black and white movie playing in the background. He tried to imagine a time when he had been a child and happy.

He watched as the man let his finger slide off the guard and onto the trigger.

"They have three million dollars!" shouted Eduardo.

Strauss blinked. He thought he had been shot. Everyone turned.

"The Americans," continued Eduardo. "They have three million dollars cash. That's what they're running with."

Ordo pushed forward, moving the rifle aside and passing between Strauss and his would-be killer.

"How much did you say?"

"Three million."

"Why didn't you say this before?"

"Would you have told me?"

"I'm the one with all the guns."

"And I'm the one with all the money," said Eduardo.

Strauss himself wasn't sure how Ordo would take that, especially since it had been said in front of his men. The gun was down, but pointing at his left knee. He didn't even know if Guillermo was still out there.

"Wouldn't you rather be the man with the money?"

Ordo's face turned ugly. It turned uglier still when he smiled. His mouth was broad and happy.

"I want to be the man with the guns and the money," he said, and he clapped Eduardo on the shoulder. Strauss felt blood rush through his body.

"I need this man," said Eduardo, motioning to Strauss.

"What for? He is old and hasn't done you much good."

"I need his connections. We have other business together. Let him be. You and I have more important things to do."

Ordo thought about it. Thinking hard seemed to take a physical effort. Lines of stress crisscrossed his face. Ordo looked at Strauss for a long time.

"Let him be," he said. The man lowered his rifle. He did not lower his eyes.

"He knows how close he came," said Ordo.

The Honda and the BMW tore up dirt as they drove out of the field. As Strauss watched the dust drift and settle, he could see the useless legs of the young hiker in the field.

"Thank you, Mister Mendes," he said sincerely.

Eduardo was dusting himself off and straightening his clothes. "I did it for myself," he said. "You're the only civilized man left in Mexico."

It was both more clear and yet much more dark in the desert. The sky was free of pollution, and the light of the moon traveled that much further. Curtis turned just in time to see Virgil projectile vomit into the air.

Virgil dropped to his knees, coughing. When he didn't get up, Curtis pulled him to his feet.

"Do you feel better?" Curtis asked.

"No," said Virgil.

"Know what's good for a queasy stomach?"

"No," said Virgil.

"Walking," Curtis told him. He tried securing the ropes around his friend, but they just fell loose around Virgil.

"Lean into it."

"I am."

He wasn't. He was swaying in place. Virgil laughed. Then he winced, like the laugh hurt. Curtis saw the ropes tighten as his weight took hold. He patted Virgil on the back and told him he was doing a good job. Virgil grunted. The ropes rose high.

Then Virgil fell onto his face.

He was wrapped in the ropes, and as he tried to get up, he became tangled.

"I don't know what happened," said Virgil.

"That's okay," said Curtis. He brushed sand off of him. "Do you think you can walk on your own?"

"No," he said. "I can help."

"I know you can," said Curtis. He picked up the shotgun. He cracked open the breach and took out two shells. He locked it up again. "I need you to carry this. Put your weight on it."

"Like a cane?" said Virgil.

"Like a walking stick," he said. He put it in his hands. Then, Curtis bent and picked up the ropes, all of them, and carefully, one at a time, slung them over his shoulders. The lower reaches of his mind once again began calculating the weight versus the dollar amount and attempting to find a figure. He took a deep breath and pushed.

He went nowhere.

The first step is the hardest, he said to himself. He saw Virgil stagger into the night. He pushed again and felt the money move behind him.

The ropes had torn into the skin on his chest, and Curtis was glad it was dark. He couldn't see it, but he could feel a deep X of raw, burning flesh across his torso.

His back hurt more. His back and his thighs. He stopped to breathe at one point, and his thighs felt like they were exploding. He stretched and squatted, but it worsened. He started pulling again, and the pain was bearable. So he pulled some more.

His feet hurt for a while, but that pain blurred into a dull discomfort. Then they went numb.

What affected him most was the cold. Now that the sun was down, the heat was gone, and the cold had found the wet clothes. It had found the wet skin. The cold reached into his muscles and threatened to enter his bones. So he kept moving.

Curtis didn't know how far he had walked. It was one arduous step at a time, with the brutal weight of the money and the unforgiving flat blandness of the land. He pushed all thoughts from his mind and tried to hypnotize himself. He focused on the sound of his footsteps, and the sound of the fortune being pulled through the sand. It was slow and steady and soft, and one day it would end.

It was his lonely walk through the desert, with an inhuman load trying to break his body. He put his left foot forward. He knew it touched ground. His knees groaned, but he repeated with the other leg. He thought of sitting alone by the fire with a warm whiskey drink in hand.

It hit him. He came to a complete stop and listened. Curtis no longer heard his footsteps. He no longer heard money being dragged. He no longer heard anything.

He couldn't hear Virgil. He looked around and couldn't see him either.

He called and heard no response. He tugged off the ropes and his skin screamed. Curtis felt his thighs tighten, like a giant fist was squeezing them, and it pinched deeper and deeper until he was free of the ropes and calling for Virgil again.

He had the flashlight out and on, but it only shone a short distance. There was no Virgil in sight.

Panic filled his chest. He felt the grip on his thighs return. He shouted Virgil's name as loud as he could. Then he screamed it.

Curtis told himself to stop. When he was calm, he breathed through his nose. This was remarkably clean air. He'd always heeded the warnings of the Mexican water, but it didn't apply to the air. This was good stuff.

Curtis shined the light on his feet. They were planted in the sand. His legs were beginning to shake. He looked a little further in the sand and saw a footprint. Then another. He slowly walked back in the dark, following the long flat seam in the ground from where the bundle had dragged. The bag had erased almost all of his footprints.

He was pulling. He was directly in front of it. Virgil, however, had been walking and stumbling alongside. He had gone almost three hundred feet and had begun to doubt his methods. That was when he wondered if they had been followed. That was when he wondered if maybe something more hadn't happened. How quietly could a man be killed? Very quietly, if he were sick. Even a strong man could be killed quietly if he were sick.

The flashlight strayed a few feet from the track, and at the edge, Curtis spotted a footprint in the sand. There was another a few feet away. Curtis followed them. They wandered through the dark and into the sand, then right up to a pair of shoes with feet in them. Virgil turned slowly and blinked when he saw the light.

"What are you doing?" Curtis asked.

"I was walking," replied Virgil. His tone was spacey and his eyes unfocused. When he spoke, his breath came out in little clouds.

"Where were you going?"

The question seemed to confuse him. He had his eyes closed.

"I see people dancing."

Curtis put his hand to Virgil's forehead. He was burning hot. He smelled bad too. In the cool crisp clean air, there was no hiding.

"You're having a fever dream."

They backtracked to the money with Virgil stumbling alongside. Curtis pulled the ropes over his chest. It hurt putting them on, but what hurt more were Virgil's pleas.

"I don't need this money," he said.

"You're sick."

"I'm not."

Curtis had taken the small bag that carried the ammunition. He hung it on Virgil. He unclipped the strap, hooked it around the ropes, and fastened it again.

"This is a leash," said Virgil.

Curtis gave him the shotgun.

"We need this," he said.

"I know."

"Don't lose it."

"I won't," said Virgil.

Curtis leaned into the ropes. They bit back.

***

His body did what he wanted it to do even if his mind refused.

Curtis ordered his foot to rise. He ordered it to trudge forward. Fresh air now had the weight of water, like sloshing through a muddy river. He ordered the foot to drop. Then came the hard part. The pull.

His mind, however, was running amuck. He had remembered the weight of a dollar bill. It was a tiny fact learned from the IRS, buried under layers of more important stuff, but once it was out, the calculator started. It worked on its own.

Each bill weighed one gram. From there, it was just adding zeros. He couldn't stop himself. He focused on the money. He focused on the heft. He focused on the slow, painstaking movements, because keeping his mind busy kept his body busy. His mind busied itself more and more, stack by stack, case by case, million by million, until a huge number began to materialize in his mind. Suddenly, the big blue bundle of cash that he was dragging through the sand had been struck by the force of gravity. The number, already in the hundreds of pounds, would be that much worse if he realized it.

Curtis noticed the satchel that was tethered to Virgil. It was sinking closer and closer to the ground. Virgil crashed through the ropes and landed in the dirt himself. Curtis felt himself being dragged backward. He ordered his legs to drop out from under him, and he landed on his hands.

"I'm sorry," said Virgil.

"That's okay," said Curtis. "You need to get up." Curtis had the weight of the money and Virgil's weight on his shoulders.

"I know," said Virgil, but he didn't. He just lay where he was.

"You need to get up," Curtis said again when he hadn't moved.

He still didn't move.

"Can you help me?" Virgil asked. It was a pathetic voice.

The ropes came down on him like rails. Virgil was putting all of his weight on them now. His mind calculated the pounds in Virgil's body, even though he told it not to. He added that weight. He felt that weight.

"Get up!" Curtis shouted. It came out of nowhere. How far did sound travel through the desert at night? His voice might have travelled for miles.

Gradually, he saw an arm rise. Then he saw a foot kicking for purchase. Virgil was tangled up in the ropes again. Curtis helped him.

"Why are we walking?"

"Men are after us."

"They're going to kill us," Virgil said. He said it calmly and in a light tone, as if it weren't bad news.

"Not me, they're not," said Curtis. He managed a smile. He strapped himself back into the load. He cleared his mind. He took a breath. He told his body to move.

His body obeyed.

The sun was up, and Curtis looked at where he was. He was in the middle of vast flatness. There was nothing distinguishing about this place. He could dig a hole right now and drop the money and be guaranteed of nothing except never finding it again.

There was one jug left, and only half of the water remained in that. His mind started to calculate, but he stopped it. Whatever it was, it was tiny, and it had to be divided by two. Virgil stumbled, as if his feet had read Curtis' mind. Divided by two, and one of them was dying.

He had pretended through the night that Virgil was only sick. When the sun had risen, Virgil's damaged skin was visible. The wound looked worse. It smelled worse. Its brightness was even brighter, and its swollenness more pronounced. The wound didn't look angry. It was positively furious and waiting to explode.

"When can we bury the money and go home?" Virgil asked.

Curtis agreed that it was a good question. He found the satchel that tethered Virgil to the money. One pocket had the shotgun shells. One had the matches. He found the pocket with the binoculars.

He scanned the horizon in front of them. This was where they were headed. All they needed was one point of distinction. A building would do. An electrical tower would work. A mailbox on the side of the road with a number on it.

Instead, all he saw were miles and miles of nothing. He had to cover that distance when he was moving inches by the minute.

He looked to either side, hoping for something different. He turned around and did the same. He saw where they had been.

What he saw made his jaw drop.

The boy remembered the advice that Strauss had given. In close, they will kill you.

He dropped.

He had almost run up on them. There was still distance between them. A handgun was too far to hurt him, but when he had frozen, his vision had frozen as well. He saw a massive blue bag. It had caused the trench. He saw the one in the bright shirt and he saw the one in the dark shirt. The one in the dark shirt had killed his father. The one in the dark shirt was holding a long gun.

Curtis tackled Virgil and held him down. Suddenly, Virgil came alive and wanted to struggle. He shouted, and Curtis covered his mouth. "There's a sniper out there."

"A sniper?" Virgil asked.

"Someone followed us."

"Who?"

"I don't know," said Curtis, but he did. He knew very well. He knew as soon as he saw him in the binoculars.

"It's the boy," he said.

"What boy?" asked a completely perplexed Virgil.

"The boy from the barn."

He could see from his face that Virgil still hadn't made the connection His face was too red to be pale, but it was a weak pink. His lips were blistering. There was an unhealthy sheen to his skin.

"The boy who thinks you killed his father," said Curtis. When he saw Virgil's eyes dilate, he knew his words had registered.

"What's he doing?" Virgil asked.

"He's coming for us," said Curtis.

***

When the boy finally poked his head up, he did so very, very slowly, and with that long gun in the forefront of his mind. He thought of what his father had taught him. He moved slower than any human being ever should. He moved like the plants grew, so gradually that not even an animal would notice. He moved slower than a cloud, and with less sound.

When he could see, the men were gone. The blue bag was still there. That meant the men were there too. The trench was a few feet away from him. No man would carry a weight like that through the desert and then leave it without a fight.

He had seen the Americans, and they had seen him. They wouldn't be hiding if they hadn't.

The killer had a long gun. That was all he saw. If it were a shotgun, he had nothing to fear at this range. If it wasn't a shotgun, that meant a rifle. He had a twenty-two. That was as small as rifles went. They were still out of his range. If they had a larger caliber, he might not be out of theirs.

He tilted the rifle so the rear sights were closer to his mouth. He pursed his lips and pointed down, leaving his eyes on the desert. He blew any dust out of the aperture.

His eyes were dry. His sights were clean. He was ready.

Curtis leaned out again, very cautiously. It was a gamble. The boy was alone. They might be able to wait him out, wear him down, force his impatience. A boy wouldn't be good at waiting. A boy would make a mistake.

"I'm sorry about your father," he heard Virgil calling.

Curtis turned to see Virgil on his feet. He was walking back where they had come, right toward the boy. He walked past the money and into the firing line.

The American stood up and began to walk toward him. The boy put a round in the chamber.

He wore the same black shirt. He wore the same blue jeans. He looked dirty. He was shouting in English. He held his arms out wide.

Stop. Count to three. He ignored the voice in his head. Before him, his father's killer kept walking. The boy climbed to his knees and brought the rifle to his eyes. He saw him clearly. He watched him turn to a dark blur as he disappeared behind the front sight.

Count to three.

He remembered the long gun they had. He remembered there was another man. He remembered the range, and the caliber. He felt his finger touch the trigger.

His eye caught movement. He ordered himself not to shoot. He lowered the sight just in time to see the American drop to the ground. The boy dropped down too.

Curtis held him down, and this time, for good. Virgil kept calling to the boy.

"What are you doing?" Curtis hissed. He had Virgil in a headlock and was trying to pull him backward, behind the money, to the one spot with cover in the entire desert.

"I'm trying to say I'm sorry," Virgil said.

"Pull it together!" Curtis hissed.

Virgil tried to get loose. He thrashed and kicked dust into the air. It was in their faces and their eyes. It was in their mouths.

"I'm sorry!" Virgil shouted.

"It doesn't matter!" Curtis screamed. "Some things you can't apologize for!"

The boy let out a breath as gravity hit him. His belly was on the dirt again where it belonged.

It was a trap. Strauss had told him to beware of these men and he hadn't listened. They had lured him. One had presented himself as a target, and, like a fool, he had taken the bait. When he stood to take the shot, he had given away his position. He had stood when he couldn't see the other man: the skinny one with the glasses and the stupid yellow shirt.

He thought of the lessons he had been taught. Caution and control had been drilled into him. His father hated thrill seekers and risk takers. He watched the field in front of him. He could see the top of the blue bag. He could not see the Americans.

The water bottle was in Virgil's hands. It was almost empty. Curtis peeked at the area around them. There was no sign of the boy, but he was out there. This boy was patient.

Curtis rested his head on the blue tarp. It felt good under his head. It was softer than he had expected. The miles of being dragged and shifted had softened the load. He closed his eyes for the tiniest of seconds.

"Virgil, can you hear me?" he asked.

"Yeah."

"I mean, can you really hear me?" He looked to see which version of the man he knew was with him. Would it be the sick and dazed Marc Virgil, who had barely a notion of what was at stake, or an alert but damaged Marc Virgil, who was a proven survivor?

"We need to talk about that boy out there."

"You should have killed him when you had the chance," Virgil said. He laughed a little.

"Maybe I should have. But I didn't. Now he's here."

"Where do you think he is?"

"I don't know. He was a hundred or so yards that way. He moved."

"How do you know?"

"I think he can hunt. I think he knows what he's doing."

"The hole in my stomach agrees with you."

"If he has his chance, he's going to put more holes in you. You understand that, right?"

"Of course." The sick and hazy Virgil was gone, at least for now.

"He can wait. We can't. We're dehydrated now. We're going to get worse. We haven't slept in days. Eventually, I'm going to close my eyes for a minute and I won't wake up. And you're not well. You're not yourself."

"I know. I'm sorry."

"It's not your fault. You didn't get shot on purpose."

Curtis broke open the shotgun, blew on the action, and slid in two shells.

"What do you think we should do?" asked Virgil. He was well enough to be aware that there was a point to this conversation. He was well enough to see that whatever was on Curtis' mind wasn't good.

"I think we should split up," Curtis said.

Stop. Count to three. It usually worked. But when the man who killed his father stood for the second time that day, the words turned to mist, and blood shot throughout his body.

He saw him, dark t-shirt, the shotgun in hand, climb to his feet. He had his back to the boy. The boy had no problem with shooting him in the back. That was a kill. He saw the American look over his shoulder once, quickly, and then lean. The blue bag moved again, and he realized that the American was pulling it.

The bag was heavy, and the man walked slowly. If he had been closer, he might have risked a shot. He was glad he was not closer. The other one was still in hiding.

He brought the rifle up and set a bead on him. He found him in the rear sight and brought the front sight to bear on him. He desperately wanted to do it.

He realized the second man was on his feet and walking away from him. He was walking away from his partner. His ridiculous yellow shirt hung loose as he headed to the north.

This was a trick. They couldn't find him, and they couldn't wait him out, so they would force his hand. He asked himself which one they wanted him to follow, but he only had to ask once. He knew who he would follow.

The fool in the yellow shirt walked quickly. Soon, he was almost out of sight. That meant nothing. He had found their tracks effortlessly. It would take nothing to double back and hunt him. He would have to constantly look behind himself.

Meanwhile, the man who had killed his father trudged on, loudly, obviously, and painfully slow. The boy knew it was a trap, but he didn't care. He could live by the rules.

Keep one just out of range. Watch for the other. Beware the long gun.

The boy still hadn't moved. He didn't need to. It would take nothing to follow this man. He watched the American as he grew smaller and darker and further away, hunched over from the weight.

The first time this man stopped or let his guard down, he was dead.

When Curtis stood, he expected to be shot in the back of the head. It wasn't fear. It was a certainty, and one he accepted. When Curtis got to his feet, he paused, figuring that this was it. Every muscle in his body tightened and strained. The hard part was releasing when it never came. There was nothing left to do but walk.

Curtis walked. Virgil walked. They both walked slowly. The sun was high and hot. They needed more water to recover from yesterday, not counting today, and today was just hitting its stride. Today might kill them.

He felt overwhelmingly guilty. It grew worse when he saw Virgil, though soon, he knew, he wouldn't see him at all. He tried to avert his eyes. He could see Virgil struggling. He knew Virgil needed help. Instead, he walked.

Virgil was going to die in this desert. Curtis knew that. He also understood that there was no use in accepting it or lying around getting sicker waiting for it to happen. Waiting for the sun or the heat to wear them down, or for the boy to surprise them with a gunshot to the face. Hiding behind that huge pile of money, they were dying.

Walking off in different directions, they had a chance. One of them might live. Waiting where they were, they both would die.

Virgil had been in his right mind when they parted. His handshake was weak, where it never had been before.

"I'll see you in America," Virgil said. He meant it to sound confident, but it sounded like a question. Virgil was too tired and too beaten to smile, so Curtis did it for him.

"Of course you will," Curtis said. "Where else would I be?"

He hoped it made sense to Virgil. He hoped that everything he said had made sense to Virgil, that it had sunk in, or that he had been in a healthy enough place to retain it.

"Which way are you going?" Curtis asked. Virgil pointed north. "That way," he said.

"In the morning, keep the sun on your right. In the afternoon, keep the sun on your left."

Curtis thought of saying good luck, but didn't. He pulled Virgil's dark shirt over his head. It had been run through with sweat and blood and sickness. Virgil had on Curtis' yellow Hawaiian shirt, with little hula girls all over it. He couldn't work the buttons and he was exposed.

Curtis picked up the ropes and slung them over his shoulders and tried not to think of the bullet that he would never hear. He lashed the ropes tight and held the shotgun like a cane. He had a doubt, but he erased it. He was dressed as Virgil, so he must think as Virgil. Virgil never second guessed himself.

The first step from stand still was the toughest, and he said a tiny prayer as he pushed.

Please let the boy believe it.

Chapter Fourteen

Virgil – Nuevo Leon, MX

Virgil woke up and realized that he had fallen asleep. He didn't know for how long. The sun was still out and about. It wasn't a new day.

He had the empty water bottle with him. His tongue was huge, to the point where he tried to spit it out of his mouth. He felt like he had eaten sand.

He walked. The sun was on his left. He would find someone soon. He thought he used to know the Spanish word for water. He could ask for water in Spanish and he could call someone an asshole in Spanish. He hoped he would remember the word if he met a person on the road. It would be terrible if he just couldn't remember the word for water. It would be worse if he accidentally called them assholes. He laughed.

Virgil took inventory of himself. His skin tingled. From time to time, there would be an intense itch, and he had to scratch it. There was no negotiating with the itch. It would be impossible to ignore. It had to be scratched right then and hard. After the scratch, there was a fleeting moment of relief. Then the pain brought him to his knees.

It felt like he had torn his skin apart. The pain wasn't just on the surface, but it burrowed into his face, layer after layer ripping and screaming. Virgil squeezed his eyes shut. He cradled his head and laid his arms in the dirt until it subsided. When it was over, he knew he should have had tears in his eyes, but his eyes were dry.

He searched himself. He had a gun. He left that alone. His pockets were full. He pulled out a handful of money. There was a paper strap around the middle to hold it together. One stack fell to the ground. He reached in and found more, and then more in the other pocket. He had one in the shirt pocket too.

He tried to do the math, but his head was pounding. Math was Curtis' job. He had a memory of Curtis telling him to lie still and pulling bills out of the big blue tarp. He didn't remember Curtis giving him money. He hadn't felt it, but he was feeling less and less from his body. He had an itch, though, on his forehead. He scratched it and the pain brought him to his knees.

He woke up and found the money all around him. He found a stack of bills in his underwear. He didn't know why it was in his underwear, but he put it back, in case it served a purpose he couldn't remember. He found another one in his sock. He left that where it was. He still had his gun, so he got to his feet, found the sun on his right, and walked. He walked, and the sun sank lower and the sky grew dark and still, he kept walking.

He walked and realized that he had no idea where to keep the moon. The sun was to his right in the morning and his left in the afternoon. Curtis made no mention of the moon. He thought about lying down, but he knew that lying down meant never getting up. So he walked.

At midnight, his left leg stopped working. At first, it wouldn't complete a full gait. Then it was half a gait. Before long, he was dragging it.

Virgil thought about the marines. They had taken leave in Hawaii and he ended up in Kauai, floating peacefully at the base of a waterfall surrounded by jungle. There had been water everywhere then.

When the sun came up, he had the presence of mind to be horrified by how his skin looked. It was thin and papery. It was coming off in flakes. The skin below it looked worse. This was no sunburn, he thought. He was glad the sun was up again. He didn't know why it was on his left when it was supposed to be on his right in the morning, so he turned around and kept walking.

His head pounded, but he found that it was almost tolerable if he set his foot down in the same rhythm as the throb of pain. That consolidated the hurt. He dragged on like that, his right leg barely helping, his left knee aching, and a strange sound coming from his hip.

One time, in the marines, he had eaten a bunny's eyeball. They had marched them up a mountain and when they said they would pick them up, after they had rationed and eaten all their food, the instructors said, "See you next week." So they found their own food and he found a bunny. They'd made him eat the eye ball cold.

He had walked off that mountain. He was skinny and he was hungry, but he was alive. Lost in the desert, Virgil made himself walk a little further.

The coughing slowed him. He didn't know when it started, but he had been thinking of the waterfall in Kauai and watching a bunny when he realized he was on his knees, coughing uncontrollably. Virgil couldn't breathe. His lungs wouldn't accept any air. He sank further to the ground, his eyes bulging from his head, until a tiny pinprick of air filtered into his chest. More air followed. When he could, he breathed like a greedy man. He put his head down, and when he lifted it, the sun was in the sky. He stood up and walked.

He discovered trash. At first, it was just wrappers. Dirty wisps of paper with rotten food flittered about him. There was a bag on the ground. It had been torn open by animals or people.

Virgil tried to bend but couldn't. Instead, he walked into the bag until more and more fell from it and all of the trash was on the desert floor.

Virgil looked at what he had. He saw greasy bags and empty cans and pieces of drywall. There was broken glass, wood shards, and Mexican shingles. Virgil was moving on when he saw a familiar flash of red.

The very sight filled him with hope. It felt like a warm hug that had been lost in time and finally delivered when he needed it most.

There in the pile, coated in white dust, with the red metal flare standing out from the rest, stood a twelve ounce can of Coca-Cola.

His back blazed with pain as he bent and grabbed for it. He could feel it swirling around at the bottom. Virgil put it to his lips and poured. He couldn't taste anything. He just felt the desperate overwhelming sense of relief as the mouthful of delicious wetness flooded into him. It was one mouthful. It was warm and it was all sugar. It was wonderful.

He passed a burned-out shell of a car. He found a house and stumbled through the front door. It was just walls. There was no roof. Virgil walked right on through to the other side. The sun was sinking again. He saw a pile of burnt tires. He wondered what they were doing this far out in the desert. The thought confused him so much that he barely noticed the two Mexicans.

They sat on milk crates. There was a soot covered barrel in front of them, but no fire. He remembered that he knew two words in Spanish, but he couldn't remember what they were.

"Assholes," said Virgil as friendly as he could manage, and meaning nothing by it. The two said nothing. They stared back, dumbfounded. Virgil stumbled by without stopping.

Virgil's lungs were tight. They felt shriveled. He took a breath and the same vicious dry cough attacked him. There was no way to stop it. It not only squeezed his throat, but forced a finger into it. It could have been his tongue. Virgil couldn't see. He was gagging. He fell to his knees. He felt his stomach contract. He felt his eyes go dark.

He came to with his forehead in the dirt. Virgil didn't know how long he had been gone. He knew the next fit would kill him. He knew staying here would kill him. He picked his head up and saw Jefe standing before him, leaning against a large black truck.

"Someone called the police," claimed Jefe. "Said a deranged white man just walked out of the desert. Thought I'd come by, see if it was anyone I knew."

Virgil didn't answer. He didn't know what to make of the big man. He put his good foot forward, slowly, held it in place with both hands, and then leaned into it. He pulled himself to his feet.

"How in the world are you still alive?" Jefe asked.

"I don't know," said Virgil.

The big man smiled. Then he spit. He had so much fluid in his body that he could let big gushing mouthfuls fall to the floor and seep into the sand. Virgil marveled.

"You look thirsty," said Jefe, in his lazy way. "Let me get you some water."

He turned to reach into the truck.

"Do you have any Coca-Cola?" Virgil asked.

"Coca-Cola?" asked a bemused Jefe. "I think I do."

Jefe came back with a huge Styrofoam cup with a straw poking out of the top of it. Virgil could hear the ice sloshing around inside. Jefe gently put the straw to his lips.

"Easy now," he said. "Go slow."

Virgil did. He had a mouthful and let it ease into his system. He felt the sweet liquid wet his mouth and throat with nothing more than a trickle. He could actually feel it make its way to his stomach. He felt his dry insides tingle with life. It felt like every cell in his body had lifted its head. He thought he could drink this forever when he heard the loud slurping sound coming from the cup.

"All gone," said Jefe. He tried to take the cup away, but Virgil began to raise his arms to take it from him.

"Slow down now," Jefe said. He took an ice cube from the cup and slipped it into Virgil's mouth. "Let it melt," he said.

The feeling was amazing. Virgil felt so good that he believed he could lay down and die. Jefe was laughing.

"What?" Virgil asked.

"How long have you gone without water?"

"A couple days, I think."

"Where were you?"

"By the blue bundle with Curtis. When the boy found us."

"What boy?" Jefe demanded.

"The boy who has been trying to kill me."

"Why would some boy want to kill you?"

"He thinks I killed his father."

"What is this boy's name?"

"Never got it."

"Where is he now?"

"Following Curtis."

"I doubt that."

"Why?"

"Do you want more ice?"

Virgil realized that the cube in his mouth had melted into a sliver. He very much wanted more ice.

"Then I ask the questions," said Jefe, fishing more out of the cup. "Where did this boy come from?"

"He just found us."

"Wandering around in the desert?"

"Yeah."

"And he hunted you down?"

"He shot me."

"Where?"

Virgil pulled his shirt up to his neck.

"Jesus God," said Jefe. "Who stitched you up?"

"A lady."

"A doctor?"

"No," said Virgil. "I don't think she was a doctor."

"I don't either," said Jefe, looking at the wound.

The ice was pleasurably disintegrating in his mouth. He still couldn't use his tongue. At the moment, he didn't care. He realized that Jefe had been studying him for a long time.

"How long have you been a cop?" Jefe asked seriously.

"Years," said Virgil.

"Why?" Jefe asked.

Virgil shrugged.

"It seemed like an adventure."

Jefe smiled. It was not a happy smile.

"Back home, I was nothing. Down here, things were different. The rules were different. Here, I was educated. I was bigger than everyone. There was a market for a particular kind of violence."

Jefe said as he put the last ice cube into Virgil's mouth. "I came down here to see what I was made of." Jefe looked at Virgil, and then off to the horizon, before looking back. "I found out," he said.

Jefe reached into his shirt pocket and removed two small books. Virgil looked at it and saw that they were United States passports. One belonged to him. The other belonged to Curtis.

"What do you want for these?" a stunned Virgil asked the big man with tremendous appetites.

"I want you to go home," said Jefe quietly.

Virgil put his passport into his front pocket. It didn't fit, and took up the whole pocket. He could feel it. He wanted to be sure it was with him. He held up Curtis' passport.

"What about—" Again, he didn't finish. The words hung in the air unspoken.

"He won't be needing it," said Jefe.

Virgil tried to accept it stoically. He looked at the landscape around him. He was surprised how many homes he hadn't noticed. He wondered how many people were watching from darkened windows.

"They caught up to him?" Virgil asked.

"Yeah," he said. "They caught up to him."

All Virgil wanted to do now was sleep. He started walking, but felt his vision narrow. There was wood in him that had propped him up for the last three days, and under the weight of this news, it had finally crumbled. Gruesome and unnerving as it was, he needed to know. He turned and saw Jefe still watching him.

"How did he die?"

"Walter Curtis?"

"Yeah," said Virgil, as if that was all he had left. He was so tired.

"He died well," said Jefe.

"What does that mean?" The shreds that were left of his memory were filled with images of beheadings and disembowelments. He needed sleep, but after he slept, he decided, he would drive into the desert and find Curtis, then bury whatever was left of him.

"What did they do to him?" he asked a final time.

"What did they do to him?" Jefe asked. When he repeated it, he stressed different words. In the haze of pain and sleeplessness, it sounded more like Jefe was asking what did he do to them.

Curtis watched his old friend as he turned from a man to a dark stumbling figure until finally he was nothing more than a black spot on the landscape. Then, he was gone.

He felt both heavy and light, but the part that felt light felt empowered. He paused, ran his hands across the straps, picked up the shotgun as if it were a cane he didn't need, and heaved his body forward. The money came with him.

Curtis cut a pace he hadn't achieved since he had first wrapped the ropes around his shoulders. He pushed one foot in front of the other and let the ropes dig. It hurt, and he relished it. He was glad it hurt. He walked harder so it hurt more. He told himself it was all downhill and that gravity was cheering for him. Eduardo Mendes was a clever little fancy pants. Eduardo Mendes couldn't stop him. His thugs couldn't stop him. That fat cop couldn't stop him. This boy and his little gun couldn't stop him. Mexico couldn't stop him.

He fell into the fearsome new rhythm and became hypnotized. All Curtis saw was the land falling before him. The bag tore through the sand. "Like a hot knife through butter," he said aloud to no one at all. He realized that he wasn't sweating, though he knew he should have been.

He heard the tear, but ignored it. The second tear was too long and too loud to ignore. Curtis stopped and felt the vice grip on his thighs. He vowed to keep moving. He marched in place. He had long since stopped caring about looking insane.

The ropes had torn through the blue plastic and left a jagged opening. Curtis shoved the money into the corners and pushed more away from the hole. His head began to tingle, and he remembered the boy. He watched for him, but saw only sand and heat and cash.

It had fallen out of the bag. He didn't need to worry about being followed. He was leaving a trail of US Currency. He picked them up and stuffed them back in, then wrapped himself once more in the ropes. He noticed one stack of bills left on the ground, and decided it wasn't worth the trouble. He pushed on, and the bag slid right over it.

He marched the boy deeper and deeper into the desert, and at one point in the early afternoon, it occurred to Curtis that he wasn't killing himself. He was killing the boy too.

He was thirsty. His whole body craved water. He could feel its demands. Curtis could feel himself going dry from the inside out. It remembered that he had almost drowned in fresh water as a boy, and he laughed. He had once had so much water that it almost killed him. Now he needed nothing more than fresh water, and he had none. He laughed as he went, and he never let go.

He saw the wasteland that lay in front of him. There was nothing here. There was no reason why any creature would exist in this place. It had been placed here to torment human beings. That was its only purpose.

He put his head down and drove on through the desert. He tried to think of home. When home became Virgil, he pushed those thoughts out as well. He let his thoughts overwhelm him and he dug his feet, one after another, through the sand and onward until one moment he happened to look up and saw a house.

It was a small structure, and it was the same color as the ground. He might have missed it had he not been looking right at it. He turned and looked at his path. He saw a massive straight line, miles long, beginning on a forgotten road from days ago. It led him directly here.

The house was nothing but walls and a roof. There were holes in the roof. The walls were clay and stone. The door was made of beaten, broken wood slats.

He didn't wonder how old this place was, or how it had come to be here. This had obviously been the barn. Long ago, some man came here for solitude and a place to make his mark. Curtis had no doubt how it had ended. Men weren't meant to live here.

He opened the door and saw sweet, calm shade. Sunlight poured in through the gaping holes in the ceiling. It was fifteen degrees cooler inside the barn. He stepped into the dark room, and the sun let go of him.

Curtis felt as if steam were rising from his body. The cool of the dark was like a blanket. He had been awake for days. He had walked for miles, carrying an inhuman load. A revenge-filled boy with a rifle had traveled miles to kill him. All of it turned to mist and evaporated.

Something stopped him. He reached for his gun before he looked. He laughed. The huge, ragged bundle of money couldn't fit through the door. Curtis pulled and tugged and kicked, and finally the load eased its way inside.

Curtis let go of the ropes. He watched through the open front door. He saw no boy. He pulled the rickety old door shut and lay down on the money.

He had been awake for days. He needed to rest. It would only be for a moment, he told himself.

The boy sipped water. He had sand and tiny rocks in his pants. They had worked their way in as he slithered over yard after yard to approach the old barn. The place was falling apart, but it was still standing. There were no windows. The door was broken and there were beams missing, but he couldn't see through it.

It was quiet here, and the wind was dead. He watched and waited. It might have been another trick, but he didn't think so. Sound travelled, and what the boy heard was the steady sound of deep sleep. It was snoring.

He remembered his father's snoring. How many times had his father jumped from the depth of sleep to wide awake and ready to fire, shotgun to his shoulder? He held the bolt action rifle in his hands. It was a small game gun. He remembered the advice from the man Strauss.

He reached into the bag. He had more water. He reached in again, this time finding the phone Strauss had given him. He wanted very much to kill this American, but he wanted more than anything to see him dead.

He compared the compass and studied the old map. He made a note in pencil. Then he was on his back, keeping his head down, slipping his shoulders through the straps of his bag. He listened to the snoring. It remained deep and heavy. He rolled to his belly, jumped to his feet, and ran. He had the rifle in one hand, the phone in the other. He ran until the phone began to ring.

Curtis opened his eyes, and the light was a different color. He understood immediately what had happened. He was angry with himself. He rolled to his side and slid on more money. He tried to stand, but the bills moved under his feet. He felt money falling around him.

Then he realized what had woken him.

He shot to his feet. The speed was agonizing. His whole body ached, and his joints refused to bend. Painfully, he hobbled straight legged to the door. He didn't dare open it.

The noise had been brakes. They were old and needed changing. He peered through a broken slat in the door and saw a white truck fifty yards in the field. Four men climbed out of it. Then the driver did too. He had a rifle.

It wasn't the only vehicle. There was Jeep on the right. The roof was loose, and it flapped in the breeze. A teenager sat on the hood, his feet dangling and kicking in the air. He held a shotgun in his lap. A bottle of water rested next to him. Another man leaned on the open door, smoking a cigarette. A pickup stood in the distance.

Then Curtis saw him, and he knew how this had happened. He was crouched behind the Jeep, a small black shadow, much smaller than the others. The boy had been there all along. Curtis smiled a little smile. He had been undone by a twelve -year old boy.

The boy had dug in tight. The rest wandered about in front like fearless targets. They carried guns as if they were toys and without a care in the world. They knew he was here. Curtis wanted to know why they hadn't come to get him, but he knew. They had been told to wait.

Behind them, in the distance, a plume of dust rose into the sky. Someone else was coming. He thought of the last words that Eduardo Mendes had spoken to him back in Monterrey, and the gruesome fate he had planned. Eduardo Mendes was riding at the forefront of that cloud.

Curtis sat down on his soft pile of money. He thought it might have been the most expensive chair in history. He held the shotgun, broke it open, and removed the shells. He blew sand from the barrel and put it back together again. He thought about water and the life he had lived.

"Which American is in there?" Eduardo asked. Anger and desperation filled his voice.

The boy didn't answer. Eduardo sighed and swore. Strauss interrupted.

"The man who you followed. What was he wearing?"

"A black shirt."

"And the other man who you did not follow. Where is he?"

The boy pointed north.

"What was he wearing?" Strauss asked.

"A silly yellow shirt."

"Very good," said Strauss. "This man in the black shirt. Did he have anything with him? Maybe a bag?"

"Yes. He was dragging it."

"How big was it?" Strauss asked.

"Good work, boy," said Eduardo suddenly, cutting him off before he could answer. Eduardo had a huge smile on his face. None of this escaped Strauss.

"How big was the bag?" he asked the boy again, this time in a softer tone.

"He found the right man," said Eduardo. "Who cares how big it is?"

"Your new friends will," said Strauss. Eduardo pretended he hadn't heard him.

A gray Ford Bronco roared through the group and stopped directly in front of the barn. Ordo and The Russian were in the cab. There was a blood on the driver's side door. Ordo jumped out with his arms in the air, as if he were expecting applause.

"What do you got there?" Ordo asked as he laid eyes on Guillermo's Uzi.

"It was my grandmother's," said Guillermo.

As if on cue, the Russian pulled a large duffel bag from the Bronco and set it on the hood of the Jeep. The Russian opened the bag and handed Ordo a long, sleek, unblemished black rifle. Ordo held it to his lips and kissed it.

Strauss watched the Russian remove another rifle. It was a cut down AR with iron sights and black tape on the grip. It was scratched and battered, and the Russian had screwed a silencer onto the barrel. Strauss watched the entire process. He had no doubt this rifle had been fired before.

"What are we doing?" Eduardo asked. He was speaking to Strauss. Strauss pointed at Ordo.

"My opinion doesn't matter here, Mister Mendes. What I do is subtle. Subtlety has no place in what we're about to do."

"You said we," pointed out Eduardo.

"There are no clean hands here," said Strauss.

The Russian came directly to Strauss and stood on the same side of the truck, keeping his eyes on the old barn. Ordo came over, laughing and talking, making it seem careless and indirect. The others wandered over, hovering near Ordo, taking none of it seriously. "What do we have?" the Russian asked.

"One barricaded American," answered Strauss.

"How do we get him out?" Eduardo asked.

"He isn't coming out," shouted Ordo, as if it were the most obvious fact in the world.

Eduardo looked to Strauss to see if that was true.

"After your comments to Agent Curtis in regard to what you planned to do to him, I doubt he'll believe we're going to let him go," said Strauss.

"The boy said he walked through the desert by himself?" Ordo asked.

"He did."

"He must be almost dead. Why not walk in and kill him?"

"Be my guest," said Strauss, motioning toward the barn.

The Russian volunteered.

"The roof is broken. You can see right through. I can climb up, shoot him through the opening."

"It's dangerous," said Strauss. The Russian shrugged.

Strauss pointed to the huge GMC Denali. It had been the second truck to arrive.

"If I had a stake in this," started Strauss, still leaning on the Navigator, "I would find a brave man and drive that truck right through the barn. Take out that wall. Go straight on through. Have your shooters in the field. When the wall comes down, the roof is going with it. Open up with everything you have. There shouldn't be much left of him after that."

Ordo waited for Eduardo's reaction. Eduardo had no idea, but he had raised an intrigued eyebrow. That was enough.

Some of the men filtered back to their cars. The Russian seemed to prefer his idea. He continued to study the little building, moving further from the group. The boy stayed by Strauss's side. He was almost invisible.

"Ordo," said Strauss. He waved him closer so he could speak quietly.

"Mister Mendes is watching," was all Strauss said. They both turned.

Eduardo couldn't hear them. Eduardo was hopelessly out of place in his silk shirt and black suit pants, and anyone should have seen it. Ordo didn't. Ordo saw who he wanted to be. He turned back to Strauss.

"He's looking for a man with balls," said Strauss. "Show him something."

Ordo spent some time thinking on it. His eyes darted when thinking, and his lips moved with his thoughts. Strauss wondered if he was dumb enough to drive the truck into the barn all by himself.

Ordo pulled his shirt off and was bare-chested. He hung the expensive shirt on the radio antenna. Then he grabbed the gun by the grip and held it straight to the sky. He opened his mouth to speak.

"There he is!" It was Eduardo's voice. Everyone turned. There was no one outside the little structure. However, in the late afternoon light, and through the broken slats in the door, shadows and figures could be seen moving, clear as day. The light jumped and ran, high and low, back and forth.

"What am I seeing?" Eduardo asked.

It looked like wild dancing. The shadows bounced on the inside of the door, the cracks spilling its secrets. It showed a crazy, irrational man. It showed a man who had walked into the desert with a fortune and lost his mind in the process.

"Smoke," said the Russian.

They could see tendrils of smoke rising through the gaps in the roof. One hole in the center had the most, but small tips of smoke were sneaking through the others, slipping into the open air. Eduardo saw a wisp of smoke appear at the front door.

"What the hell is he doing?" Ordo said loudly.

They all stood and watched, their guns useless at their sides, dumbfounded.

Suddenly, Eduardo knew what he was doing. He knew why smoke was rising through the holes in the roof and through the door. He knew why there were wild and unpredictable shadows being cast.

He couldn't believe what he was seeing. His mind wouldn't allow it. He felt like he had awoken and found he had been thrown from an airplane. His mind struggled to process it all.

"He's burning it," Eduardo mumbled. He thought of the implications. Curtis was in there, he had a fortune in US Currency, and he had set fire to it.

"Who the hell burns three million dollars?" gasped Ordo.

"There's twenty million dollars in there," said Eduardo, as if in a trance. Every man heard him. Every man turned to see if they heard him correctly, or to see if he had lost his mind.

Eduardo had not lost his mind. He was simply overcome by emotion. He was overcome by a single-minded desire to not lose, not to the little man inside that barn who had made a fool of him.

"There's twenty million dollars in there," repeated Eduardo. The news landed among them like grenades. It took a moment for the news to detonate. When it did, the frenzy began.

In an instant, the same terrible idea formed in every man's head. They turned to look at one another. All of their eyes went wide. Some of their jaws hung open. There was twenty million dollars on the other side of a rickety door, where a skinny madman was feeding it to a fire.

Guillermo was the first spark. All he did was pivot. He was fast for a man his age, even with the extra weight. He broke into a run. Then the others did too. They all did. They exploded in a feverish sprint toward the flames.

Curtis felt the force of the fire licking at his back. It had grown faster than expected. Outside, he saw the desired effect.

He began to count them, but when they started moving, he lost it. He had a dozen, but he knew there were more. They were running straight at him.

He stayed close to the door, and to the cracks. He breathed fresh air. They had to know he was there, and yet they came anyway.

Curtis studied the crowd. There was one man with an AK-47. There were two with AR-15s, but one of them was out of sight. He had no time to worry about where that man had gone. He looked through the crowd for the AK-47. The man holding it had a hard face that looked as if a knife had been sharpened against it. He saw a shotgun, then another. He looked and lost the AK. He saw an Uzi in the front row. It was held in dark, brown hands and arms shining with sweat. He looked no higher. The Uzi would get there first.

Curtis pushed the door open. The men who were running had no time to stop or to understand what was happening. They came on full force. Curtis fired.

The shotgun slug was a bolt of metal the size of his thumb, and it hit Guillermo in the throat. It spun inside then exploded through the back of his neck. Blood sailed into the air. It floated like a mist as the men behind him ran through it. It landed wet and heavy on their faces and clothes. Guillermo landed on his back.

The Mexicans stopped. Some ducked. Their feet kicked up dirt. Guillermo choked and jerked. Curtis looked for the AK. He found it. The man who held it looked away from Guillermo in time. He moved behind one of Ordo's teenage fighters, who held his pistol grip shotgun at the waist. Curtis shot that boy in the stomach. Then he ran.

The door to the barn exploded. He felt stone dust and pebbles bounce against his head and shoulders. Each rifle blast reverberated through his chest.

Then they were all firing. Daylight filtered through the door, and tiny shards of wood and rock shook through the air. Curtis crouched and broke open the shotgun. He had the satchel around his neck, but had two rounds perched in his back pocket. He snapped it back together.

An unseen hand flung the door open. Another hand pushed a handgun across the threshold. It fired blindly.

Curtis heard a machine gun. He saw the stream of fire, then he saw the gun. Ordo ran through the door, unloading the clip on full automatic. His foot slid into a trench just past the threshold to the doorway. It caught the earth on the other side. Ordo dropped the rifle, doubled at the waist, and stumbled uncontrollably face first into the pile of burning money. His face and hands went into the flames.

Curtis had dug three long slits in the ground. Each was the length of the doorway. Each had been designed with that purpose in mind. Curtis brought his gun up to eye level and breathed.

The AK appeared. The man holding it stopped before his foot sank into the trench, his free hand gripping the door to hold his balance. Ordo sat up and began screaming. Curtis leveled his shotgun on the man with the AK. His hard face showed only surprise. Curtis shot him in the chest.

He told himself to move. He rushed out of the corner. The hand appeared again, and this time, the gun it held unloaded into the corner where Curtis had just been. He swung the shotgun toward the hand and tried to align his sights. He heard another explosion. He saw a thin little man fly over the trenches.

When the shooting started, the Russian ran. He ran fast and dove hard into the base of the little building. The stone walls shook from the heavy rifle rounds landing. He heard one fly over his head with a zip.

He was counting. The shotgun blasts had started it. He was on the other side and had no way to know, not this fast, but he bet the shotgun belonged to the American. The American was trained. He was not to be underestimated.

He climbed. Smoke hit him in the face. He heard gun shots. Part of the roof blew away on the other side of the barn. There were many others, but he listened. He distinctly heard .40 caliber. No one in the world carried .40 caliber except for American police. He heard six of them. He reared back to clear his eyes and breathe. The smoke was black now, thick and ugly. There was a big hole in the roof. He could drop through it, but the smoke obscured his vision. He would be dropping blind.

***

Ordo screamed again. The man danced right over him. His foot landed in the low flames, touched ground for a second, sent sparks flying, and took flight once more. He had a gun in his hand. Curtis fired at his head.

The round flew past him and blew part of the roof into the air. The dancing man hadn't seen Curtis, but he did now. He turned in mid air. He came down hard but couldn't stop. Curtis threw the shotgun at him and drew his second gun. The dancing man tried to adjust on the fly, but no man can dance forever. Curtis shot him in the shoulder.

It didn't knock him off his feet, but it did knock him back. The dancing man fired his gun into the wall. Curtis heard an explosion from the field. Then he shot the dancing man five times in the chest.

Curtis saw the muzzle flash, and it came from the first man he had killed. He brought his gun up and saw a Mexican with a shotgun using the dead body for cover. He fired twice, and the Mexican ducked. The hand came around the corner once more. The gun it held was long and silver. He fired blindly throughout the room. Curtis fired twice at him too, and the gun slid behind the corner again. When he fired, he watched the man hiding behind the dead body.

He saw the shotgun tilted to the sky, and the hand came up and racked another round into the chamber. He brought his head up and the gun down and searched for a target over Guillermo's body. Toxic black smoke filled the small room.

Curtis fired, and the head went down, seeking cover. He fired into Guillermo's body, which wouldn't stop all of his bullets. He fired until he was empty. He heard screaming.

The Russian knew guns. He knew their sounds. He knew killing people. He heard thirteen rounds. He let go of the wall, took the fore grip in his hand, and prepared himself. He heard two more shots. Empty. He dropped into the black smoke.

***

He needed to move. The training had buried it in Curtis' mind. His left hand went to his belt for the extra clip. It was in his pocket. He fumbled. Curtis sensed movement. He turned and saw a man fall from the ceiling.

The man had a rifle and held it like a soldier. He brought it level. Curtis tried to get the magazine. He knew he was in his sights. Instinctively, he let go of the clip and put his hand in front of him, as if that would stop a bullet.

The Russian shot him twice.

Curtis lay on the ground, clutching his wounded stomach. He expected the Russian to calmly walk over and put another round into his head. He saw the Russian approach with the rifle in hand, preparing to do just that. He waited to be executed. He refused to close his eyes.

Sparks flew. Then gunshots. He saw tiny dots of daylight through the ceiling. The Russian dove.

"Stop," he heard the Russian shouting.

"Who is it?" a distant voice called.

"The Russian. Stop shooting."

Curtis had been shot in the hand, but refused to look. He tried to move it, and lightning bolts of pain shot through his nervous system. He had a hole in his upper abdomen. He had another in his lower chest. He breathed. He could still breathe.

He had pain in his back. It didn't hurt like he knew it should, and he knew that was bad. Curtis could still feel his feet, which hurt, and his knees, which hurt. He wasn't paralyzed.

Curtis realized how hot he was. He was facing the fire. The whole pile was engulfed now. He saw the blue tarp curling at the edges. There was a man in the barn who was going to kill him. Suddenly, he realized that there were two.

"Is he dead?" a voice asked from far too close.

"I have him," said the Russian. "Help me."

The fire was so close. He had seen a man fall into it and survive. That man was also still in the room somewhere.

"Where is the money?" the voice called, almost immediately behind him. Curtis couldn't see the man, but he could see parts of him. He pushed away from the fire and had a hand up to his face. The other hand was at his side, and it held a large silver gun.

"I cannot see," said the Russian.

"Is he dead?"

"Yes, he is dead. I have smoke in my eyes," he said. Curtis couldn't see him. The Russian was somewhere behind him. He saw that man take the long silver gun and tuck it into the back of his pants.

Curtis wondered if he could sneak out of this. All he had to do was wait out the fire. As soon as he thought it, the tarp folded into itself and brought fresh, unburned cash into the heat of the flame. The fire roared.

In the light of the sudden burst of heat, Curtis found his gun. It was on the ground just an arm's length away from him.

"Where are you?" the voice called. Black smoke had choked the lighter smoke into submission. The fire was fat and greedy.

Curtis had the gun in his hand. It was empty.

"Here," said the Russian. He was close.

Curtis tried to work his left hand. There was a huge hole in the middle of his palm. His fingers flexed wide, but that was all they did. Curtis couldn't move them or make a fist. He looked through his hand and saw fire.

He was still curled up in a ball. Curtis tucked the gun between his knees. With his good hand, he reached into the pocket of his pants for the spare magazine.

He slid it into the open end of the grip between his knees. He felt it connect. He took the gun, still at lock back, and felt for the slide release.

"Here," said the other man.

Curtis pressed down on the tiny lever, and the slide loudly slid forward, slamming another round into the chamber, ready to fire.

"What was that?" said the Russian, somehow, impossibly, hearing the sound of the gun working.

Curtis rolled. His ribs were tiny razors that cut into his insides. His left hand felt like it was breaking again. The two men were next to each other, but only the Russian was looking. He opened his lips, either as a warning or a protest, just in time for a bullet to fly between them. A halo of red mist instantly appeared behind his head.

The man with the silver gun began to run at him. His hand was behind his back. The gun was coming out of his pants. Curtis fired, but he kept coming. He fired again and again, and the man dove. Curtis anticipated feeling his hands around his throat any second, but the man soared over and past him. Curtis fired the entire time.

He rolled again, his gun up, and ready to keep fighting this man. His long silver gun was in the dirt. His head was in the fire. His legs were not even twitching.

When the shooting started, Eduardo scrambled desperately to the top of the Navigator so he wouldn't miss a shot. The boy had hidden under the truck. Strauss hadn't moved, staying safely where he was, sipping coffee, and watching it all happen.

Dead bodies lay piled up outside the little barn. Smoke was racing out from every crack in the roof in dark plumes. A man was crawling away with one arm. His other arm was dragging beside him, bloody and useless. He called to Ordo's men for help, but none of them came. They went the other way. All around, men with guns crouched or tucked themselves behind trucks, waiting for whatever was inside to come out for them.

When the boy saw what was happening, he dove. He crawled gun first into a secure spot. He threw his pack down and rested the stock of the rifle on top. He kept his head up and shifted into a natural firing position.

He had seen the look of disdain on the rich man's face. The boy could read his face, and he knew the man called Eduardo thought he was hiding. There was a world of difference between hiding and hunting. Eduardo was the man who didn't want to get dirty. He should have stayed out of Mexico.

The boy watched as man after man fell outside the barn or ran inside and never returned. This American was vicious. He realized in that instant that he had somehow been fooled.

He pointed the rifle at the door. He looked over the sights. He told his eyes not to see the fire.

Curtis moved in slow, tiny footsteps, each of which was more painful than the last. He lowered himself to his knees just outside the door by the trenches. This was where it had started.

Opposite him on the other side, Ordo sat with his back to the wall. He held his ruined hands up and stared at them. His flesh was red and black. Ordo shivered uncontrollably. Curtis saw bone.

He told himself not to scream when he pulled his shirt over his head. He used the shirt to wrap his wounded hand.

He inspected the wounds on his torso. He looked up to see Ordo staring at him. Curtis looked at the man who had come to kill him. His voice was rough, and he had very little air left in his lungs. The fire behind him crackled and roared as it spread to the roof.

"What if I told you there was three million dollars buried in the desert?" Curtis asked.

One of Ordo's men had dropped to the ground and stayed down for the gunfight. It had been a good decision. Then he had moved, and Eduardo had seen him. Eduardo shouted and demanded that he pick up a gun and go into the barn. The young man chose the Uzi, and looked back for Eduardo's approval. He turned just in time for Curtis to send a bullet through his forehead.

Walter Curtis walked out of the fire and into the field. Every man took a step back.

He stood bare-chested with open wounds and soft wisps of smoke rising from his shoulders. He had soot and blood splashed across his body, and the ropes had cut a large X in ragged flesh across his chest. He walked slowly into the field and stopped in front of all of them.

The desert was silent save for the fire. None of the men spoke or moved or raised a weapon. Curtis looked at them. He saw men young and old, men with handguns or shotguns, and one with a rifle. They were hard Mexican killers, all of them, and he was holding them at bay with a look.

One man was without a gun. Curtis knew the slim profile and the luxurious head of hair at a glance. He had met this man in America, come here at his invitation, and walked himself to death to avoid him.

For the first time in his life, Walter Curtis gave no weight to doubt or hesitation.

"Good afternoon, Mister Mendes," he said, and he shot Eduardo in the face.

A flash came from under the truck. He felt it. Then he heard it. Curtis stumbled. A bullet flew into his neck, ricocheted off his spine, and burst out the other side. He saw Eduardo Mendes fall. He felt his own blood spurting out of his neck. He saw Ordo crawling away frantically on his knees and elbows. Then he found himself falling inside the walls of the barn.

The fire was everywhere. Even the stone was burning. Curtis had stopped worrying about dying. He had let go of panic. His nose filled with smoke. His throat filled with blood. Just before the lights went out, he realized he was drowning.

They watched it burn until there was nothing left but black smoke, cinders, and scorched roofless walls. Even the door burned.

Those who had survived and weren't injured studied the dead from a distance until the roof collapsed and no one else came out and it was clearly, definitely over and done. They asked themselves what they should do with the bodies, whether they should leave them or stack them or cut off their hands so they could never be identified. One Mexican suggested burial, but no one responded and it wasn't brought up again. Finally, when Strauss could take no more, he said they should burn them.

The first two men had their belongings stripped and sorted into little piles next to their bodies. They all had guns, some money, and a little gold. The pile next to the third man was smaller than the first two, and the fourth smaller than that. When Strauss looked back at the first two bodies, their piles were gone. Guillermo had eight US dollars in his pocket, and a bunch of Mexican coins. Strauss thought for a moment that he should be the one to throw him to the fire, but he thought too long. Two Mexicans took Guillermo by the feet and the hands and did it for him.

Eduardo was tossed roughly into the back of a pickup truck. He lay in the fetal position, saying nothing and not moving, though he was very much alive. He had a horrible gash that started just after his mouth, ran the length of his face, and had severed his ear. His expensive coat was his bandage. He held his eyes shut tight. The tailgate was flipped up and locked.

Strauss found the boy waiting for him. He had the rifle in one hand and by the forestock, far away from the trigger. The sun was almost down, and he looked cold.

"You killed him," said Strauss.

The boy said nothing. Strauss understood that he was both immensely proud and terribly sad. He said it and let the boy think about it for a time.

Strauss opened the front passenger side door.

"Get in," he said.

It was midnight in the ER. Doctors shouted orders. There was blood on the floor, and a man was losing consciousness. Jefe said nothing, but calmly busied himself with the shreds of the black suit that had been cut off the man on the table. The man was Eduardo Mendes.

At the end of the hall, a police officer in an ornate uniform screamed into a phone. He was the comandante of the station from which the Americans had escaped. He was in a rage.

Jefe found a scrap of paper in the coat pocket. There was one drop of blood in the corner. On it, the name Felipe was written, along with an address and a number.

Jefe's fat fingers punched numbers into the phone. Dejo came up, covered in sweat. "The comandante says he's not taking the blame for this. He says he's going to tell people about us."

"Us?" asked Jefe, barely paying attention.

"You," said Dejo. "He says someone has to pay for this." He saw one man in a suit enter the hall. He had bushy hair and tired, honest eyes.

"An agent from the Federal Police just showed up," said Dejo, who saw him shake hands with the comandante and look in their direction. "This is bad."

Jefe put the phone to his ear. He listened for a time.

Jefe looked at the little comandante and his chest covered with metal. He looked at Eduardo Mendes. He couldn't see him through the scrum of doctors, but he could see his blood on the floor below. He looked back at the note in his hand.

"What is that?" Dejo asked.

Jefe smiled. His teeth were brown.

"Salvation," he said.

Chapter Fifteen

Virgil – Nuevo Leon, MX

He was sharp enough now to understand that he was going to die. If he didn't get medical attention, he would be dead before the sun came up, and all the Coca-Cola in Mexico wouldn't stop it. He laughed. He stumbled and staggered, chuckling to himself amid a sea of identical homes, when he opened his eyes to see a brutally injured man.

"I know him," said Virgil.

The man was bleeding from the feet, the side, and his head. His arms had been stretched out painfully. The look on his face was grotesque. It was a statue, but whoever had built it had gone to great artistic lengths to capture a look of pure agony.

Virgil looked at where he was. The sign read La Iglesia de San Miguel. He knew what Miguel meant.

It was a small white building with a cross affixed to the very top. The front doors were nine feet tall and formed an arch. There was a steeple in the back. There was a cross on that too.

Virgil remembered what Curtis had said about landmarks.

With one leg almost completely useless, he moved to the back of the little church and looked around. There was a house in the distance, and the lights were on, but in between there were space, grass, and bushes. He found an ancient tree in the back.

"They ain't making fire wood out of you any time soon."

Virgil got on his knees and dug a hole with his bare hands. He didn't expect it to be so hard, and when he was done, he was thirsty. One of these houses had Coca-Cola. He was sure of it.

Slowly, he pulled off the shirt he was wearing. He remembered it as yellow, but now it looked brown. He could still see little hula girls, dancing and smiling in between the grime and the blood. He flattened it out on the ground. He put his gun on it. He put in the money he had in his pockets and the money he had in his sock. He found money in his pants, but he remembered that he might need money to get around, so he put that back. Finally, he put the passports on the shirt, which he twisted up and tied into a ball and then buried in the ground by the tree behind the church.

When he found the road, Virgil walked shirtless right down the middle. Cars honked as they passed him. Men swore. The lights blinded him, but he kept his thumb out where people could see it. Eventually, a yellow car stopped for him. Virgil had almost forgotten why he wanted it.

The driver spoke to him in Spanish. "I need to go to the doctor," he said. The man only spoke more rapid Spanish.

From a hazy dream that had happened a hundred years ago, he remembered something Curtis had said to a stranger on the road on a rainy, violent night.

"Medico."

"Si," said the driver, clearly understanding what Virgil needed. "Muestreme el dinero."

The man was talking about money. He reached into his pants and took out his last stack of money. He had no idea how much it was. He handed it to the driver.

At first, the driver recoiled. His face showed disgust. Then his eyes had opened, and he realized what was being offered. He looked from the money to Virgil and back again, then took the stack and pushed Virgil into his car.

The ride was short and full of lights. He realized he was downtown in some city, but he had no idea which one. The lights were dazzling and hypnotic. The cab never seemed to stop, cutting through lines and traffic. Then, just as he began to sleep, it stopped abruptly, and he was being pulled out of the car.

Virgil saw the driver clearly for the first time. He was sweaty, overweight, and smelled like cigarettes. He hadn't shaved. He smiled, but it was a bad smile, one nobody should trust.

"You good," he said in English. He patted Virgil on the shoulder. Then he hurried back into his cab. Virgil heard the engine rise.

Virgil looked up at the sign to see where he was. The blazing blue light in front of his face said hospital.

Virgil laughed. They drove around Mexico asking for medical attention in broken English, trying new and creative ways to express themselves, when all along, the word was the same. It made him very happy and very sleepy. He didn't have to walk anymore. He was here. He felt his eyes close while he was standing. He felt his body drifting.

***

When Virgil came to in the hospital, the nice one with the clean walls and orderlies who didn't steal his dope, the doctors came and spoke to him in Spanish. Virgil could barely move, and half his face was wrapped. He could only see from one eye. His skin was horribly damaged from its time in the sun. It hurt to move at his hips, but he couldn't see why.

He knew. He knew the sun had damn near killed him. He knew the burns were severe. He knew they had operated on his leg or hip. The pain was like it had just happened, as if they had shot him again, except this time stabbed him as well.

There was a policeman in an ornate uniform beside his bed. The man was stuffy and officious and yelled in short, stocky sentences. The doctor yelled back at him. Virgil had no idea what they were saying, but he could gather enough. The police had come to take his fingerprints. His hands were too badly burned. The doctor refused.

Ultimately, his fingers and the secrets they carried remained his. The men went away. Virgil went back to sleep.

These people had no idea who he was.

Marc Virgil opened his eyes. He was awake and in pain. He saw the flickering shadow on the ceiling from the rusty old gray fan whirling by the window. He could see the nurse's head when she walked past. He could see everything he'd ever done wrong with perfect clarity.

Clearest of all was his memory. He could remember much of what happened in the desert, and most of it shamed him.

He thought of how he had let Curtis bear the load they both should have carried. He thought of how he let Curtis die by himself. He was angry and embarrassed that he had finally passed out on his feet at the steps of the hospital. He wasn't sorry though. He wasn't sorry that his mind had finally relented, had shut itself down, and gone to sleep. He wasn't sorry that he had fallen face first like a rag doll into the steps. He wasn't sorry that he had lost teeth and broken his jaw in the fall.

He felt like he deserved it.

He was glad the orderly had stolen his drugs. The pain brought clarity and punishment.

The Mexican doctors had wired his mouth shut. He hadn't uttered a word.

One day, a nurse came with the doctor. She was young and pretty. She dressed like a nurse from old times, prim and proper with a clean white nurse's hat. The doctor spoke to her in Spanish, and she spoke to Virgil in English.

"Hello, sir, how are you?"

Virgil said nothing. He stared at the ceiling.

"Can you hear me?" she said it nicely. He ignored her.

"Blink if you can hear me," she said. He tried not to blink at all. She turned to the doctor and shook her head. They went away.

At first, he slept all the time. The pain woke him whenever it got the urge. The burning skin was the worst. After a while, that went away like everything else, but there was a deeper pain in his face that emerged. He had his bandages. He found himself starting to worry about what could be under them.

At night in the hospital, Virgil didn't have to pretend. He could hoist himself to his elbows and move his head. Though he was the only one.

It was an old and poorly cared for building near an industrial park. The air was bad, and the light was muddled by dirty windows. Heavy trucks rolled past at all hours. The ceiling had water damage and was rotting. The men in the beds were too. This was a ward for destitute patients with serious brain damage.

The moans bothered him at first. There was more than one moaner, and if their minds were being tortured, no one knew or cared. There was one doctor for an entire floor, and he was more like an orderly himself. He was always in a hurry with other places to be. After a few days, Virgil realized that he was the only doctor in a warehouse sized building.

A loud crash rang out in the dark.

"Go get 'em, Thrasher," Virgil whispered. His jaw was wired so tightly that he couldn't understand himself, but he knew the substance.

The Thrasher fought them blindly and without anger. He was an instinctive rebel. He had to be strapped down, but he fought so hard that he routinely got loose. Thrasher would lay still for a while, then jerk to life with a thoughtless spasm, sending bedpans, pill jars, and food carts crashing to the floor. The orderlies hated the Thrasher, and for a long time, he was Virgil's only entertainment.

He realized that young nurse was not a nurse. She was a nun. She wore a small hat that distinguished her, but it wasn't quite a habit. She also wore a very small gold cross around her neck. She would sit and read to each man on the ward. He understood not a single word she said, for she only spoke in Spanish. Her voice was soft and lovely. She read for only ninety minutes a week, and Virgil pretended to be severely brain damaged the entire time. Each week, it was the best ninety minutes of his life.

In this young nun's voice, Spanish was a beautiful, romantic language, and not so much a foreign tongue as the secret password to a seductive life where passions ruled and rules disappeared. She was in no hurry and spoke so slowly that he could savor each word. He told himself if he listened long and carefully enough, he would learn the language himself without ever opening his mouth.

The Thrasher barked, and two metal bedpans crashed loudly to the floor. There was a distinctive weight to the sound as the metal rang out, and there was no doubt the pan had been full.

"Oh, fuck," said the young nun in English.

Virgil's mouth was wired shut. He couldn't speak. He also couldn't smile. But smiles aren't limited to the mouth. The young nun caught herself and looked about in terror. No one had seen her, and no one had heard her. No one except for Virgil. They made eye contact, and she saw the mischievous pleasure in his eye that was as obvious as a belly laugh. She also saw the recognition.

He put it away immediately. He stared at the ceiling. He played dead.

Virgil felt her study him. Then he heard the book close definitively. She left. Moments later, he heard the sounds of buckets and mops, but he kept his eye on the ceiling.

The next day, the young nun opened her book and began to read as she always did. A door closed in the distance. She shut the book, then opened it again at the beginning. She paused and cleared her throat. When she opened her lips again, the English language poured out.

She began to tell the story of an old man facing death who remembered a moment from his childhood when he had first discovered ice. It was more English than he had heard in months. He had no idea how much he had missed it, and the only thing he could compare it to was the thirst he had felt in the desert. She spoke naturally, without hesitation, and with only the slightest of accents. He wanted to hug her. He wanted to kiss her. Instead, he lay on his bed and pretended he was brain damaged.

But she knew.

Virgil heard lazy footsteps in the distance. Suddenly, the nun was leaning over him, so he couldn't avoid her.

"My name is Patricia," she whispered.

The next time she came, he turned his head to look at her. She smiled, and then she read to him. She turned the page four times. He lost track of the story when he was thinking of how wonderful she was.

One day, he was propped up, waiting for her and staring straight ahead when the man who tried to kill him in the jail cell appeared before him.

Angel slid silently into his line of sight. Virgil saw him in profile, waiting. There was no turning away. Angel wore the same, emotionless expression.

Virgil's one open eye darted about him. He was weak, and he was broken. He had virtually no way to defend himself.

Virgil decided to live in that moment. He accepted that it would hurt. When Angel came near him, he would play dead. He would wait for Angel to stab or choke him or do whatever he planned to end Virgil's life. Then Virgil would rip his eye out.

He flexed two fingers straight and made a fist with the other two. This would have hurt the day before, but now, all he felt was his heart. He'd shove those two fingers through Angel's eye and, with his other hand, pull him down to his level. Then, he would wrap his arm around Angel's neck until he stopped moving.

The doctor appeared, and then the nurse. That wouldn't stop Angel. Then Patricia came, and she looked at him and smiled. Then her smile disappeared. No one else paid Virgil any attention, but Patricia saw it. Then there was the orderly, and he realized that Angel was sitting. The orderlies stepped behind Angel, who sat in a wheelchair, and turned him in the direction the doctor pointed. Virgil saw him in full now.

One entire side of his head had caved into itself. It was just gone. Stubbly hair formed a soft tender patch of skin ringed by silver staples. Underneath it, the bone was gone.

What was there was drool. A long, solitary strand hung out of his mouth and pooled on his gown. It shimmered in the light as the orderly turned him.

The doctor gave more orders. The nurse wrote them down. The orderly wheeled. Angel drooled.

Patricia looked again, and he could see her concern. He couldn't tell her, and she couldn't ask. Virgil realized he was sweating. He told himself to calm down and go to sleep. It didn't work. Until it grew dark and then long after, he watched Angel.

Virgil sat propped up in bed, watching Angel shit himself and the orderlies changing him. When they were done, they dropped him roughly.

Patricia was reading to him. She was in mid-sentence when he reached out with one hand and closed the book.

For a man who pretended to be comatose, and who moved only one eye, this was the equivalent of an earthquake. Patricia looked frightened, and then nervous. One of her hands fumbled with her cross.

His voice was full of rust and the dry muscles in his throat hurt when they rubbed one another. His jaw was still fused shut. All he managed were grunts and hisses.

Patricia put the cross down and leaned over him. Her hair fell loosely onto Virgil's cheek. For the first time, he could smell her. All he had known was the scent of chemicals and human bodies, covered up with harsh disinfectants. She smelled of warmth and of genuine health. He saw the cross sliding along the tiny band.

He tried again and again, and on the third attempt, she could hear Virgil whisper, "What's wrong with me?"

Patricia sat down again. Her face showed deep concern. She fumbled with the cross again.

"You were shot," said Patricia.

Virgil nodded. He knew that. That was old news.

"Someone treated you, but they treated you badly," she said. That was the rough old woman they had met at the little house off the road. He remembered her well.

"Your wounds became infected," said Patricia. "The doctor thinks you might have been poisoned."

Virgil thought about that. It explained a few things, but not all of them. He gestured for her to come close.

"Why does it still hurt?"

Whatever it was, she didn't want to tell him. Patricia seemed to understand that if she did not, no one would. When she spoke, her voice had lost its whisper.

"The flesh inside of you became infected. The doctors had to cut it out."

Instinctively, he flexed his hips, and lifted his legs. Even that tiny movement ached. He wondered how much they had cut out of him.

"Can I walk?" he asked.

Patricia nodded. She pursed her lips. "But not like you did before. And it will hurt."

He was sorry that Patricia had to tell him. She clearly had not wanted to tell him, but she had done it anyway. That was duty. He motioned for her to come closer.

"What kind of nun says the f-word?" he asked.

Patricia laughed. Her eyes smiled as wide as her mouth, even though they were wet.

"I'm not a nun," she said. "I'm a postulant."

"What the hell is a postulant?" he said. The word "what" came out intelligible and the rest was garbled. Patricia understood.

"A postulant is a woman who is training to be a nun."

"You shouldn't be a nun. You should run away with a handicapped American."

"What?" she asked, still smiling. Virgil shook his head.

"Do they know who I am?" he asked as softly as he could.

She was serious again.

"They think they do," she said. "The doctor will not let them come near you. The police say you are wanted for murder."

"Here or there?" he asked.

"Both," she said. Her eyes said she didn't believe it or didn't want to. He would miss this too.

"Patricia," he began. He was getting the hang of talking this way. He touched his finger to the bandages on his face. When he did, he saw her smile disappear. Her eyes grew wetter.

"Why do I still have bandages on my face?" he asked.

He remembered the look she had worn when she didn't want to answer the question about his hip. He would have killed for a look that promising now. Her fingers began to play nervously with the cross again, and he knew.

"The flesh inside of you became infected," she began. "The doctors had to cut it out."

He stopped listening. He knew before she said another word. His eye was gone.

One day he woke and found the orderlies whispering about him.

It was the orderly who routinely helped himself to his drugs. Up close, he was emaciated. He wore long sleeve shirts when the others' were short. His skin was discolored, and he had a sore on his hand that wouldn't heal.

The other was fat and greasy. His hair was tied back in a bun and he had small ferret eyes. They both held mops. They both pretended to be doing this or that, but they weren't. They were looking at him and whispering. The junkie looked particularly intent.

A door closed down the hall. The orderlies both turned. Virgil held his breath. The junkie approached and began to frisk him. There was nothing to be had. They pulled down the covers. Virgil tried to stare at the ceiling, but it was impossible. They paid him no attention.

"Aqui," said the orderly when he came to Virgil's arm. There was obvious excitement in his voice. The other joined him. They spoke in hushed tones. Virgil understood none of it and all of it. The orderlies covered his arm again and tucked him in neatly. The junkie gave him one last look, then nodded with confidence.

It was the tattoo on his arm, the everlasting symbol of his years in the service.

Virgil had been made.

When Patricia sat down to read, Virgil reached over and closed the book in her hands.

"I need a mirror," he said.

Patricia stayed in her seat, and he saw defiance in her. Then she left. He listened to her clicking down the hall. In a moment, she returned, carrying with her an oval vanity mirror.

She held it up, but Virgil took it from her. It no longer mattered who saw him or what they thought. He sat upright in bed, and saw his new face for the first time.

He had grown a beard in the hospital. It had come in thick, which it never had before, and it covered him. He had lost weight. Virgil always thought of himself as healthy and vibrant. This man in the mirror was sick and emaciated.

"No," she said when he reached for the bandage. She tried to take the mirror, but he pulled away from her.

"Yes," he told her.

He pulled the bandage away and didn't see himself. He saw someone else. There was a gaping, terrible hole in his face. The flesh above his eye was shriveled and scarred, having been transplanted from his backside. What skin remained, all over his face, looked as if it had been ripped off and left raw.

He stopped looking at himself, and instead he looked at Patricia. She had never been there when the bandages had been changed. This was her first time too.

Her face, lovely and honest, answered all of his questions. No, she would never love him. No, no one ever would. He was a cripple now, a figure to be pitied and avoided.

He put the bandage back in place, then handed her the mirror. He cleared his throat and, though it hurt, made his jaw move. This was the last thing he would say to Patricia, and he wanted her to know it was sincere.

"Never look at me again," he said.

He waited until an hour after dark. With one arm, he threw his blankets to the side. He sat up, and his whole body creaked.

He rested at the edge of the bed. He knew it was going to be painful, and he wanted to prepare himself. Slowly, he pushed himself from the bed until his feet touched the cold tile floor. Then he stood for the first time in months.

Virgil took his first step and thought he had been stabbed. His body crashed as if a few inches were unexpectedly gone from his leg. Virgil caught himself with a bed on each side.

Virgil hobbled that way into the hall. He stopped to rest on a rail with one hand and for just one second. He could do this, he knew, and he kept walking in his painful, uneven way. He limped until he came to Angel's bed.

There was a chart. He found what he thought was the Spanish word for name, and next to it was nothing.

Angel had the most vacant eyes of any man on the ward. They were open and staring into the abyss above him. His lips and chin were chapped and raw. Virgil flicked a finger against Angel's cheek. He did it hard. There was nothing.

Virgil pulled the covers off gently. He was a small man in person, and now genuinely frail. This was the man who had come to destroy him once. Virgil hugged him. He hugged him around his upper back. He hugged him through his knees. Then he stood with the notorious Mexican killer cradled in his arms.

Walking was slow and painstaking. When he put his left foot down, it kept going. He compensated, but it never flattened out. He moved in a Frankenstein waddle, his arms burning, his shoulders tearing. His back didn't want to help. Virgil put his chin in the air and looked at the ceiling. The floor wasn't so cold, and his bare feet felt slippery.

Angel's center of gravity was sinking. He was losing him. Virgil could almost touch his hands. He hurried. He tried to run. It was a frenzied waddle. He felt his knees strike Angel's backside and he flung him, artless and aimless, as far as he could, and he landed on the edge of Virgil's bed. His body landed and bounced coming off the hard mattress. Virgil saw him rolling. He saw the body moving toward the edge. He thought of the pain he was in, and he understood that if Angel hit the floor, then he was staying on the floor. Virgil dove on top of him. He held Angel's body with one arm. He grabbed the railings and dug in with his slippery feet until he slid into the next bed and held fast.

He went through the little nightstand and found the roll of gauze. Then, he began to unspool the bandage around Angel's left eye. He didn't stop there. He rolled until he covered the eye, the forehead, and the collapsed skull and all its signs of surgery. When he was done, he examined his gift wrapping. Virgil pulled the blankets up to his neck, left Angel's arms free, and folded the blanket neatly as Patricia would have done.

He climbed into Angel's bed and waited.

At three in the morning, he heard tapping. It was a specific rhythm that he hadn't heard in years. It was the sound of authority. It was the step of a military man.

The beam of light came into the room and danced along the bedrails. It bobbed and bounced across the beds. It stopped on the bed that had been his. It was the bed that now belonged to Angel. The beam came from a long black flashlight, the kind policemen carried, and the man who held it unhooked the clipboard to examine what was written.

After name, there was nothing.

The man carefully placed the clipboard where he had found it. The light wasn't searching anymore, and Virgil could see his face clearly. He wore a suit. It was black. His shirt was sharply pressed and white. He had short, precise hair. His features were chiseled Asian. Virgil had seen him before.

Curtis, long dead now, whispered into his ear, his voice sounding as alive as ever.

"He's an assassin," Curtis had said.

Virgil remembered a conversation a million years in the past, two lifetimes ago, as Virgil sifted through the old Colon files.

"He's Japanese," Curtis had said. "He's actually from Peru."

Looking at the stoically angry face in the dark, a name he never thought he would need to remember bubbled to the surface of his mind.

"Matsumoto," whispered Curtis. It was Colon's longtime bodyguard.

Matsumoto was the only man moving in the ward. Virgil was the only man watching. Matsumoto regarded the man in the bed. Angel was sleeping with his eyes open, though one of them was now covered. He was peaceful.

Matsumoto moved deliberately, and the beam of light danced across the ceiling. He brought the flashlight around in an arc and it crashed into Angel's head. Virgil heard bone crack. The beam flew, and he heard it again. Matsumoto kept striking. The sounds turned wet and heavy. Virgil heard blood splash against the floor.

Matsumoto struck long after what was necessary, and when he was done, Virgil could hear him breathing. He did not hear Angel and knew that he would not. In the dim light, he saw the crisp white shirt had been painted with deep, dark drops. His face had too. Instinctively, Matsumoto drew a white handkerchief from a pocket. He wiped his face. Then he wiped his flashlight. He took one last look at what he thought had been Marc Virgil.

Virgil closed his eyes, in case this man was seeking witnesses. He forced them shut. His heart pounded so loudly that he thought for sure Matsumoto could hear it. He heard the hard steps of the polished shoes he never saw, squeezed his eyes shut, and braced. The footsteps grew softer. Eventually, they disappeared.

Virgil rose from bed. The floor felt hot now. He rested on the bedrail that had been his. There was no reason to go further.

Angel's head had been demolished. In its place was an unrecognizable mess. Virgil knew who this was, but he was the only one.

In Angel's nightstand was a paper bag filled with his personal items. Virgil dumped it on the bed. There was a pair of gray slacks. Virgil thought they looked tight, but they fit just fine. There was a pair of shoes. They hurt, but he wore them anyway. Then there was a tan sport coat. It was smooth and soft. It still smelled of finer living. He slid it over himself. There was a watch too. It looked fancy, with part of the face cut away to reveal a tiny device inside of it, spinning around mysteriously.

There was a clock on the wall. It was over his bed, and he had never seen it. The pieces disagreed, but he used the wall as his guide and set the fancy watch to Mexican madhouse time. He smiled in the dark.

The sun would come up soon. He needed to hurry. The locals would be out and going to mass. He had buried a package behind a church. It was filled with guns and enough money to start a new life. Someone might see him digging it up.

Made in the USA
Middletown, DE
03 July 2019